RAT QUEENS™

VOLUME ONE: SASS and SORCERY

Shadowline™

image

www.ShadowlineOnline.com

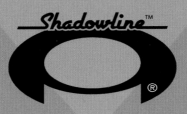

image COMICS PRESENTS

KURTIS J. WIEBE
story

ROC UPCHURCH
art
covers

ED BRISSON
letters

LAURA TAVISHATI
edits

IMAGE COMICS, INC.
Robert Kirkman – Chief Operating Officer
Erik Larsen – Chief Financial Officer
Todd McFarlane – President
Marc Silvestri – Chief Executive Officer
Jim Valentino – Vice-President

Eric Stephenson – Publisher
Corey Murphy – Director of Sales
Jeremy Sullivan – Director of Digital Sales
Kat Salazar – Director of PR & Marketing
Emily Miller – Director of Operations
Branwyn Bigglestone – Senior Accounts Manager
Sarah Mello – Accounts Manager
Drew Gill – Art Director
Jonathan Chan – Production Manager
Meredith Wallace – Print Manager
Randy Okamura – Marketing Production Designer
David Brothers – Branding Manager
Ally Power – Content Manager
Addison Duke – Production Artist
Vincent Kukua – Production Artist
Sasha Head – Production Artist
Tricia Ramos – Production Artist
Emilio Bautista – Sales Assistant
Chloe Ramos-Peterson – Administrative Assistant
IMAGECOMICS.COM

JIM VALENTINO
publisher/book design

A
Shadowline
PRODUCTION

image

FOURTH PRINTING: AUGUST, 2015   ISBN: 978-1-60706-945-4

MEET the QUEENS

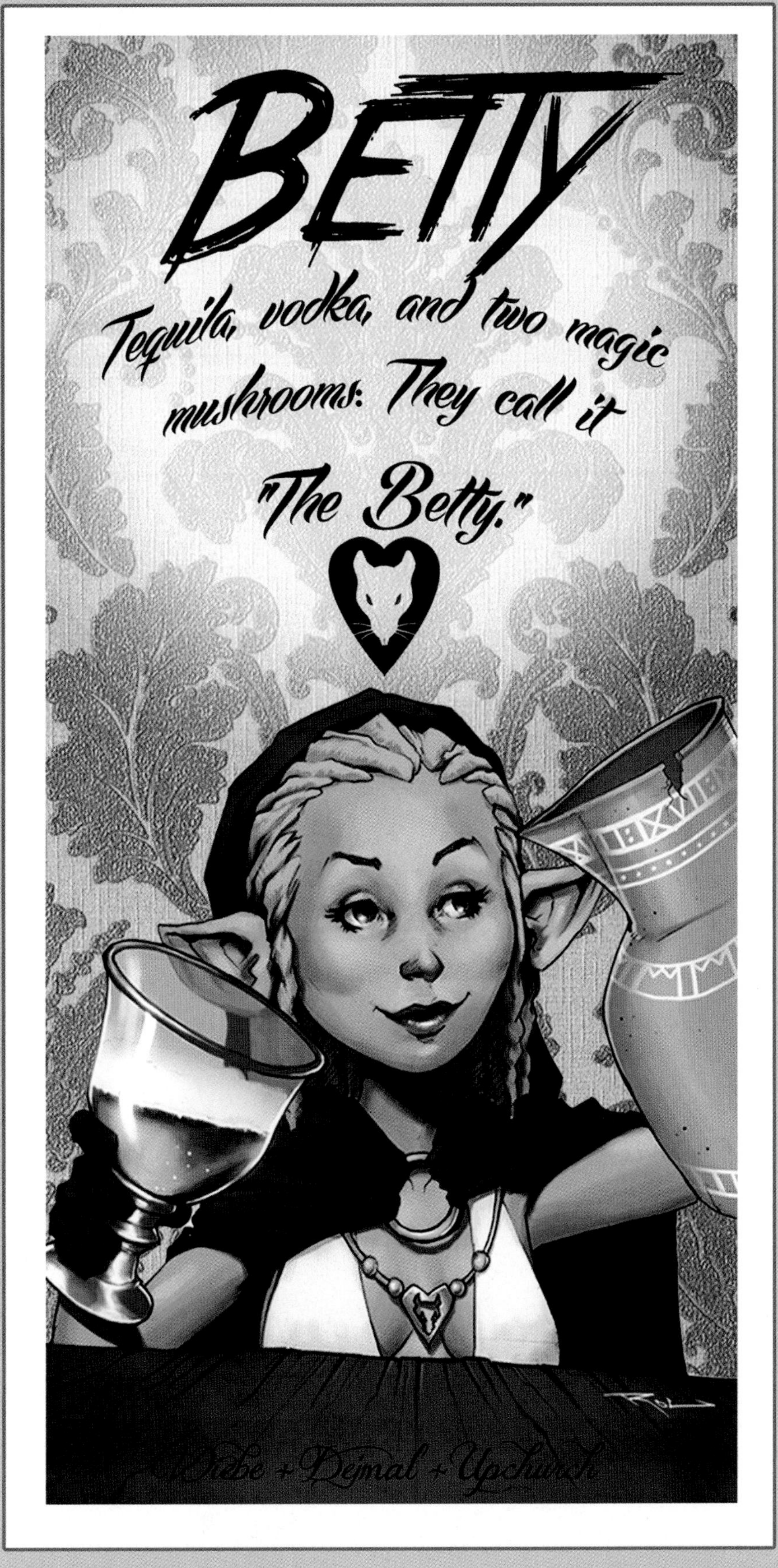
BETTY
Tequila, vodka, and two magic mushrooms. They call it "The Betty."
Wiebe + Dejmal + Upchurch

MEET the QUEENS

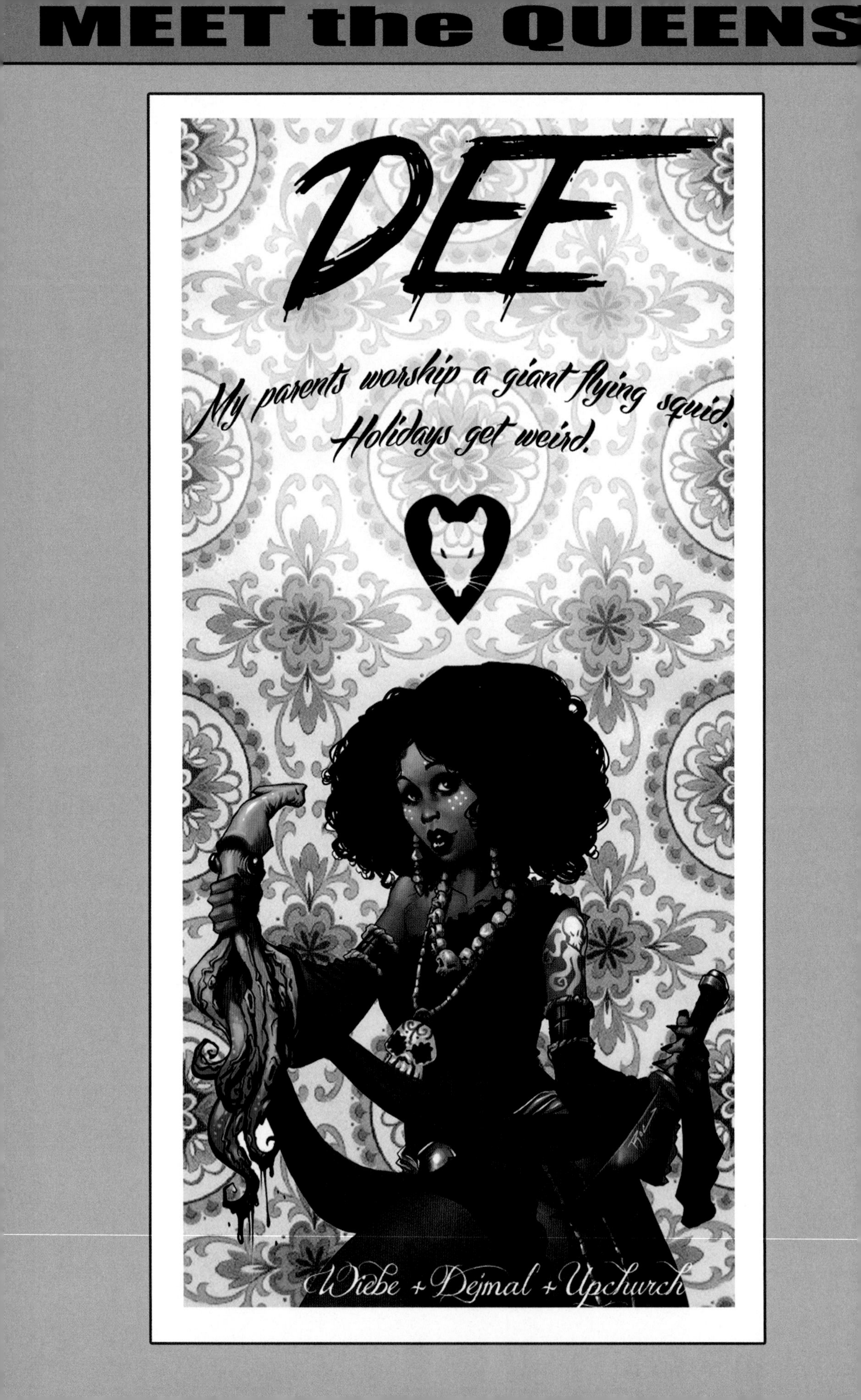

DEE
My parents worship a giant flying squid.
Holidays get weird.
Wiebe + Dejmal + Upchurch

MEET the QUEENS

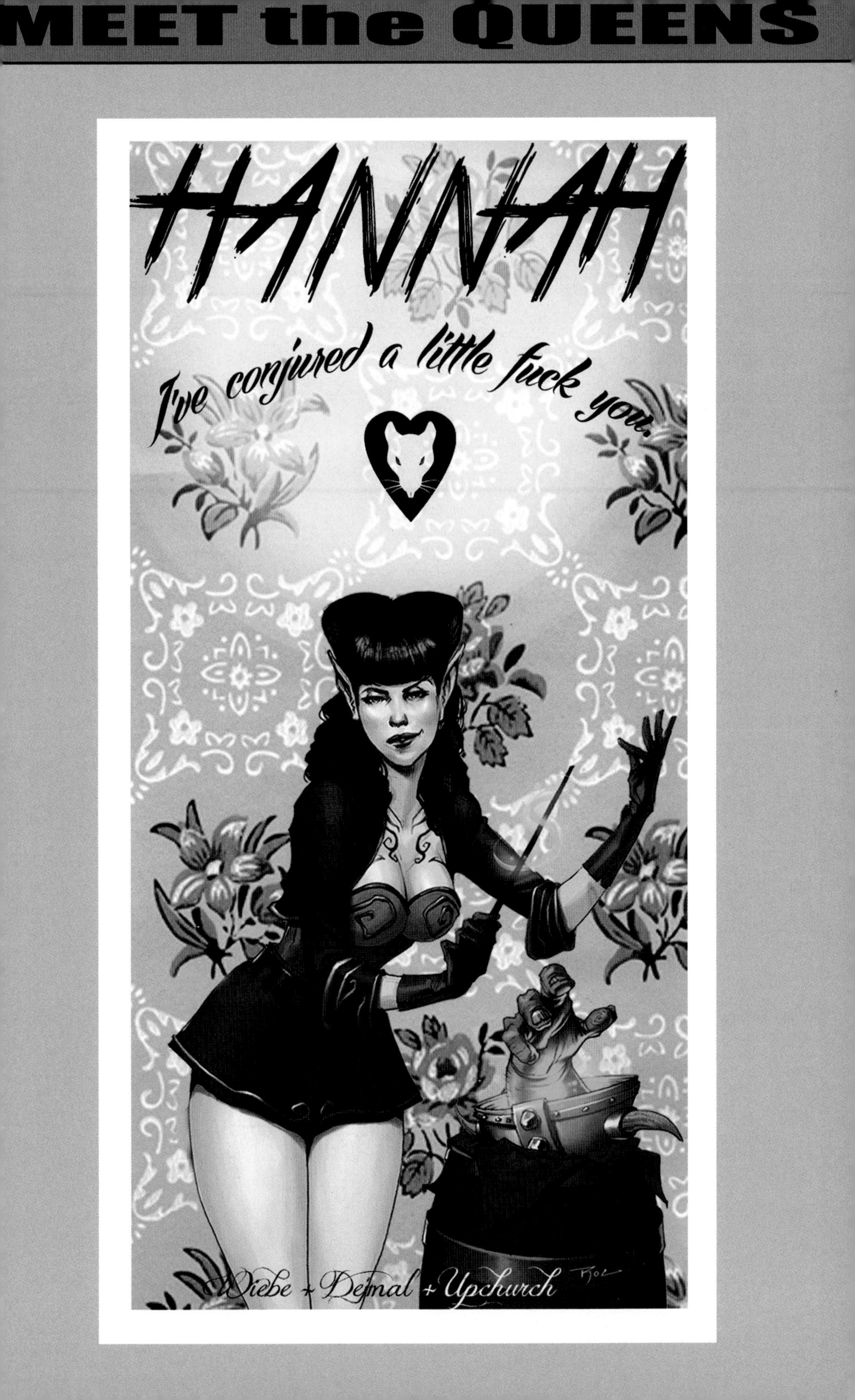
HANNAH
I've conjured a little fuck you.
Wiebe + Dejmal + Upchurch

MEET the QUEENS

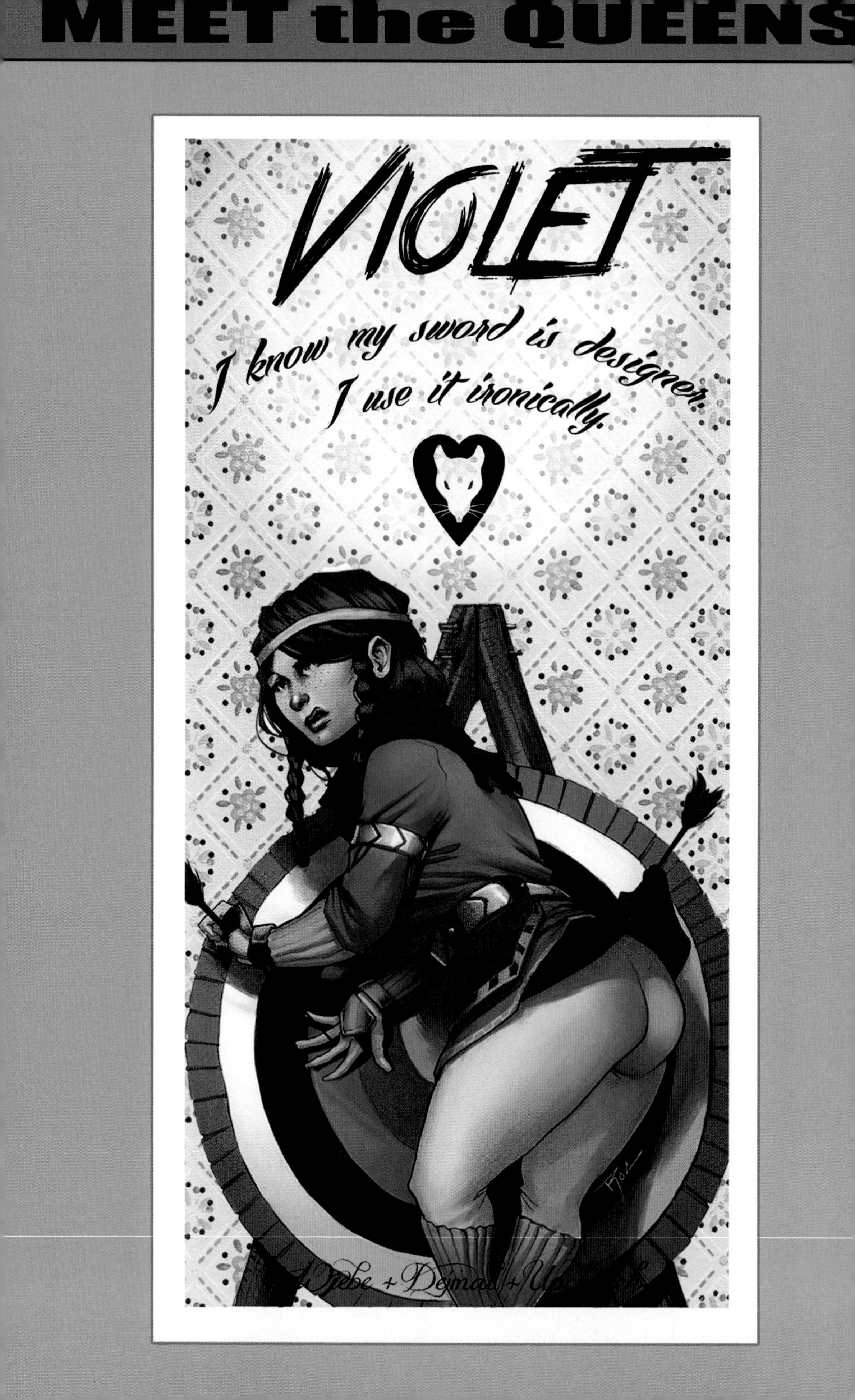
VIOLET
I know my sword is designer.
I use it ironically.

CHAPTER ONE

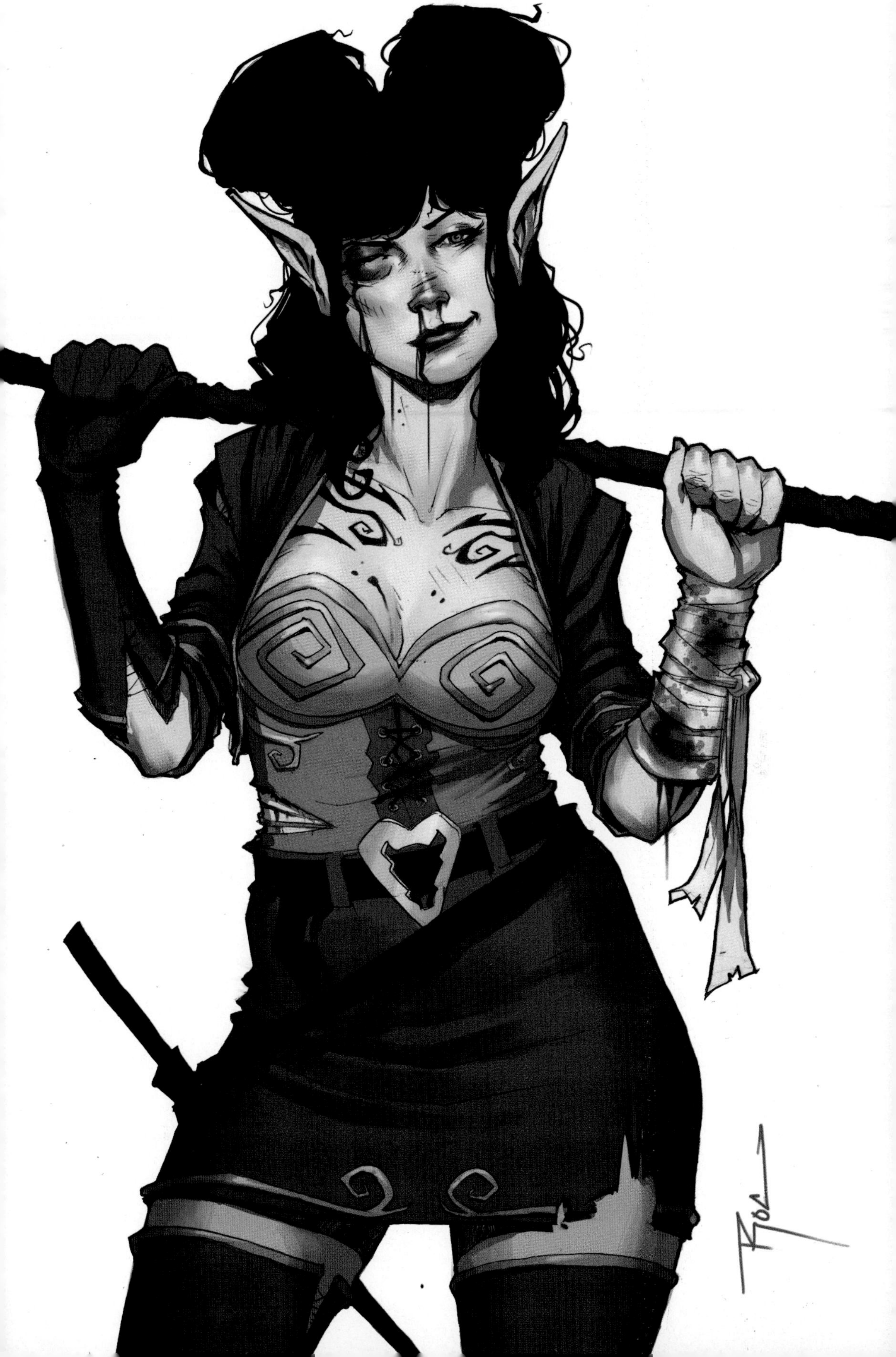

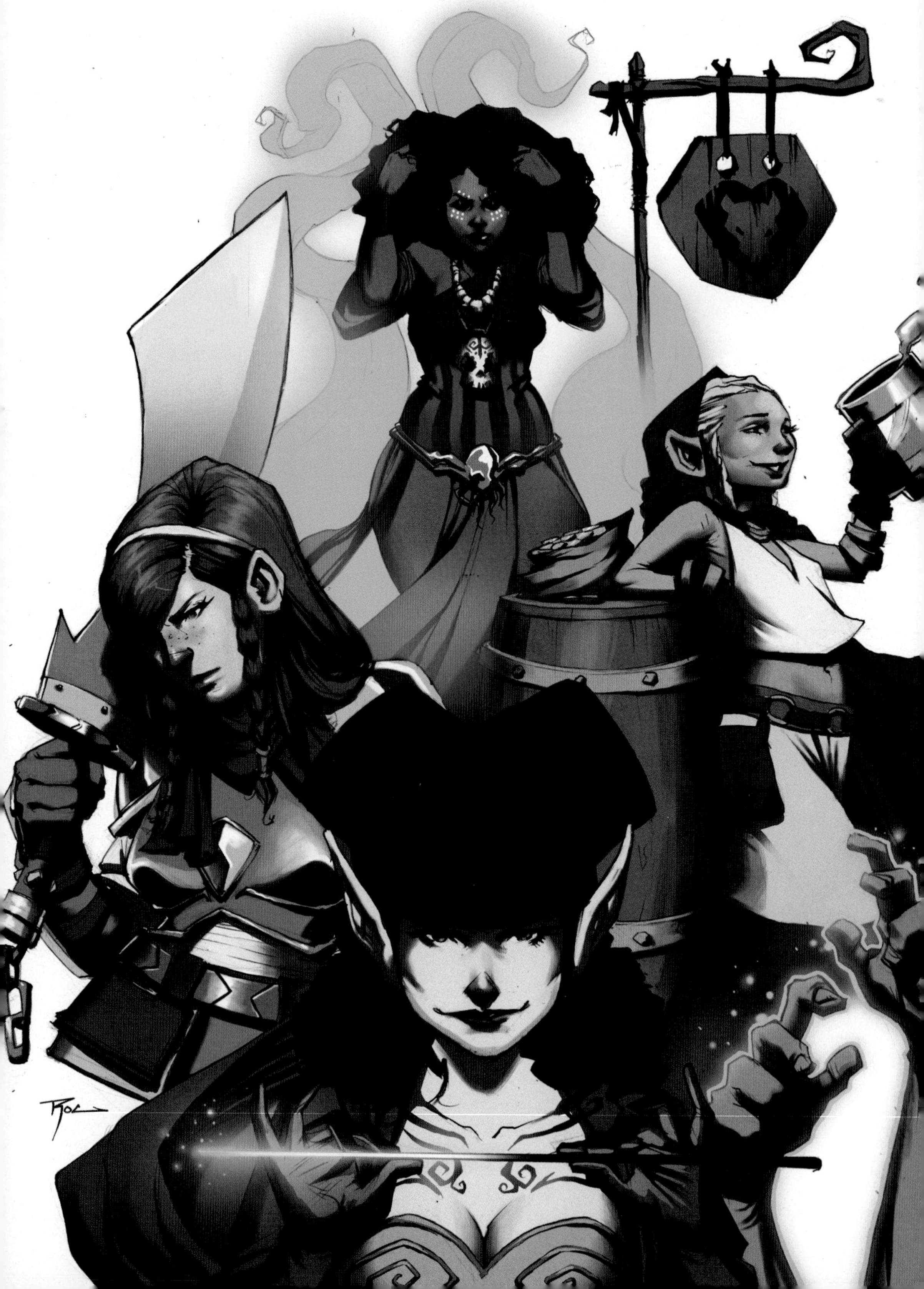

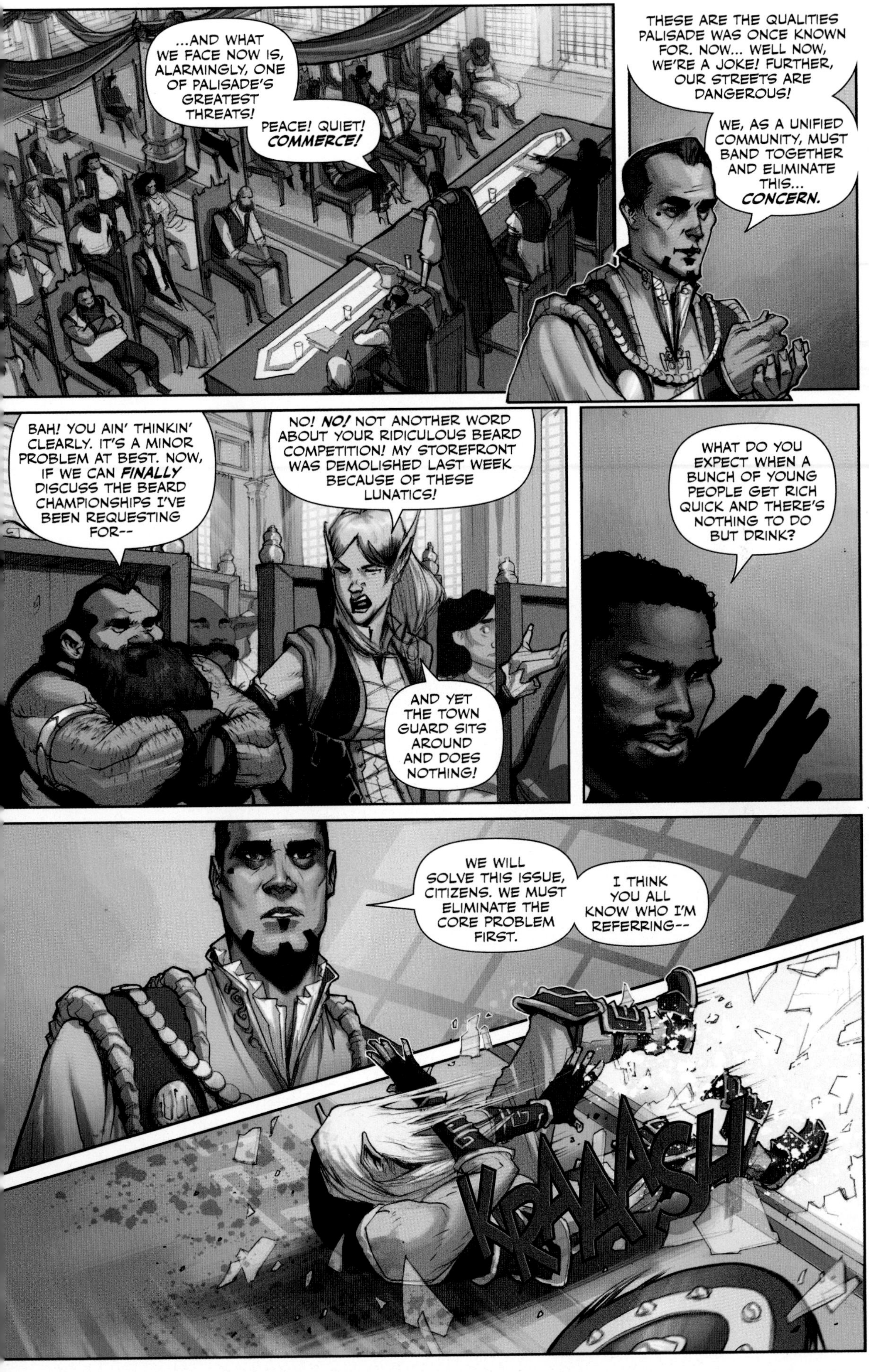

...AND WHAT WE FACE NOW IS, ALARMINGLY, ONE OF PALISADE'S GREATEST THREATS!
PEACE! QUIET! COMMERCE!
THESE ARE THE QUALITIES PALISADE WAS ONCE KNOWN FOR. NOW... WELL NOW, WE'RE A JOKE! FURTHER, OUR STREETS ARE DANGEROUS!
WE, AS A UNIFIED COMMUNITY, MUST BAND TOGETHER AND ELIMINATE THIS... CONCERN.
BAH! YOU AIN' THINKIN' CLEARLY. IT'S A MINOR PROBLEM AT BEST. NOW, IF WE CAN FINALLY DISCUSS THE BEARD CHAMPIONSHIPS I'VE BEEN REQUESTING FOR--
NO! NO! NOT ANOTHER WORD ABOUT YOUR RIDICULOUS BEARD COMPETITION! MY STOREFRONT WAS DEMOLISHED LAST WEEK BECAUSE OF THESE LUNATICS!
AND YET THE TOWN GUARD SITS AROUND AND DOES NOTHING!
WHAT DO YOU EXPECT WHEN A BUNCH OF YOUNG PEOPLE GET RICH QUICK AND THERE'S NOTHING TO DO BUT DRINK?
WE WILL SOLVE THIS ISSUE, CITIZENS. WE MUST ELIMINATE THE CORE PROBLEM FIRST.
I THINK YOU ALL KNOW WHO I'M REFERRING--
KRAASH!

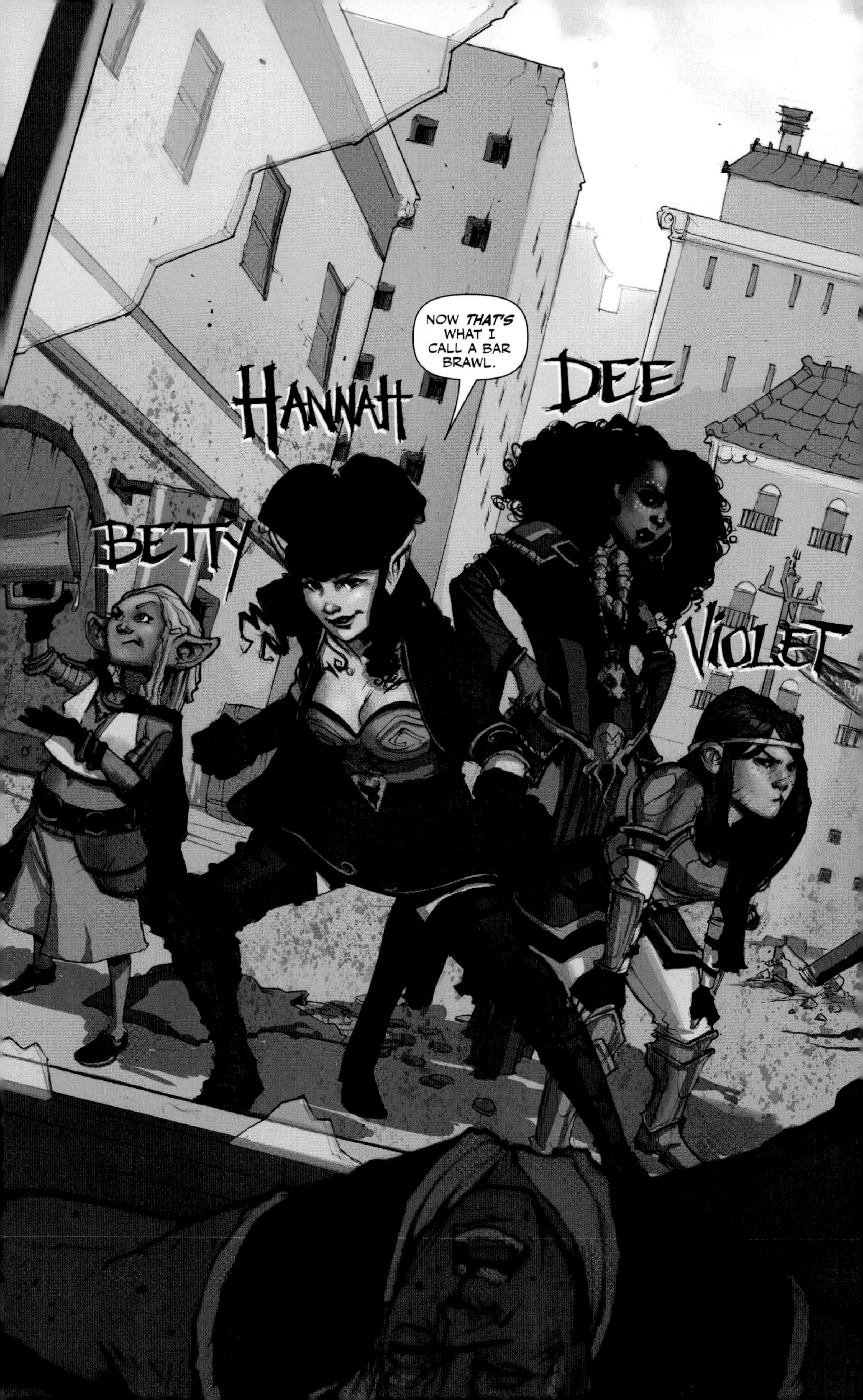
NOW *THAT'S* WHAT I CALL A BAR BRAWL.
HANNAH
DEE
BETTY
VIOLET

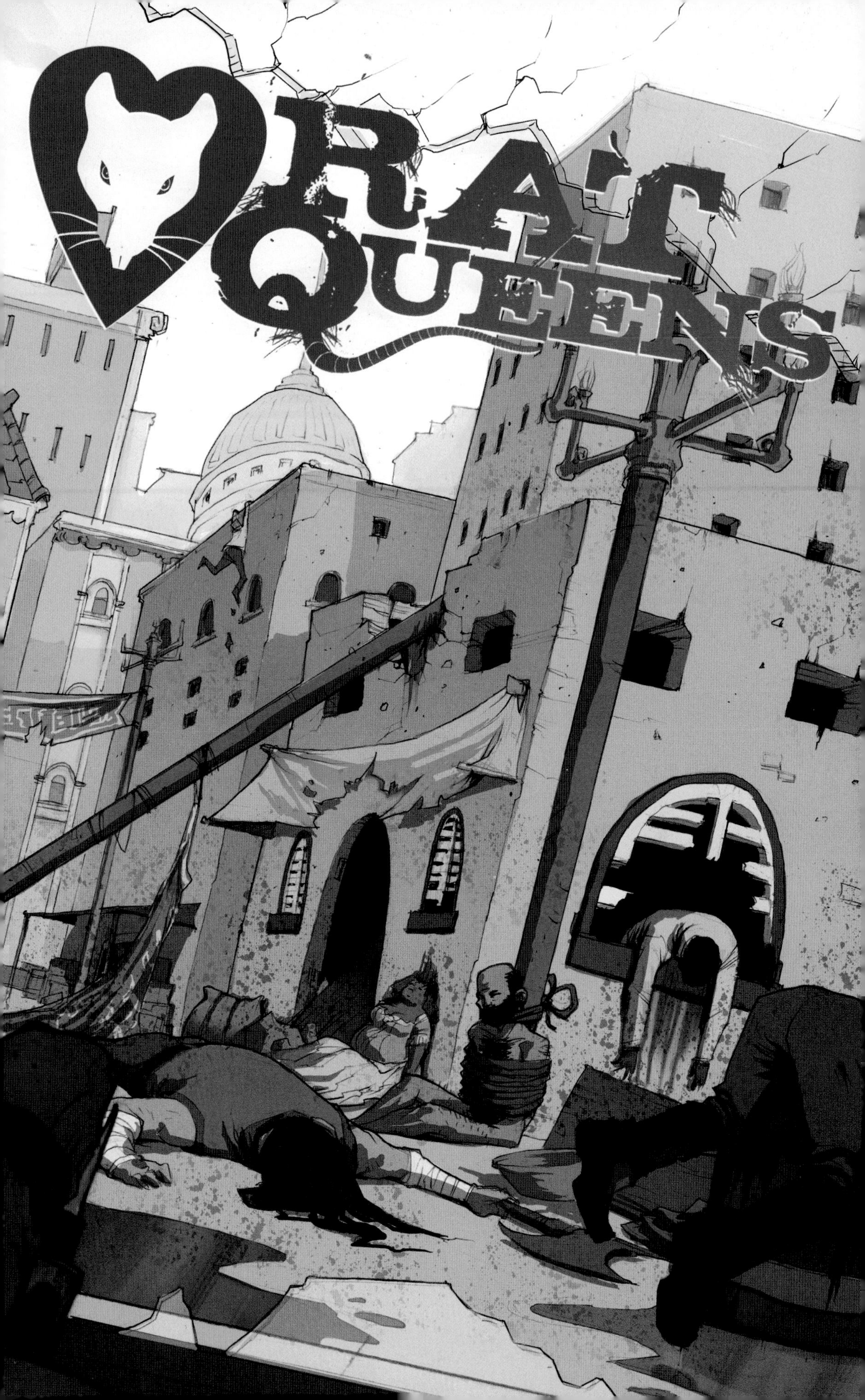
RAT
QUEENS

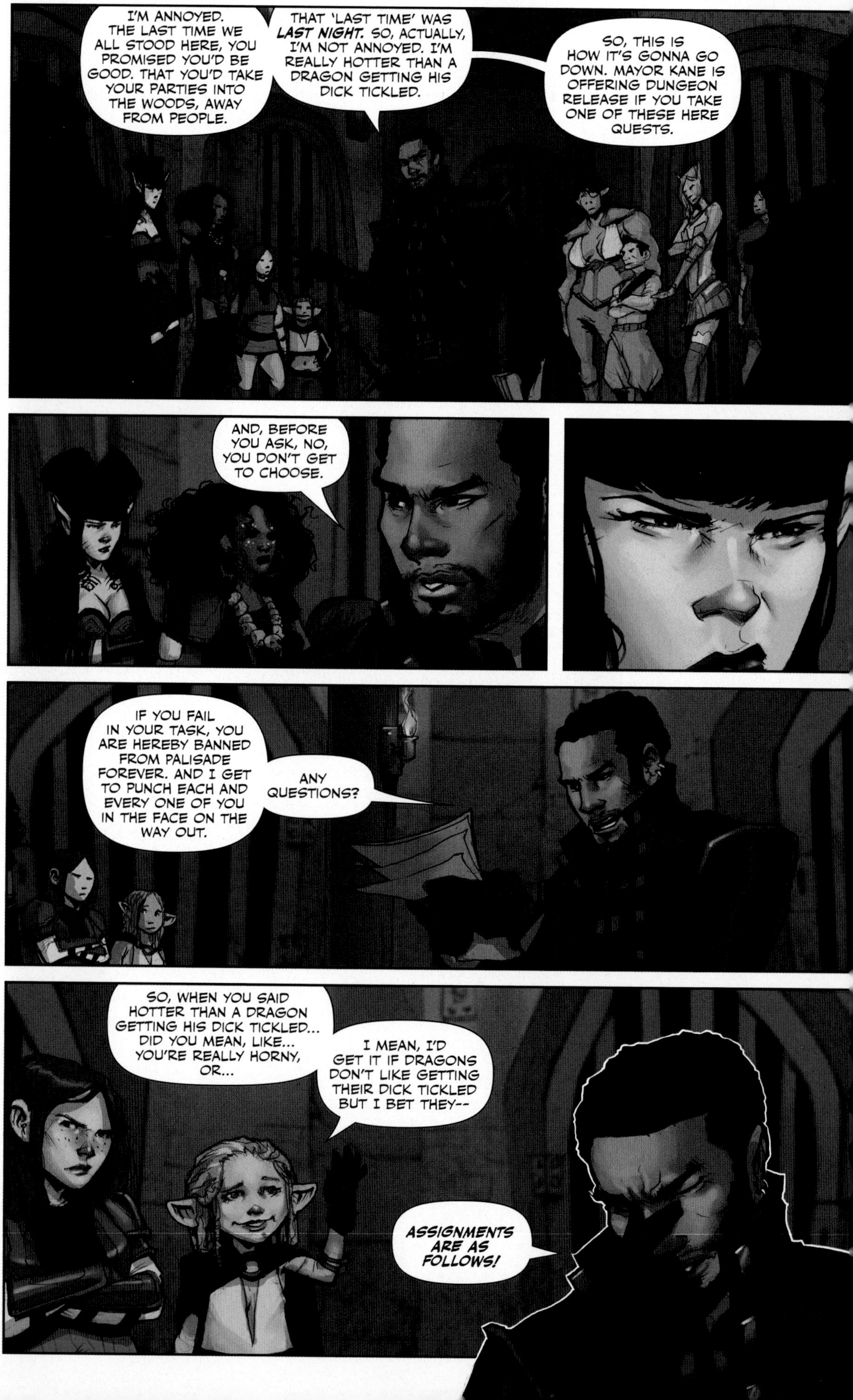
I'M ANNOYED. THE LAST TIME WE ALL STOOD HERE, YOU PROMISED YOU'D BE GOOD. THAT YOU'D TAKE YOUR PARTIES INTO THE WOODS, AWAY FROM PEOPLE.
THAT 'LAST TIME' WAS LAST NIGHT. SO, ACTUALLY, I'M NOT ANNOYED. I'M REALLY HOTTER THAN A DRAGON GETTING HIS DICK TICKLED.
SO, THIS IS HOW IT'S GONNA GO DOWN. MAYOR KANE IS OFFERING DUNGEON RELEASE IF YOU TAKE ONE OF THESE HERE QUESTS.
AND, BEFORE YOU ASK, NO, YOU DON'T GET TO CHOOSE.
IF YOU FAIL IN YOUR TASK, YOU ARE HEREBY BANNED FROM PALISADE FOREVER. AND I GET TO PUNCH EACH AND EVERY ONE OF YOU IN THE FACE ON THE WAY OUT.
ANY QUESTIONS?
SO, WHEN YOU SAID HOTTER THAN A DRAGON GETTING HIS DICK TICKLED... DID YOU MEAN, LIKE... YOU'RE REALLY HORNY, OR...
I MEAN, I'D GET IT IF DRAGONS DON'T LIKE GETTING THEIR DICK TICKLED BUT I BET THEY--
ASSIGNMENTS ARE AS FOLLOWS!

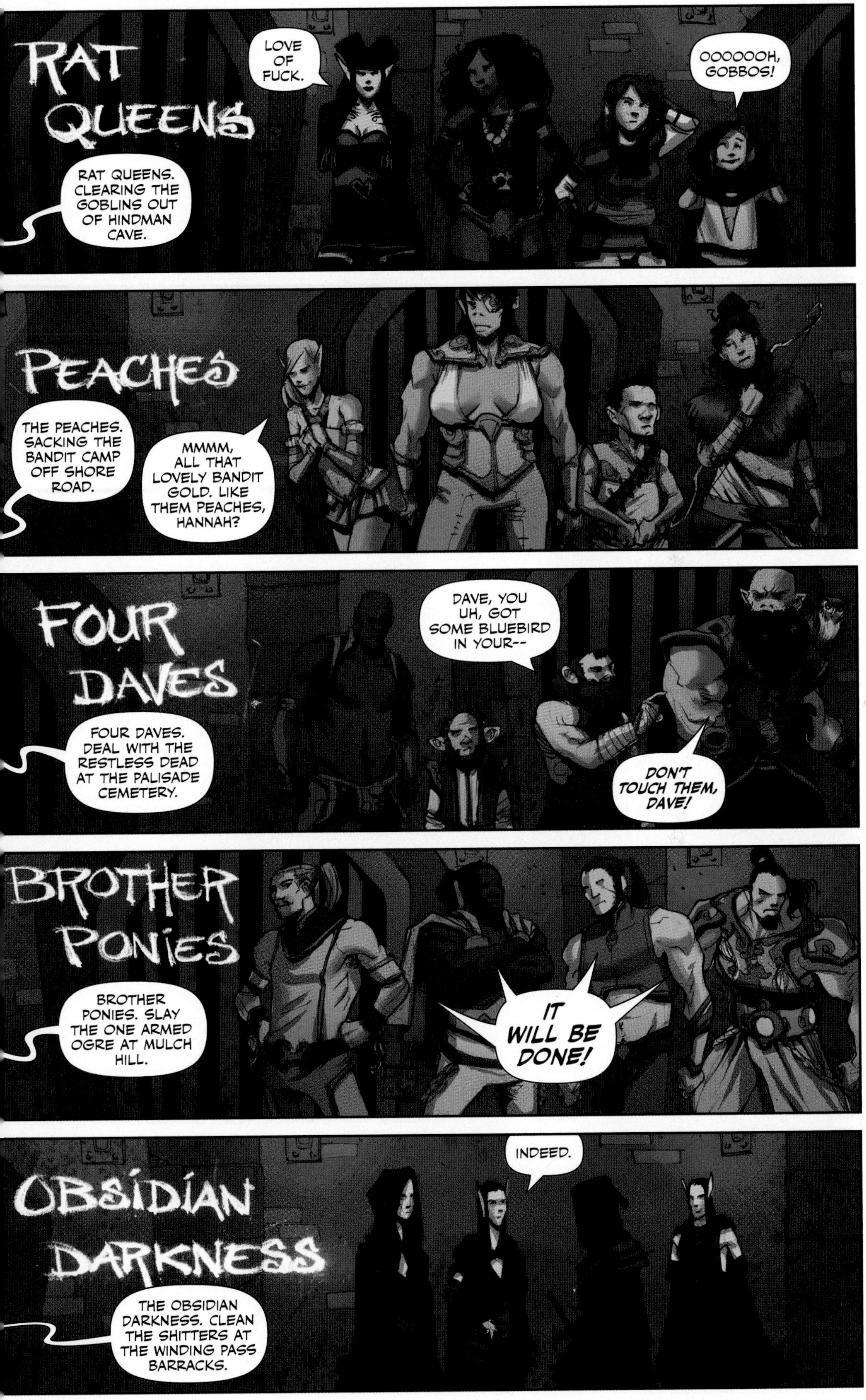
RAT QUEENS
LOVE OF FUCK.
OOOOOOH, GOBBOS!
RAT QUEENS. CLEARING THE GOBLINS OUT OF HINDMAN CAVE.
PEACHES
THE PEACHES. SACKING THE BANDIT CAMP OFF SHORE ROAD.
MMMM, ALL THAT LOVELY BANDIT GOLD. LIKE THEM PEACHES, HANNAH?
FOUR DAVES
DAVE, YOU UH, GOT SOME BLUEBIRD IN YOUR--
FOUR DAVES. DEAL WITH THE RESTLESS DEAD AT THE PALISADE CEMETERY.
DON'T TOUCH THEM, DAVE!
BROTHER PONIES
BROTHER PONIES. SLAY THE ONE ARMED OGRE AT MULCH HILL.
IT WILL BE DONE!
OBSIDIAN DARKNESS
INDEED.
THE OBSIDIAN DARKNESS. CLEAN THE SHITTERS AT THE WINDING PASS BARRACKS.

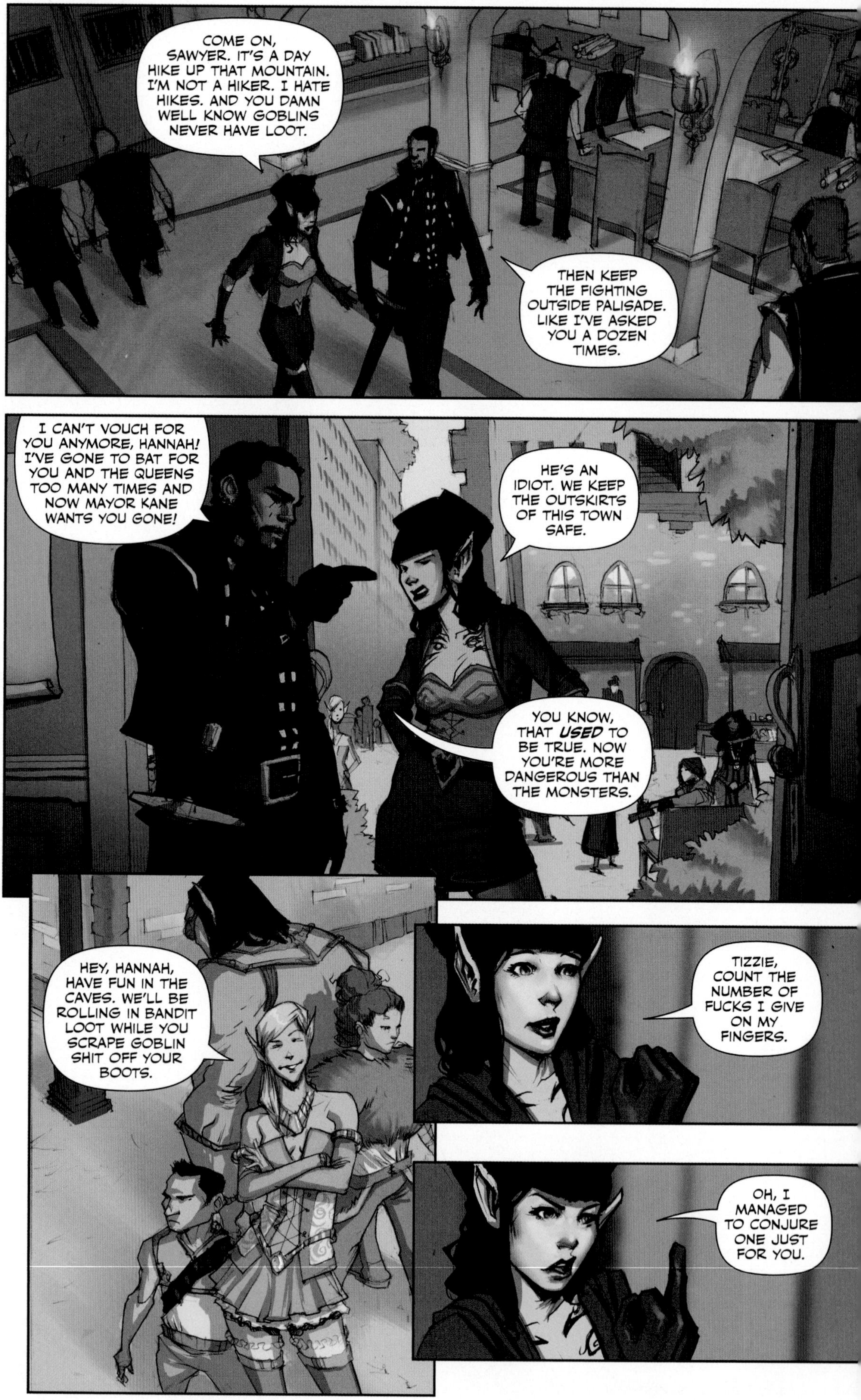
COME ON, SAWYER. IT'S A DAY HIKE UP THAT MOUNTAIN. I'M NOT A HIKER. I HATE HIKES. AND YOU DAMN WELL KNOW GOBLINS NEVER HAVE LOOT.
THEN KEEP THE FIGHTING OUTSIDE PALISADE. LIKE I'VE ASKED YOU A DOZEN TIMES.
I CAN'T VOUCH FOR YOU ANYMORE, HANNAH! I'VE GONE TO BAT FOR YOU AND THE QUEENS TOO MANY TIMES AND NOW MAYOR KANE WANTS YOU GONE!
HE'S AN IDIOT. WE KEEP THE OUTSKIRTS OF THIS TOWN SAFE.
YOU KNOW, THAT USED TO BE TRUE. NOW YOU'RE MORE DANGEROUS THAN THE MONSTERS.
HEY, HANNAH, HAVE FUN IN THE CAVES. WE'LL BE ROLLING IN BANDIT LOOT WHILE YOU SCRAPE GOBLIN SHIT OFF YOUR BOOTS.
TIZZIE, COUNT THE NUMBER OF FUCKS I GIVE ON MY FINGERS.
OH, I MANAGED TO CONJURE ONE JUST FOR YOU.

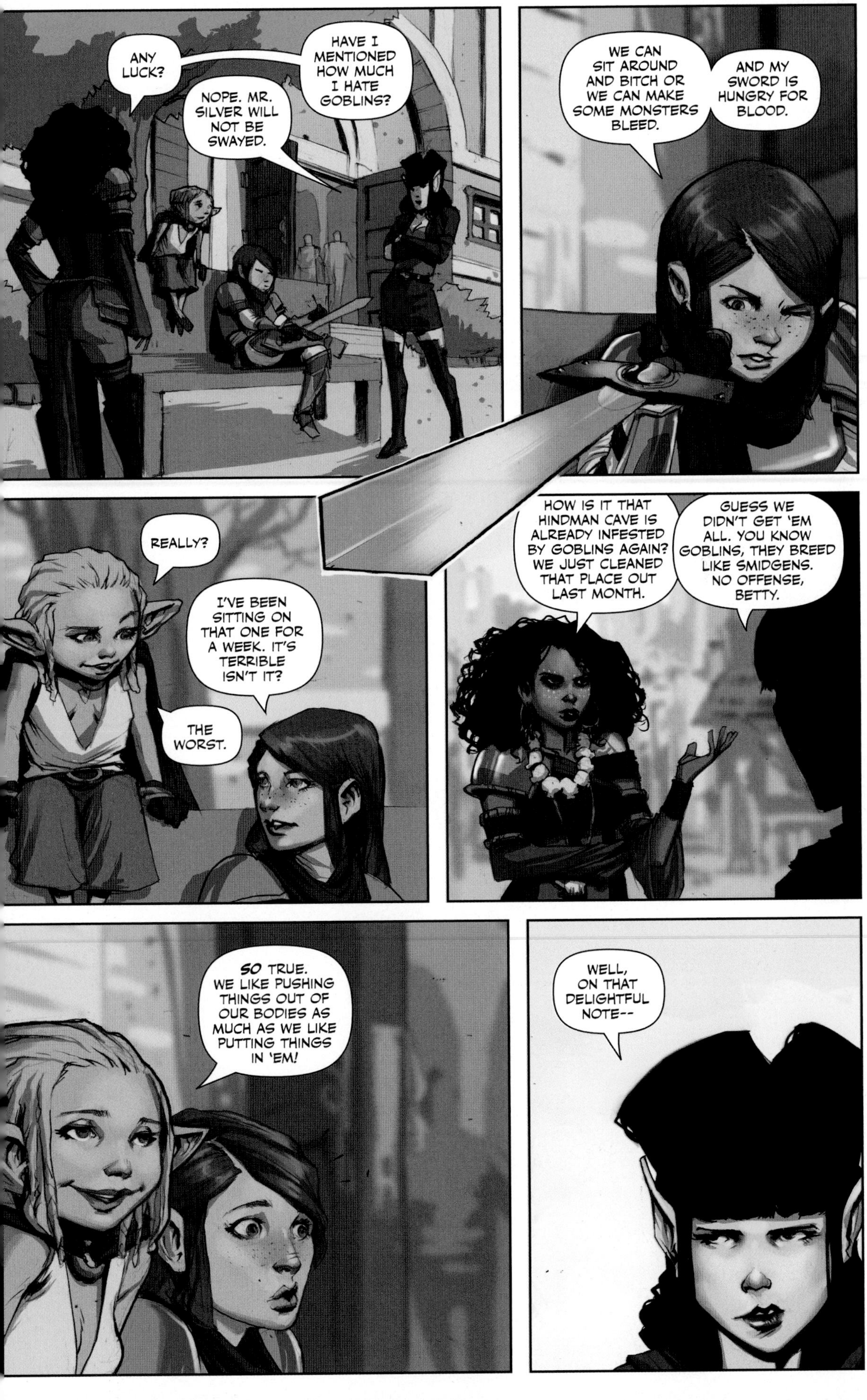
ANY LUCK?
HAVE I MENTIONED HOW MUCH I HATE GOBLINS?
NOPE. MR. SILVER WILL NOT BE SWAYED.
WE CAN SIT AROUND AND BITCH OR WE CAN MAKE SOME MONSTERS BLEED.
AND MY SWORD IS HUNGRY FOR BLOOD.
REALLY?
I'VE BEEN SITTING ON THAT ONE FOR A WEEK. IT'S TERRIBLE ISN'T IT?
THE WORST.
HOW IS IT THAT HINDMAN CAVE IS ALREADY INFESTED BY GOBLINS AGAIN? WE JUST CLEANED THAT PLACE OUT LAST MONTH.
GUESS WE DIDN'T GET 'EM ALL. YOU KNOW GOBLINS, THEY BREED LIKE SMIDGENS. NO OFFENSE, BETTY.
SO TRUE. WE LIKE PUSHING THINGS OUT OF OUR BODIES AS MUCH AS WE LIKE PUTTING THINGS IN 'EM!
WELL, ON THAT DELIGHTFUL NOTE--

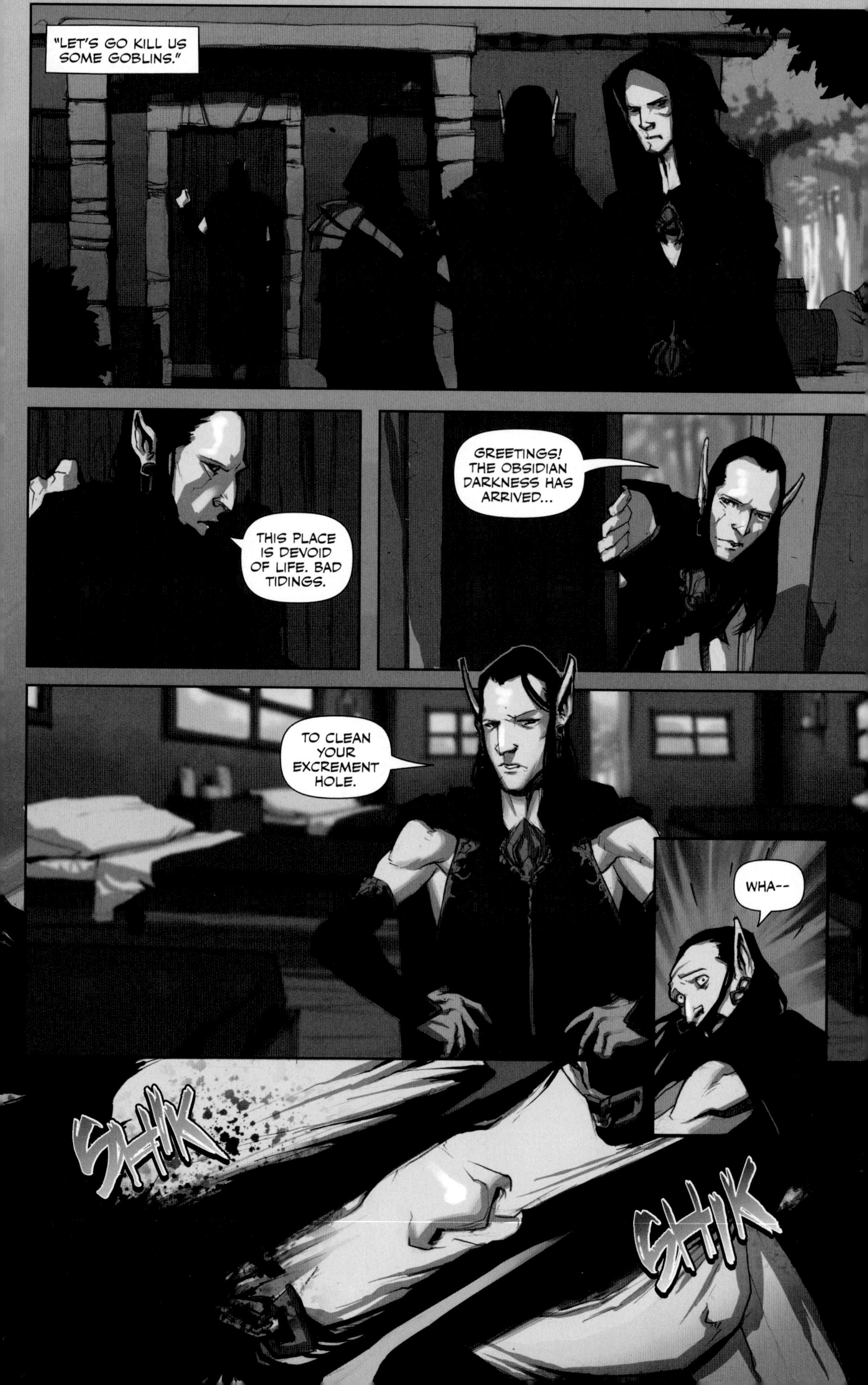
"LET'S GO KILL US SOME GOBLINS."
THIS PLACE IS DEVOID OF LIFE. BAD TIDINGS.
GREETINGS! THE OBSIDIAN DARKNESS HAS ARRIVED...
TO CLEAN YOUR EXCREMENT HOLE.
WHA--
SHIK
SHIK

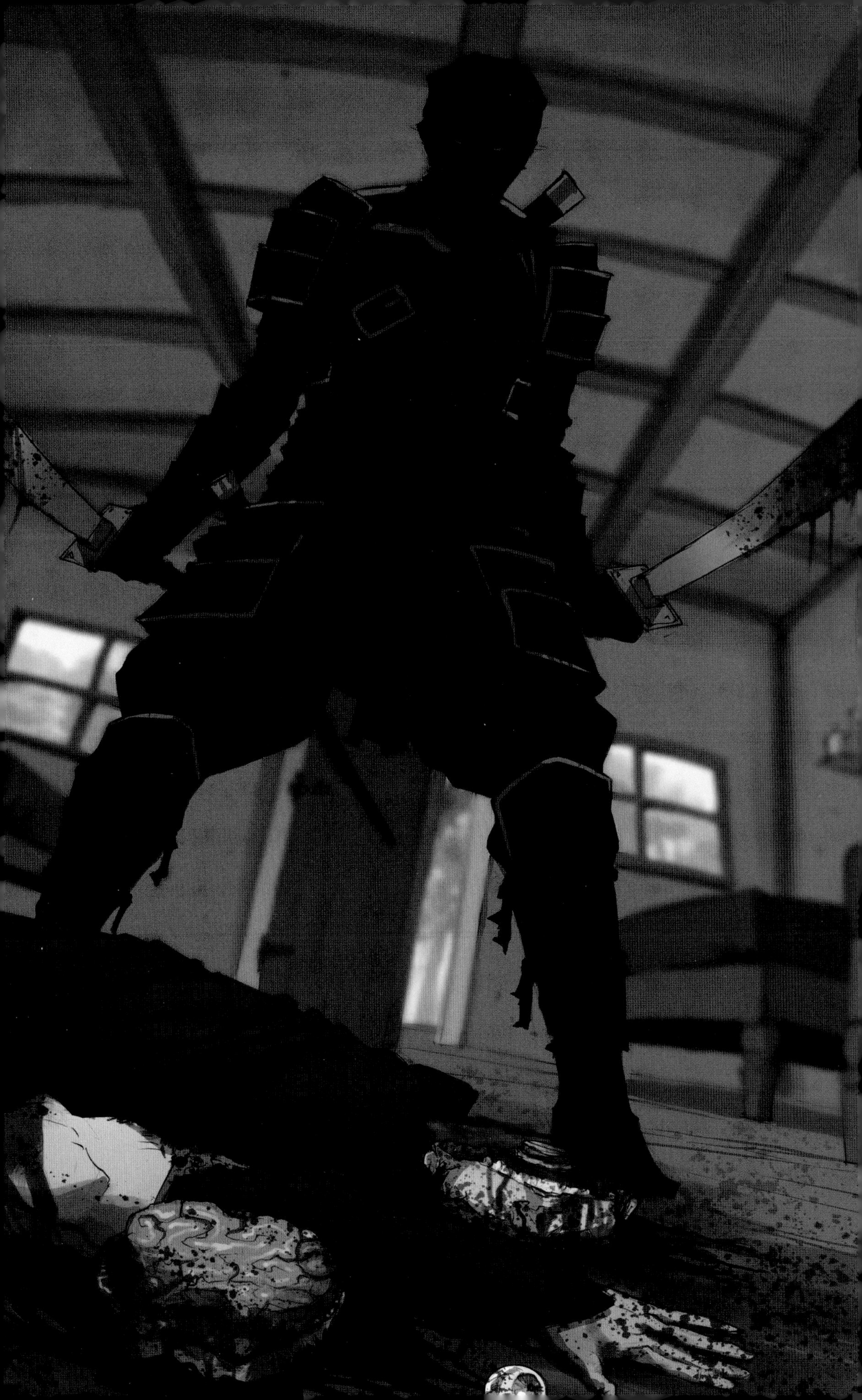

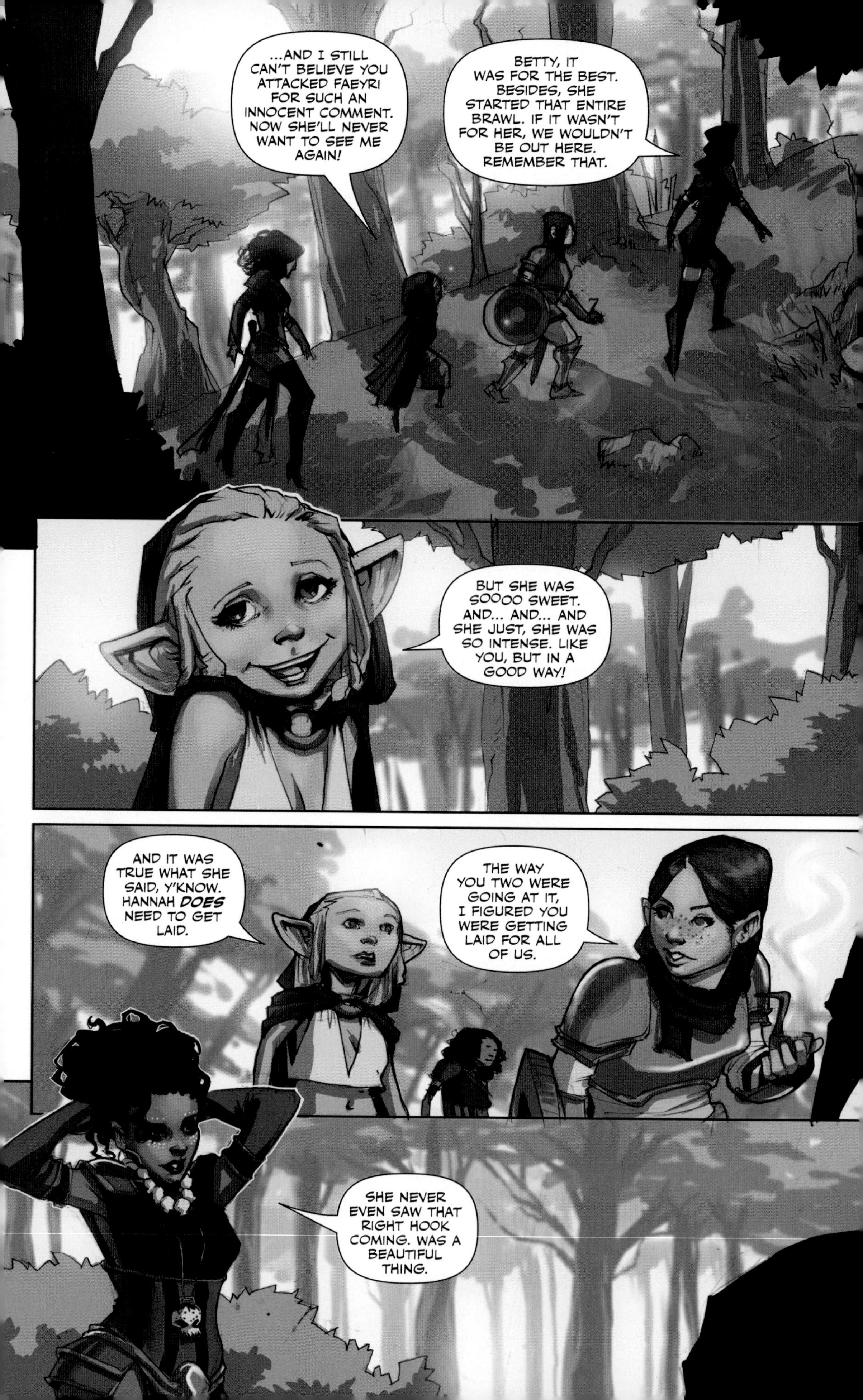
...AND I STILL CAN'T BELIEVE YOU ATTACKED FAEYRI FOR SUCH AN INNOCENT COMMENT. NOW SHE'LL NEVER WANT TO SEE ME AGAIN!
BETTY, IT WAS FOR THE BEST. BESIDES, SHE STARTED THAT ENTIRE BRAWL. IF IT WASN'T FOR HER, WE WOULDN'T BE OUT HERE. REMEMBER THAT.
BUT SHE WAS SOOOO SWEET. AND... AND... AND SHE JUST, SHE WAS SO INTENSE. LIKE YOU, BUT IN A GOOD WAY!
AND IT WAS TRUE WHAT SHE SAID, Y'KNOW. HANNAH *DOES* NEED TO GET LAID.
THE WAY YOU TWO WERE GOING AT IT, I FIGURED YOU WERE GETTING LAID FOR ALL OF US.
SHE NEVER EVEN SAW THAT RIGHT HOOK COMING. WAS A BEAUTIFUL THING.

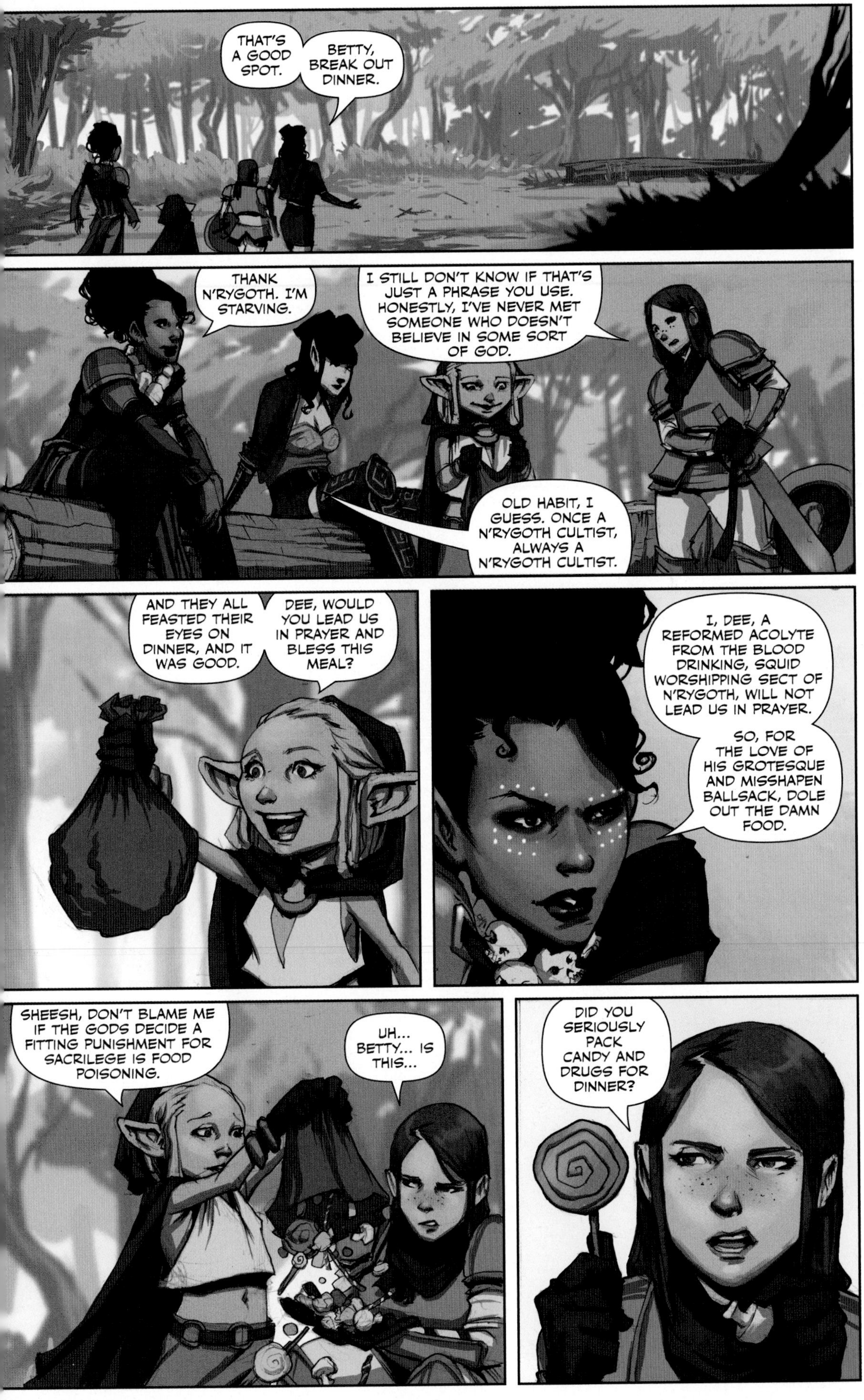
THAT'S A GOOD SPOT.
BETTY, BREAK OUT DINNER.
THANK N'RYGOTH. I'M STARVING.
I STILL DON'T KNOW IF THAT'S JUST A PHRASE YOU USE. HONESTLY, I'VE NEVER MET SOMEONE WHO DOESN'T BELIEVE IN SOME SORT OF GOD.
OLD HABIT, I GUESS. ONCE A N'RYGOTH CULTIST, ALWAYS A N'RYGOTH CULTIST.
AND THEY ALL FEASTED THEIR EYES ON DINNER, AND IT WAS GOOD.
DEE, WOULD YOU LEAD US IN PRAYER AND BLESS THIS MEAL?
I, DEE, A REFORMED ACOLYTE FROM THE BLOOD DRINKING, SQUID WORSHIPPING SECT OF N'RYGOTH, WILL NOT LEAD US IN PRAYER.
SO, FOR THE LOVE OF HIS GROTESQUE AND MISSHAPEN BALLSACK, DOLE OUT THE DAMN FOOD.
SHEESH, DON'T BLAME ME IF THE GODS DECIDE A FITTING PUNISHMENT FOR SACRILEGE IS FOOD POISONING.
UH... BETTY... IS THIS...
DID YOU SERIOUSLY PACK CANDY AND DRUGS FOR DINNER?

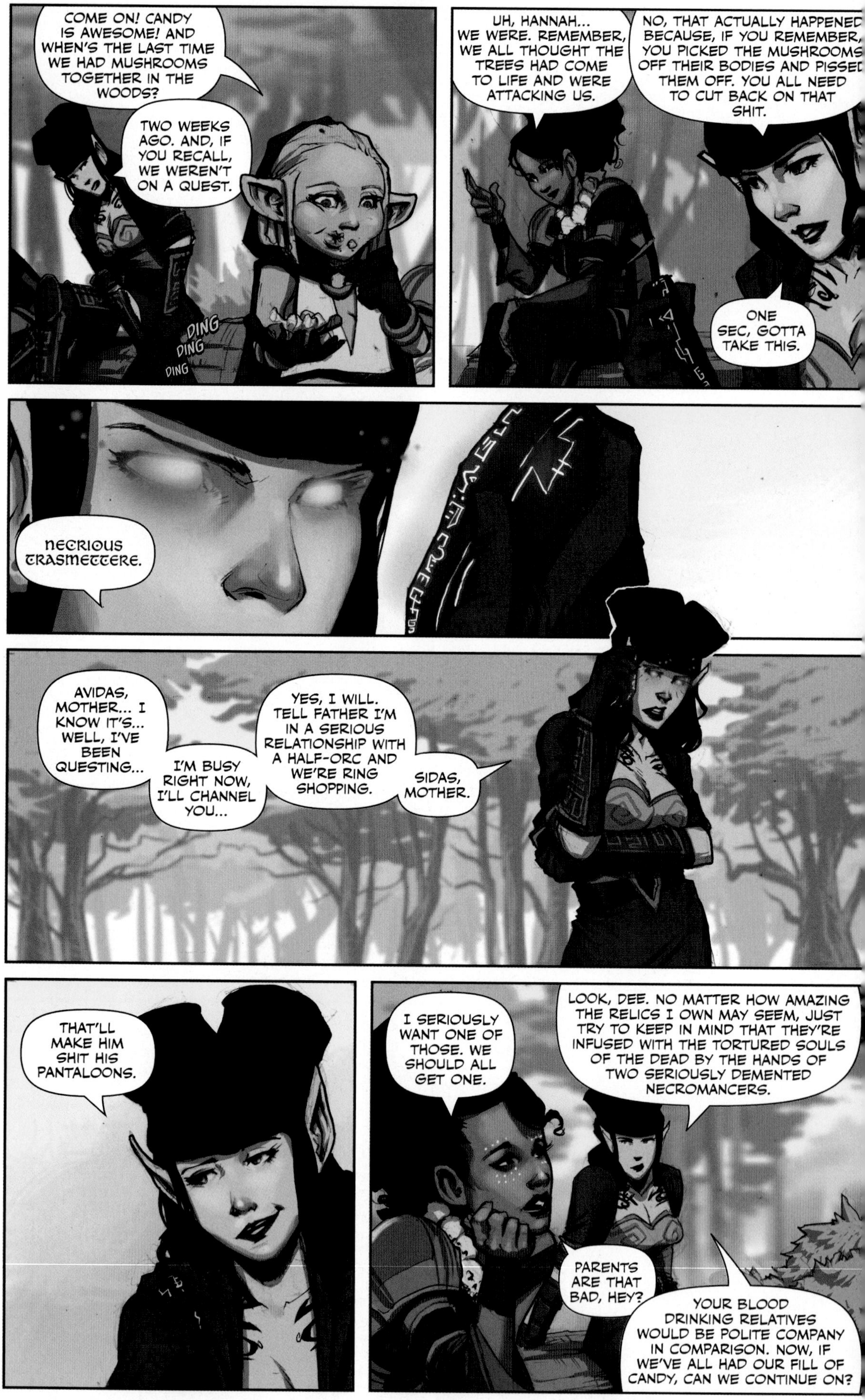

COME ON! CANDY IS AWESOME! AND WHEN'S THE LAST TIME WE HAD MUSHROOMS TOGETHER IN THE WOODS?
TWO WEEKS AGO. AND, IF YOU RECALL, WE WEREN'T ON A QUEST.
DING DING DING
UH, HANNAH... WE WERE. REMEMBER, WE ALL THOUGHT THE TREES HAD COME TO LIFE AND WERE ATTACKING US.
NO, THAT ACTUALLY HAPPENED BECAUSE, IF YOU REMEMBER, YOU PICKED THE MUSHROOMS OFF THEIR BODIES AND PISSED THEM OFF. YOU ALL NEED TO CUT BACK ON THAT SHIT.
ONE SEC, GOTTA TAKE THIS.
NECRIOUS TRASMETTERE.
AVIDAS, MOTHER... I KNOW IT'S... WELL, I'VE BEEN QUESTING...
I'M BUSY RIGHT NOW, I'LL CHANNEL YOU...
YES, I WILL. TELL FATHER I'M IN A SERIOUS RELATIONSHIP WITH A HALF-ORC AND WE'RE RING SHOPPING.
SIDAS, MOTHER.
THAT'LL MAKE HIM SHIT HIS PANTALOONS.
I SERIOUSLY WANT ONE OF THOSE. WE SHOULD ALL GET ONE.
LOOK, DEE. NO MATTER HOW AMAZING THE RELICS I OWN MAY SEEM, JUST TRY TO KEEP IN MIND THAT THEY'RE INFUSED WITH THE TORTURED SOULS OF THE DEAD BY THE HANDS OF TWO SERIOUSLY DEMENTED NECROMANCERS.
PARENTS ARE THAT BAD, HEY?
YOUR BLOOD DRINKING RELATIVES WOULD BE POLITE COMPANY IN COMPARISON. NOW, IF WE'VE ALL HAD OUR FILL OF CANDY, CAN WE CONTINUE ON?

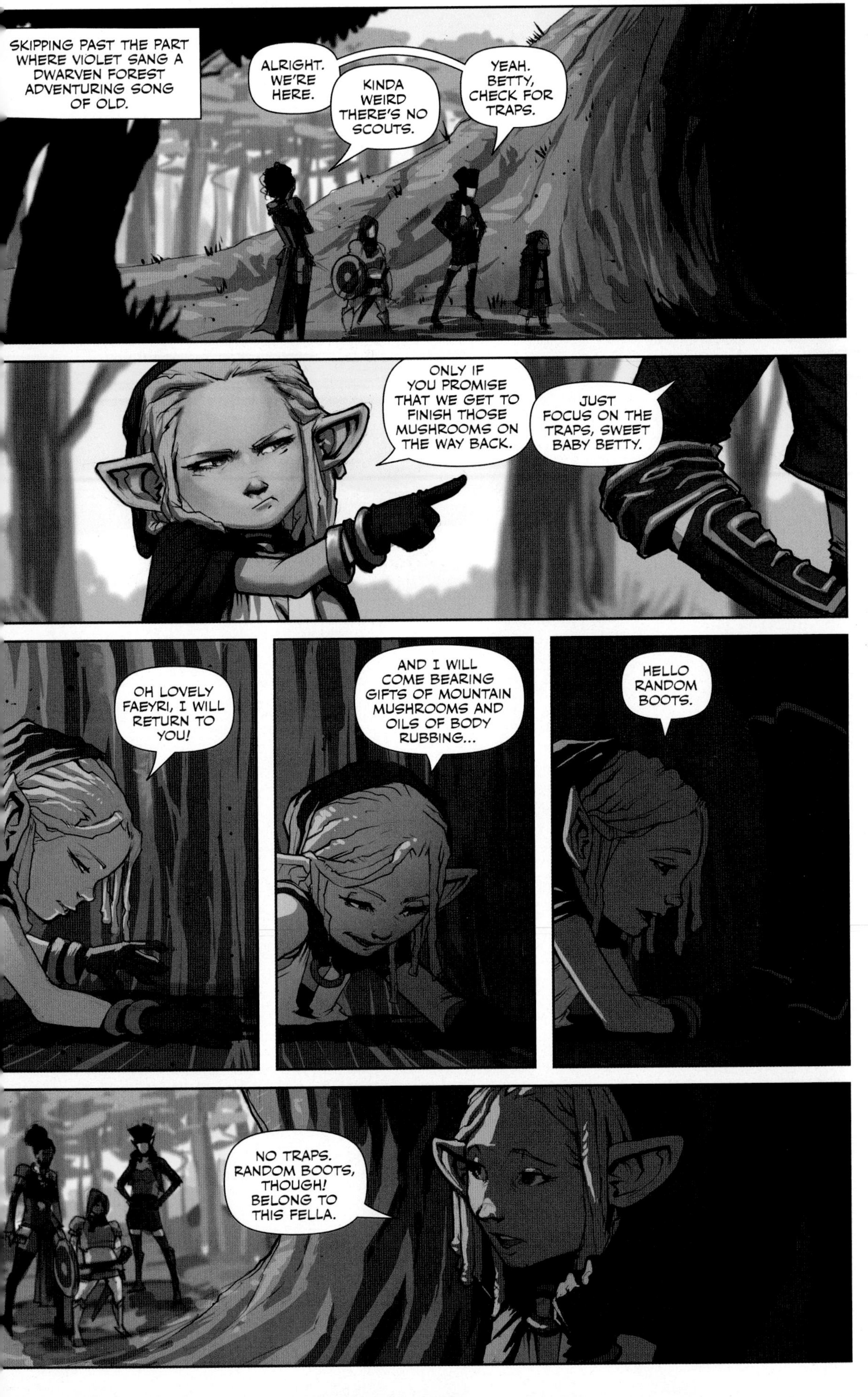
SKIPPING PAST THE PART WHERE VIOLET SANG A DWARVEN FOREST ADVENTURING SONG OF OLD.
ALRIGHT. WE'RE HERE.
KINDA WEIRD THERE'S NO SCOUTS.
YEAH. BETTY, CHECK FOR TRAPS.
ONLY IF YOU PROMISE THAT WE GET TO FINISH THOSE MUSHROOMS ON THE WAY BACK.
JUST FOCUS ON THE TRAPS, SWEET BABY BETTY.
OH LOVELY FAEYRI, I WILL RETURN TO YOU!
AND I WILL COME BEARING GIFTS OF MOUNTAIN MUSHROOMS AND OILS OF BODY RUBBING...
HELLO RANDOM BOOTS.
NO TRAPS. RANDOM BOOTS, THOUGH! BELONG TO THIS FELLA.

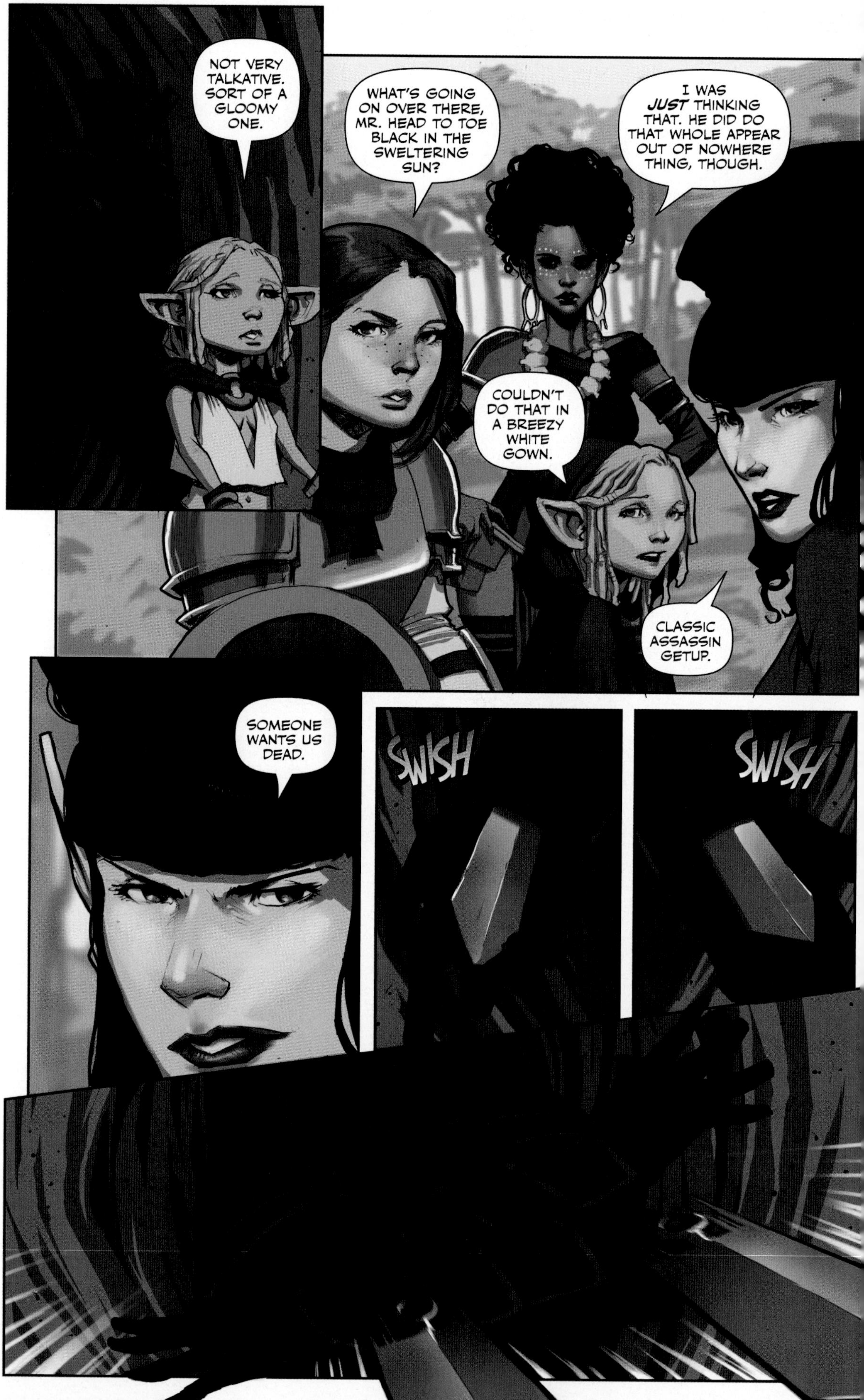
NOT VERY TALKATIVE. SORT OF A GLOOMY ONE.
WHAT'S GOING ON OVER THERE, MR. HEAD TO TOE BLACK IN THE SWELTERING SUN?
I WAS JUST THINKING THAT. HE DID DO THAT WHOLE APPEAR OUT OF NOWHERE THING, THOUGH.
COULDN'T DO THAT IN A BREEZY WHITE GOWN.
CLASSIC ASSASSIN GETUP.
SOMEONE WANTS US DEAD.
SWISH
SWISH

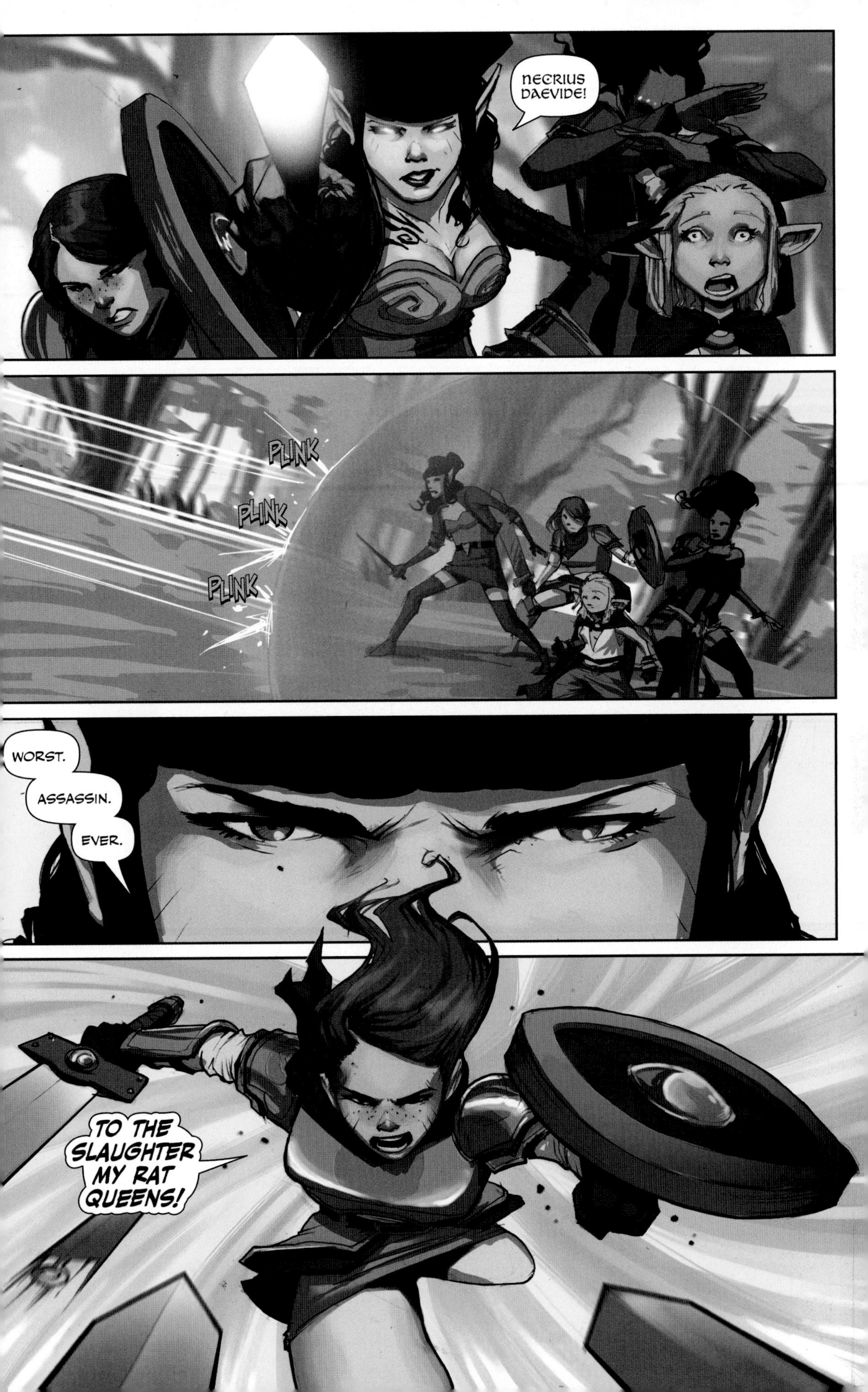
NECRIUS DAEVIDE!
PLINK
PLINK
PLINK
WORST.
ASSASSIN.
EVER.
TO THE SLAUGHTER MY RAT QUEENS!

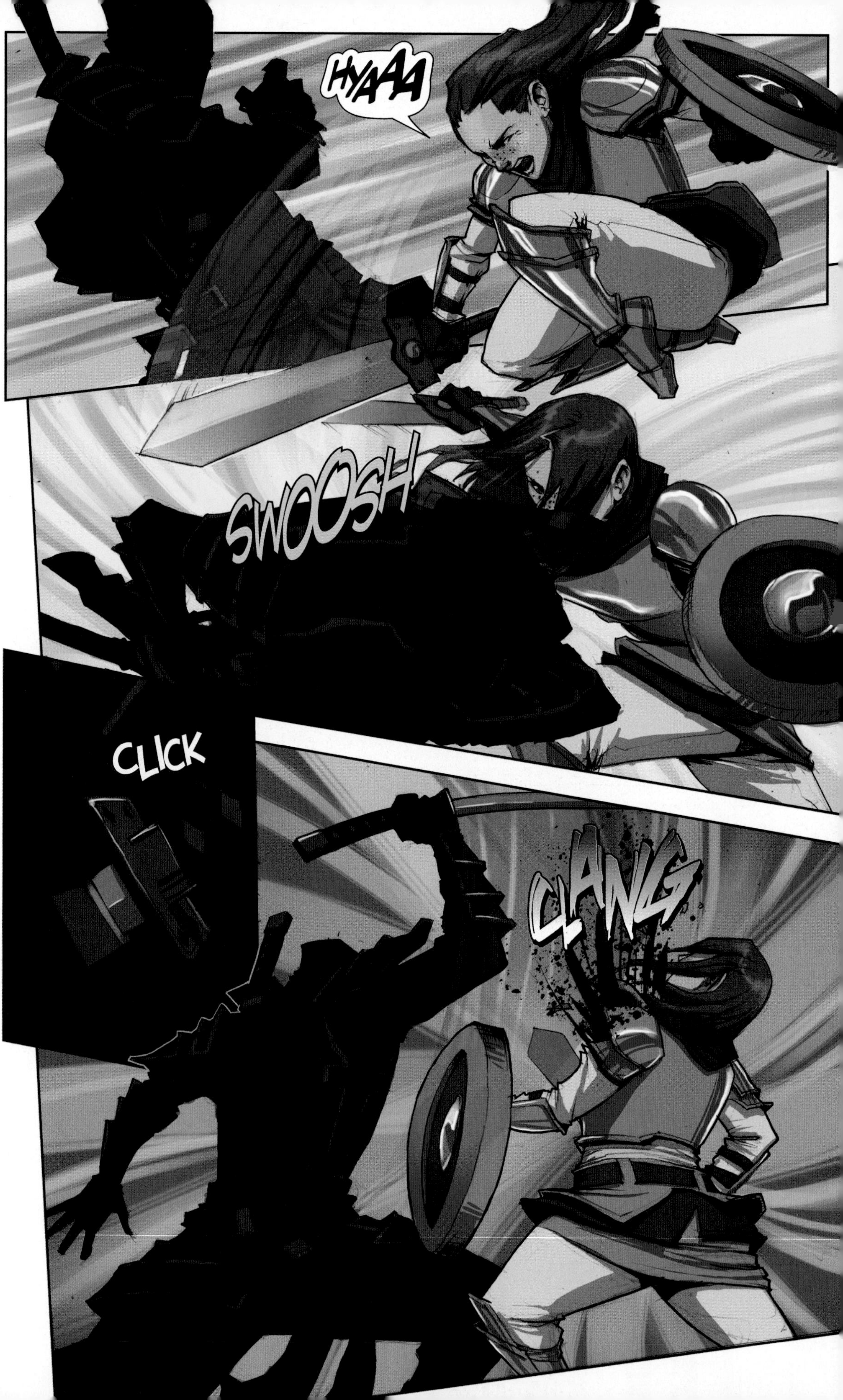
HYAAA
SWOOSH
CLICK
CLANG

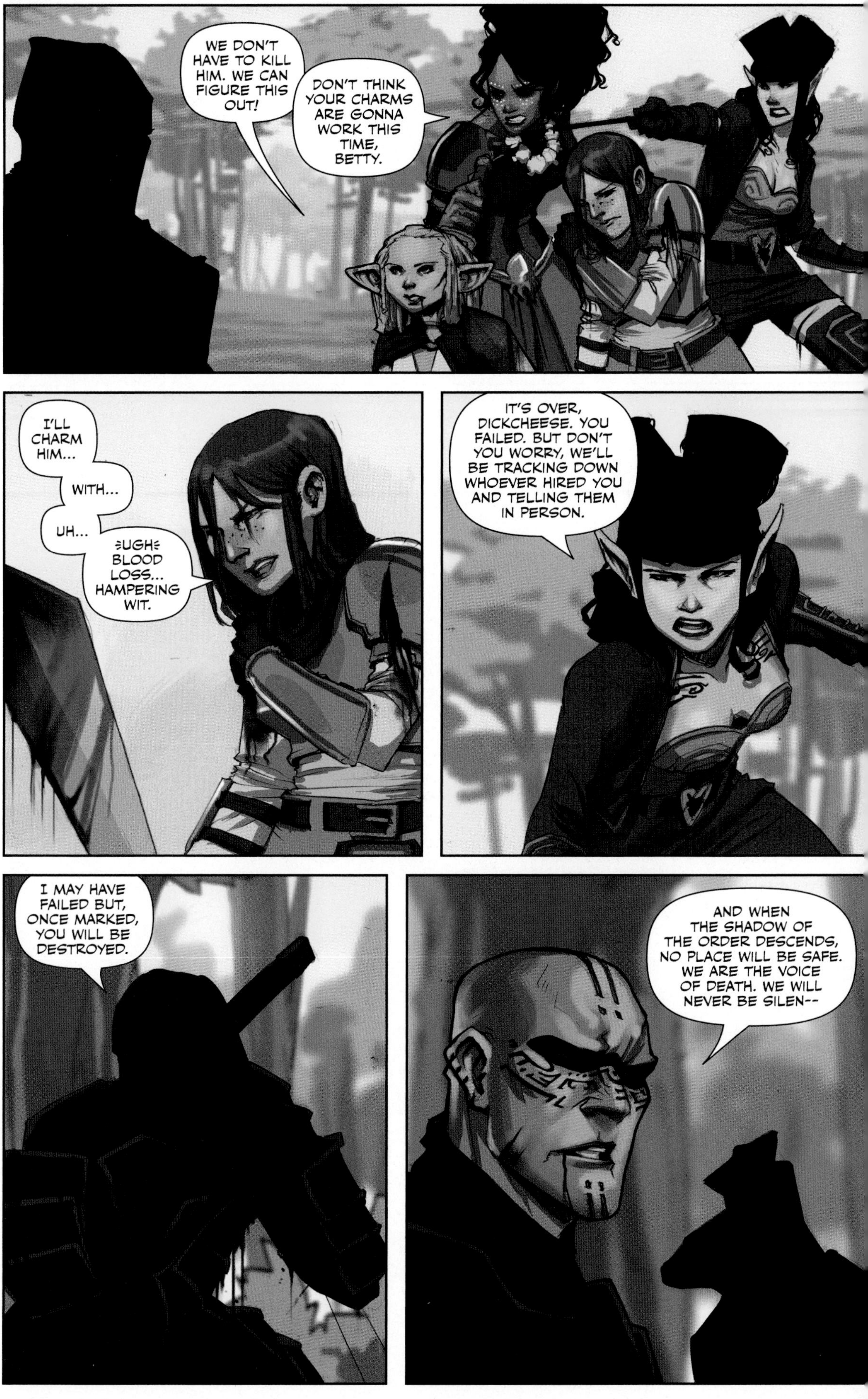
WE DON'T HAVE TO KILL HIM. WE CAN FIGURE THIS OUT!
DON'T THINK YOUR CHARMS ARE GONNA WORK THIS TIME, BETTY.
I'LL CHARM HIM...
WITH...
UH...
UGH BLOOD LOSS... HAMPERING WIT.
IT'S OVER, DICKCHEESE. YOU FAILED. BUT DON'T YOU WORRY, WE'LL BE TRACKING DOWN WHOEVER HIRED YOU AND TELLING THEM IN PERSON.
I MAY HAVE FAILED BUT, ONCE MARKED, YOU WILL BE DESTROYED.
AND WHEN THE SHADOW OF THE ORDER DESCENDS, NO PLACE WILL BE SAFE. WE ARE THE VOICE OF DEATH. WE WILL NEVER BE SILEN--

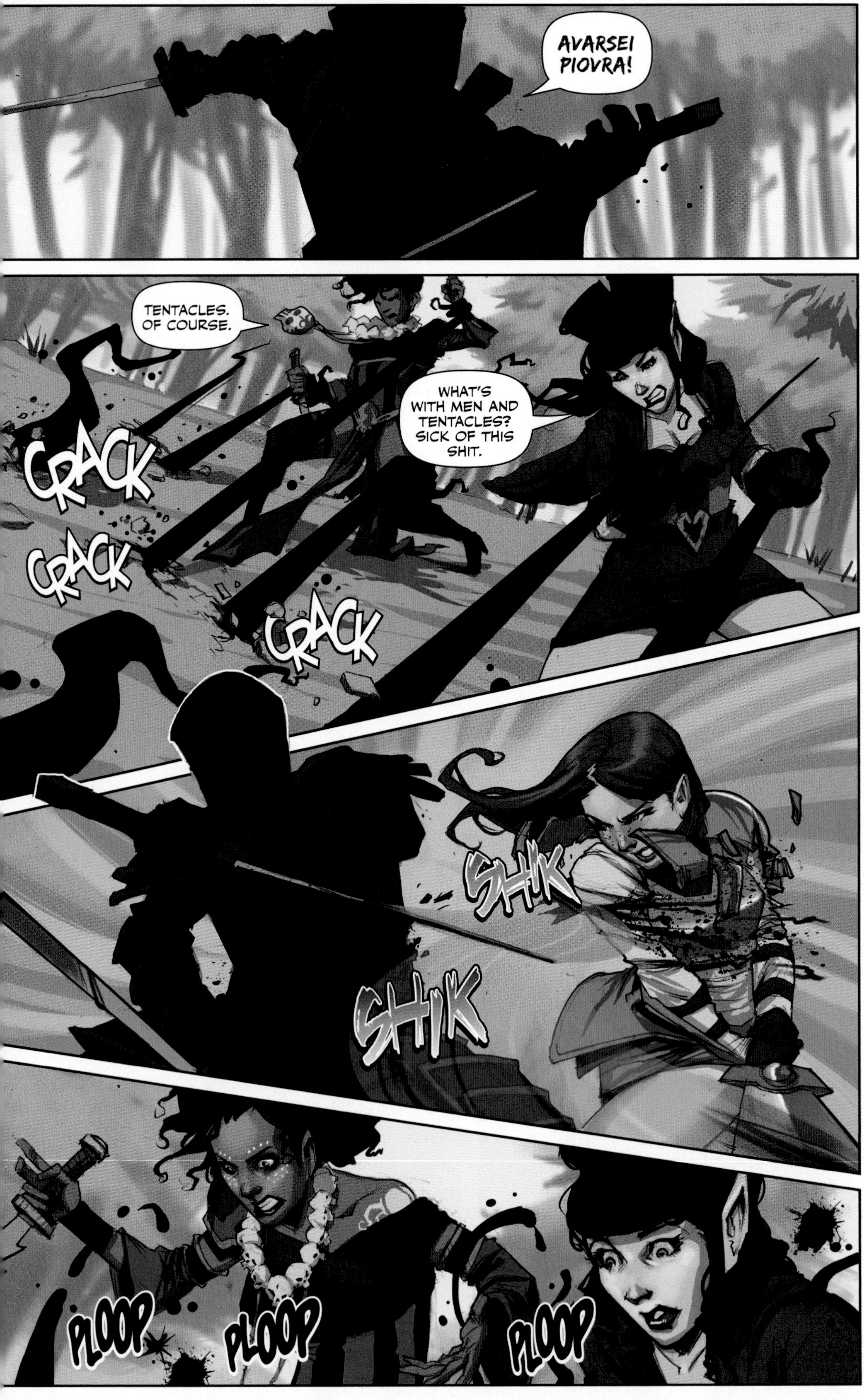
AVARSEI PIOVRA!
TENTACLES. OF COURSE.
WHAT'S WITH MEN AND TENTACLES? SICK OF THIS SHIT.
CRACK
CRACK
CRACK
SHIK
SHIK
PLOOP
PLOOP
PLOOP

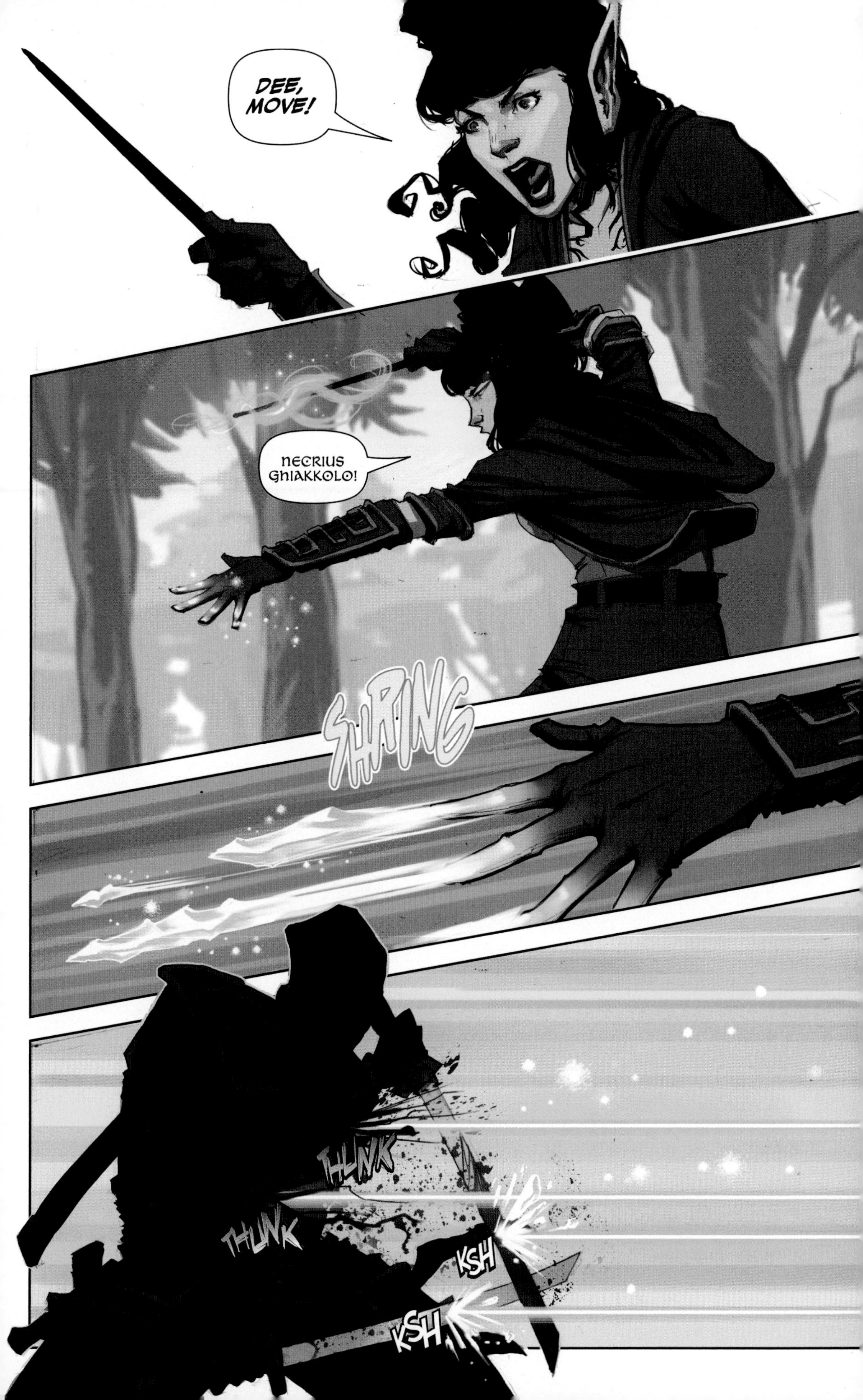
DEE, MOVE!
NECRIUS GHIAKKOLO!
SHRING
THUNK
THUNK
KSH
KSH

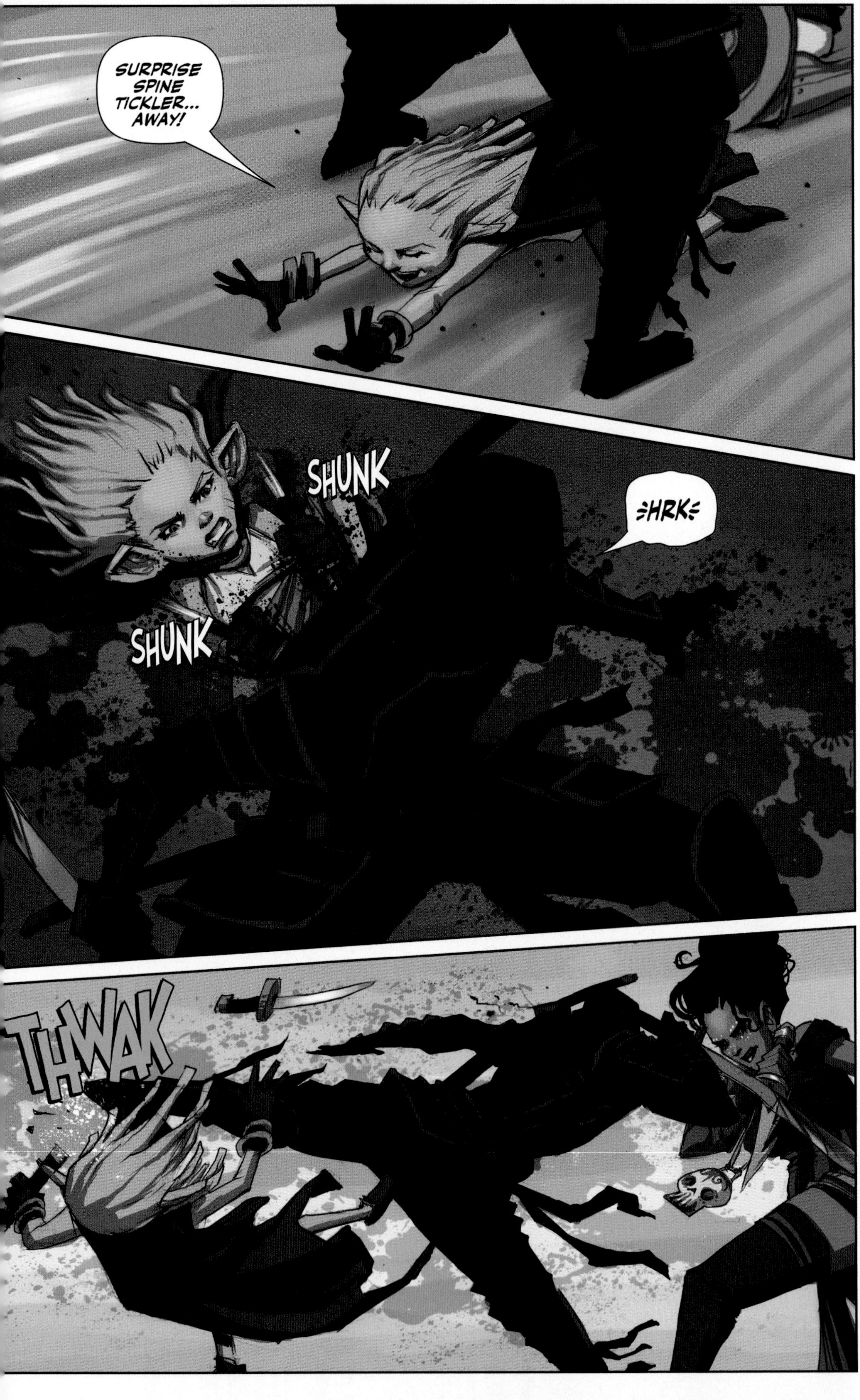
SURPRISE SPINE TICKLER... AWAY!
SHUNK
SHUNK
HRK
THWAK

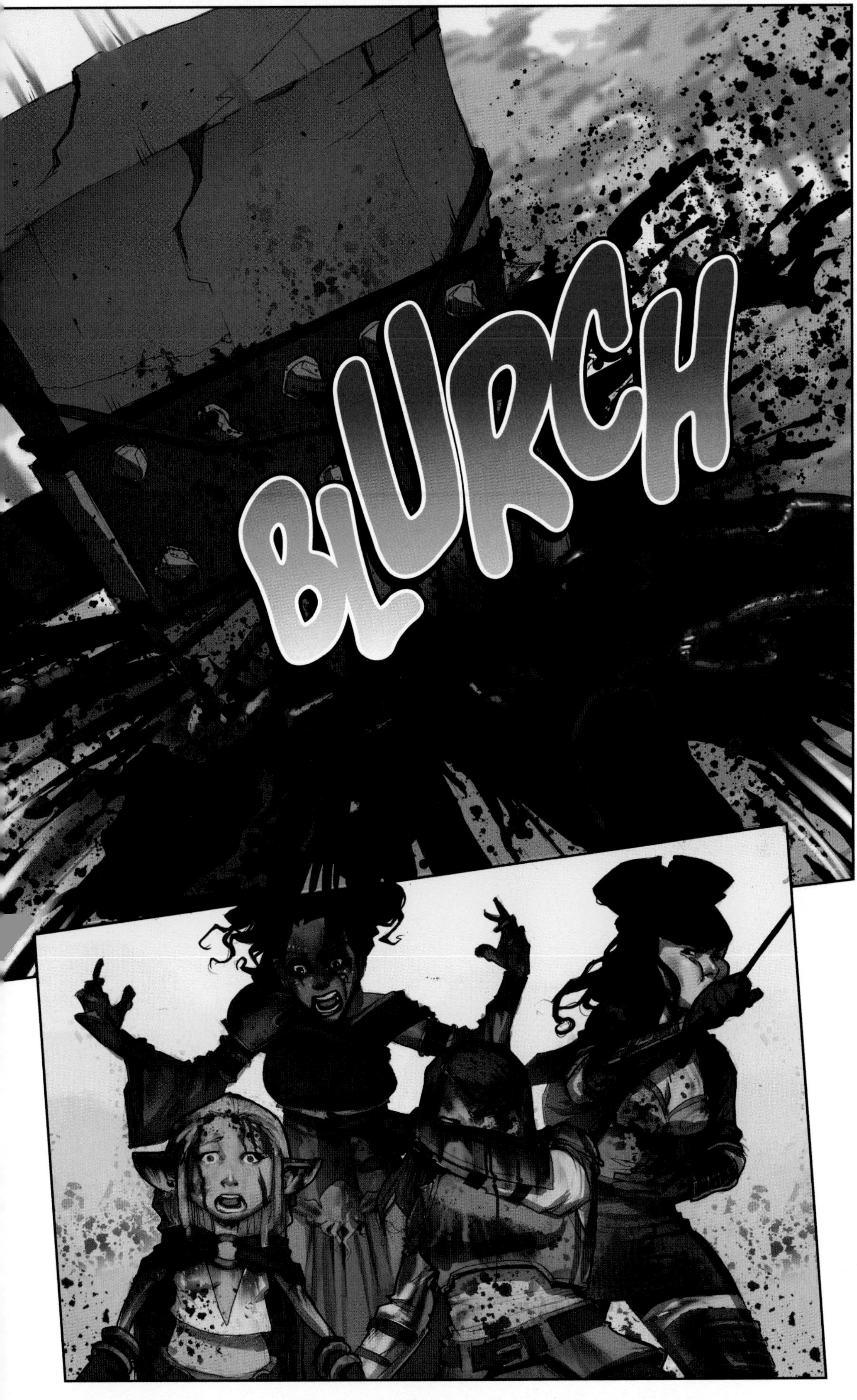
BLURCH

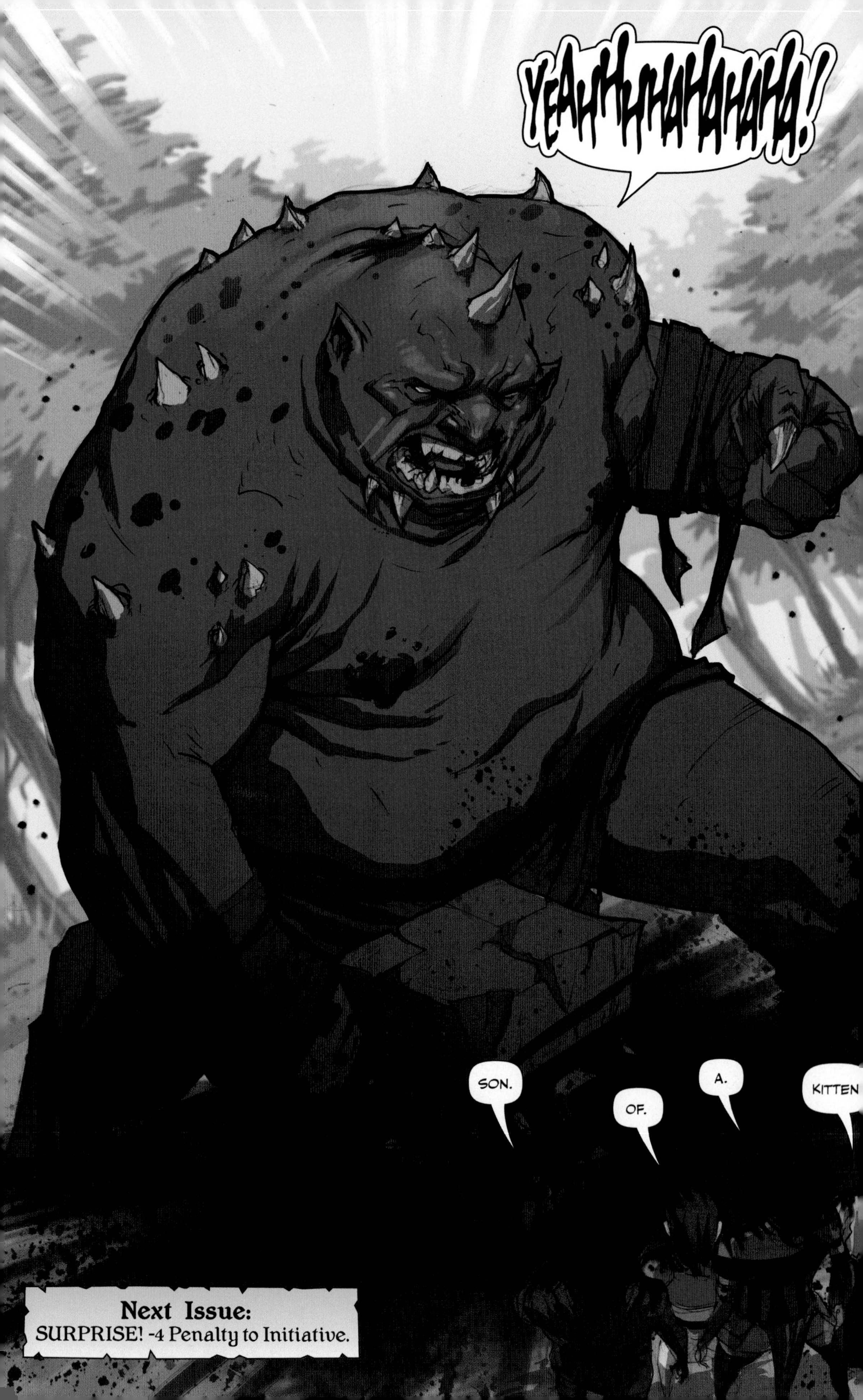

YEAHHHHAHAHAHA!
SON.
OF.
A.
KITTEN
Next Issue:
SURPRISE! -4 Penalty to Initiative.

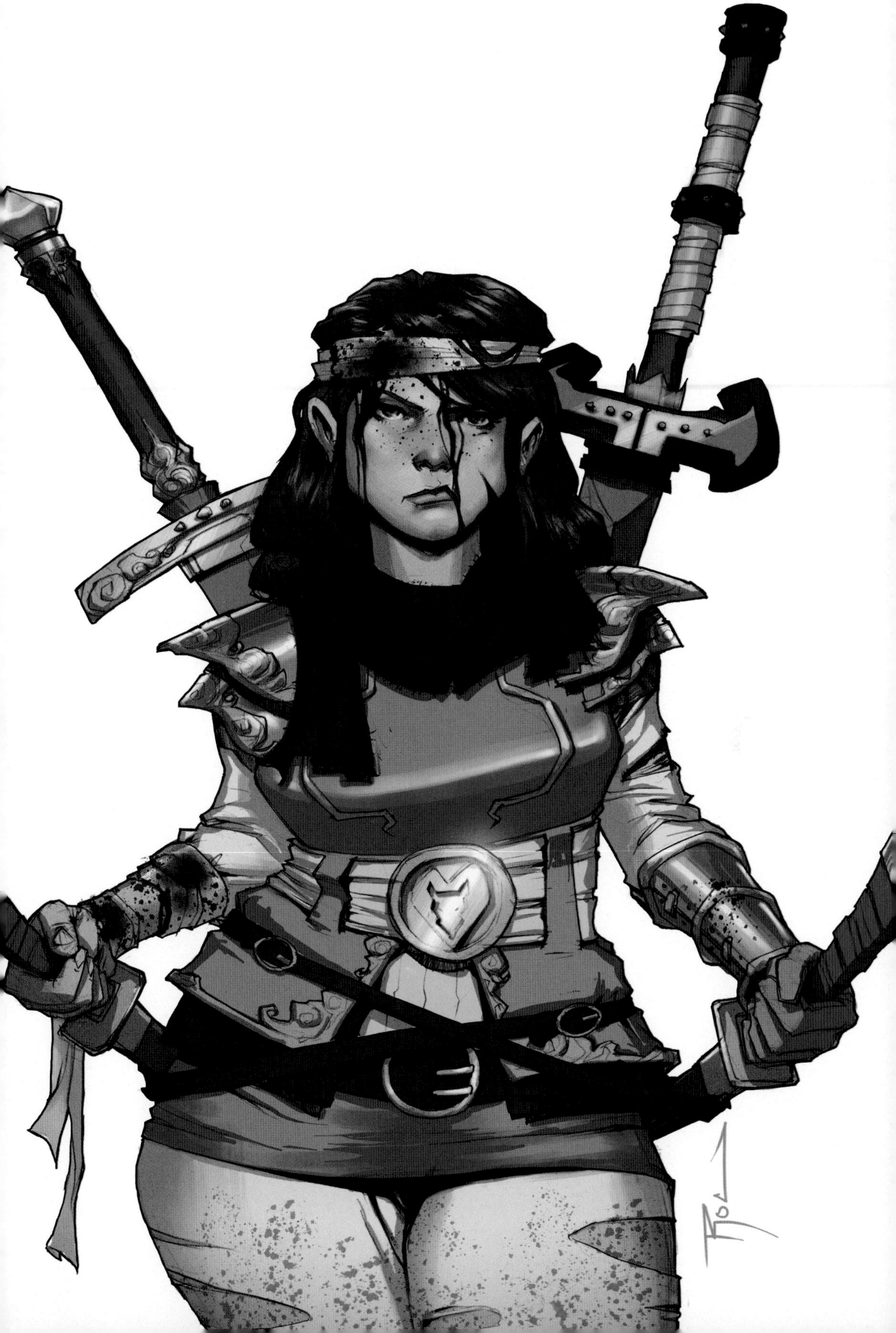

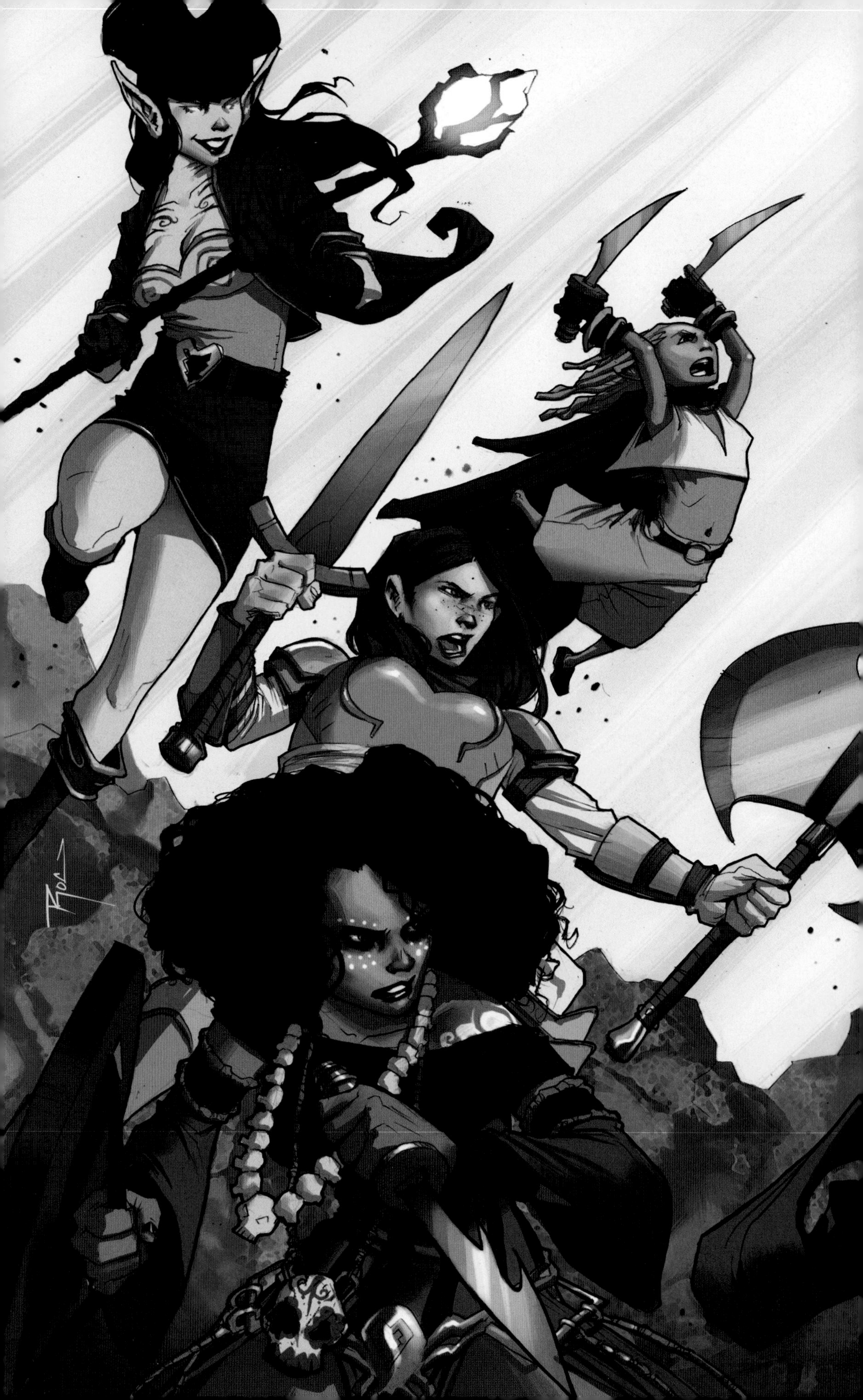

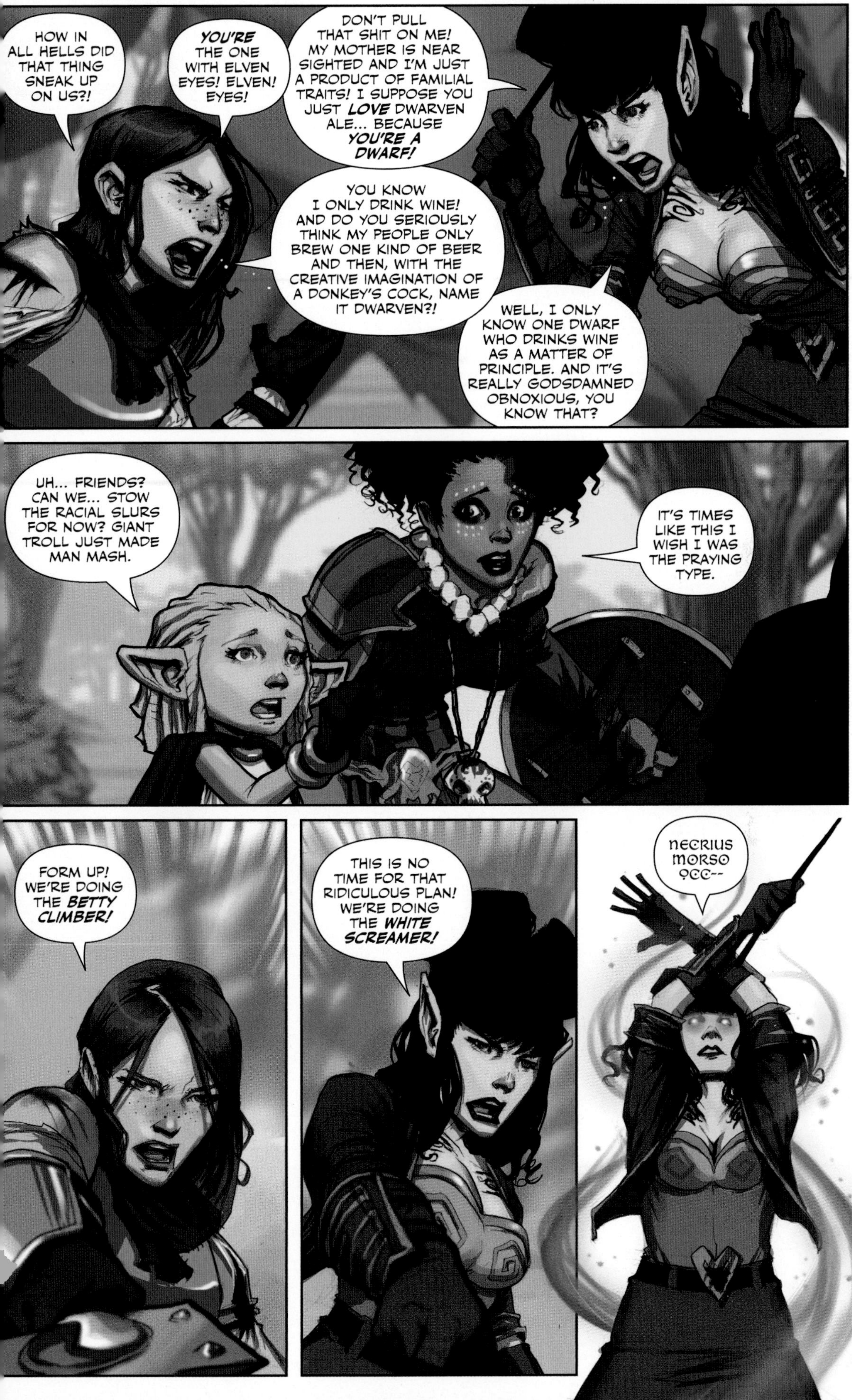
HOW IN ALL HELLS DID THAT THING SNEAK UP ON US?!
YOU'RE THE ONE WITH ELVEN EYES! ELVEN! EYES!
DON'T PULL THAT SHIT ON ME! MY MOTHER IS NEAR SIGHTED AND I'M JUST A PRODUCT OF FAMILIAL TRAITS! I SUPPOSE YOU JUST LOVE DWARVEN ALE... BECAUSE YOU'RE A DWARF!
YOU KNOW I ONLY DRINK WINE! AND DO YOU SERIOUSLY THINK MY PEOPLE ONLY BREW ONE KIND OF BEER AND THEN, WITH THE CREATIVE IMAGINATION OF A DONKEY'S COCK, NAME IT DWARVEN?!
WELL, I ONLY KNOW ONE DWARF WHO DRINKS WINE AS A MATTER OF PRINCIPLE. AND IT'S REALLY GODSDAMNED OBNOXIOUS, YOU KNOW THAT?
UH... FRIENDS? CAN WE... STOW THE RACIAL SLURS FOR NOW? GIANT TROLL JUST MADE MAN MASH.
IT'S TIMES LIKE THIS I WISH I WAS THE PRAYING TYPE.
FORM UP! WE'RE DOING THE BETTY CLIMBER!
THIS IS NO TIME FOR THAT RIDICULOUS PLAN! WE'RE DOING THE WHITE SCREAMER!
NECRIUS MORSO OCC--

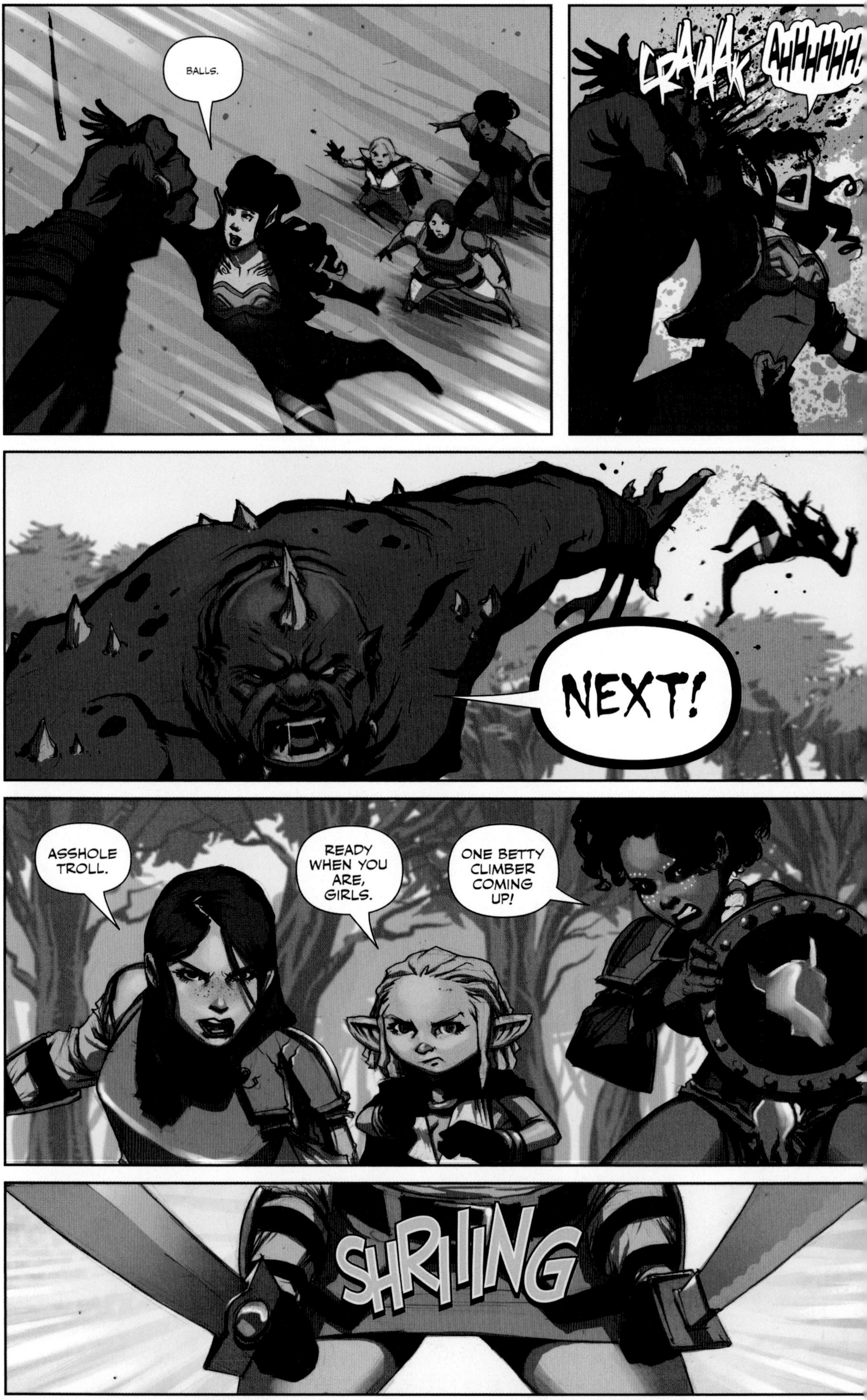
BALLS.
CRAAAAK
AHHHHHH!
NEXT!
ASSHOLE TROLL.
READY WHEN YOU ARE, GIRLS.
ONE BETTY CLIMBER COMING UP!
SHRIIING

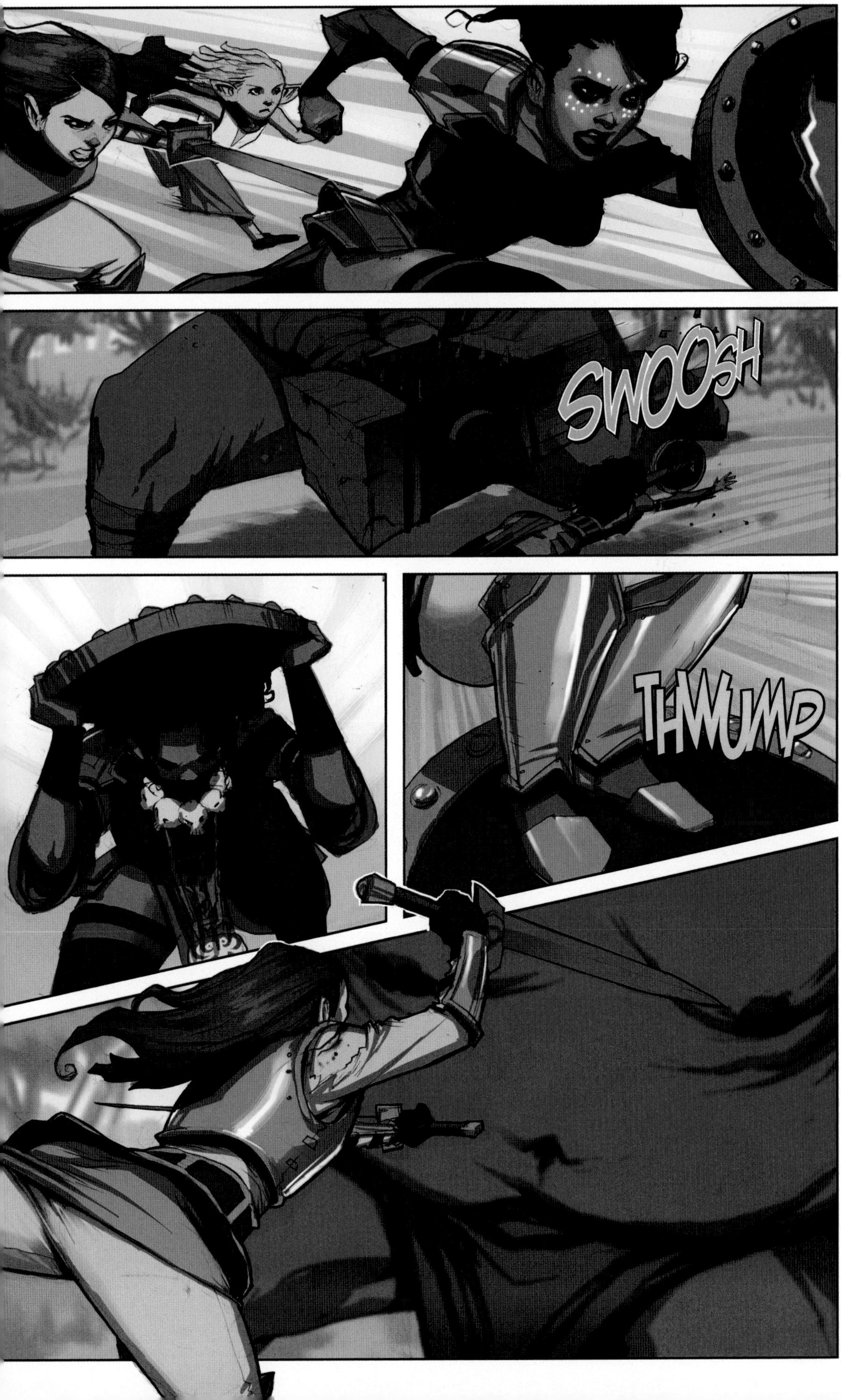
SWOOSH
THWUMP

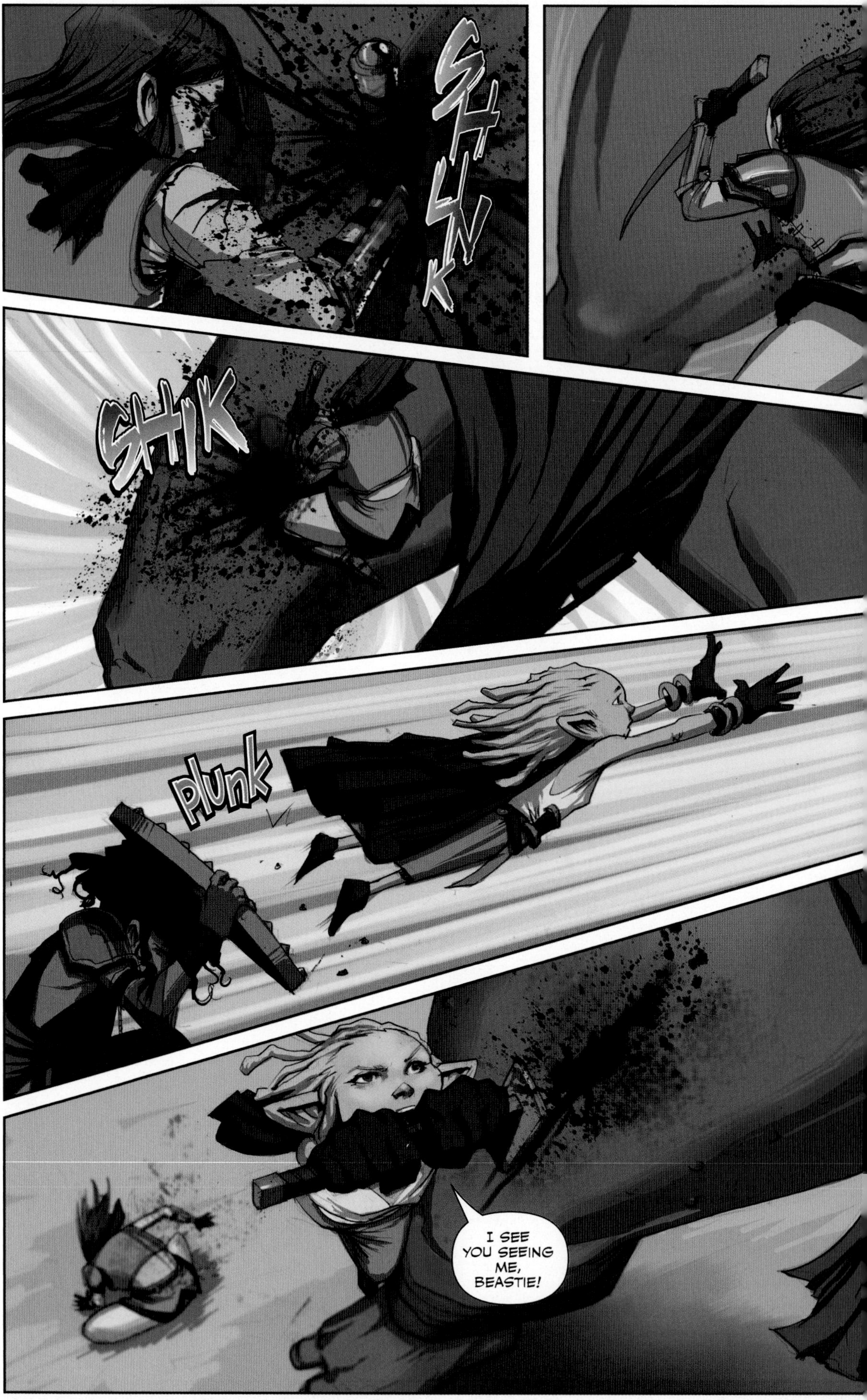
SHLNK
SHIK
plunk
I SEE YOU SEEING ME, BEASTIE!

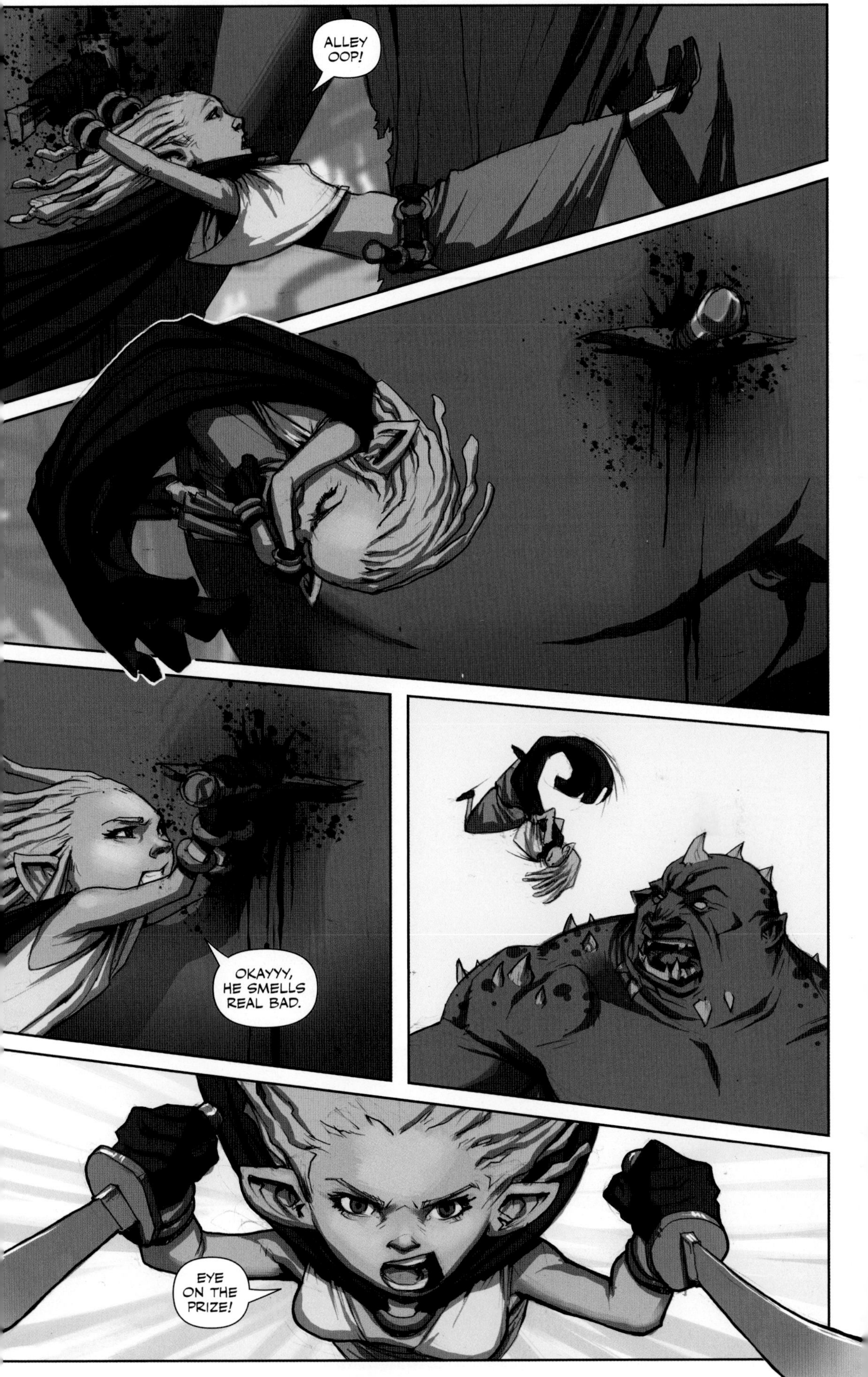
ALLEY OOP!
OKAYYY, HE SMELLS REAL BAD.
EYE ON THE PRIZE!

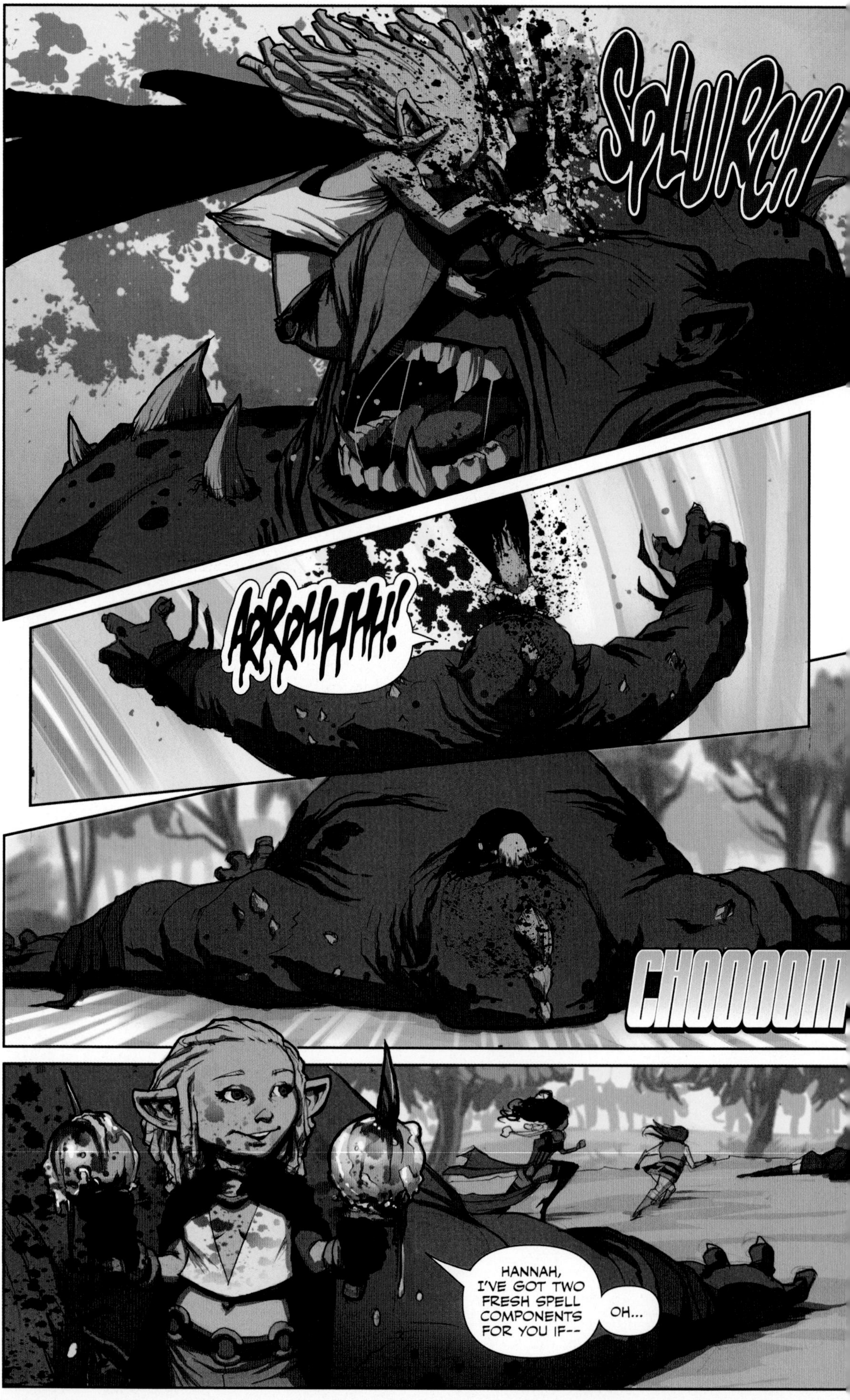
SPLURCH
ARRRHHHH!
CHOOOOM
HANNAH, I'VE GOT TWO FRESH SPELL COMPONENTS FOR YOU IF--
OH...

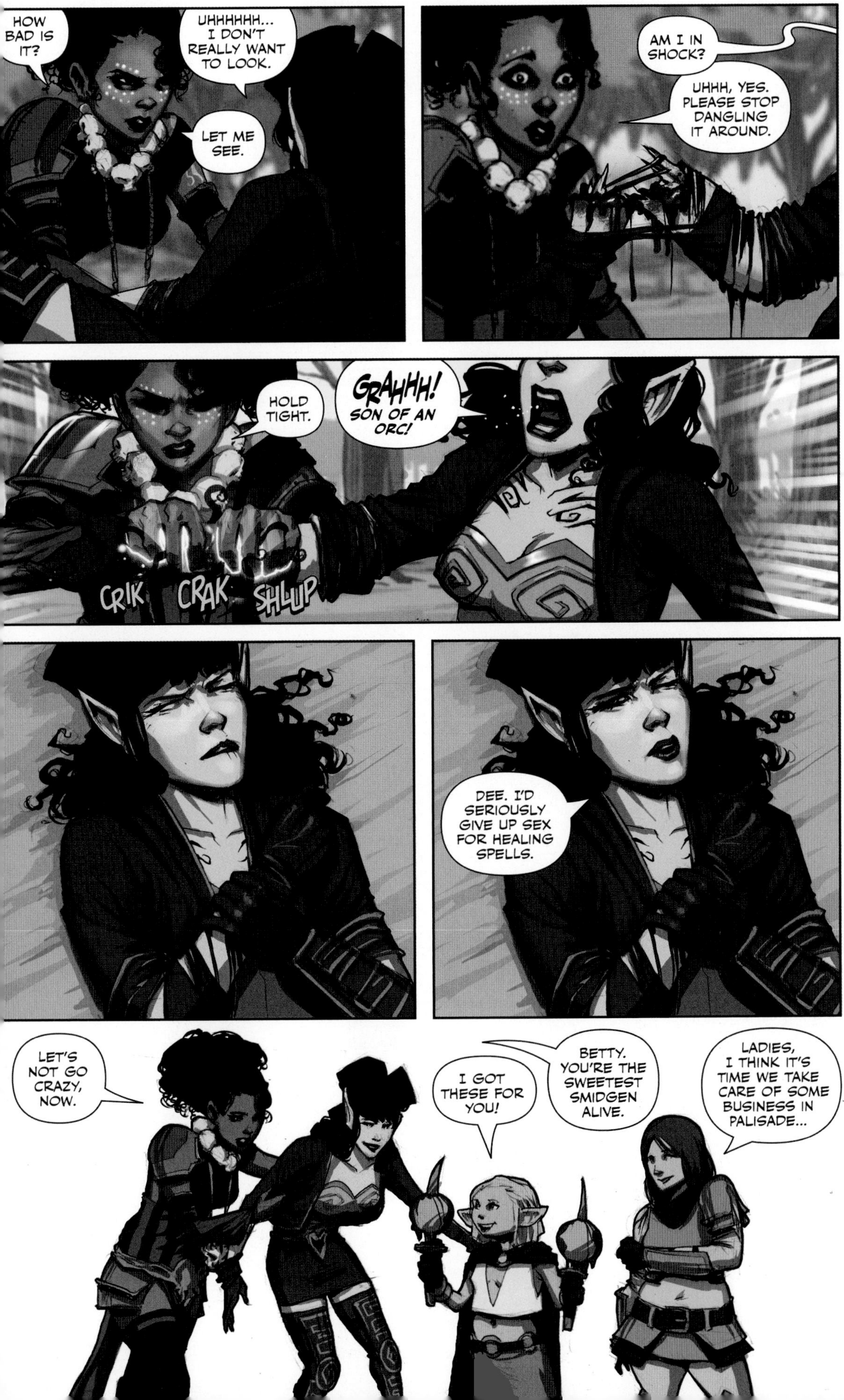
HOW BAD IS IT?
UHHHHHH... I DON'T REALLY WANT TO LOOK.
LET ME SEE.
AM I IN SHOCK?
UHHH, YES. PLEASE STOP DANGLING IT AROUND.
HOLD TIGHT.
GRAHHH! SON OF AN ORC!
CRIK
CRAK
SHLUP
DEE. I'D SERIOUSLY GIVE UP SEX FOR HEALING SPELLS.
LET'S NOT GO CRAZY, NOW.
I GOT THESE FOR YOU!
BETTY. YOU'RE THE SWEETEST SMIDGEN ALIVE.
LADIES, I THINK IT'S TIME WE TAKE CARE OF SOME BUSINESS IN PALISADE...

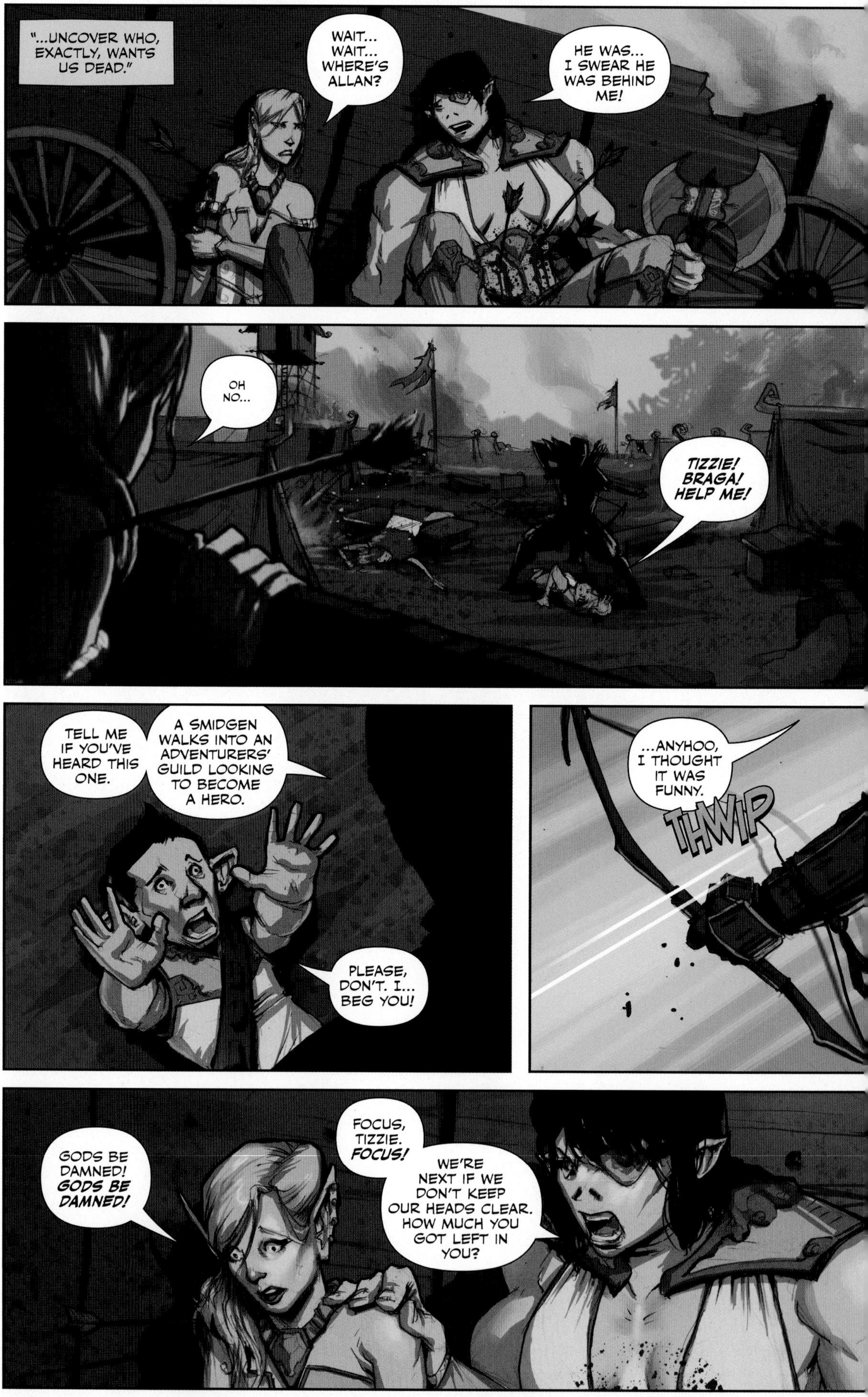
"...UNCOVER WHO, EXACTLY, WANTS US DEAD."
WAIT... WAIT... WHERE'S ALLAN?
HE WAS... I SWEAR HE WAS BEHIND ME!
OH NO...
TIZZIE! BRAGA! HELP ME!
TELL ME IF YOU'VE HEARD THIS ONE.
A SMIDGEN WALKS INTO AN ADVENTURERS' GUILD LOOKING TO BECOME A HERO.
PLEASE, DON'T. I... BEG YOU!
...ANYHOO, I THOUGHT IT WAS FUNNY.
THWIP
GODS BE DAMNED! GODS BE DAMNED!
FOCUS, TIZZIE. FOCUS!
WE'RE NEXT IF WE DON'T KEEP OUR HEADS CLEAR. HOW MUCH YOU GOT LEFT IN YOU?

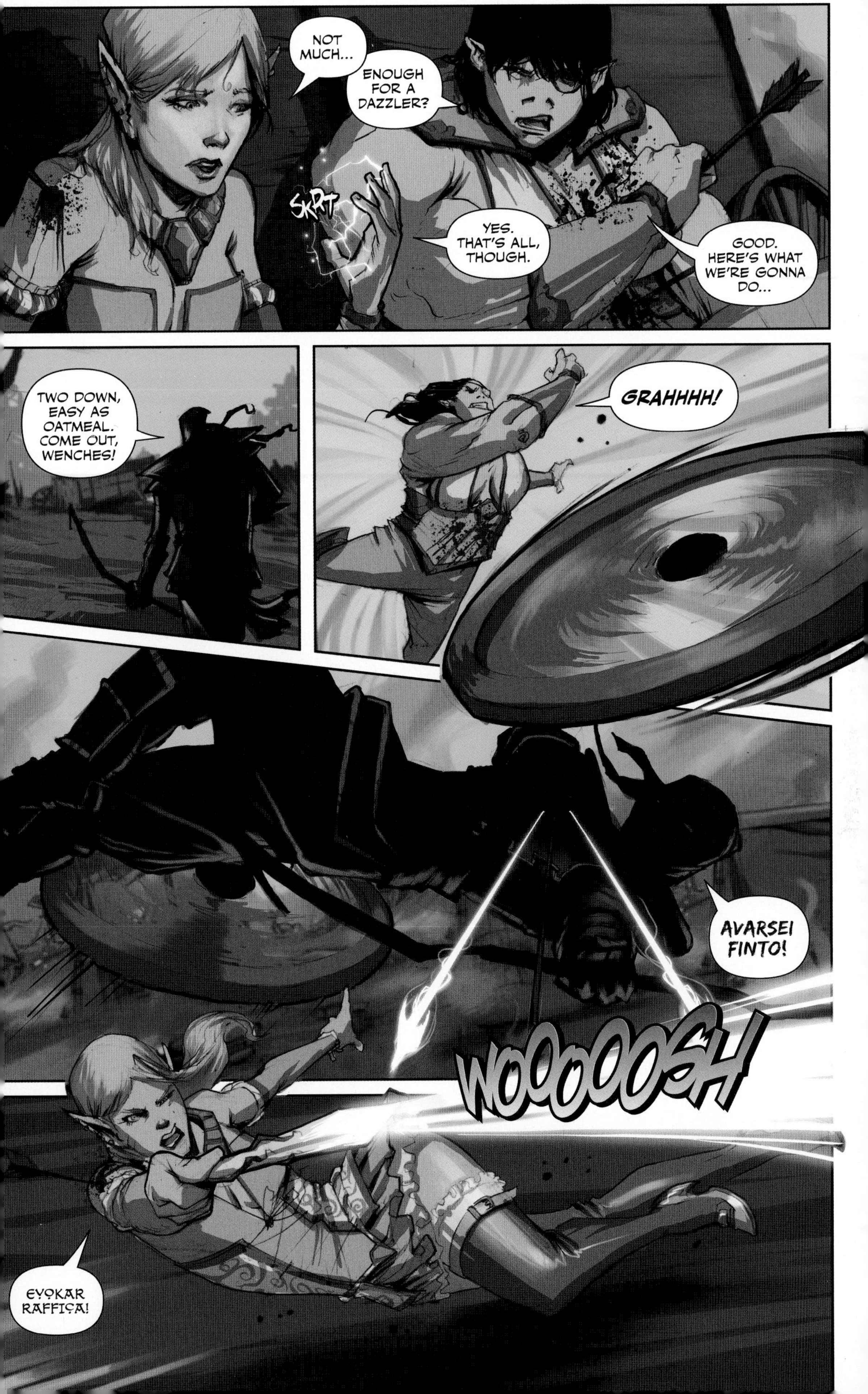
NOT MUCH...
ENOUGH FOR A DAZZLER?
SKRT
YES. THAT'S ALL, THOUGH.
GOOD. HERE'S WHAT WE'RE GONNA DO...
TWO DOWN, EASY AS OATMEAL. COME OUT, WENCHES!
GRAHHHH!
AVARSEI FINTO!
WOOOOOSH
EYOKAR RAFFIÇA!

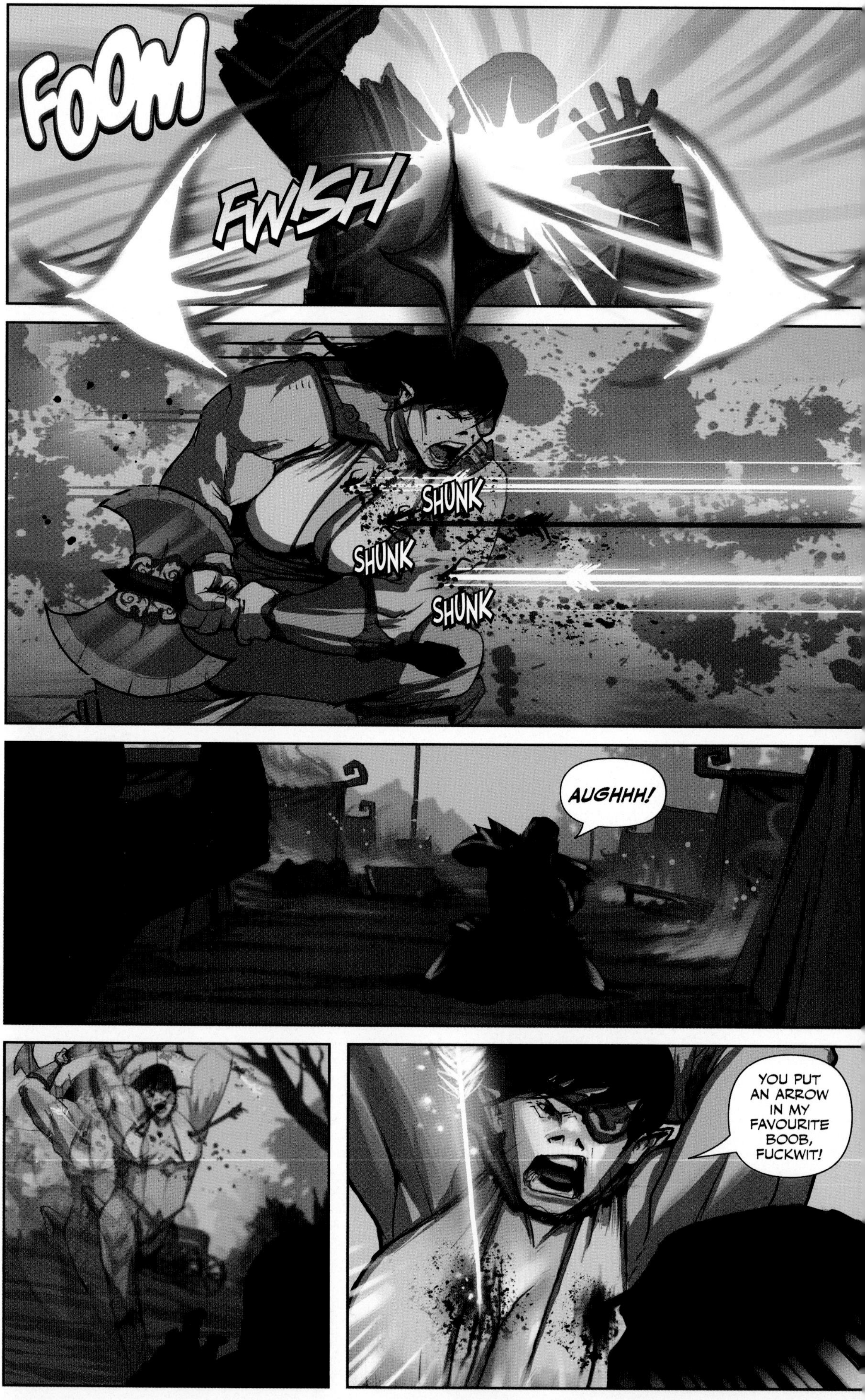
FOOM
FWISH
SHUNK
SHUNK
SHUNK
AUGHHH!
YOU PUT AN ARROW IN MY FAVOURITE BOOB, FUCKWIT!

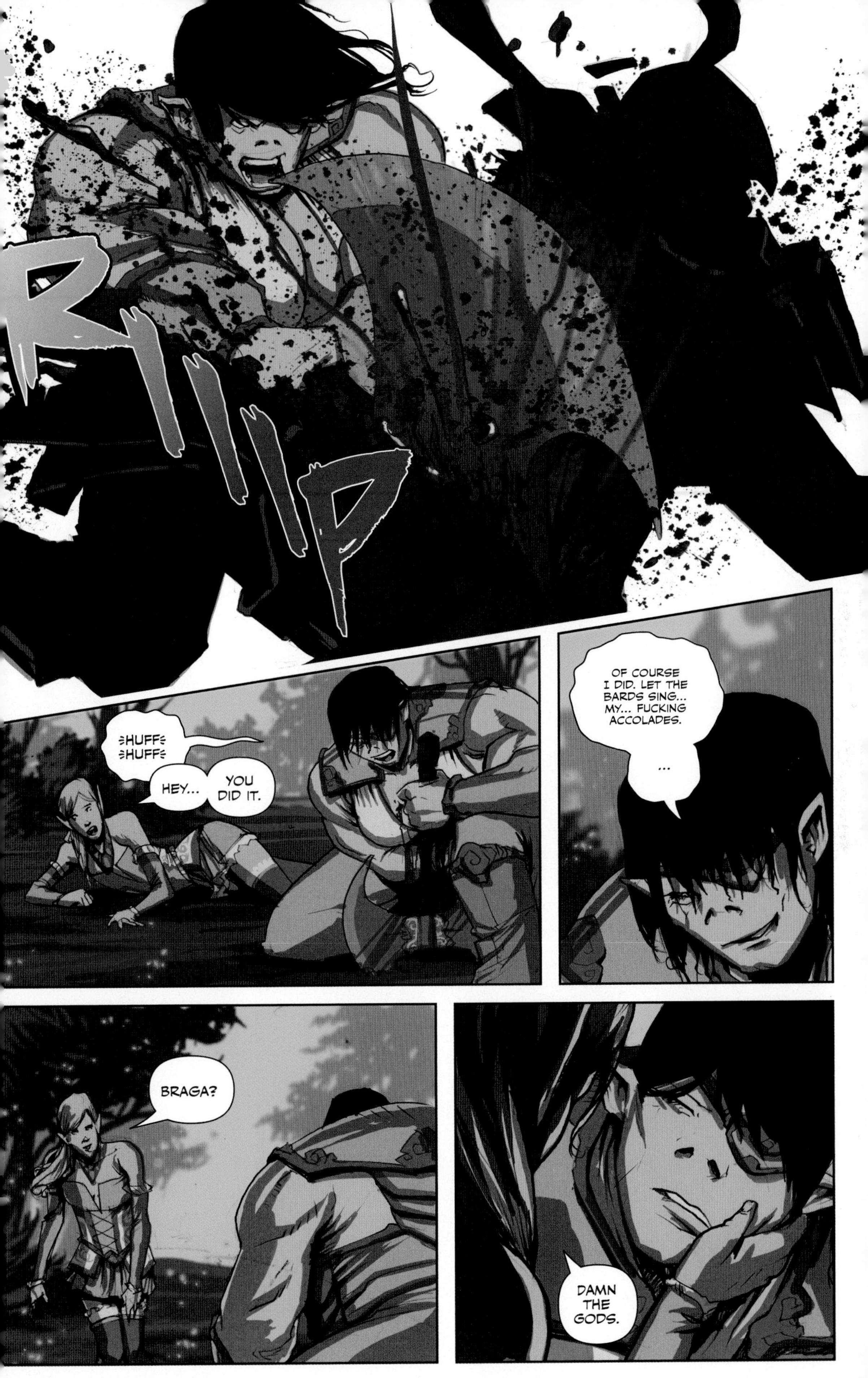
RRIIP
HUFF HUFF
HEY...
YOU DID IT.
OF COURSE I DID. LET THE BARDS SING... MY... FUCKING ACCOLADES.
...
BRAGA?
DAMN THE GODS.

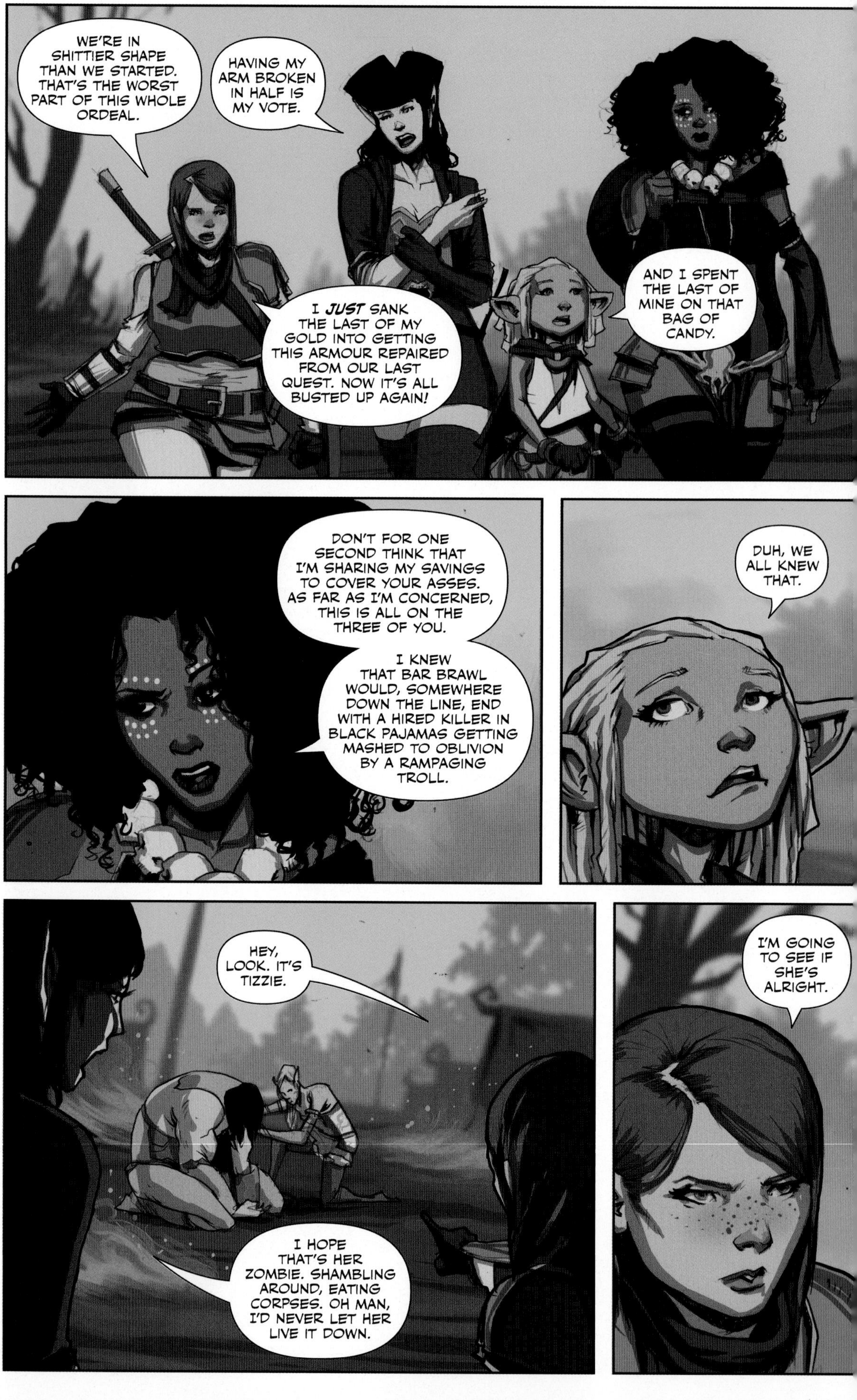
WE'RE IN SHITTIER SHAPE THAN WE STARTED. THAT'S THE WORST PART OF THIS WHOLE ORDEAL.
HAVING MY ARM BROKEN IN HALF IS MY VOTE.
I *JUST* SANK THE LAST OF MY GOLD INTO GETTING THIS ARMOUR REPAIRED FROM OUR LAST QUEST. NOW IT'S ALL BUSTED UP AGAIN!
AND I SPENT THE LAST OF MINE ON THAT BAG OF CANDY.
DON'T FOR ONE SECOND THINK THAT I'M SHARING MY SAVINGS TO COVER YOUR ASSES. AS FAR AS I'M CONCERNED, THIS IS ALL ON THE THREE OF YOU.
I KNEW THAT BAR BRAWL WOULD, SOMEWHERE DOWN THE LINE, END WITH A HIRED KILLER IN BLACK PAJAMAS GETTING MASHED TO OBLIVION BY A RAMPAGING TROLL.
DUH, WE ALL KNEW THAT.
HEY, LOOK. IT'S TIZZIE.
I HOPE THAT'S HER ZOMBIE. SHAMBLING AROUND, EATING CORPSES. OH MAN, I'D NEVER LET HER LIVE IT DOWN.
I'M GOING TO SEE IF SHE'S ALRIGHT.

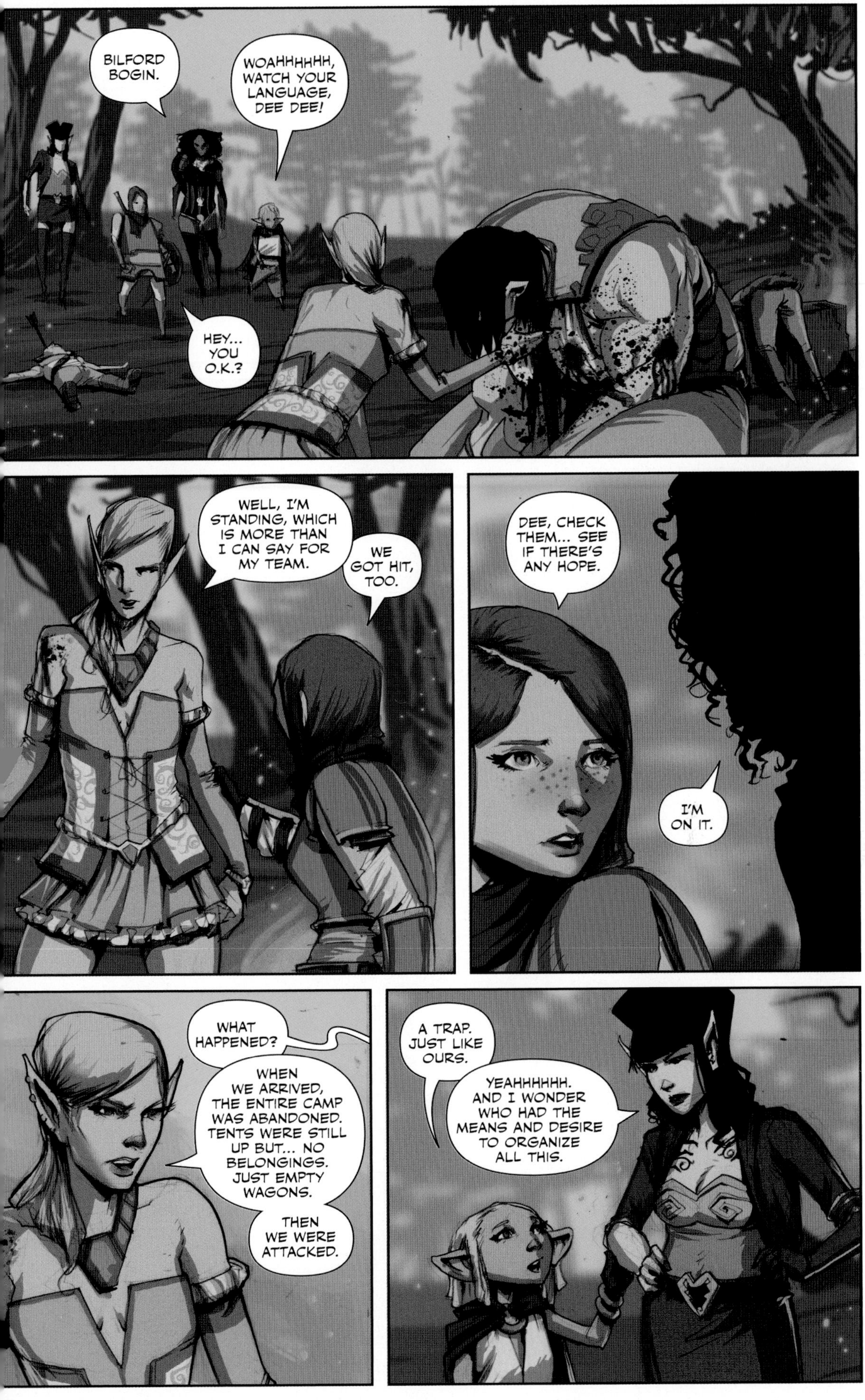
BILFORD BOGIN.
WOAHHHHHH, WATCH YOUR LANGUAGE, DEE DEE!
HEY... YOU O.K.?
WELL, I'M STANDING, WHICH IS MORE THAN I CAN SAY FOR MY TEAM.
WE GOT HIT, TOO.
DEE, CHECK THEM... SEE IF THERE'S ANY HOPE.
I'M ON IT.
WHAT HAPPENED?
WHEN WE ARRIVED, THE ENTIRE CAMP WAS ABANDONED. TENTS WERE STILL UP BUT... NO BELONGINGS. JUST EMPTY WAGONS.
THEN WE WERE ATTACKED.
A TRAP. JUST LIKE OURS.
YEAHHHHHH. AND I WONDER WHO HAD THE MEANS AND DESIRE TO ORGANIZE ALL THIS.

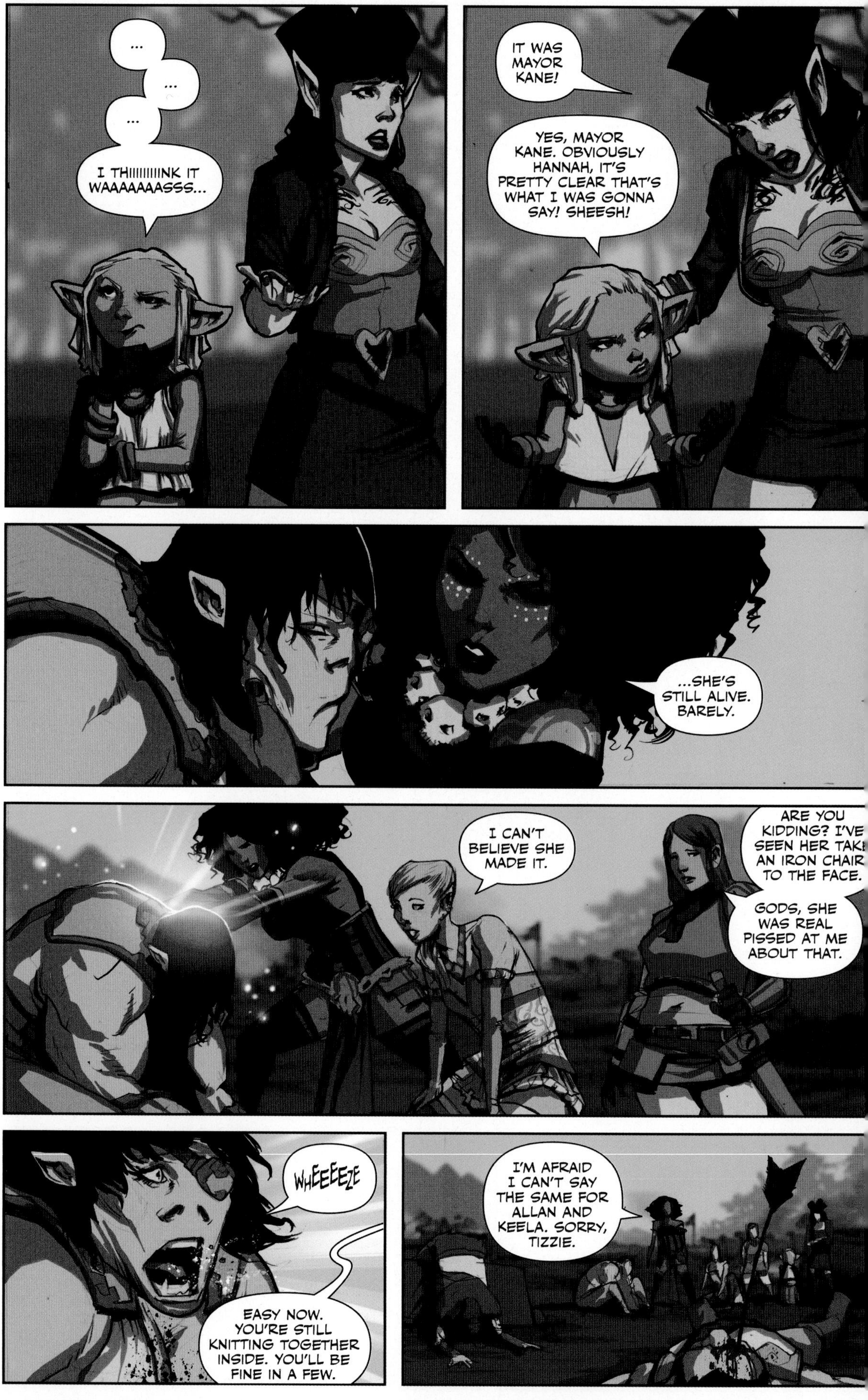
...
...
...
I THIIIIIIIINK IT WAAAAAAASSS...
IT WAS MAYOR KANE!
YES, MAYOR KANE. OBVIOUSLY HANNAH, IT'S PRETTY CLEAR THAT'S WHAT I WAS GONNA SAY! SHEESH!
...SHE'S STILL ALIVE. BARELY.
I CAN'T BELIEVE SHE MADE IT.
ARE YOU KIDDING? I'VE SEEN HER TAKE AN IRON CHAIR TO THE FACE.
GODS, SHE WAS REAL PISSED AT ME ABOUT THAT.
WHEEEEZE
EASY NOW. YOU'RE STILL KNITTING TOGETHER INSIDE. YOU'LL BE FINE IN A FEW.
I'M AFRAID I CAN'T SAY THE SAME FOR ALLAN AND KEELA. SORRY, TIZZIE.

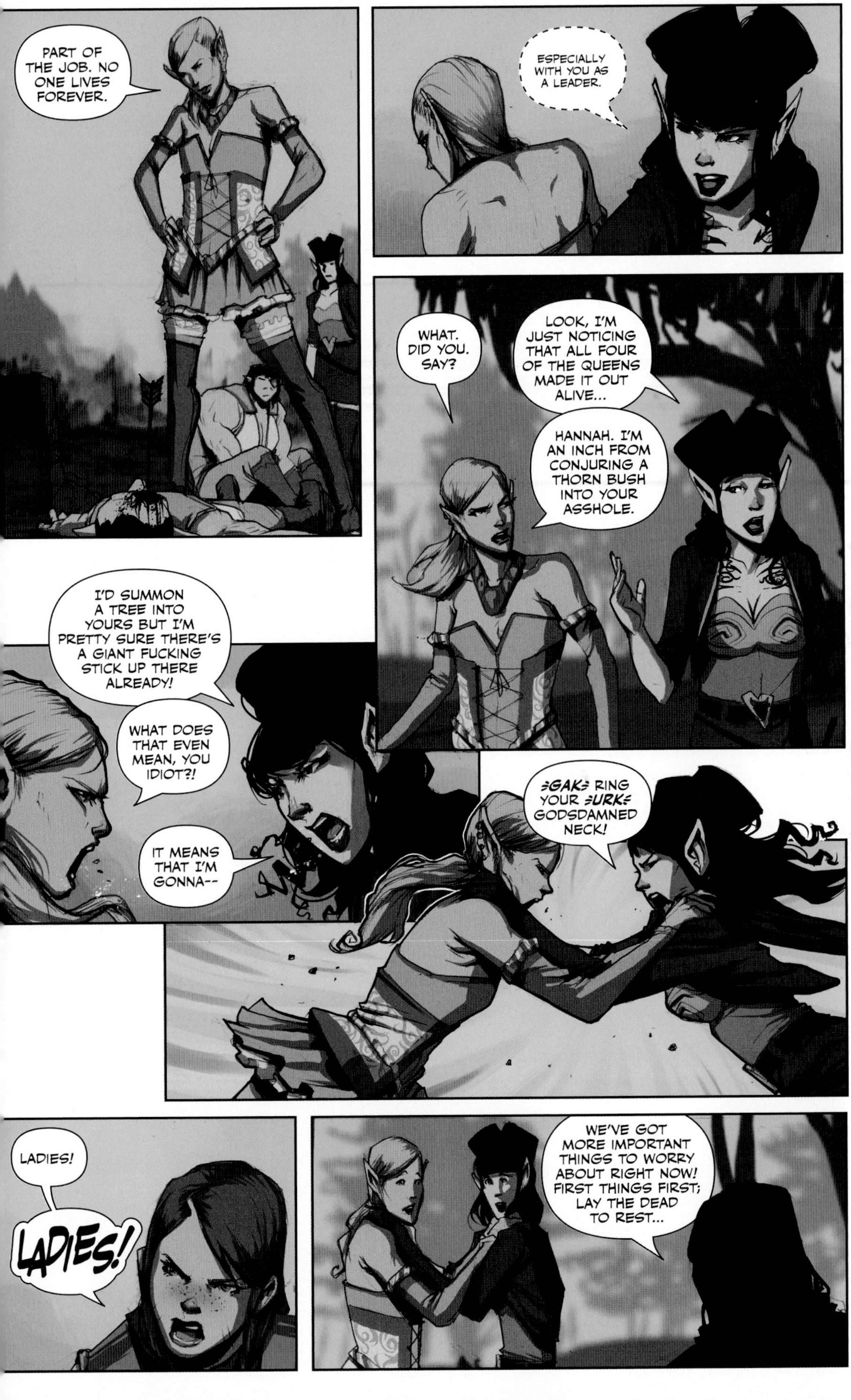
PART OF THE JOB. NO ONE LIVES FOREVER.
ESPECIALLY WITH YOU AS A LEADER.
WHAT. DID YOU. SAY?
LOOK, I'M JUST NOTICING THAT ALL FOUR OF THE QUEENS MADE IT OUT ALIVE...
HANNAH. I'M AN INCH FROM CONJURING A THORN BUSH INTO YOUR ASSHOLE.
I'D SUMMON A TREE INTO YOURS BUT I'M PRETTY SURE THERE'S A GIANT FUCKING STICK UP THERE ALREADY!
WHAT DOES THAT EVEN MEAN, YOU IDIOT?!
IT MEANS THAT I'M GONNA--
GAK RING YOUR URK GODSDAMNED NECK!
LADIES!
LADIES!
WE'VE GOT MORE IMPORTANT THINGS TO WORRY ABOUT RIGHT NOW! FIRST THINGS FIRST; LAY THE DEAD TO REST...

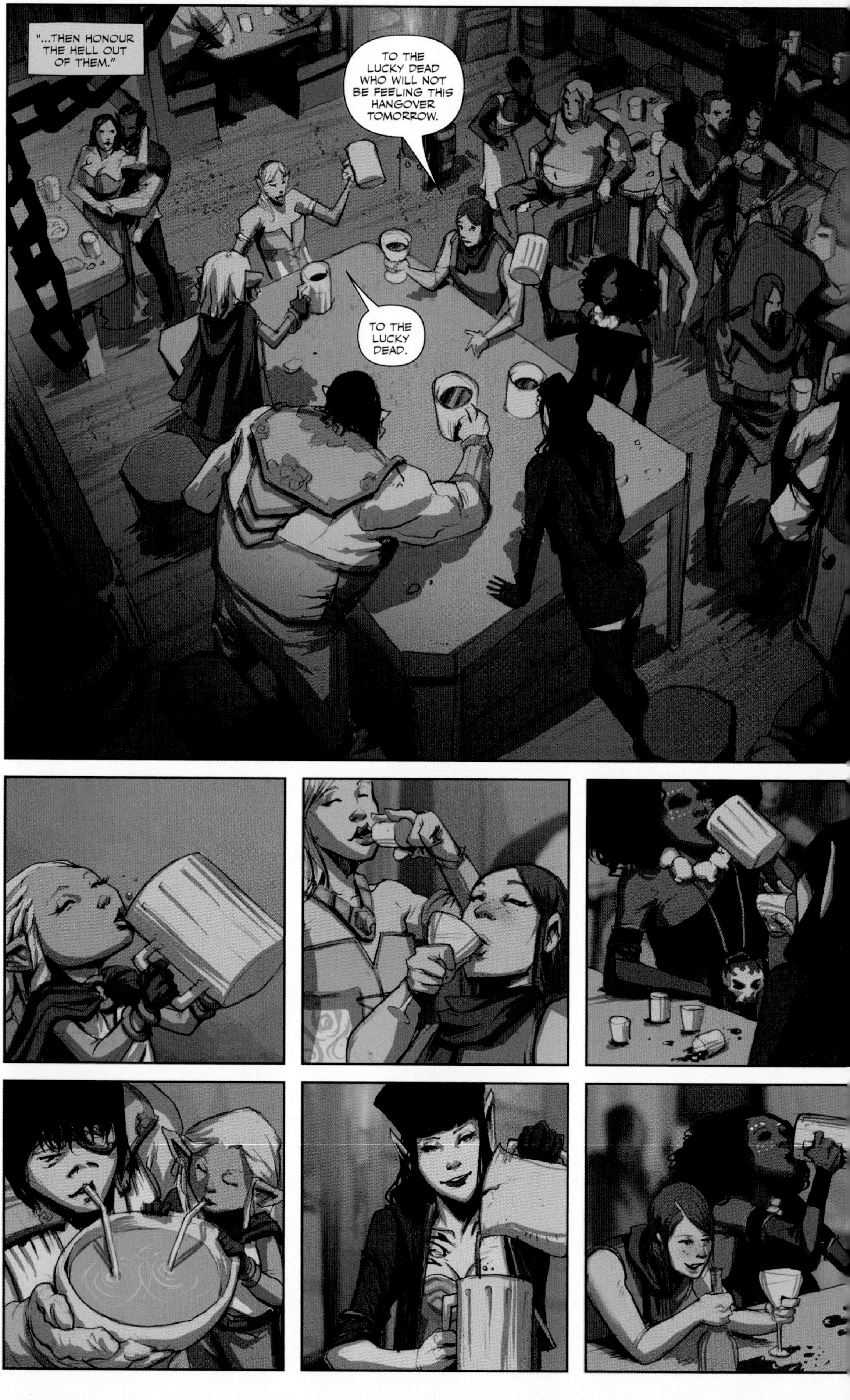
"...THEN HONOUR THE HELL OUT OF THEM."
TO THE LUCKY DEAD WHO WILL NOT BE FEELING THIS HANGOVER TOMORROW.
TO THE LUCKY DEAD.

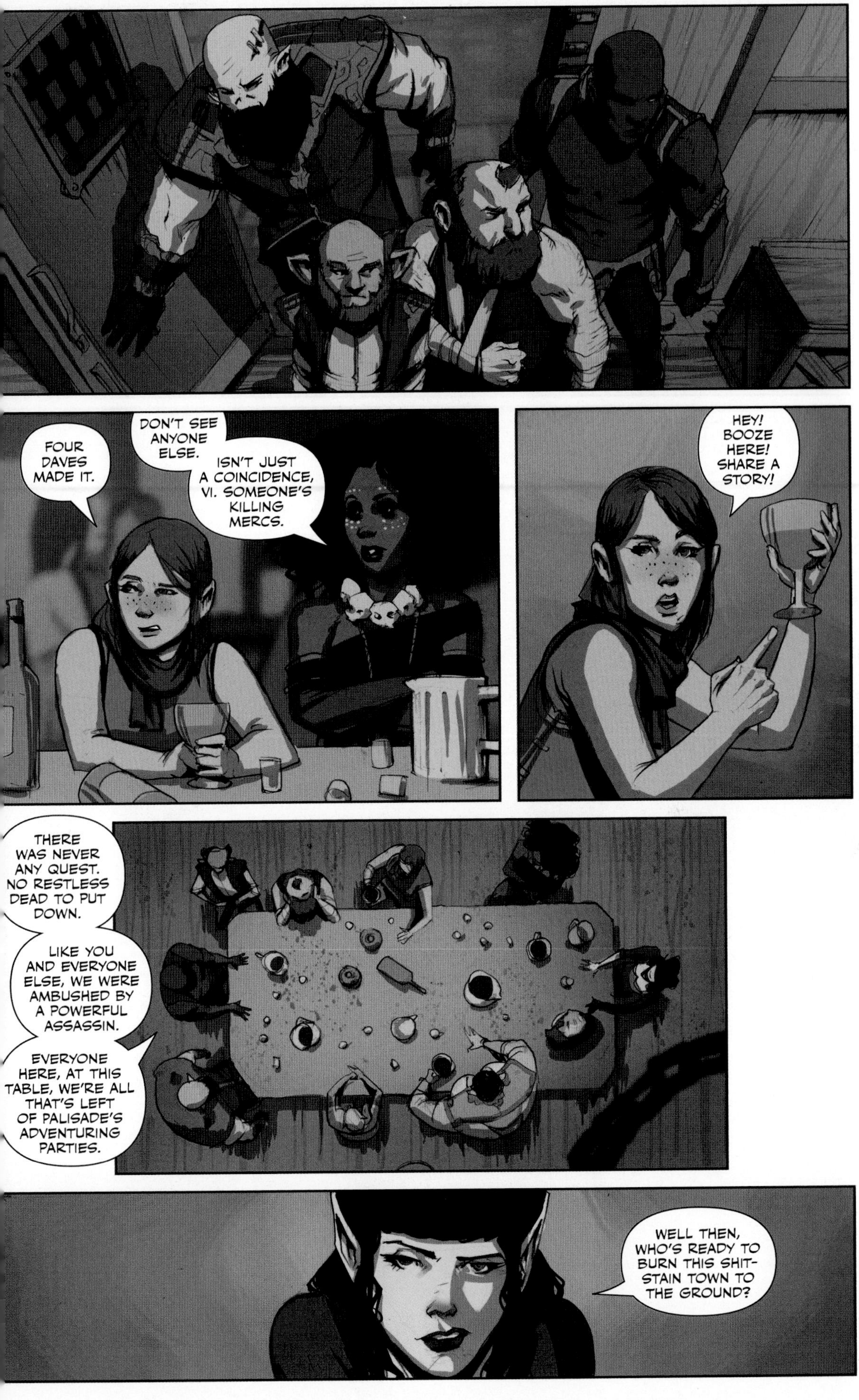
FOUR DAVES MADE IT.
DON'T SEE ANYONE ELSE.
ISN'T JUST A COINCIDENCE, VI. SOMEONE'S KILLING MERCS.
HEY! BOOZE HERE! SHARE A STORY!
THERE WAS NEVER ANY QUEST. NO RESTLESS DEAD TO PUT DOWN.
LIKE YOU AND EVERYONE ELSE, WE WERE AMBUSHED BY A POWERFUL ASSASSIN.
EVERYONE HERE, AT THIS TABLE, WE'RE ALL THAT'S LEFT OF PALISADE'S ADVENTURING PARTIES.
WELL THEN, WHO'S READY TO BURN THIS SHIT-STAIN TOWN TO THE GROUND?

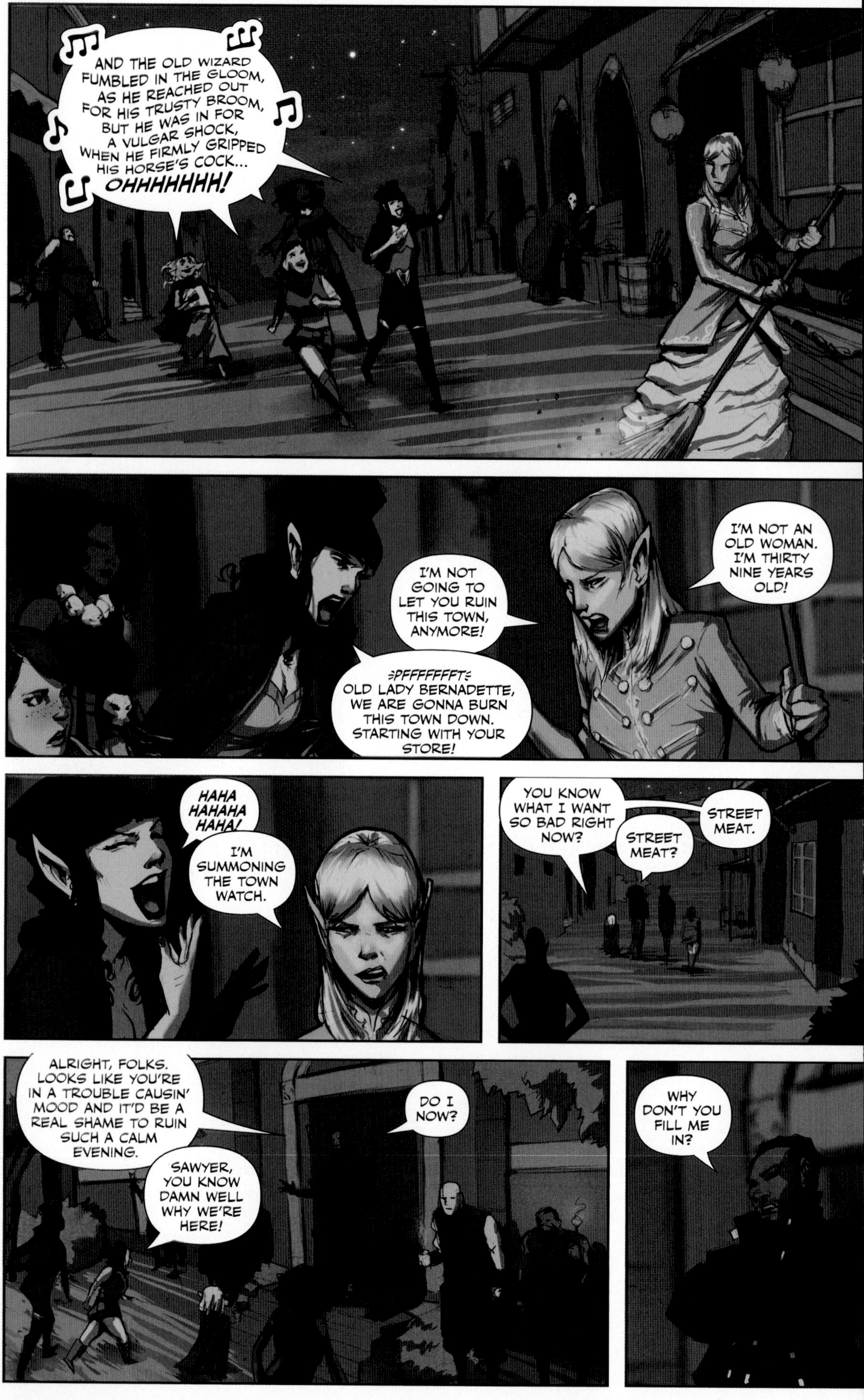
AND THE OLD WIZARD FUMBLED IN THE GLOOM, AS HE REACHED OUT FOR HIS TRUSTY BROOM, BUT HE WAS IN FOR A VULGAR SHOCK, WHEN HE FIRMLY GRIPPED HIS HORSE'S COCK... OHHHHHHH!
I'M NOT AN OLD WOMAN. I'M THIRTY NINE YEARS OLD!
I'M NOT GOING TO LET YOU RUIN THIS TOWN, ANYMORE!
PFFFFFFFT OLD LADY BERNADETTE, WE ARE GONNA BURN THIS TOWN DOWN. STARTING WITH YOUR STORE!
HAHA HAHAHA HAHA!
I'M SUMMONING THE TOWN WATCH.
YOU KNOW WHAT I WANT SO BAD RIGHT NOW?
STREET MEAT.
STREET MEAT?
ALRIGHT, FOLKS. LOOKS LIKE YOU'RE IN A TROUBLE CAUSIN' MOOD AND IT'D BE A REAL SHAME TO RUIN SUCH A CALM EVENING.
SAWYER, YOU KNOW DAMN WELL WHY WE'RE HERE!
DO I NOW?
WHY DON'T YOU FILL ME IN?

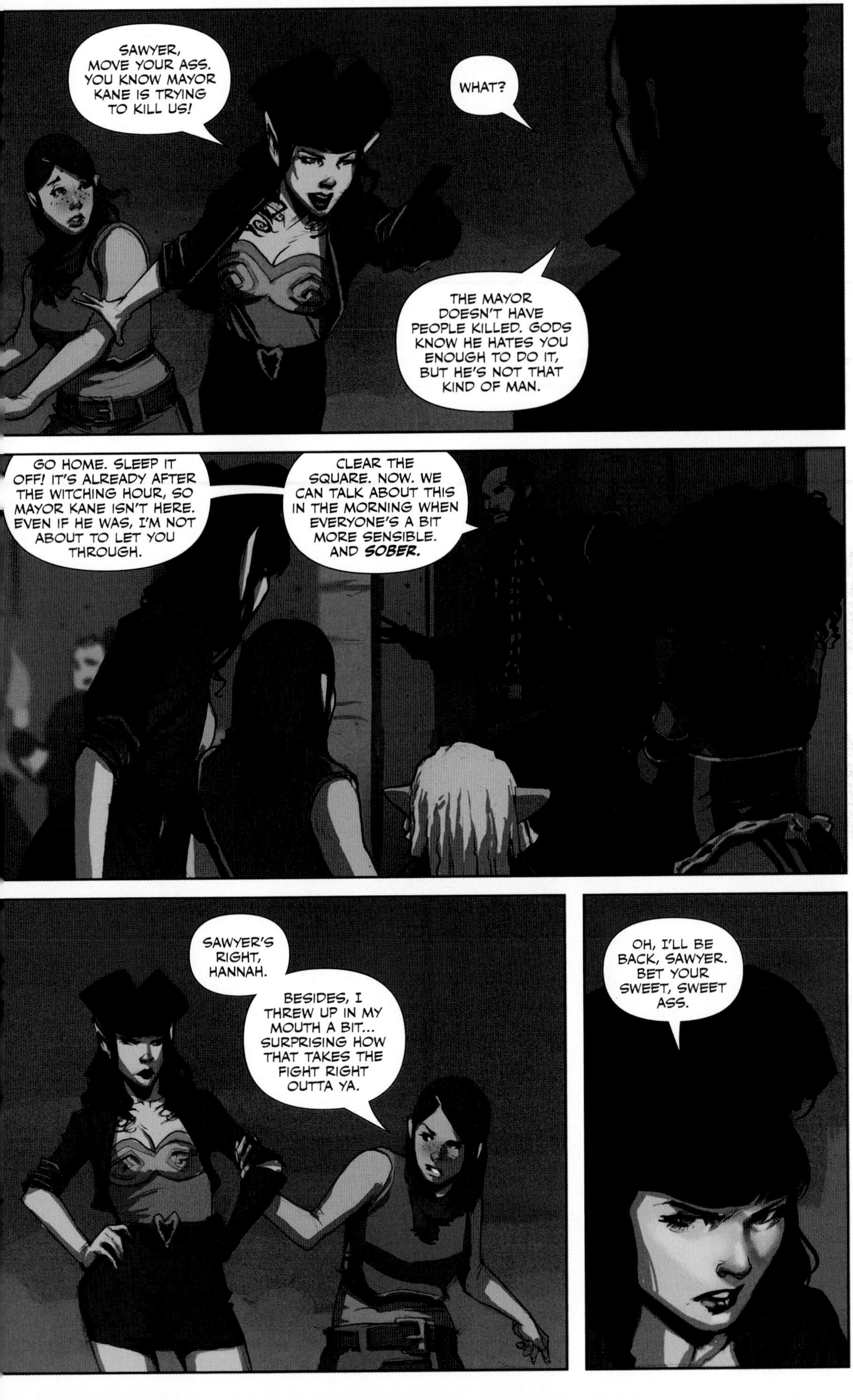
SAWYER, MOVE YOUR ASS. YOU KNOW MAYOR KANE IS TRYING TO KILL US!
WHAT?
THE MAYOR DOESN'T HAVE PEOPLE KILLED. GODS KNOW HE HATES YOU ENOUGH TO DO IT, BUT HE'S NOT THAT KIND OF MAN.
GO HOME. SLEEP IT OFF! IT'S ALREADY AFTER THE WITCHING HOUR, SO MAYOR KANE ISN'T HERE. EVEN IF HE WAS, I'M NOT ABOUT TO LET YOU THROUGH.
CLEAR THE SQUARE. NOW. WE CAN TALK ABOUT THIS IN THE MORNING WHEN EVERYONE'S A BIT MORE SENSIBLE. AND *SOBER.*
SAWYER'S RIGHT, HANNAH.
BESIDES, I THREW UP IN MY MOUTH A BIT... SURPRISING HOW THAT TAKES THE FIGHT RIGHT OUTTA YA.
OH, I'LL BE BACK, SAWYER. BET YOUR SWEET, SWEET ASS.

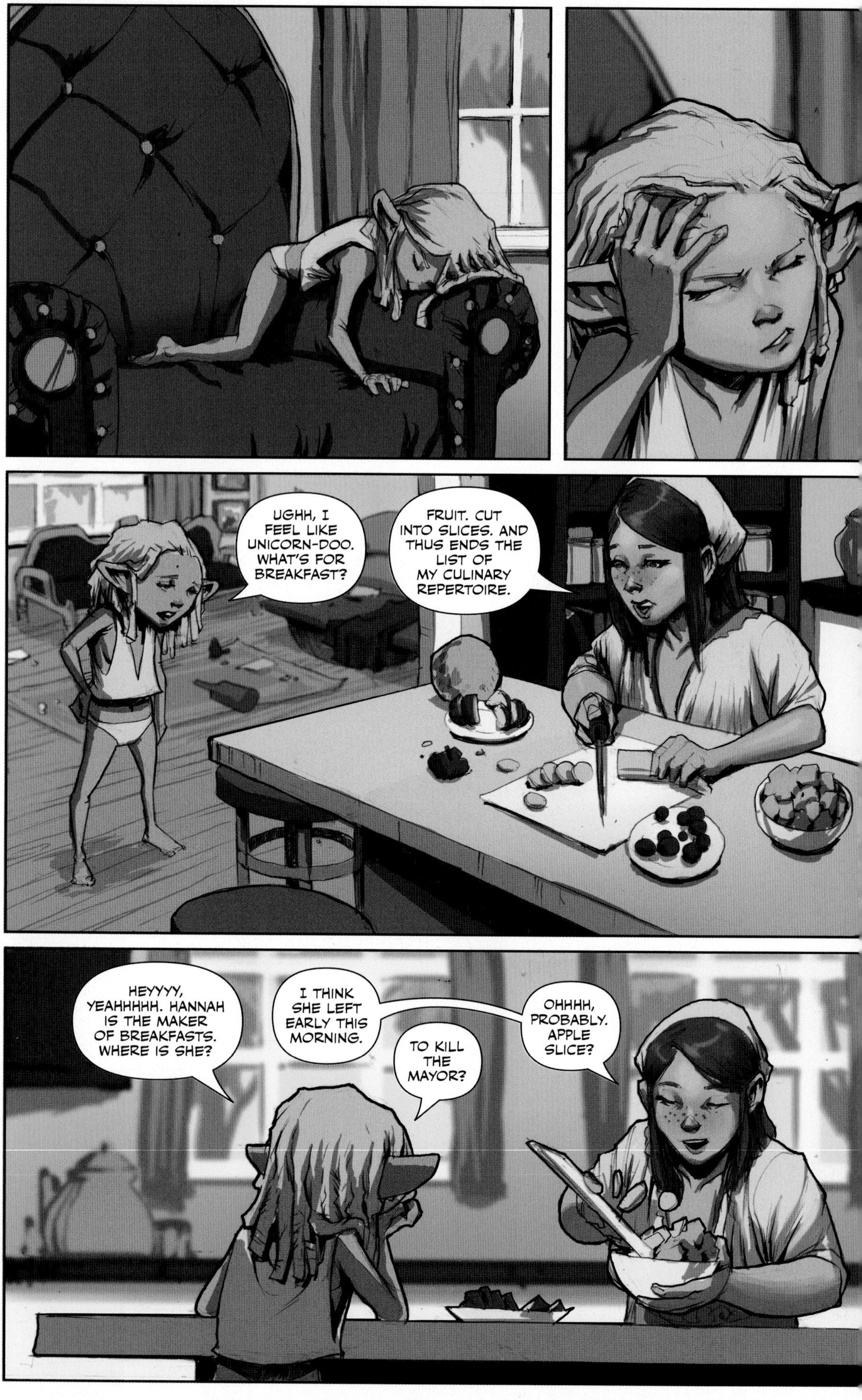
UGHH, I FEEL LIKE UNICORN-DOO. WHAT'S FOR BREAKFAST?
FRUIT. CUT INTO SLICES. AND THUS ENDS THE LIST OF MY CULINARY REPERTOIRE.
HEYYYY, YEAHHHHH. HANNAH IS THE MAKER OF BREAKFASTS. WHERE IS SHE?
I THINK SHE LEFT EARLY THIS MORNING.
TO KILL THE MAYOR?
OHHHH, PROBABLY. APPLE SLICE?

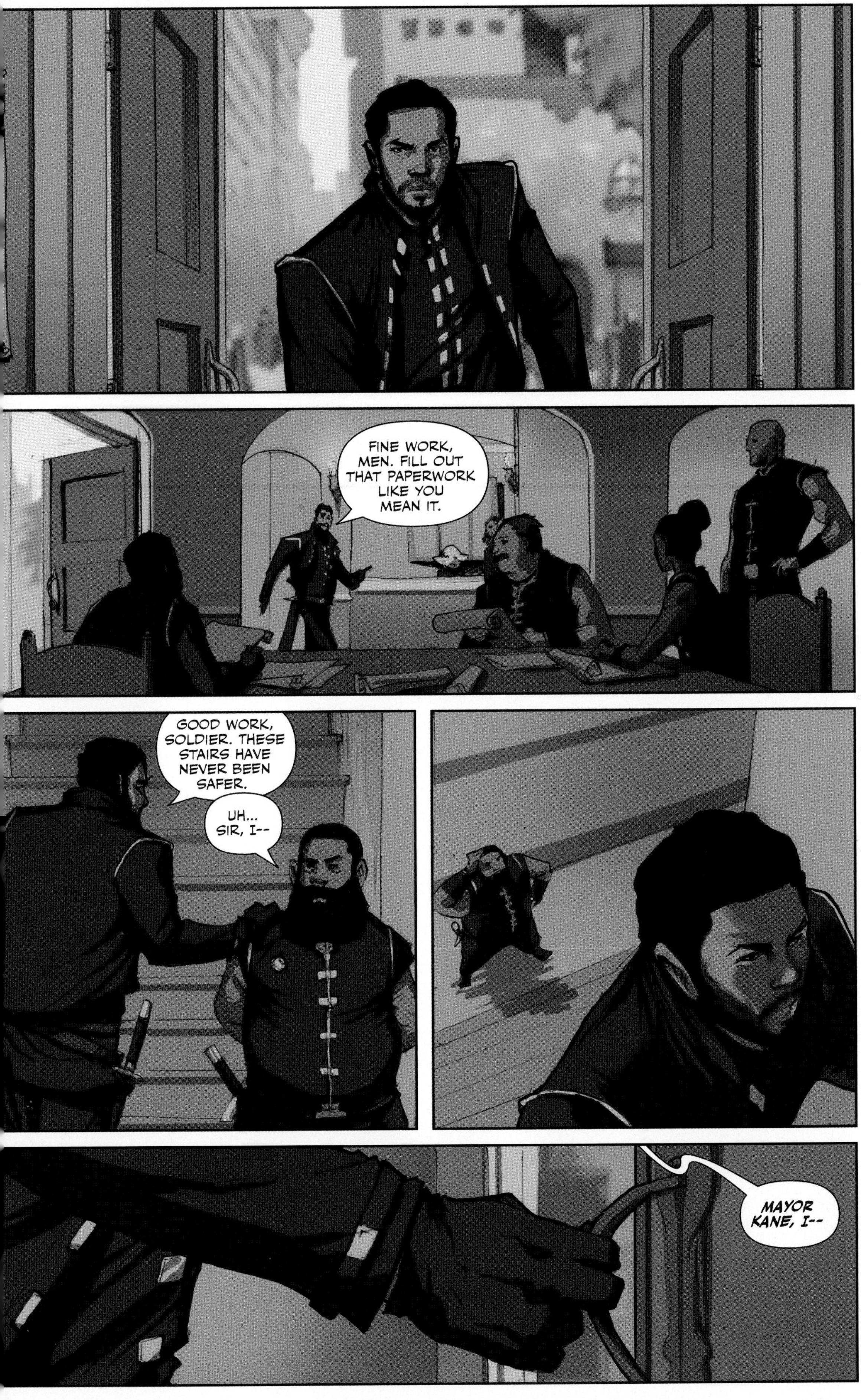
FINE WORK, MEN. FILL OUT THAT PAPERWORK LIKE YOU MEAN IT.
GOOD WORK, SOLDIER. THESE STAIRS HAVE NEVER BEEN SAFER.
UH... SIR, I--
MAYOR KANE, I--

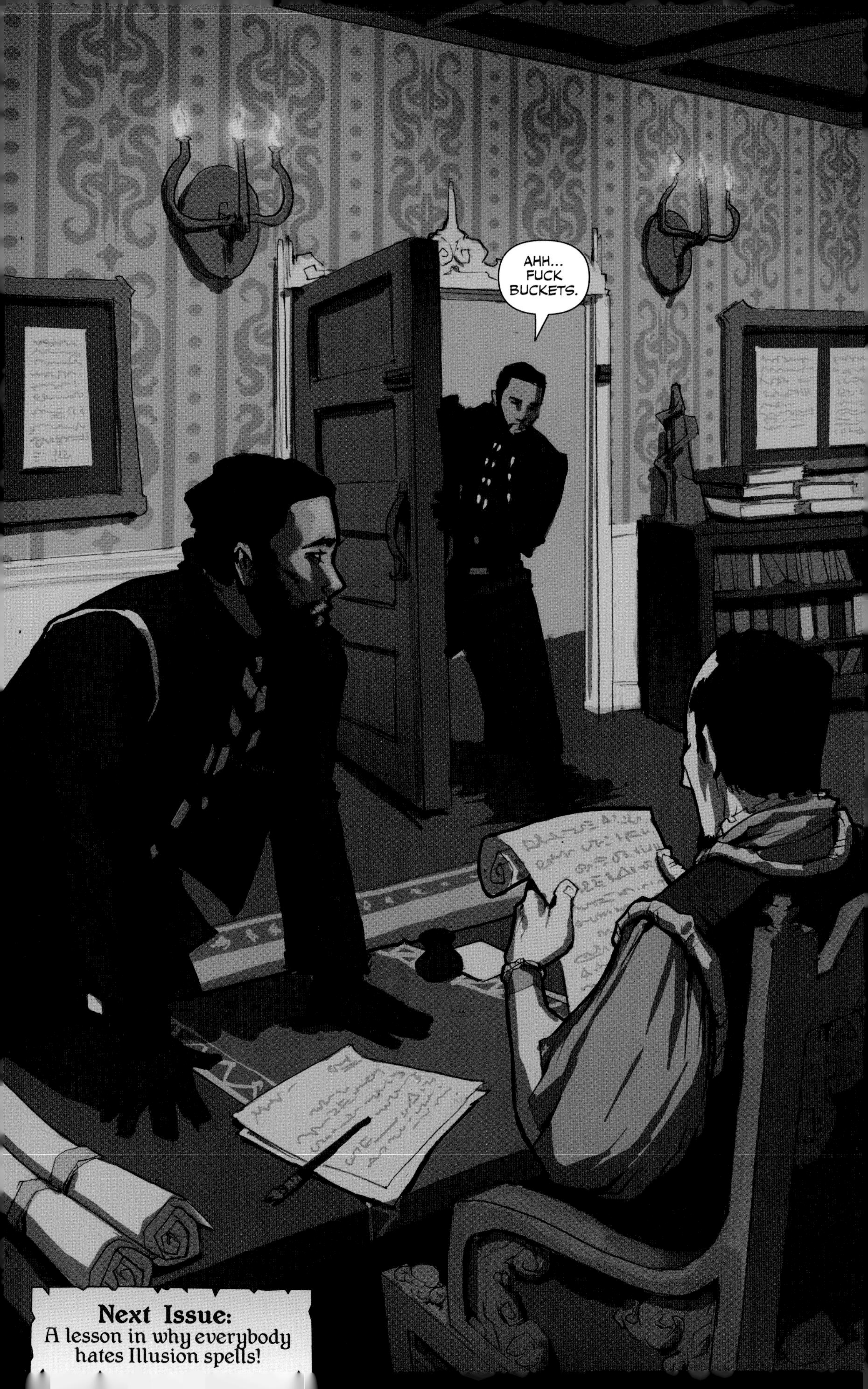
AHH... FUCK BUCKETS.
Next Issue:
A lesson in why everybody hates Illusion spells!

CHAPTER THREE

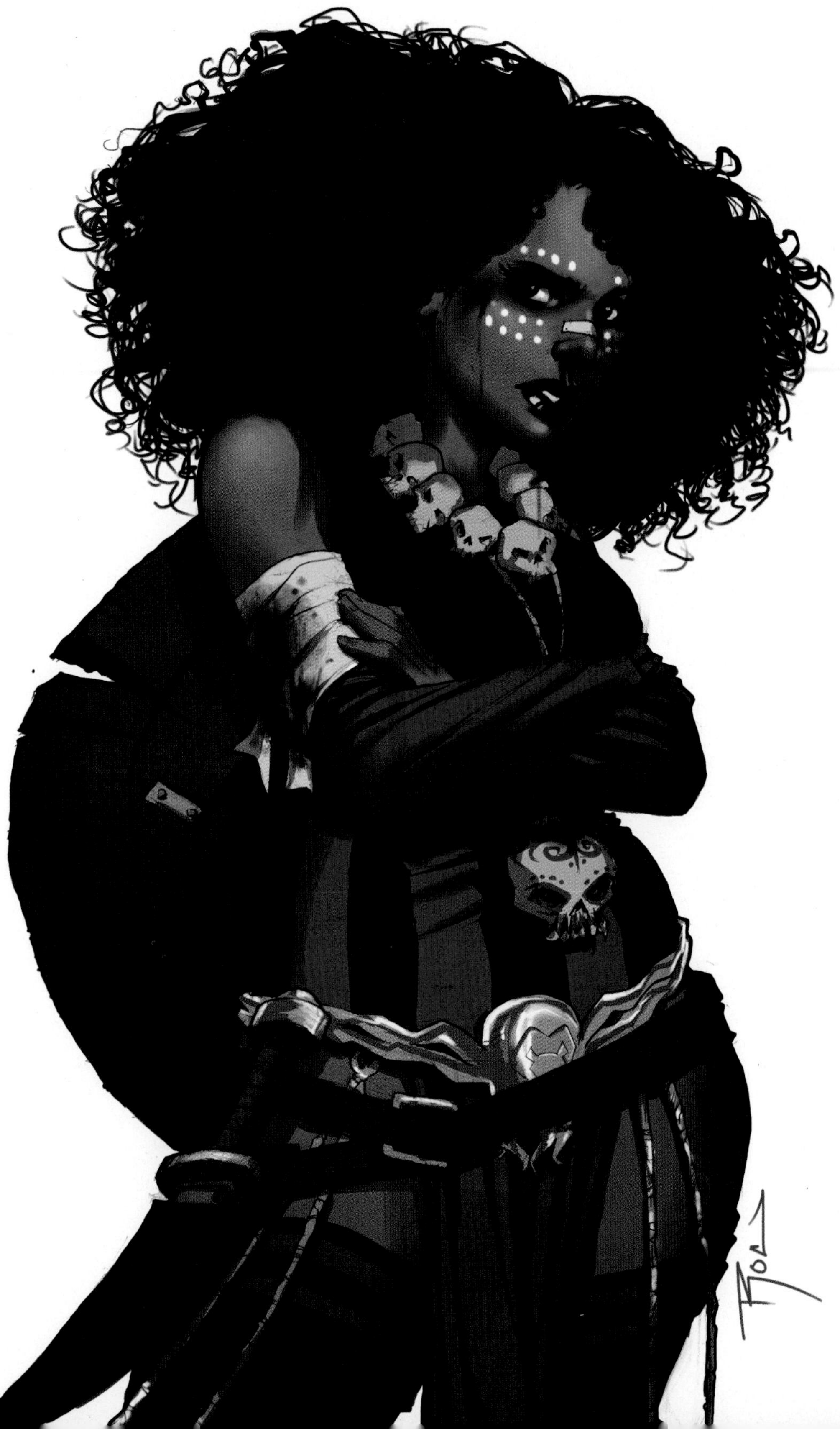

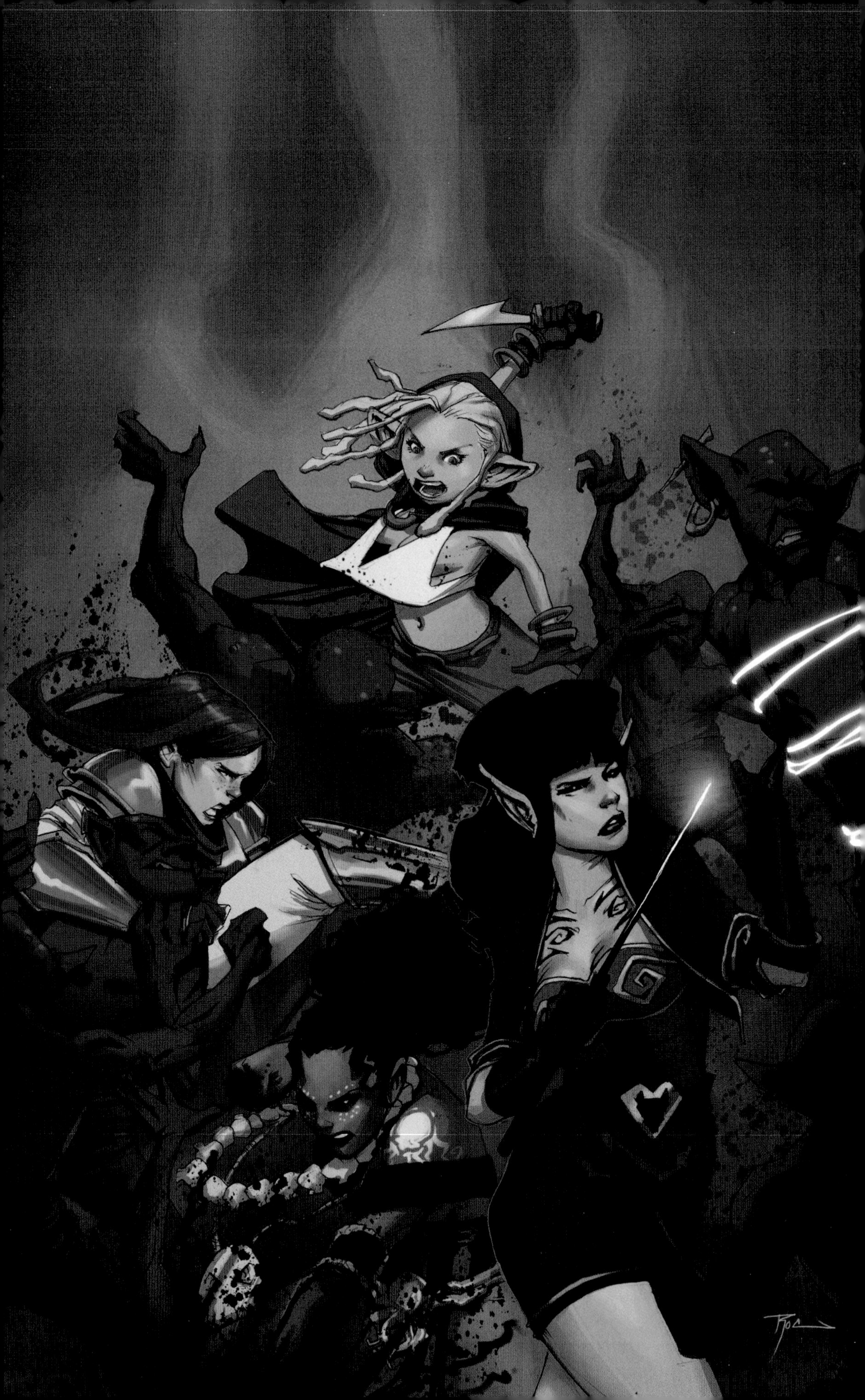

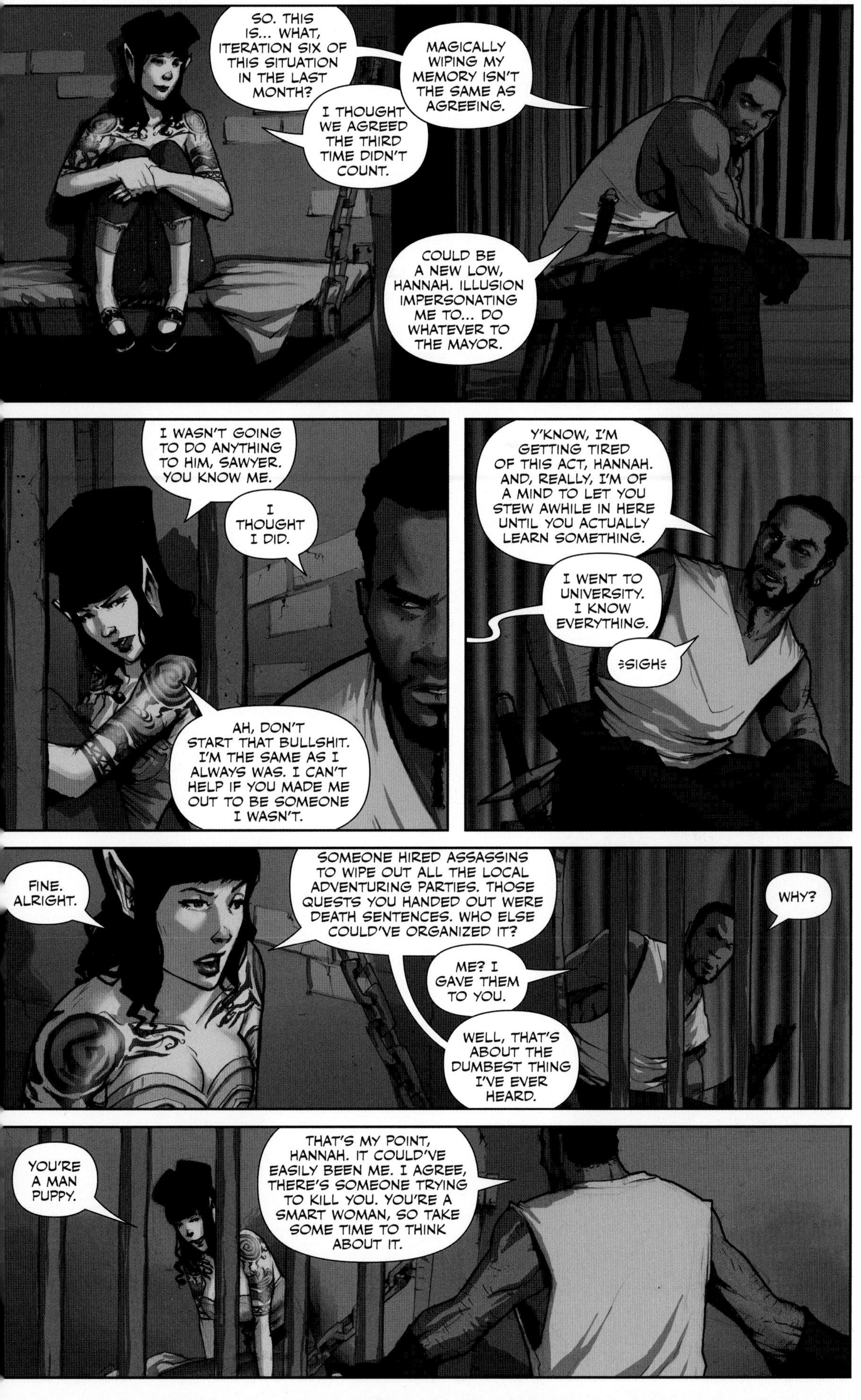
SO. THIS IS... WHAT, ITERATION SIX OF THIS SITUATION IN THE LAST MONTH?
MAGICALLY WIPING MY MEMORY ISN'T THE SAME AS AGREEING.
I THOUGHT WE AGREED THE THIRD TIME DIDN'T COUNT.
COULD BE A NEW LOW, HANNAH. ILLUSION IMPERSONATING ME TO... DO WHATEVER TO THE MAYOR.
I WASN'T GOING TO DO ANYTHING TO HIM, SAWYER. YOU KNOW ME.
I THOUGHT I DID.
AH, DON'T START THAT BULLSHIT. I'M THE SAME AS I ALWAYS WAS. I CAN'T HELP IF YOU MADE ME OUT TO BE SOMEONE I WASN'T.
Y'KNOW, I'M GETTING TIRED OF THIS ACT, HANNAH. AND, REALLY, I'M OF A MIND TO LET YOU STEW AWHILE IN HERE UNTIL YOU ACTUALLY LEARN SOMETHING.
I WENT TO UNIVERSITY. I KNOW EVERYTHING.
SIGH
FINE. ALRIGHT.
SOMEONE HIRED ASSASSINS TO WIPE OUT ALL THE LOCAL ADVENTURING PARTIES. THOSE QUESTS YOU HANDED OUT WERE DEATH SENTENCES. WHO ELSE COULD'VE ORGANIZED IT?
WHY?
ME? I GAVE THEM TO YOU.
WELL, THAT'S ABOUT THE DUMBEST THING I'VE EVER HEARD.
YOU'RE A MAN PUPPY.
THAT'S MY POINT, HANNAH. IT COULD'VE EASILY BEEN ME. I AGREE, THERE'S SOMEONE TRYING TO KILL YOU. YOU'RE A SMART WOMAN, SO TAKE SOME TIME TO THINK ABOUT IT.

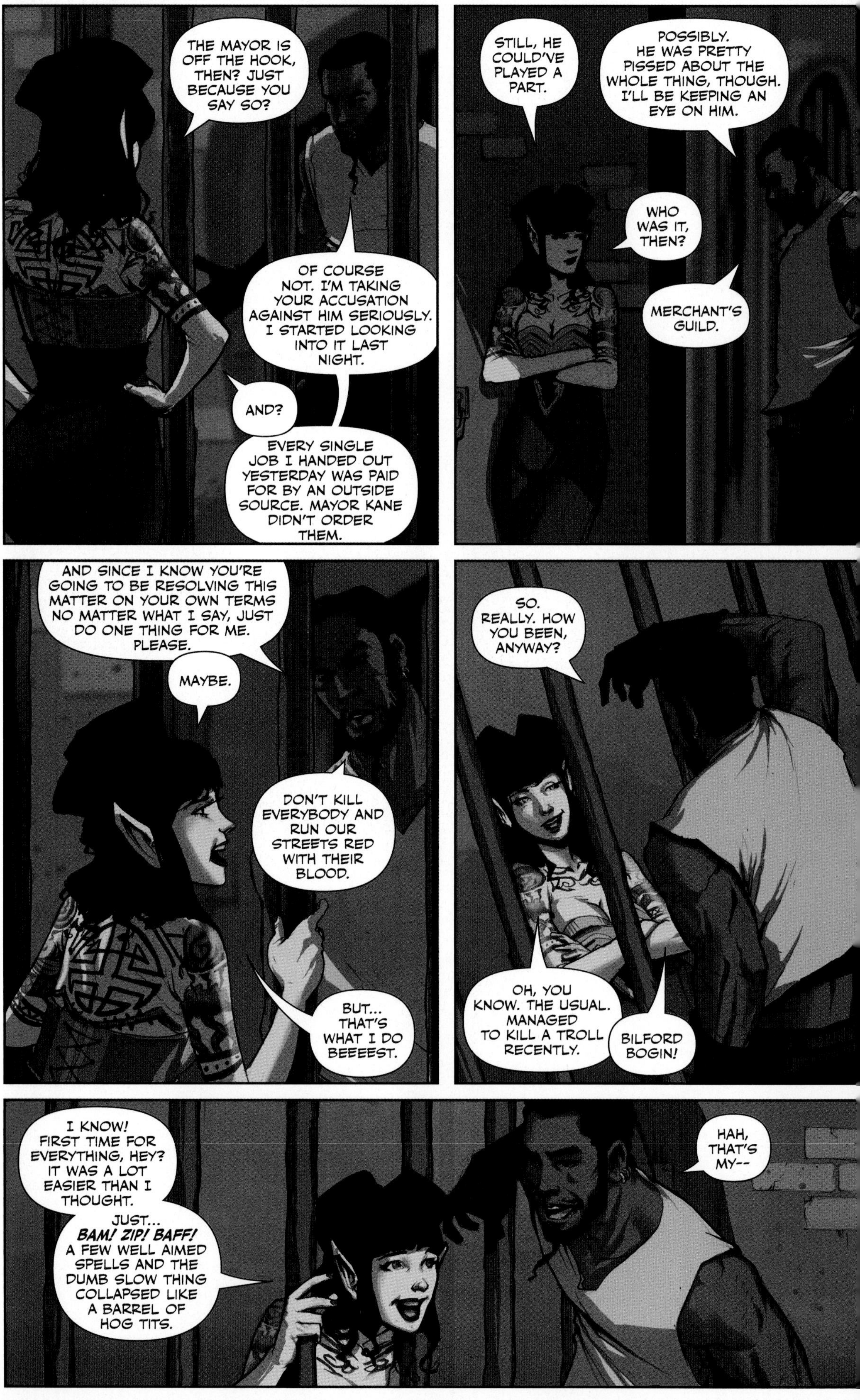
THE MAYOR IS OFF THE HOOK, THEN? JUST BECAUSE YOU SAY SO?
OF COURSE NOT. I'M TAKING YOUR ACCUSATION AGAINST HIM SERIOUSLY. I STARTED LOOKING INTO IT LAST NIGHT.
AND?
EVERY SINGLE JOB I HANDED OUT YESTERDAY WAS PAID FOR BY AN OUTSIDE SOURCE. MAYOR KANE DIDN'T ORDER THEM.
STILL, HE COULD'VE PLAYED A PART.
POSSIBLY. HE WAS PRETTY PISSED ABOUT THE WHOLE THING, THOUGH. I'LL BE KEEPING AN EYE ON HIM.
WHO WAS IT, THEN?
MERCHANT'S GUILD.
AND SINCE I KNOW YOU'RE GOING TO BE RESOLVING THIS MATTER ON YOUR OWN TERMS NO MATTER WHAT I SAY, JUST DO ONE THING FOR ME. PLEASE.
MAYBE.
DON'T KILL EVERYBODY AND RUN OUR STREETS RED WITH THEIR BLOOD.
BUT... THAT'S WHAT I DO BEEEEST.
SO. REALLY. HOW YOU BEEN, ANYWAY?
OH, YOU KNOW. THE USUAL. MANAGED TO KILL A TROLL RECENTLY.
BILFORD BOGIN!
I KNOW! FIRST TIME FOR EVERYTHING, HEY? IT WAS A LOT EASIER THAN I THOUGHT.
JUST... BAM! ZIP! BAFF! A FEW WELL AIMED SPELLS AND THE DUMB SLOW THING COLLAPSED LIKE A BARREL OF HOG TITS.
HAH, THAT'S MY--

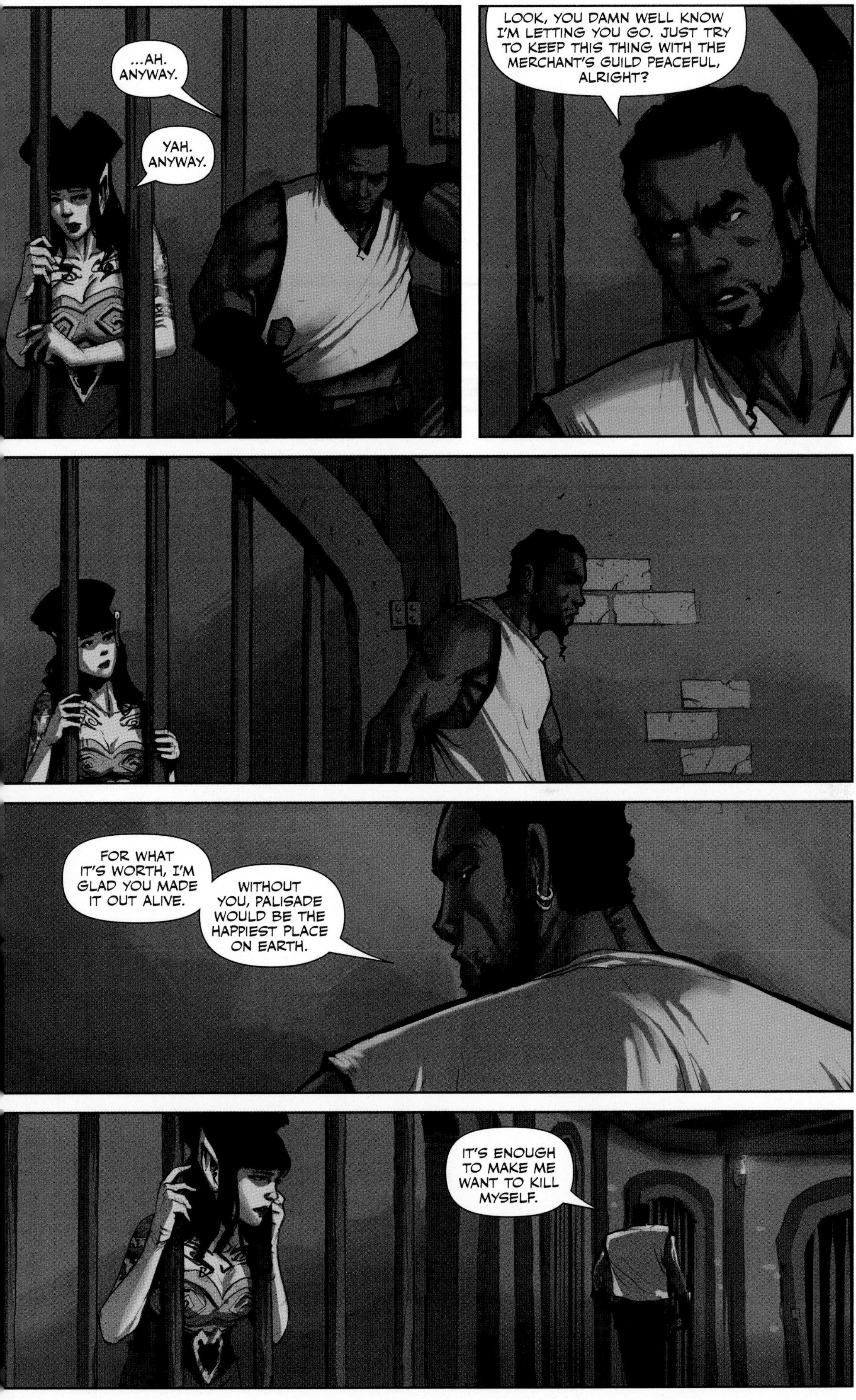
...AH. ANYWAY.
YAH. ANYWAY.
LOOK, YOU DAMN WELL KNOW I'M LETTING YOU GO. JUST TRY TO KEEP THIS THING WITH THE MERCHANT'S GUILD PEACEFUL, ALRIGHT?
FOR WHAT IT'S WORTH, I'M GLAD YOU MADE IT OUT ALIVE.
WITHOUT YOU, PALISADE WOULD BE THE HAPPIEST PLACE ON EARTH.
IT'S ENOUGH TO MAKE ME WANT TO KILL MYSELF.

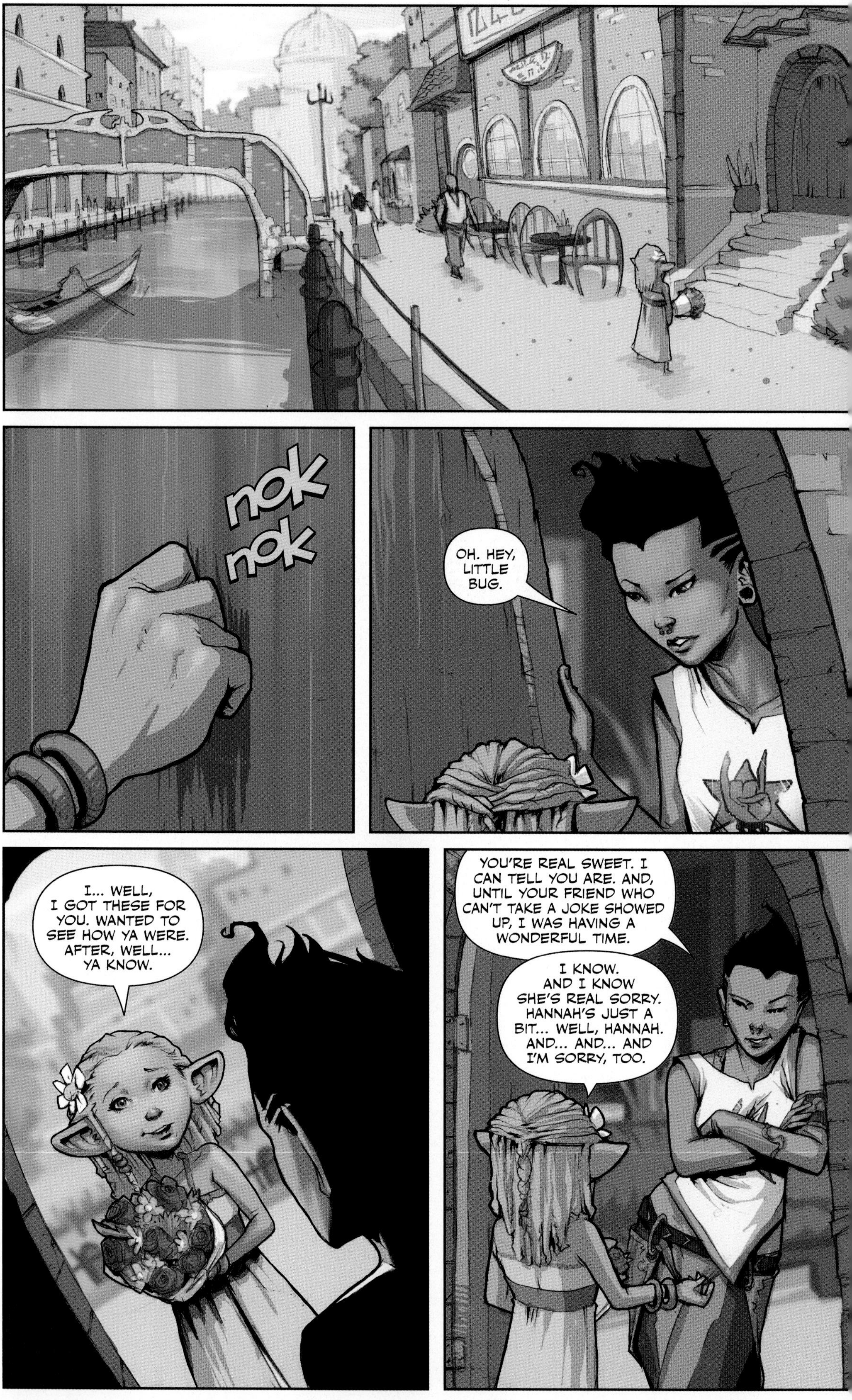
nok nok
OH. HEY, LITTLE BUG.
I... WELL, I GOT THESE FOR YOU. WANTED TO SEE HOW YA WERE. AFTER, WELL... YA KNOW.
YOU'RE REAL SWEET. I CAN TELL YOU ARE. AND, UNTIL YOUR FRIEND WHO CAN'T TAKE A JOKE SHOWED UP, I WAS HAVING A WONDERFUL TIME.
I KNOW. AND I KNOW SHE'S REAL SORRY. HANNAH'S JUST A BIT... WELL, HANNAH. AND... AND... AND I'M SORRY, TOO.

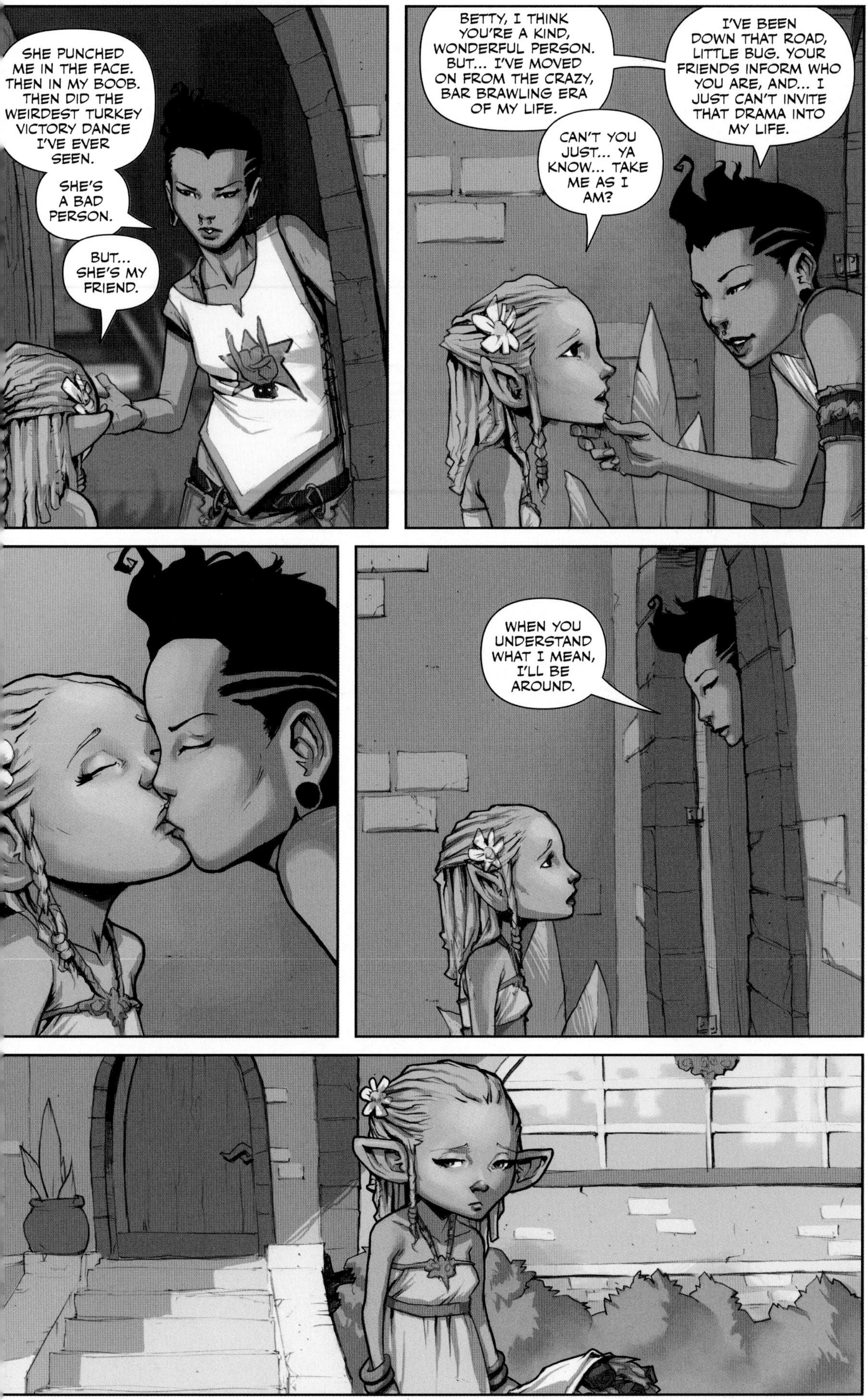
SHE PUNCHED ME IN THE FACE. THEN IN MY BOOB. THEN DID THE WEIRDEST TURKEY VICTORY DANCE I'VE EVER SEEN.
SHE'S A BAD PERSON.
BUT... SHE'S MY FRIEND.
BETTY, I THINK YOU'RE A KIND, WONDERFUL PERSON. BUT... I'VE MOVED ON FROM THE CRAZY, BAR BRAWLING ERA OF MY LIFE.
I'VE BEEN DOWN THAT ROAD, LITTLE BUG. YOUR FRIENDS INFORM WHO YOU ARE, AND... I JUST CAN'T INVITE THAT DRAMA INTO MY LIFE.
CAN'T YOU JUST... YA KNOW... TAKE ME AS I AM?
WHEN YOU UNDERSTAND WHAT I MEAN, I'LL BE AROUND.

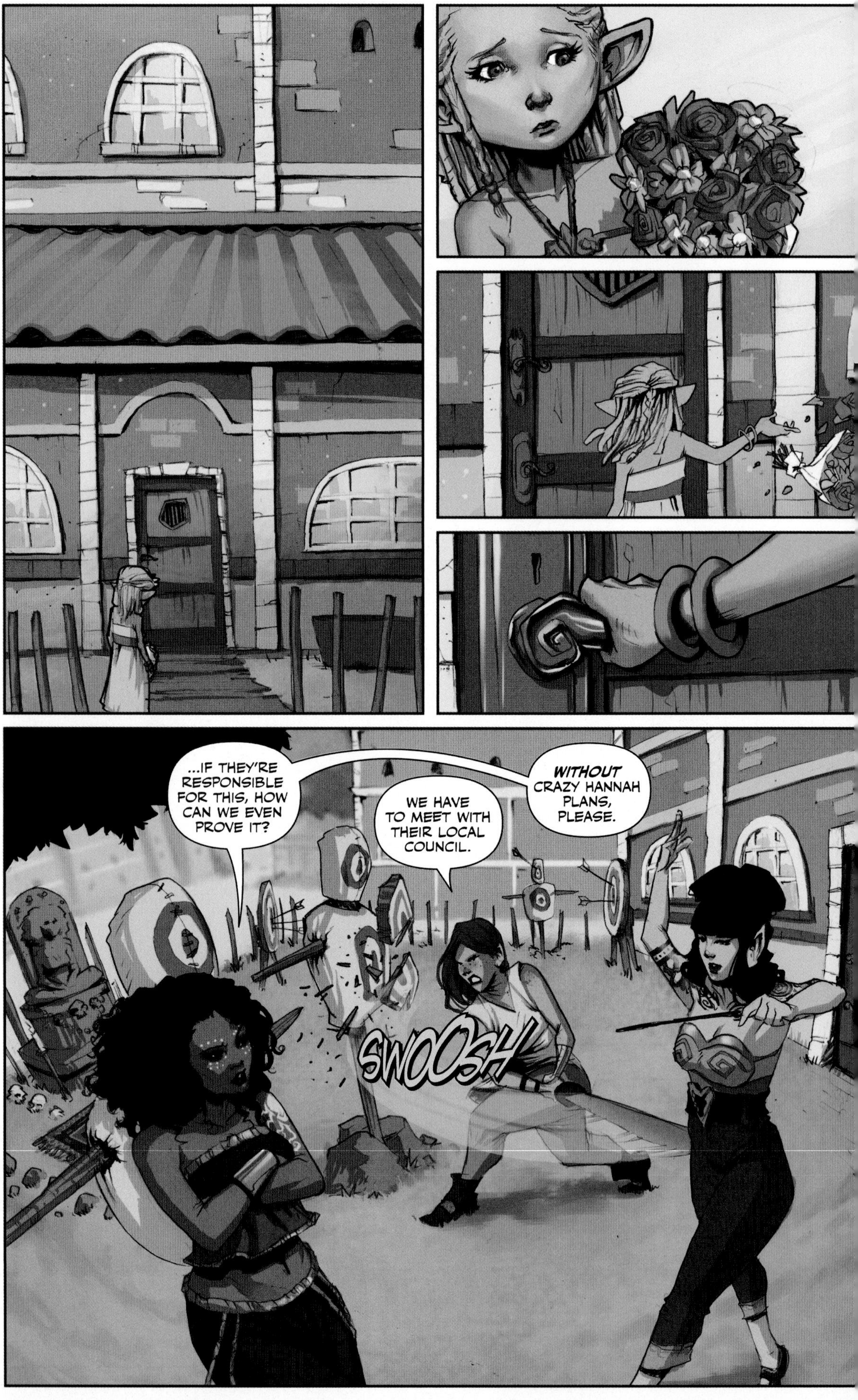
...IF THEY'RE RESPONSIBLE FOR THIS, HOW CAN WE EVEN PROVE IT?
WE HAVE TO MEET WITH THEIR LOCAL COUNCIL.
WITHOUT CRAZY HANNAH PLANS, PLEASE.
SWOOSH

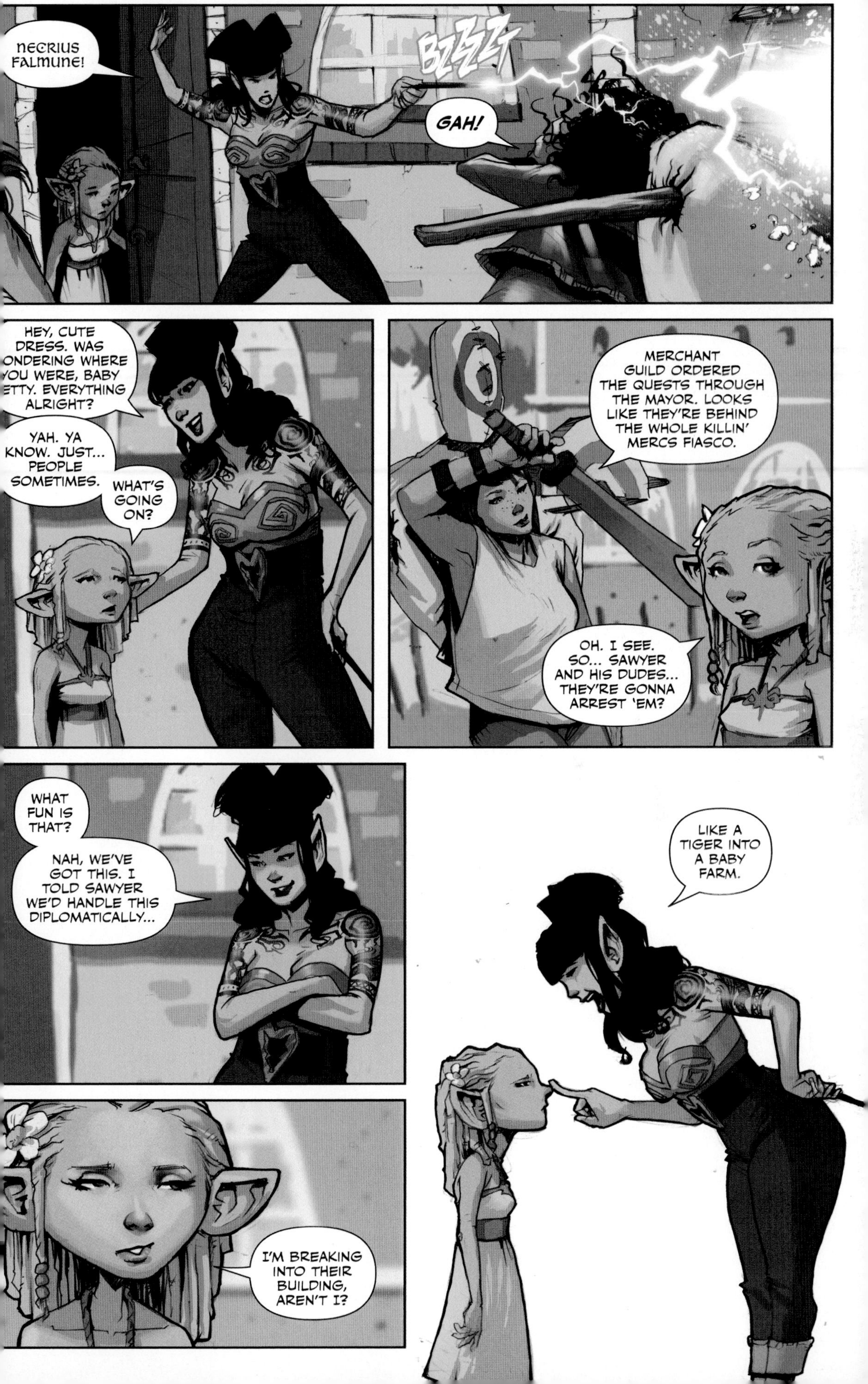
NECRIUS FALMUNE!
BZZZZT
GAH!
HEY, CUTE DRESS. WAS ONDERING WHERE YOU WERE, BABY ETTY. EVERYTHING ALRIGHT?
YAH. YA KNOW. JUST... PEOPLE SOMETIMES.
WHAT'S GOING ON?
MERCHANT GUILD ORDERED THE QUESTS THROUGH THE MAYOR. LOOKS LIKE THEY'RE BEHIND THE WHOLE KILLIN' MERCS FIASCO.
OH. I SEE. SO... SAWYER AND HIS DUDES... THEY'RE GONNA ARREST 'EM?
WHAT FUN IS THAT?
NAH, WE'VE GOT THIS. I TOLD SAWYER WE'D HANDLE THIS DIPLOMATICALLY...
I'M BREAKING INTO THEIR BUILDING, AREN'T I?
LIKE A TIGER INTO A BABY FARM.

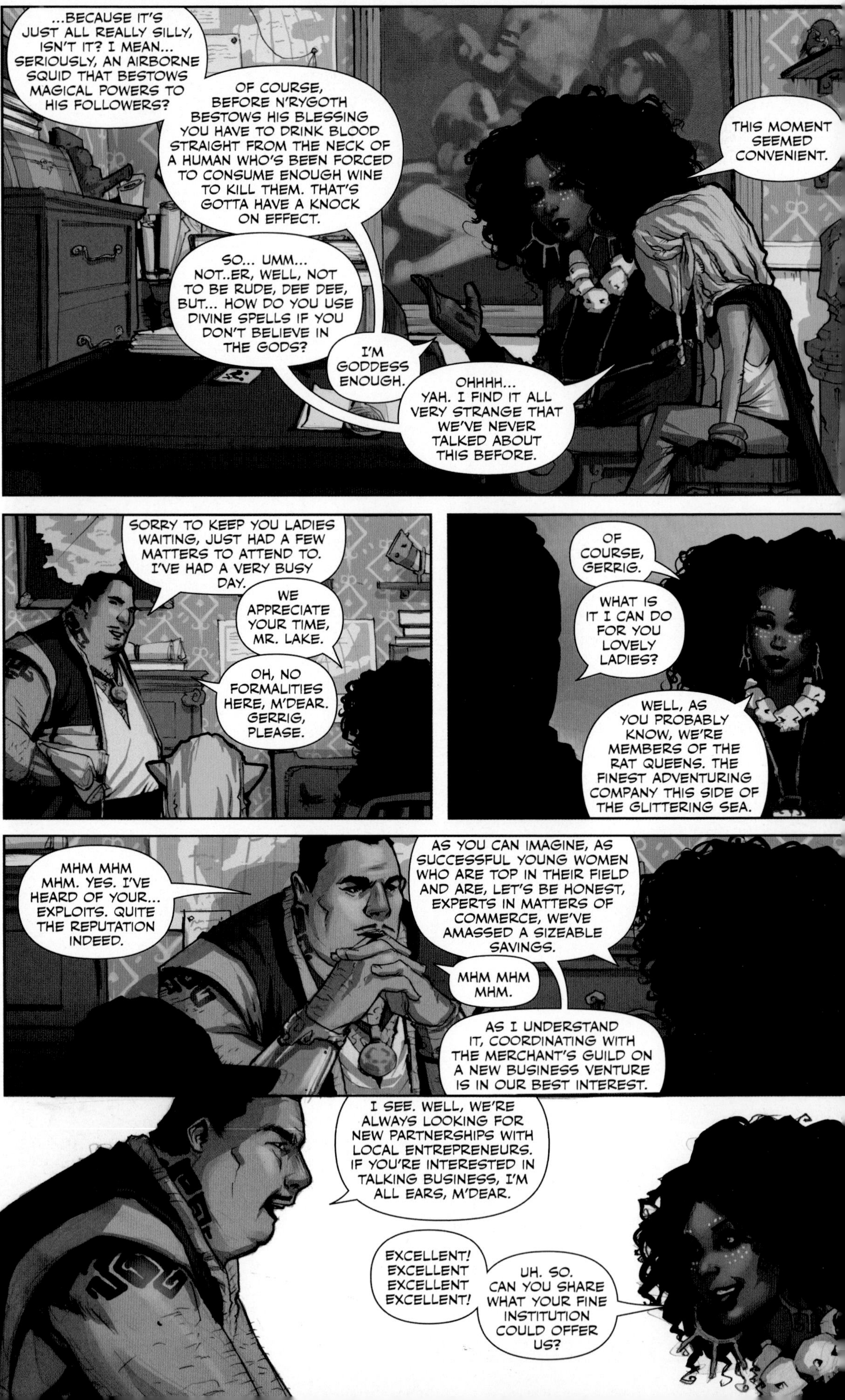
...BECAUSE IT'S JUST ALL REALLY SILLY, ISN'T IT? I MEAN... SERIOUSLY, AN AIRBORNE SQUID THAT BESTOWS MAGICAL POWERS TO HIS FOLLOWERS?
OF COURSE, BEFORE N'RYGOTH BESTOWS HIS BLESSING YOU HAVE TO DRINK BLOOD STRAIGHT FROM THE NECK OF A HUMAN WHO'S BEEN FORCED TO CONSUME ENOUGH WINE TO KILL THEM. THAT'S GOTTA HAVE A KNOCK ON EFFECT.
THIS MOMENT SEEMED CONVENIENT.
SO... UMM... NOT..ER, WELL, NOT TO BE RUDE, DEE DEE, BUT... HOW DO YOU USE DIVINE SPELLS IF YOU DON'T BELIEVE IN THE GODS?
I'M GODDESS ENOUGH.
OHHHH... YAH. I FIND IT ALL VERY STRANGE THAT WE'VE NEVER TALKED ABOUT THIS BEFORE.
SORRY TO KEEP YOU LADIES WAITING, JUST HAD A FEW MATTERS TO ATTEND TO. I'VE HAD A VERY BUSY DAY.
WE APPRECIATE YOUR TIME, MR. LAKE.
OH, NO FORMALITIES HERE, M'DEAR. GERRIG, PLEASE.
OF COURSE, GERRIG.
WHAT IS IT I CAN DO FOR YOU LOVELY LADIES?
WELL, AS YOU PROBABLY KNOW, WE'RE MEMBERS OF THE RAT QUEENS. THE FINEST ADVENTURING COMPANY THIS SIDE OF THE GLITTERING SEA.
MHM MHM MHM. YES. I'VE HEARD OF YOUR... EXPLOITS. QUITE THE REPUTATION INDEED.
AS YOU CAN IMAGINE, AS SUCCESSFUL YOUNG WOMEN WHO ARE TOP IN THEIR FIELD AND ARE, LET'S BE HONEST, EXPERTS IN MATTERS OF COMMERCE, WE'VE AMASSED A SIZEABLE SAVINGS.
MHM MHM MHM.
AS I UNDERSTAND IT, COORDINATING WITH THE MERCHANT'S GUILD ON A NEW BUSINESS VENTURE IS IN OUR BEST INTEREST.
I SEE. WELL, WE'RE ALWAYS LOOKING FOR NEW PARTNERSHIPS WITH LOCAL ENTREPRENEURS. IF YOU'RE INTERESTED IN TALKING BUSINESS, I'M ALL EARS, M'DEAR.
EXCELLENT! EXCELLENT EXCELLENT EXCELLENT!
UH. SO. CAN YOU SHARE WHAT YOUR FINE INSTITUTION COULD OFFER US?

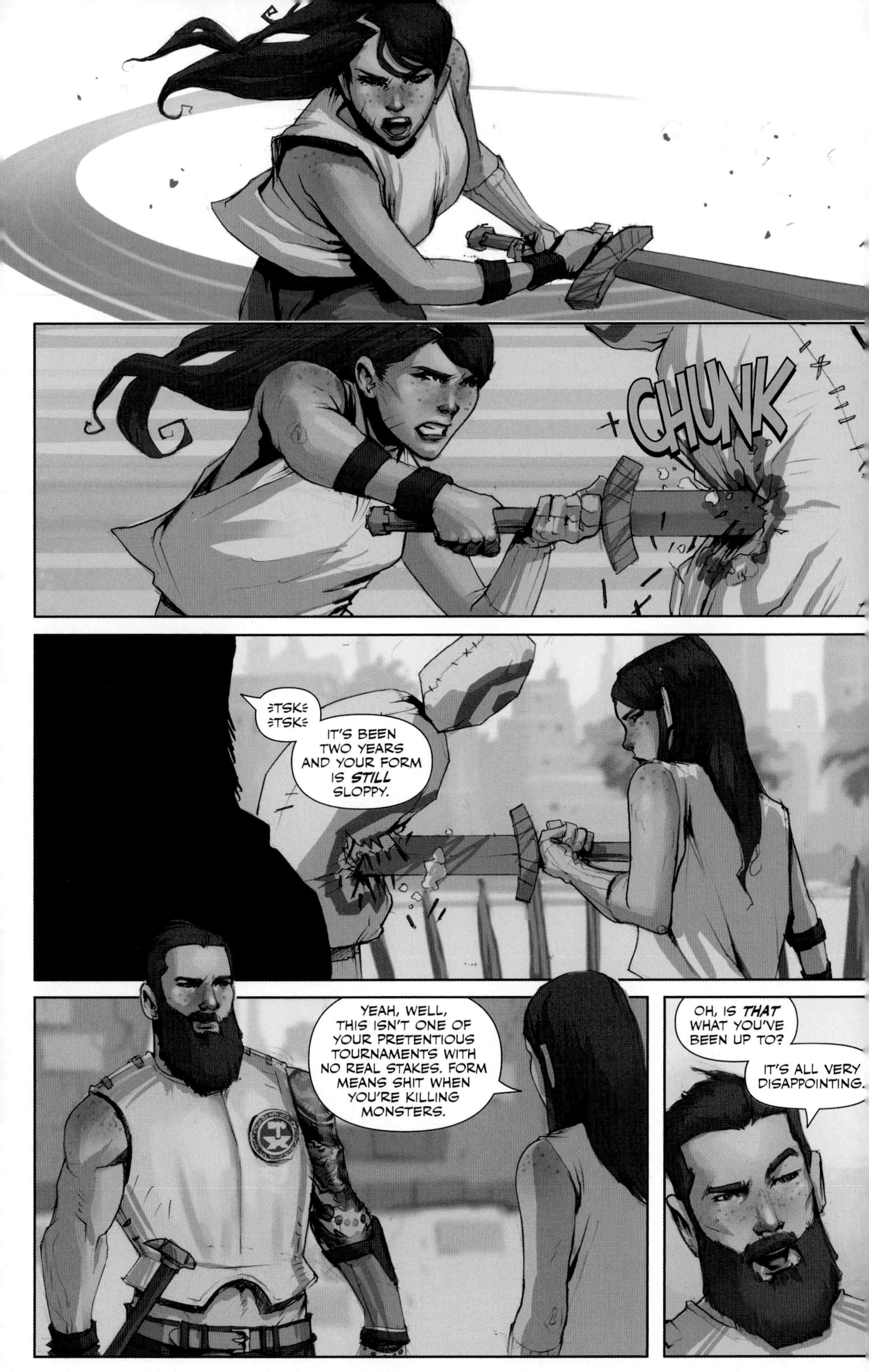
CHUNK
TSK TSK
IT'S BEEN TWO YEARS AND YOUR FORM IS STILL SLOPPY.
YEAH, WELL, THIS ISN'T ONE OF YOUR PRETENTIOUS TOURNAMENTS WITH NO REAL STAKES. FORM MEANS SHIT WHEN YOU'RE KILLING MONSTERS.
OH, IS THAT WHAT YOU'VE BEEN UP TO?
IT'S ALL VERY DISAPPOINTING.

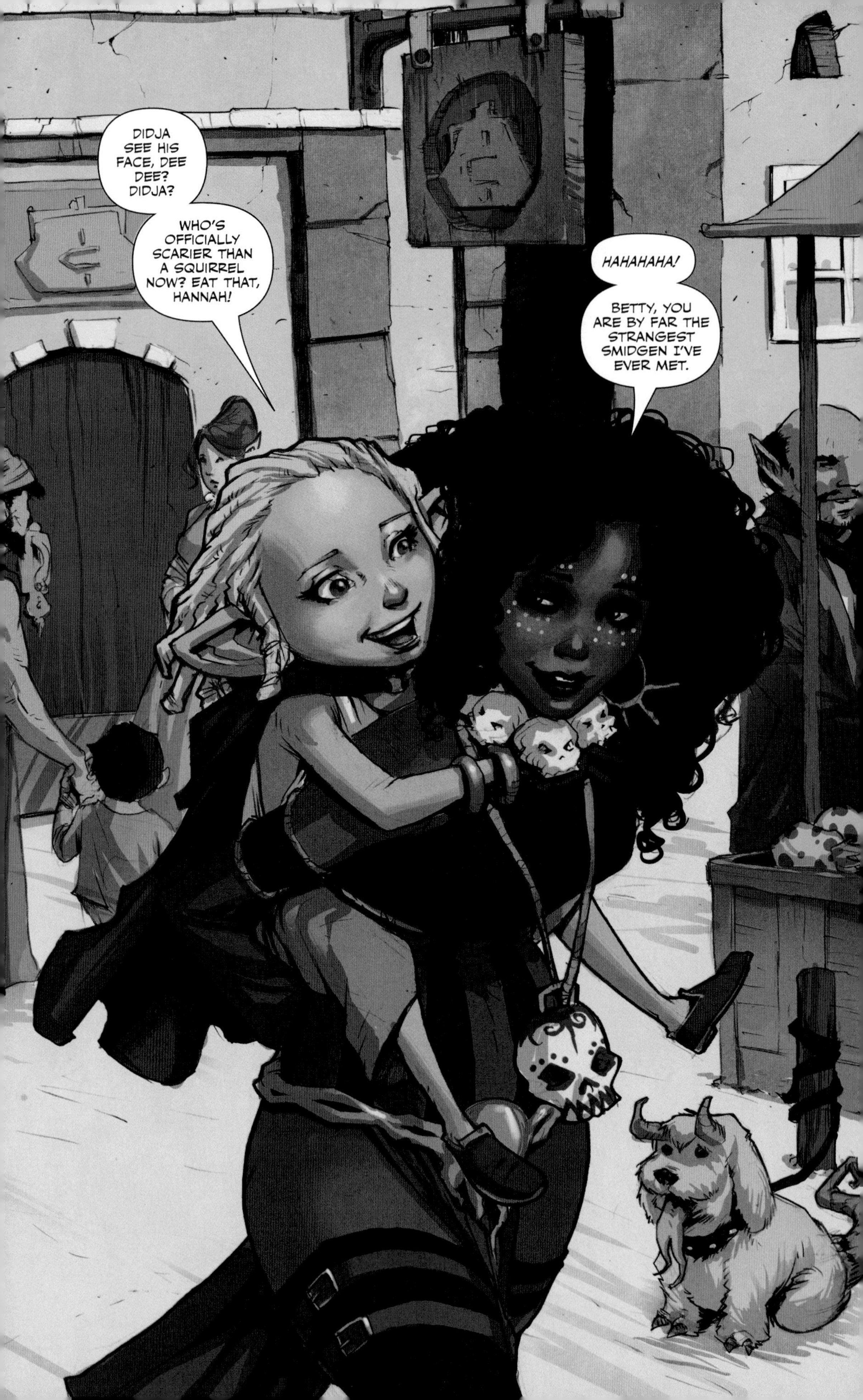
DIDJA SEE HIS FACE, DEE DEE? DIDJA?
WHO'S OFFICIALLY SCARIER THAN A SQUIRREL NOW? EAT THAT, HANNAH!
HAHAHAHA!
BETTY, YOU ARE BY FAR THE STRANGEST SMIDGEN I'VE EVER MET.

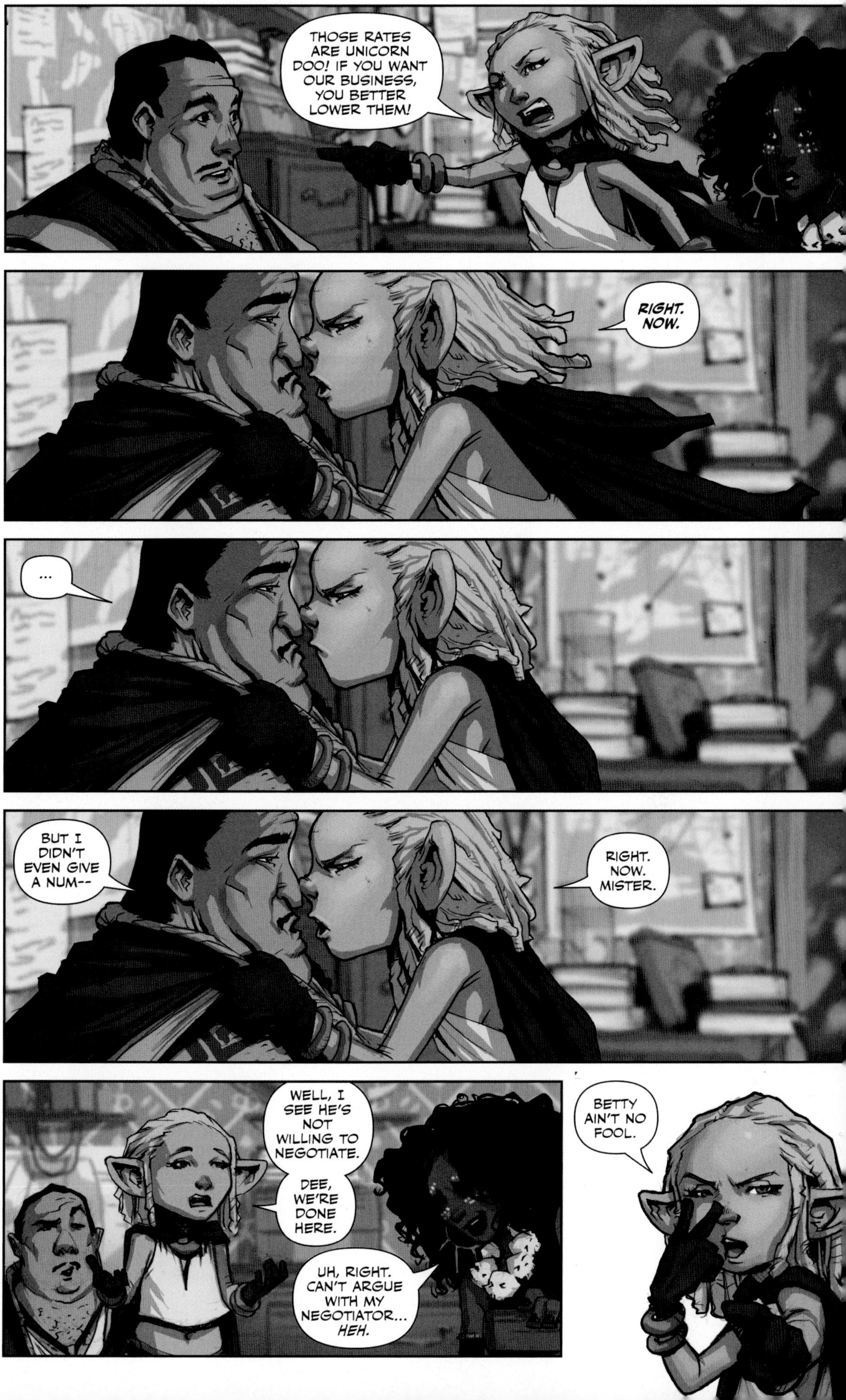
THOSE RATES ARE UNICORN DOO! IF YOU WANT OUR BUSINESS, YOU BETTER LOWER THEM!
RIGHT. NOW.
...
BUT I DIDN'T EVEN GIVE A NUM--
RIGHT. NOW. MISTER.
WELL, I SEE HE'S NOT WILLING TO NEGOTIATE.
DEE, WE'RE DONE HERE.
UH, RIGHT. CAN'T ARGUE WITH MY NEGOTIATOR... HEH.
BETTY AIN'T NO FOOL.

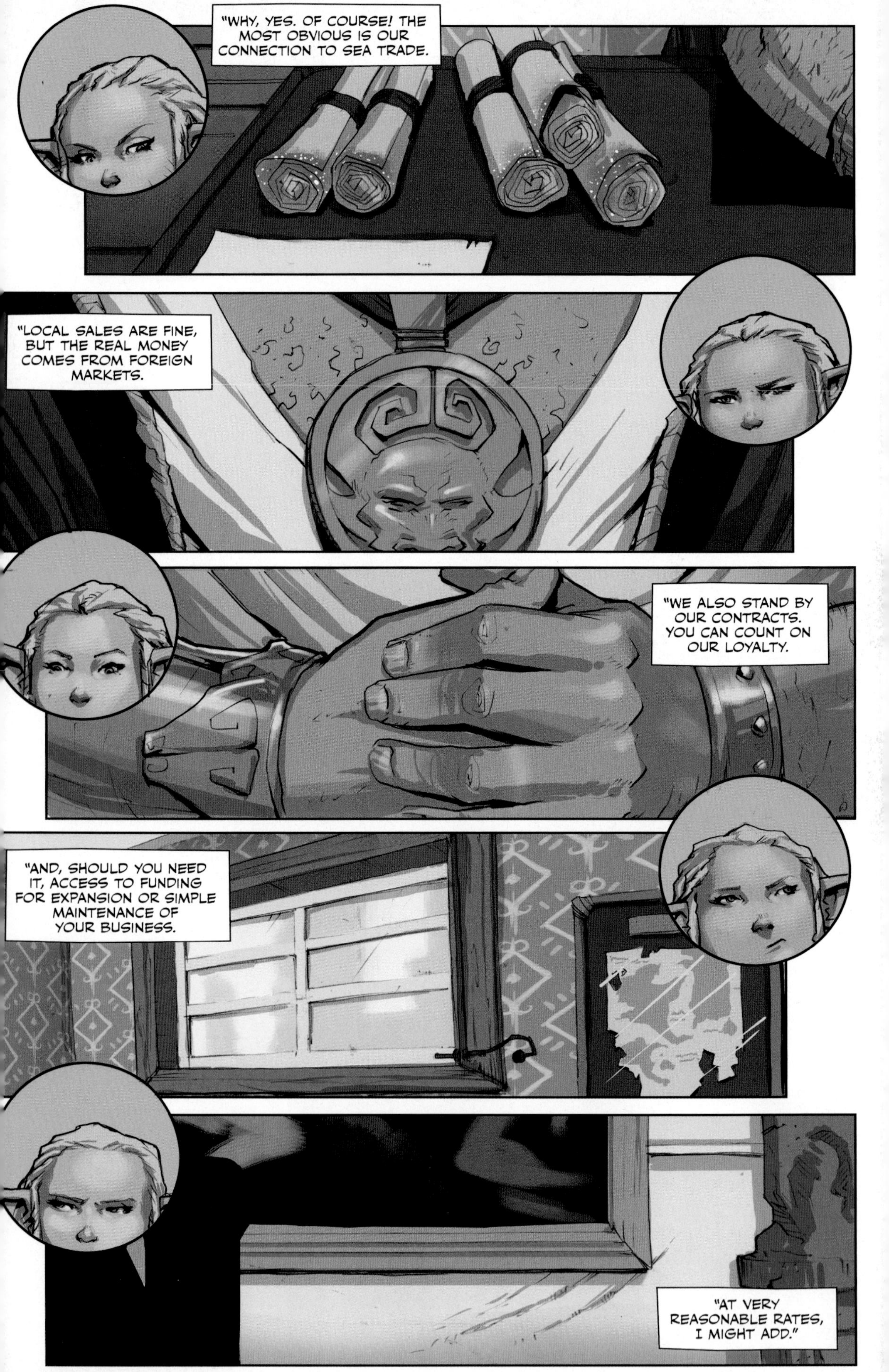
"WHY, YES. OF COURSE! THE MOST OBVIOUS IS OUR CONNECTION TO SEA TRADE.
"LOCAL SALES ARE FINE, BUT THE REAL MONEY COMES FROM FOREIGN MARKETS.
"WE ALSO STAND BY OUR CONTRACTS. YOU CAN COUNT ON OUR LOYALTY.
"AND, SHOULD YOU NEED IT, ACCESS TO FUNDING FOR EXPANSION OR SIMPLE MAINTENANCE OF YOUR BUSINESS.
"AT VERY REASONABLE RATES, I MIGHT ADD."

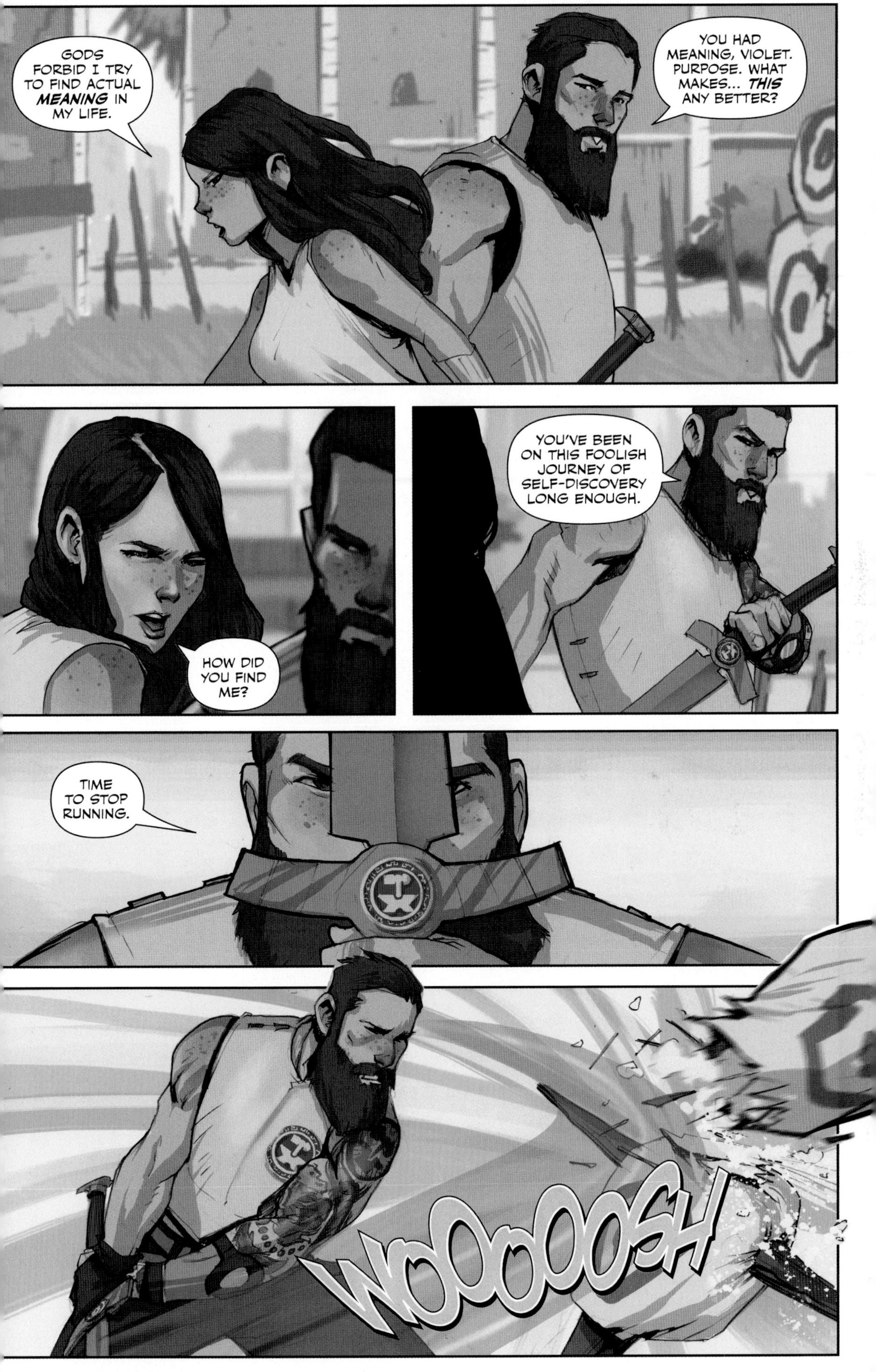
GODS FORBID I TRY TO FIND ACTUAL *MEANING* IN MY LIFE.
YOU HAD MEANING, VIOLET. PURPOSE. WHAT MAKES... *THIS* ANY BETTER?
HOW DID YOU FIND ME?
YOU'VE BEEN ON THIS FOOLISH JOURNEY OF SELF-DISCOVERY LONG ENOUGH.
TIME TO STOP RUNNING.
WOOOOOOSH

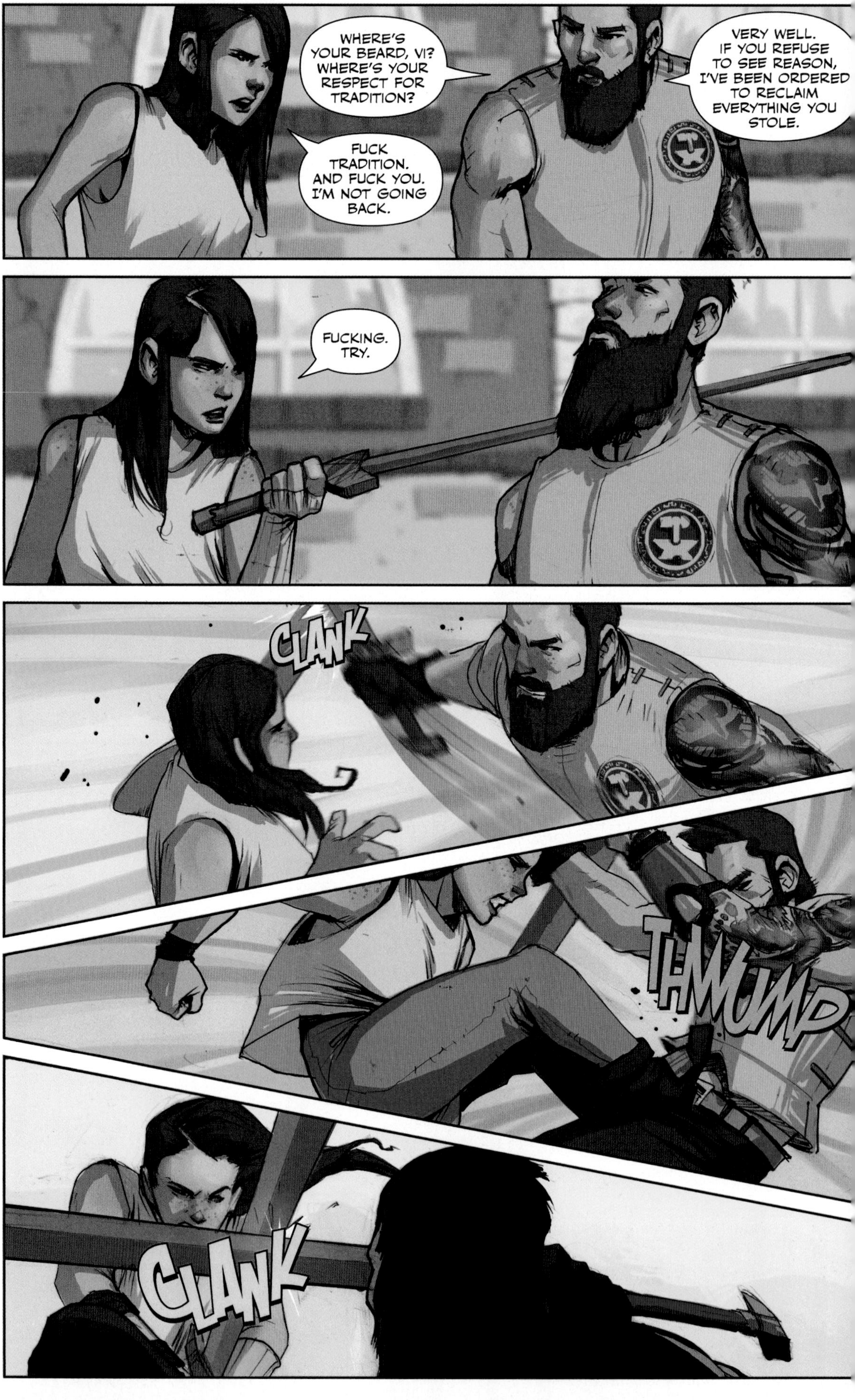
WHERE'S YOUR BEARD, VI? WHERE'S YOUR RESPECT FOR TRADITION?
VERY WELL. IF YOU REFUSE TO SEE REASON, I'VE BEEN ORDERED TO RECLAIM EVERYTHING YOU STOLE.
FUCK TRADITION. AND FUCK YOU. I'M NOT GOING BACK.
FUCKING. TRY.
CLANK
THWUMP
CLANK

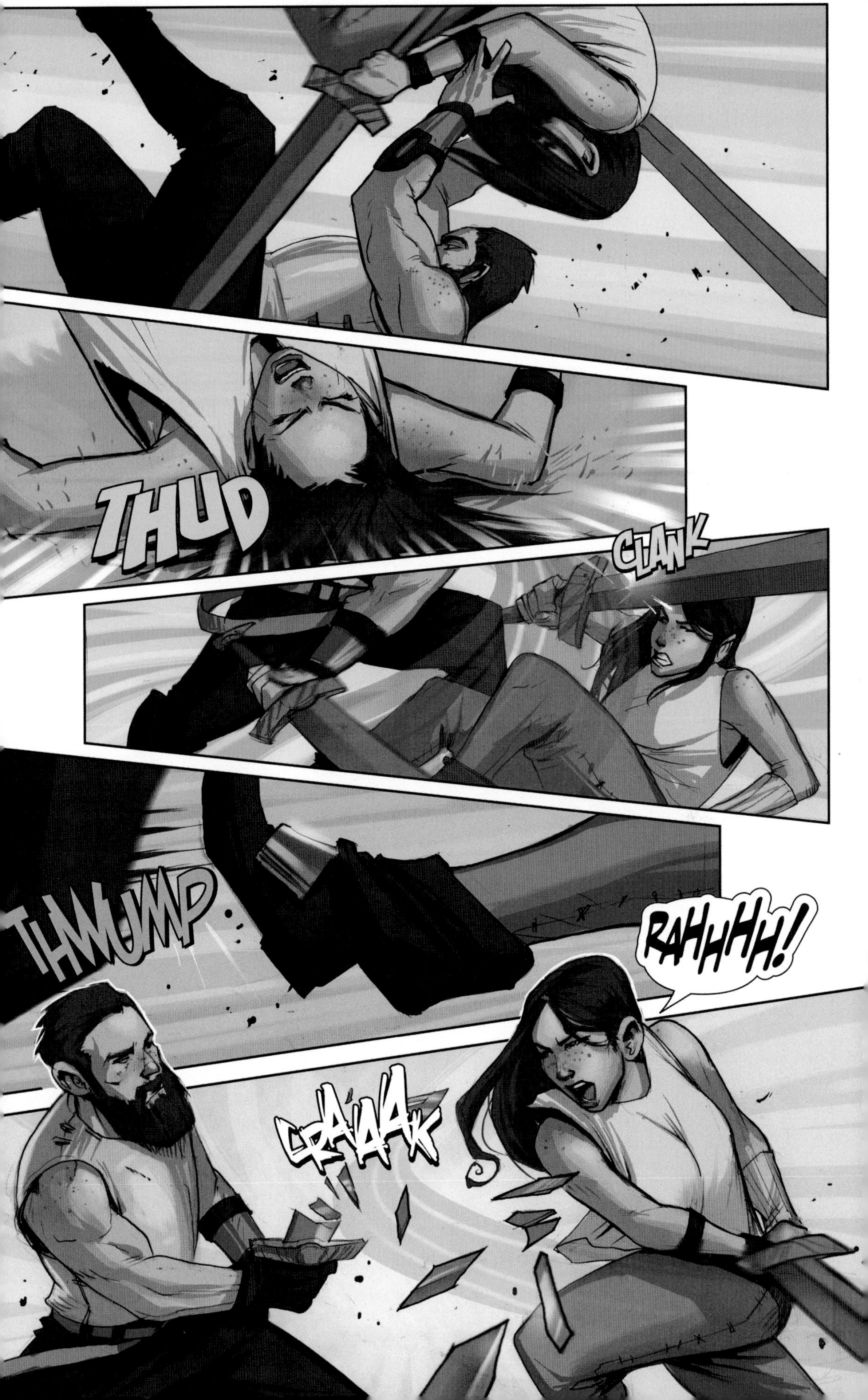
THUD
CLANK
THWUMP
RAHHHH!
CRAAAK

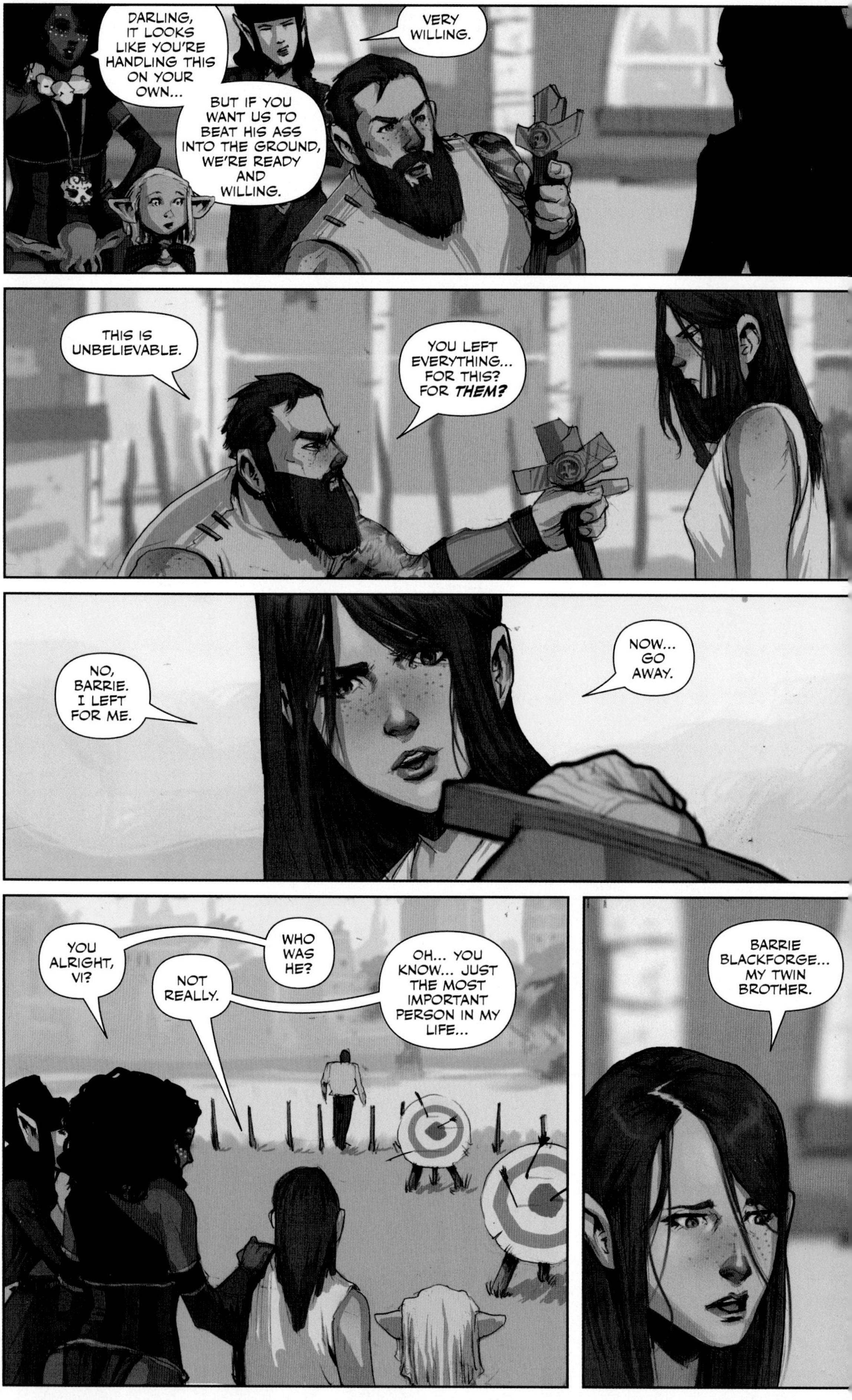
DARLING, IT LOOKS LIKE YOU'RE HANDLING THIS ON YOUR OWN...
BUT IF YOU WANT US TO BEAT HIS ASS INTO THE GROUND, WE'RE READY AND WILLING.
VERY WILLING.
THIS IS UNBELIEVABLE.
YOU LEFT EVERYTHING... FOR THIS? FOR *THEM?*
NO, BARRIE. I LEFT FOR ME.
NOW... GO AWAY.
YOU ALRIGHT, VI?
NOT REALLY.
WHO WAS HE?
OH... YOU KNOW... JUST THE MOST IMPORTANT PERSON IN MY LIFE...
BARRIE BLACKFORGE... MY TWIN BROTHER.

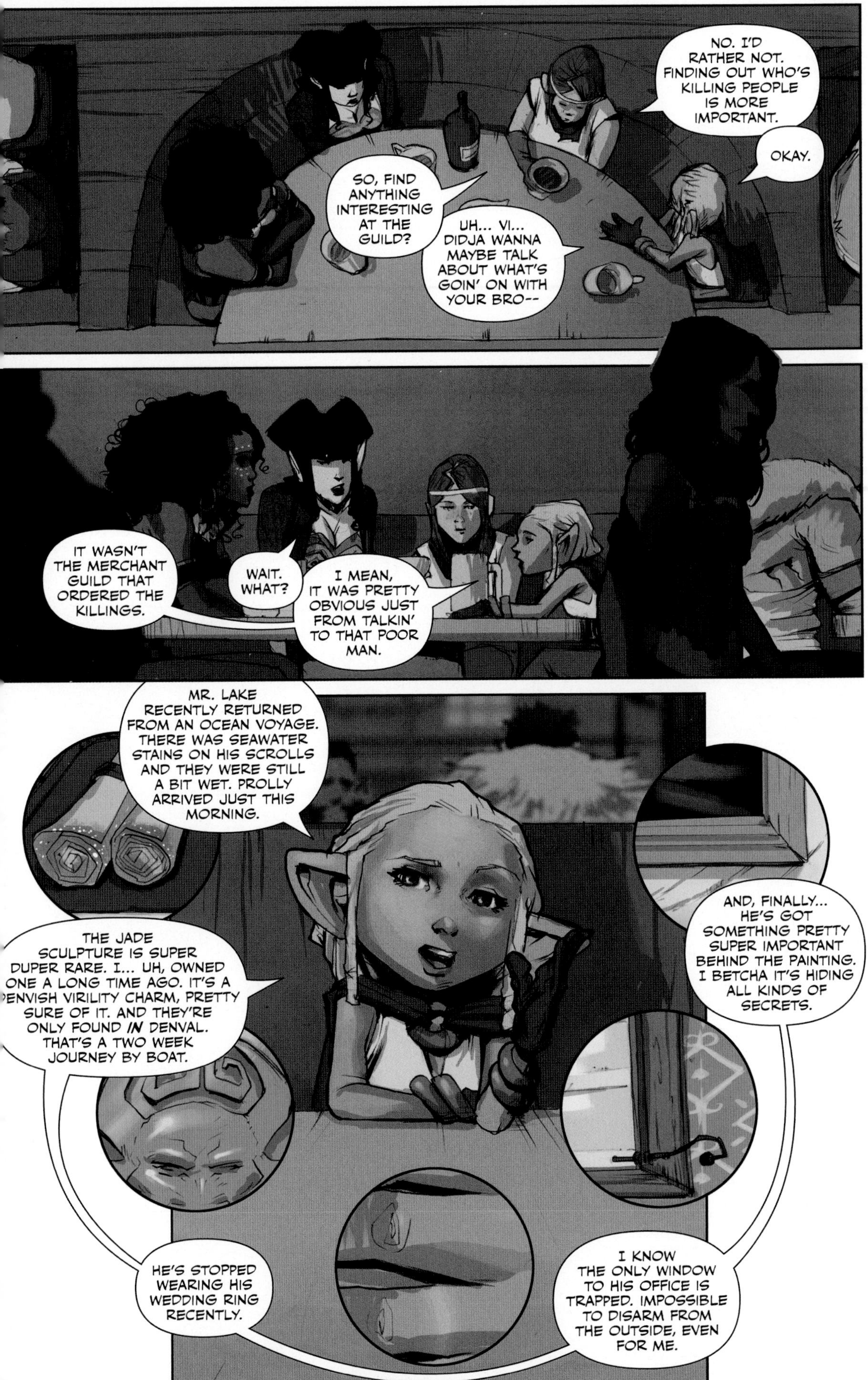
NO. I'D RATHER NOT. FINDING OUT WHO'S KILLING PEOPLE IS MORE IMPORTANT.
OKAY.
SO, FIND ANYTHING INTERESTING AT THE GUILD?
UH... VI... DIDJA WANNA MAYBE TALK ABOUT WHAT'S GOIN' ON WITH YOUR BRO--
IT WASN'T THE MERCHANT GUILD THAT ORDERED THE KILLINGS.
WAIT. WHAT?
I MEAN, IT WAS PRETTY OBVIOUS JUST FROM TALKIN' TO THAT POOR MAN.
MR. LAKE RECENTLY RETURNED FROM AN OCEAN VOYAGE. THERE WAS SEAWATER STAINS ON HIS SCROLLS AND THEY WERE STILL A BIT WET. PROLLY ARRIVED JUST THIS MORNING.
THE JADE SCULPTURE IS SUPER DUPER RARE. I... UH, OWNED ONE A LONG TIME AGO. IT'S A DENVISH VIRILITY CHARM, PRETTY SURE OF IT. AND THEY'RE ONLY FOUND *IN* DENVAL. THAT'S A TWO WEEK JOURNEY BY BOAT.
HE'S STOPPED WEARING HIS WEDDING RING RECENTLY.
I KNOW THE ONLY WINDOW TO HIS OFFICE IS TRAPPED. IMPOSSIBLE TO DISARM FROM THE OUTSIDE, EVEN FOR ME.
AND, FINALLY... HE'S GOT SOMETHING PRETTY SUPER IMPORTANT BEHIND THE PAINTING. I BETCHA IT'S HIDING ALL KINDS OF SECRETS.

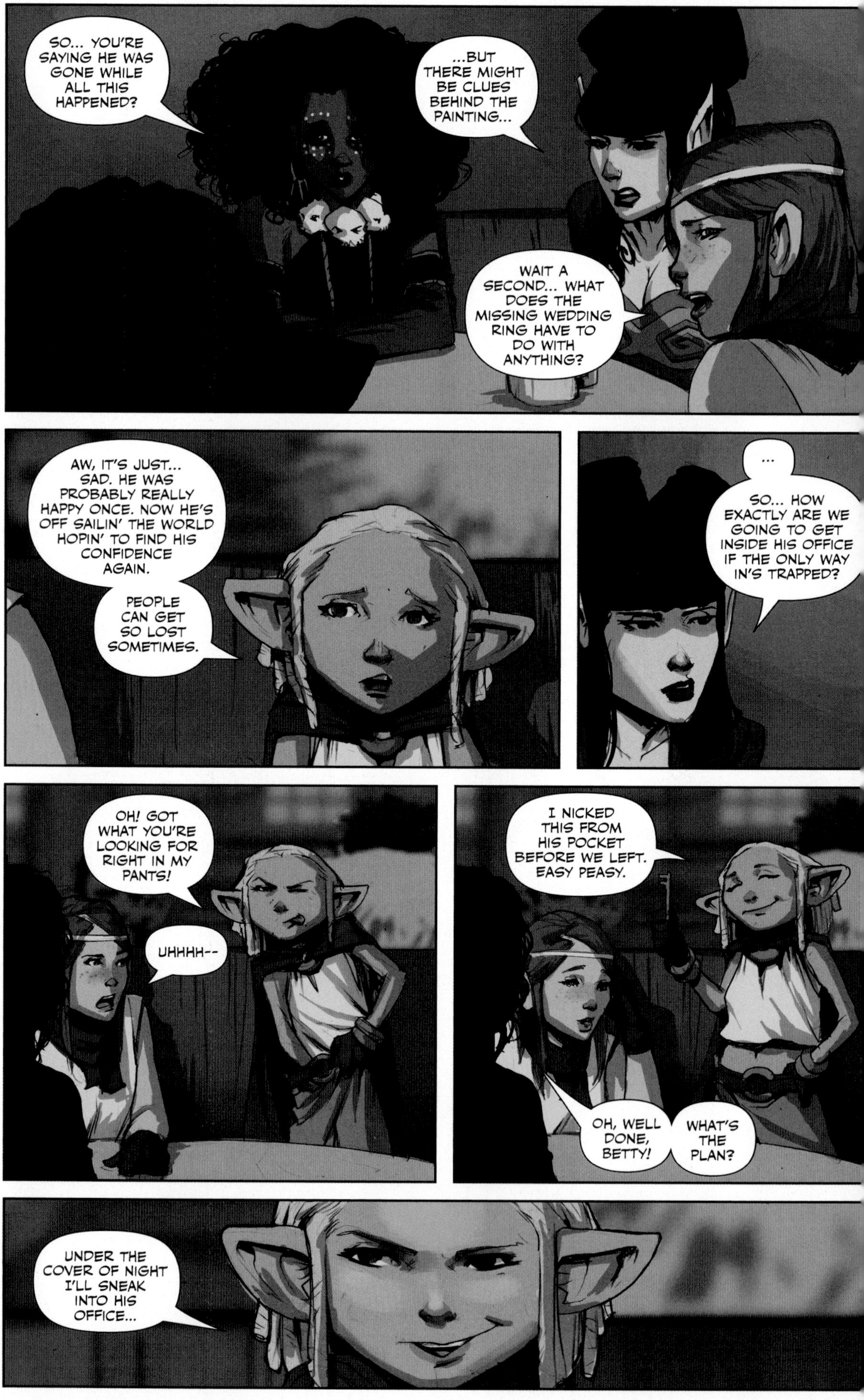
SO... YOU'RE SAYING HE WAS GONE WHILE ALL THIS HAPPENED?
...BUT THERE MIGHT BE CLUES BEHIND THE PAINTING...
WAIT A SECOND... WHAT DOES THE MISSING WEDDING RING HAVE TO DO WITH ANYTHING?
AW, IT'S JUST... SAD. HE WAS PROBABLY REALLY HAPPY ONCE. NOW HE'S OFF SAILIN' THE WORLD HOPIN' TO FIND HIS CONFIDENCE AGAIN.
PEOPLE CAN GET SO LOST SOMETIMES.
...
SO... HOW EXACTLY ARE WE GOING TO GET INSIDE HIS OFFICE IF THE ONLY WAY IN'S TRAPPED?
OH! GOT WHAT YOU'RE LOOKING FOR RIGHT IN MY PANTS!
UHHHH--
I NICKED THIS FROM HIS POCKET BEFORE WE LEFT. EASY PEASY.
OH, WELL DONE, BETTY!
WHAT'S THE PLAN?
UNDER THE COVER OF NIGHT I'LL SNEAK INTO HIS OFFICE...

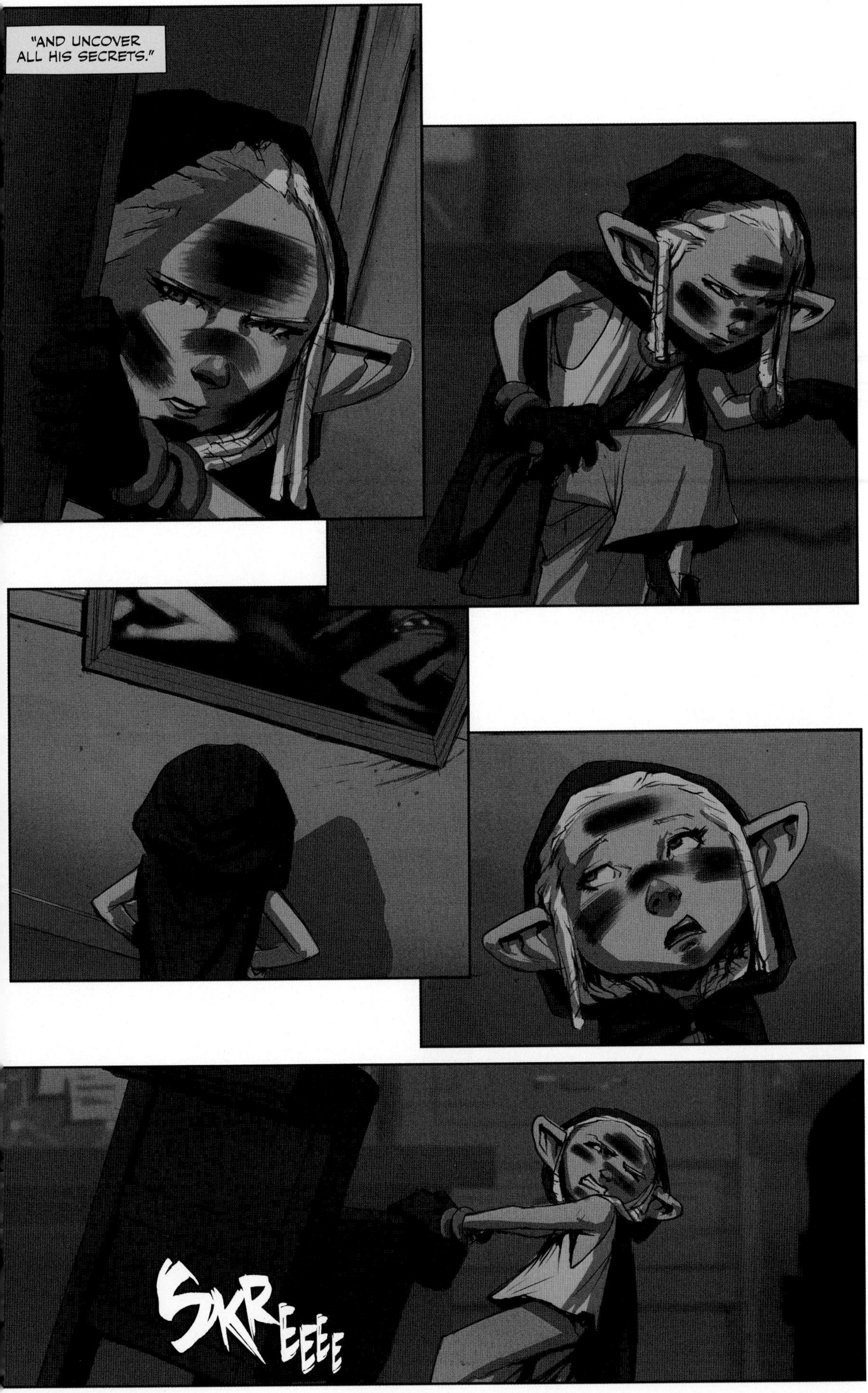
"AND UNCOVER ALL HIS SECRETS."
SKREEEE

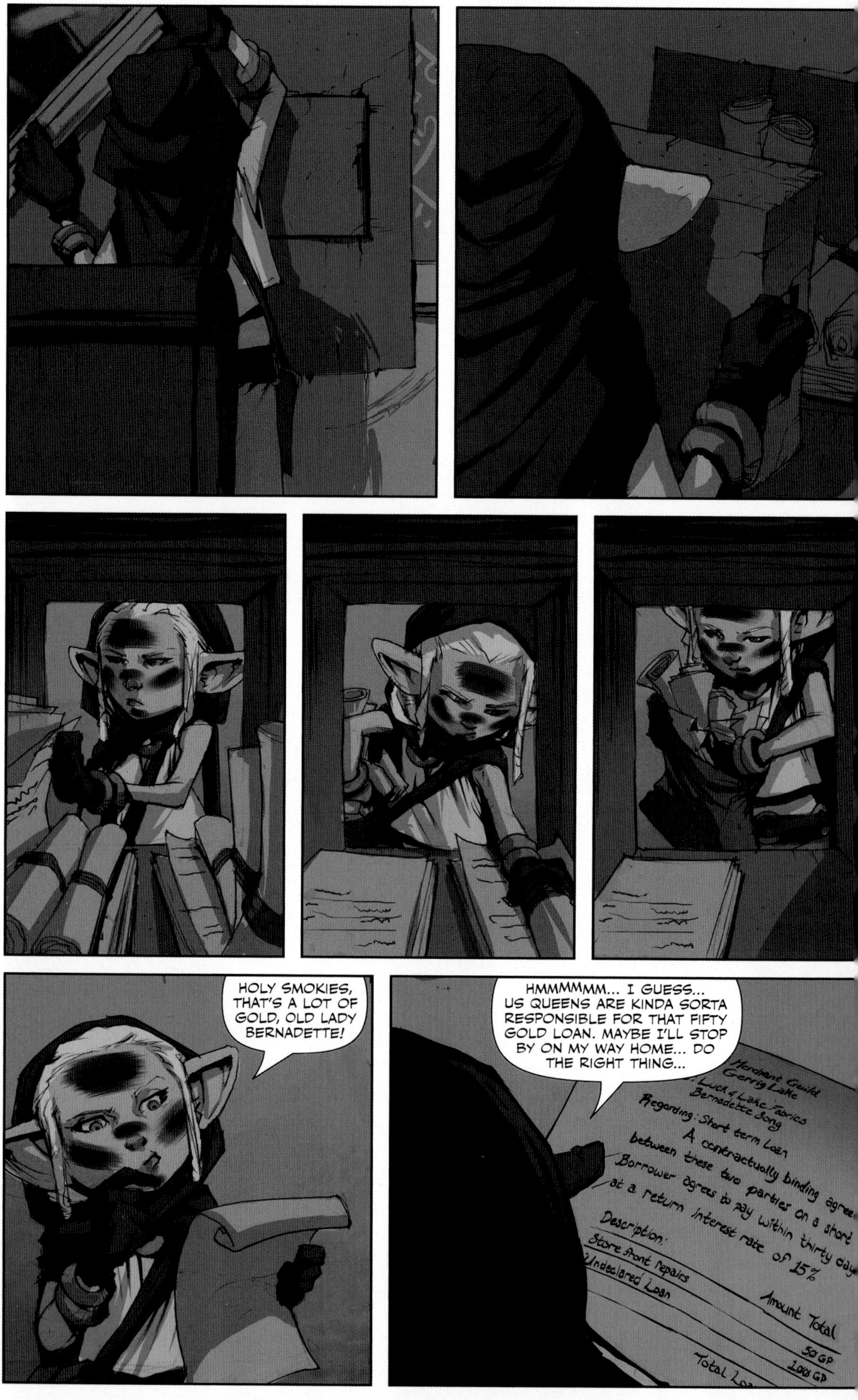
HOLY SMOKIES, THAT'S A LOT OF GOLD, OLD LADY BERNADETTE!
HMMMMMM... I GUESS... US QUEENS ARE KINDA SORTA RESPONSIBLE FOR THAT FIFTY GOLD LOAN. MAYBE I'LL STOP BY ON MY WAY HOME... DO THE RIGHT THING...
Merchant Guild
Gerrig Lake
Luck & Lake Fabrics
Bernadette Song
Regarding: Short term Loan
A contractually binding agree
between these two parties on a short
Borrower agrees to pay within thirty day
at a return interest rate of 15%
Description:
Store front repairs
Undeclared Loan
Amount Total
50 GP
100 GP
Total Lo

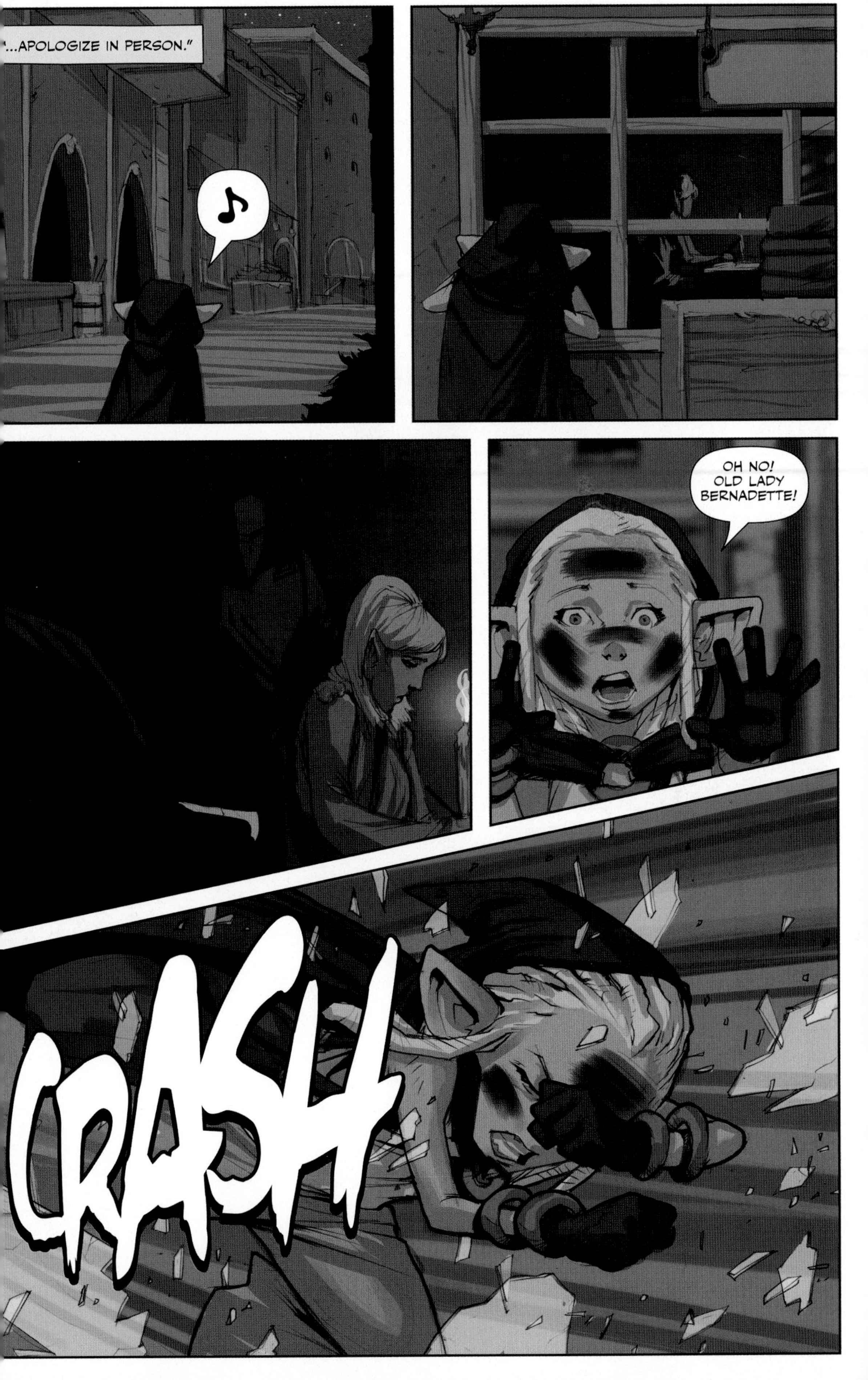
"...APOLOGIZE IN PERSON."
♪
OH NO! OLD LADY BERNADETTE!
CRASH

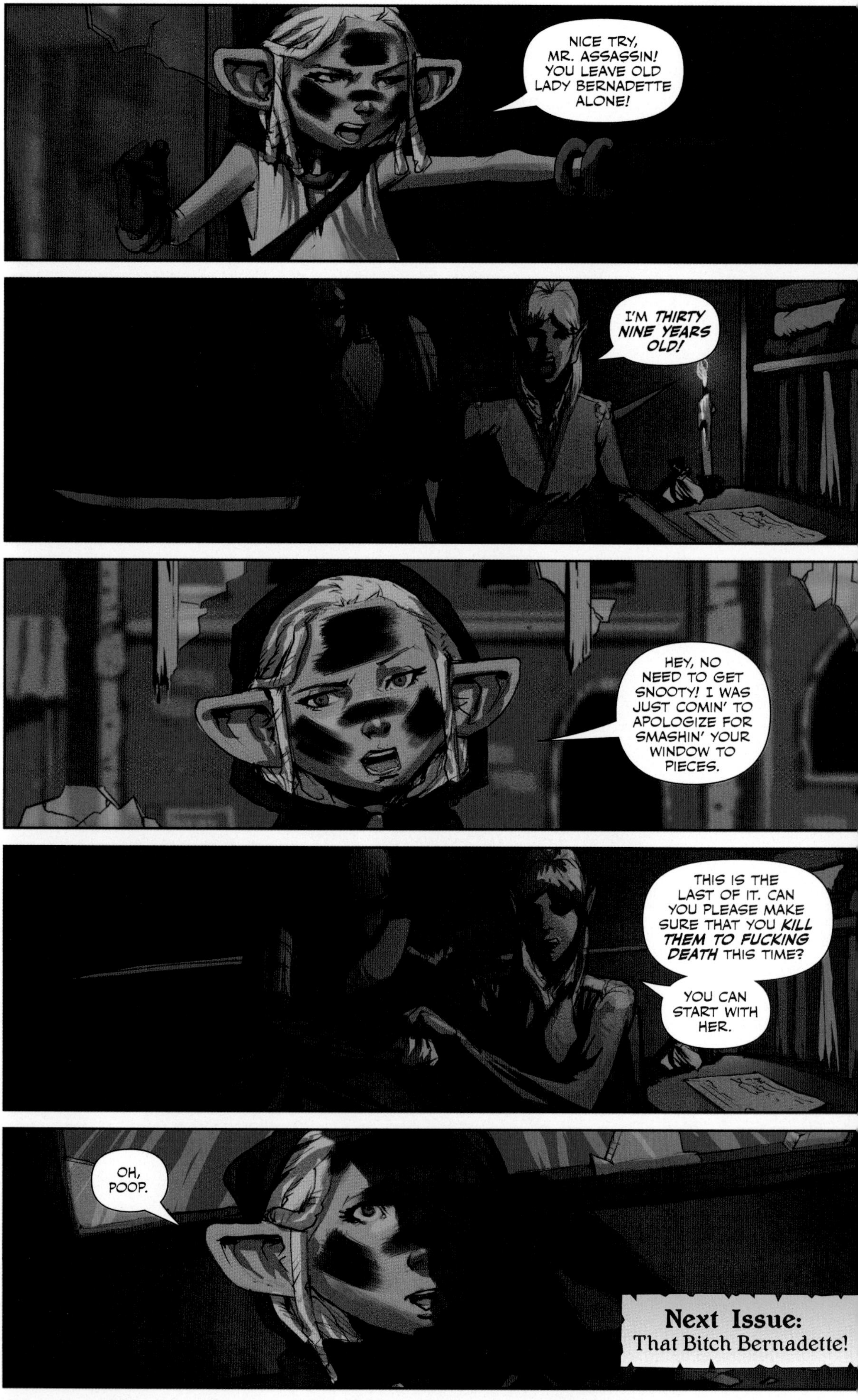
NICE TRY, MR. ASSASSIN! YOU LEAVE OLD LADY BERNADETTE ALONE!
I'M *THIRTY NINE YEARS OLD!*
HEY, NO NEED TO GET SNOOTY! I WAS JUST COMIN' TO APOLOGIZE FOR SMASHIN' YOUR WINDOW TO PIECES.
THIS IS THE LAST OF IT. CAN YOU PLEASE MAKE SURE THAT YOU *KILL THEM TO FUCKING DEATH* THIS TIME?
YOU CAN START WITH HER.
OH, POOP.
Next Issue:
That Bitch Bernadette!

CHAPTER FOUR

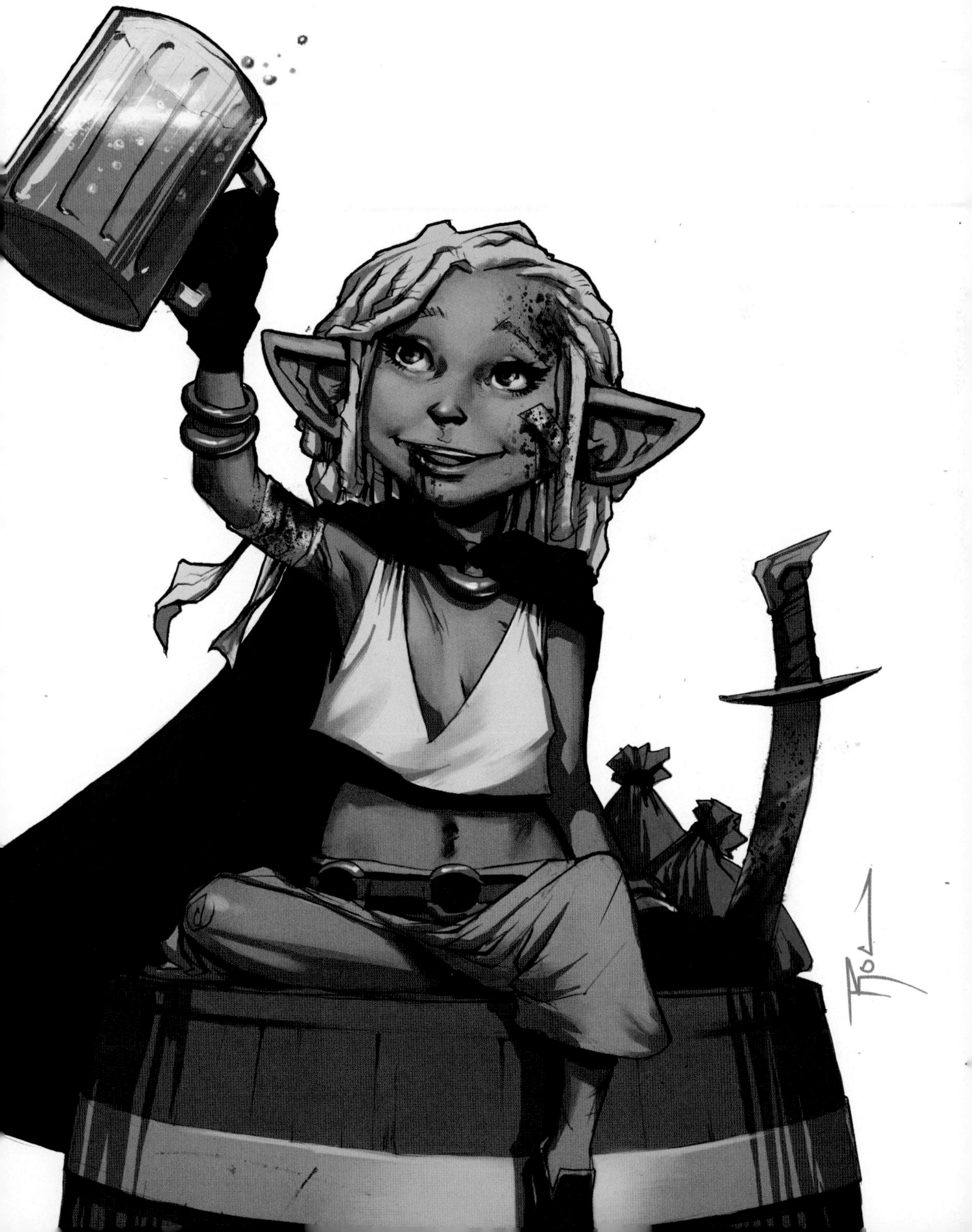

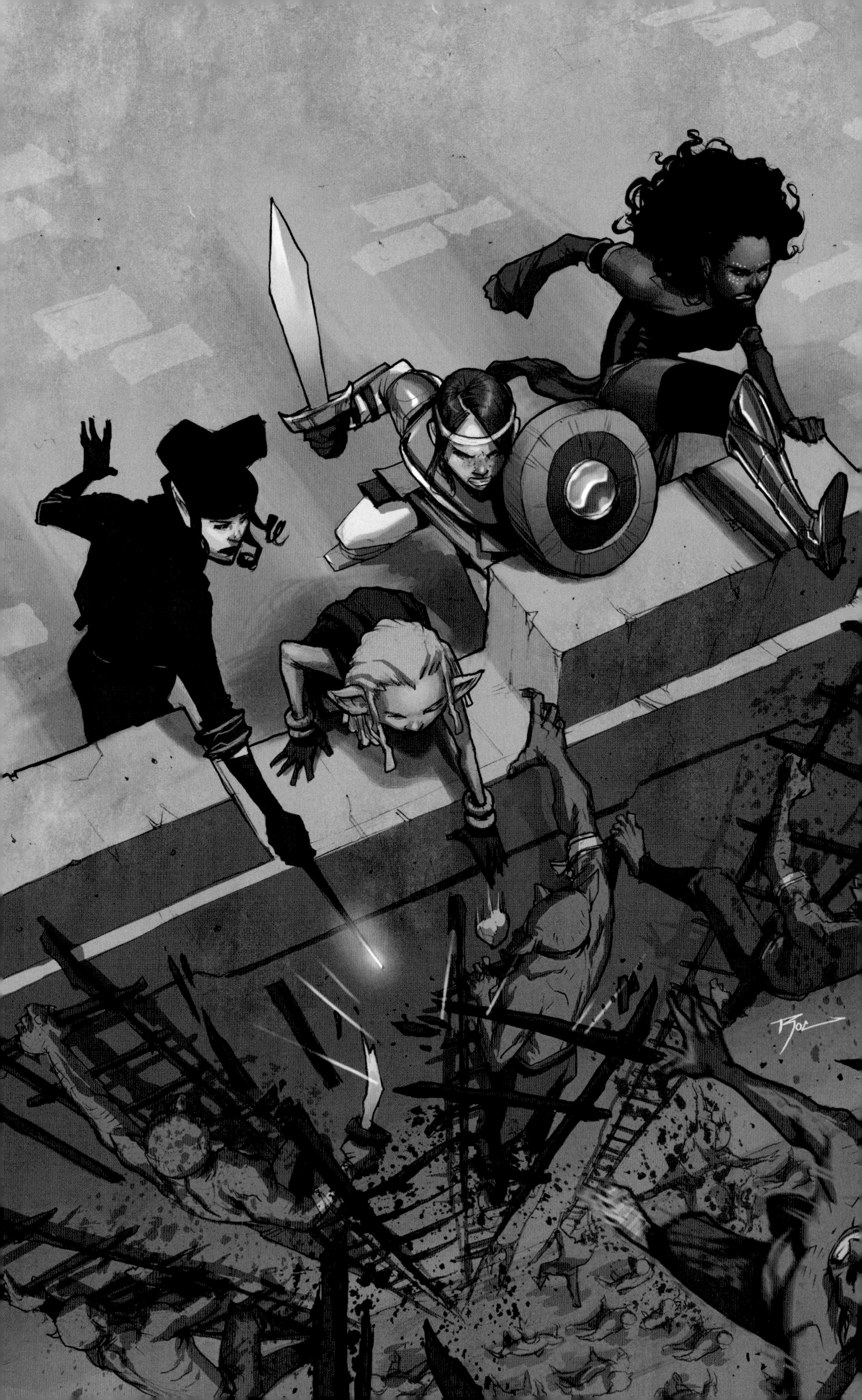

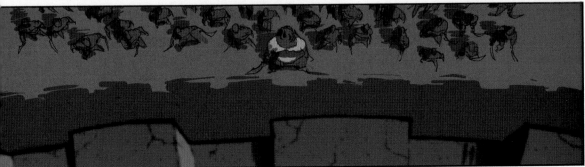

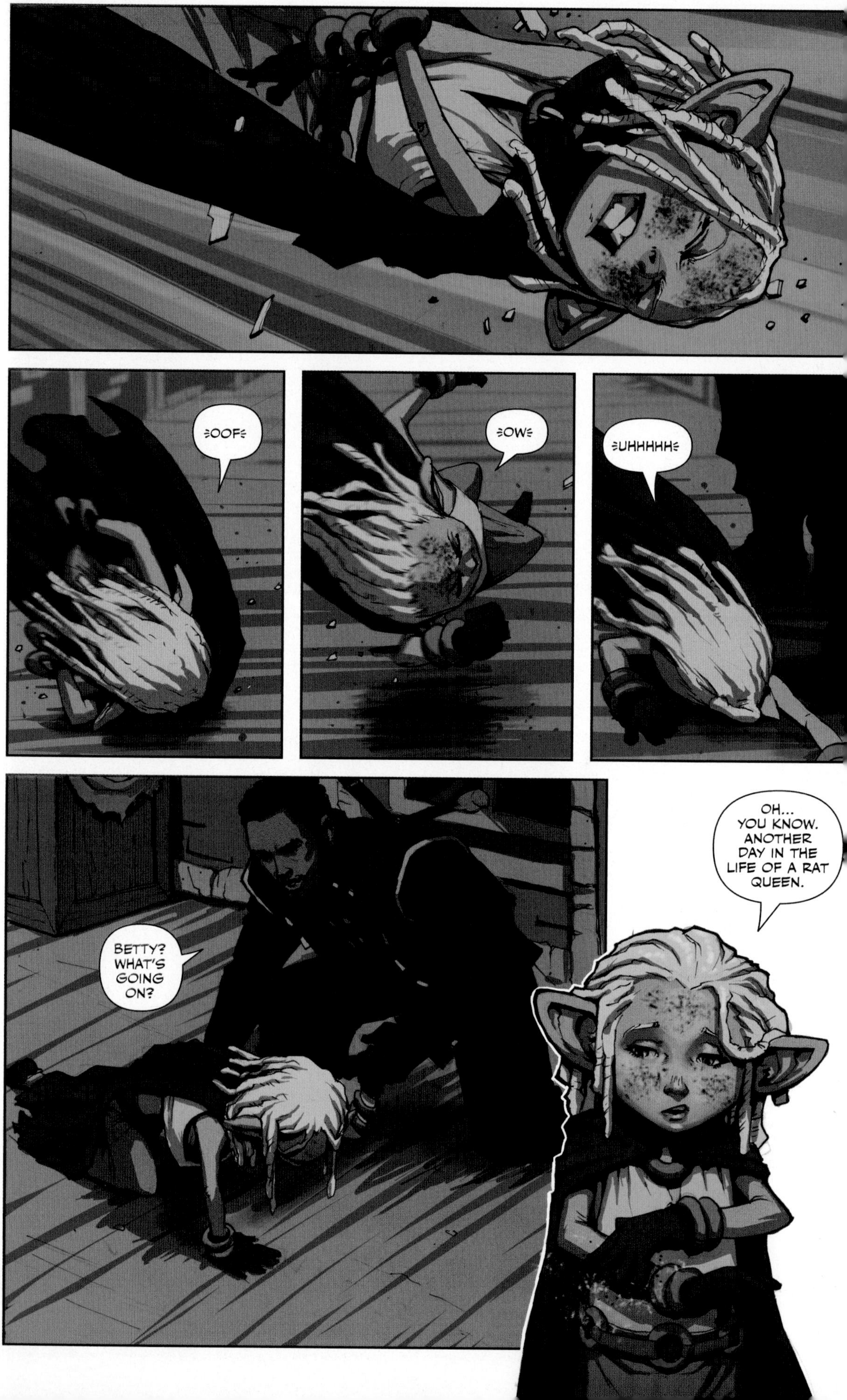
OOF
OW
UHHHHH
BETTY? WHAT'S GOING ON?
OH... YOU KNOW. ANOTHER DAY IN THE LIFE OF A RAT QUEEN.

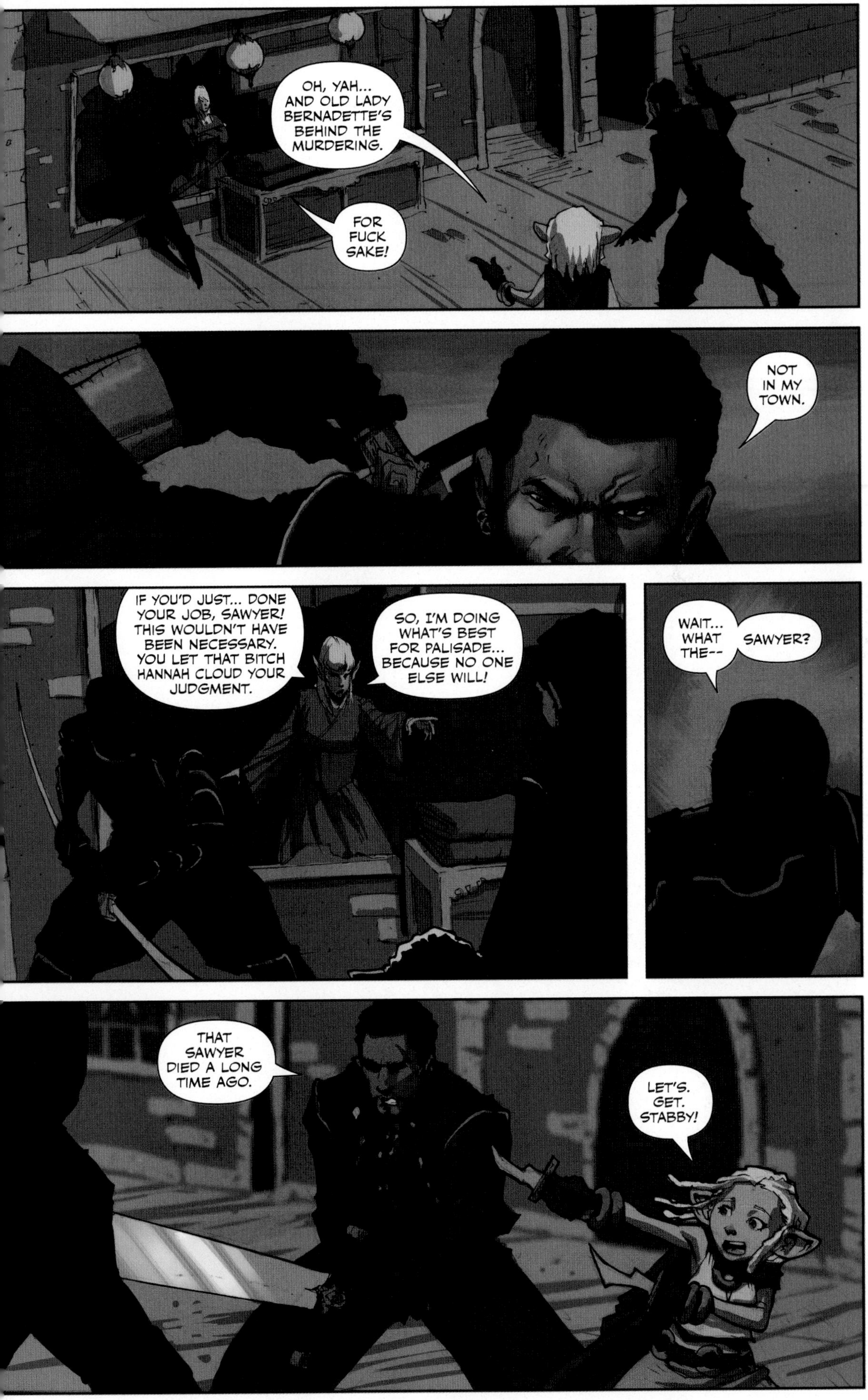
OH, YAH... AND OLD LADY BERNADETTE'S BEHIND THE MURDERING.
FOR FUCK SAKE!
NOT IN MY TOWN.
IF YOU'D JUST... DONE YOUR JOB, SAWYER! THIS WOULDN'T HAVE BEEN NECESSARY. YOU LET THAT BITCH HANNAH CLOUD YOUR JUDGMENT.
SO, I'M DOING WHAT'S BEST FOR PALISADE... BECAUSE NO ONE ELSE WILL!
WAIT... WHAT THE--
SAWYER?
THAT SAWYER DIED A LONG TIME AGO.
LET'S. GET. STABBY!

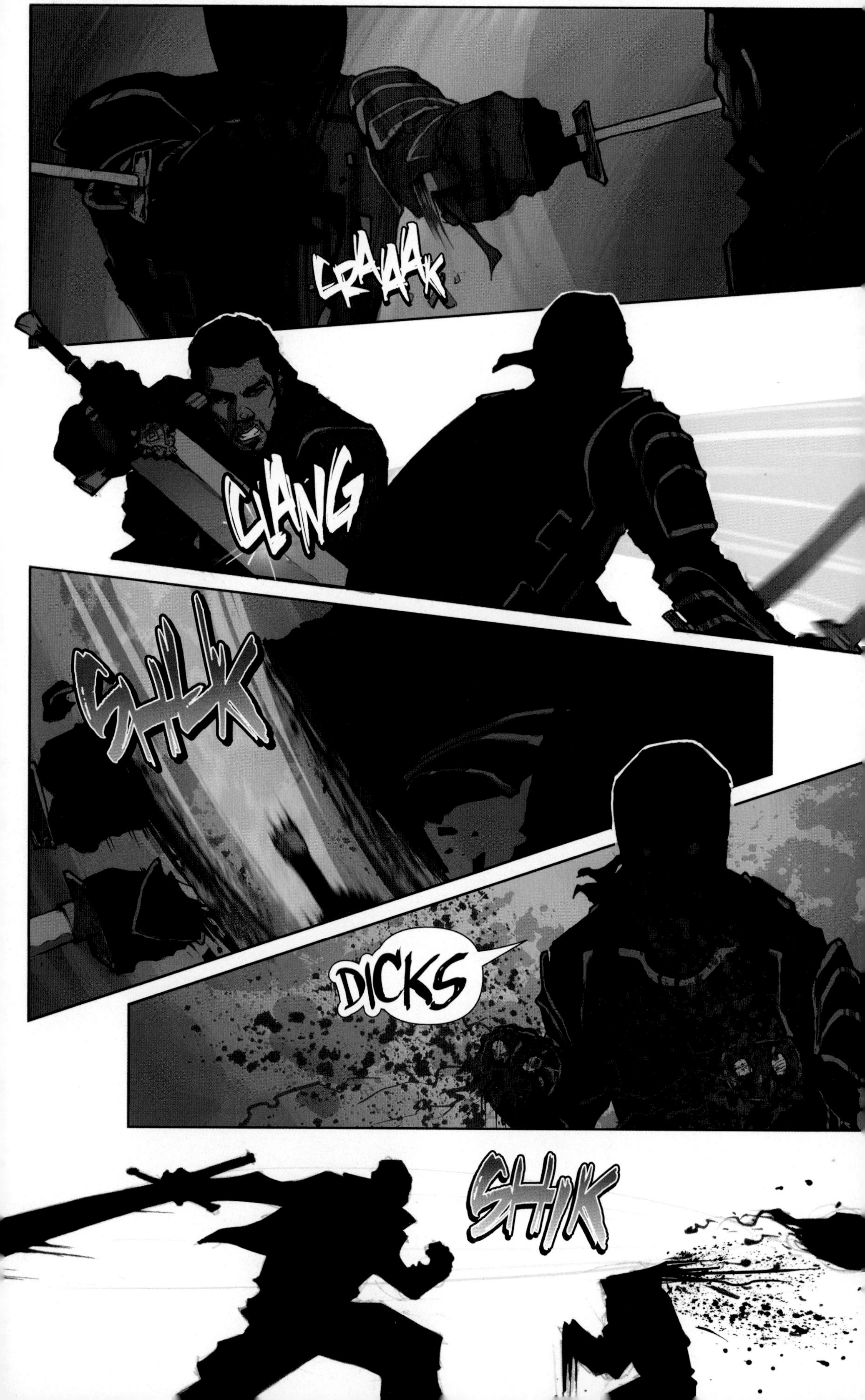
CRAAAAK
CLANG
SHLK
DICKS
SHIK

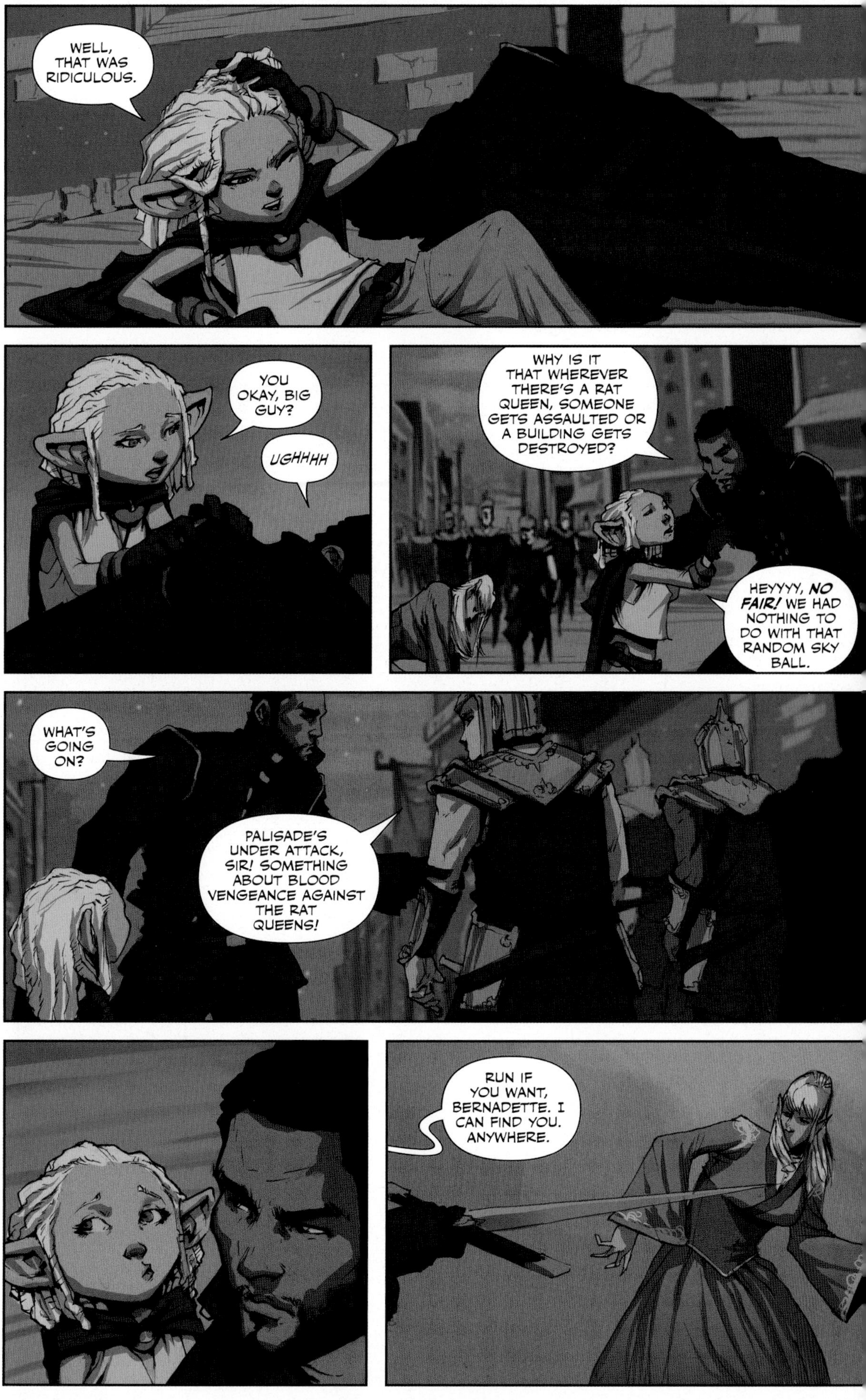
WELL, THAT WAS RIDICULOUS.
YOU OKAY, BIG GUY?
UGHHHH
WHY IS IT THAT WHEREVER THERE'S A RAT QUEEN, SOMEONE GETS ASSAULTED OR A BUILDING GETS DESTROYED?
HEYYYY, NO FAIR! WE HAD NOTHING TO DO WITH THAT RANDOM SKY BALL.
WHAT'S GOING ON?
PALISADE'S UNDER ATTACK, SIR! SOMETHING ABOUT BLOOD VENGEANCE AGAINST THE RAT QUEENS!
RUN IF YOU WANT, BERNADETTE. I CAN FIND YOU. ANYWHERE.

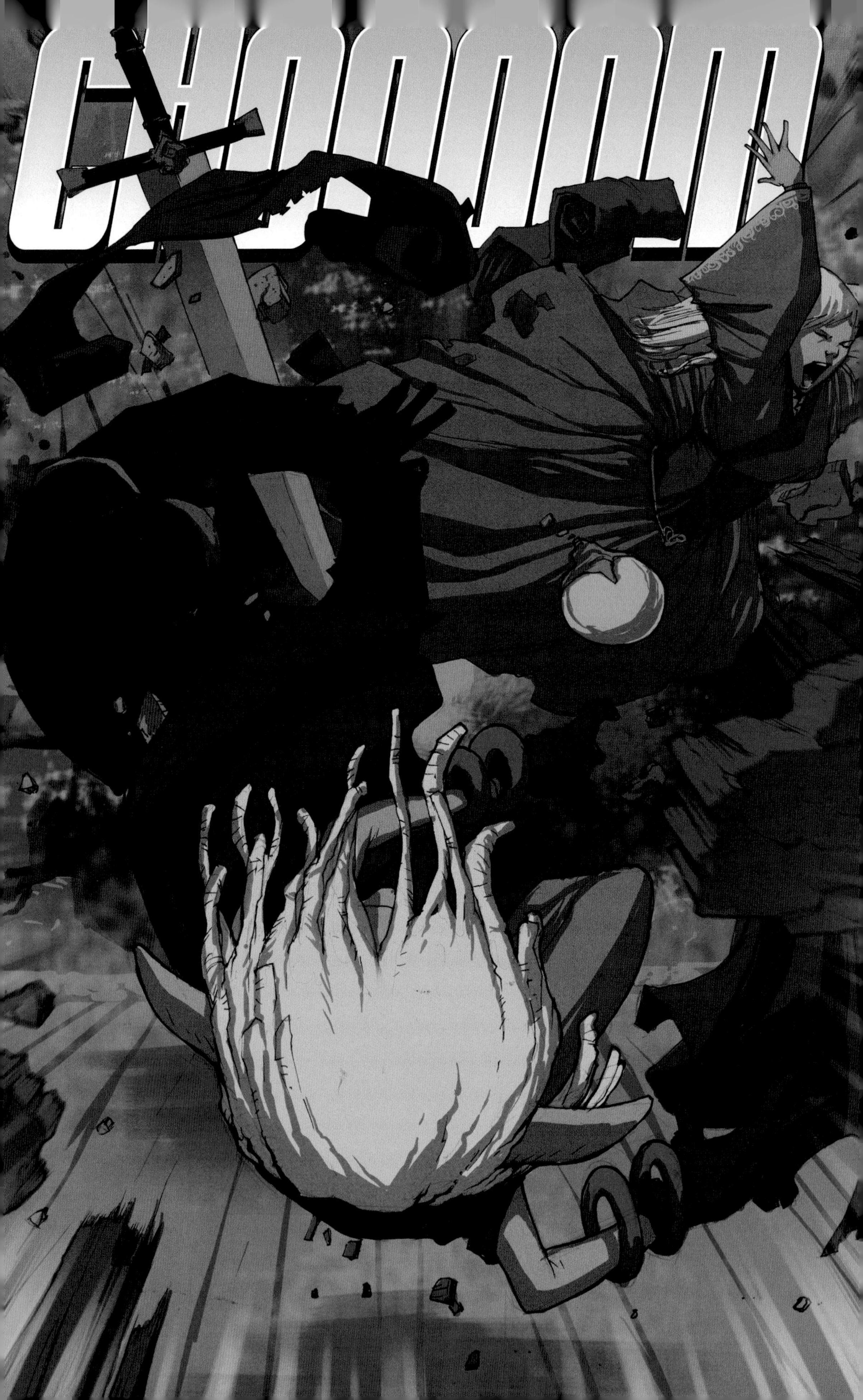
CHOOOOM

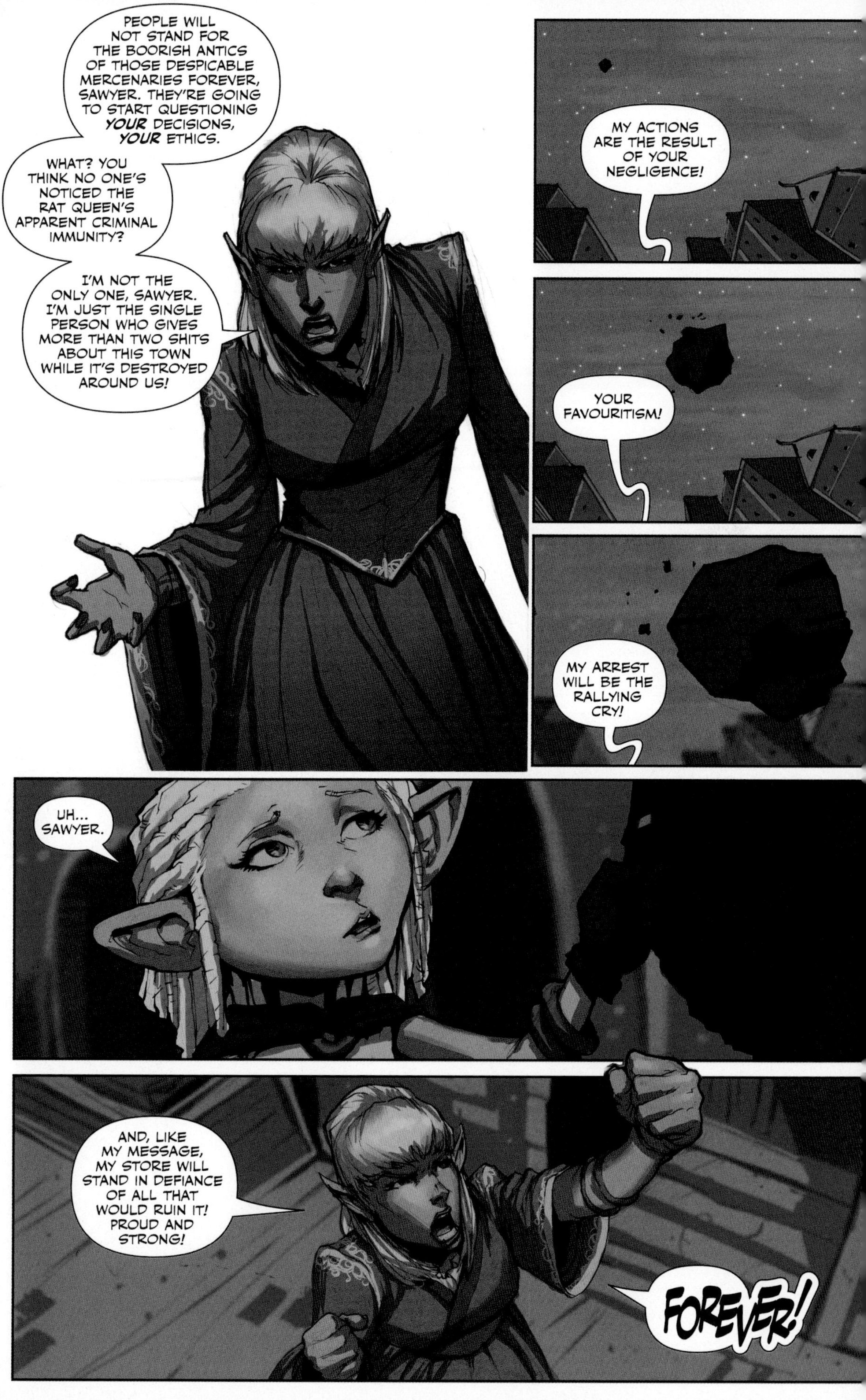
PEOPLE WILL NOT STAND FOR THE BOORISH ANTICS OF THOSE DESPICABLE MERCENARIES FOREVER, SAWYER. THEY'RE GOING TO START QUESTIONING *YOUR* DECISIONS, *YOUR* ETHICS.
WHAT? YOU THINK NO ONE'S NOTICED THE RAT QUEEN'S APPARENT CRIMINAL IMMUNITY?
I'M NOT THE ONLY ONE, SAWYER. I'M JUST THE SINGLE PERSON WHO GIVES MORE THAN TWO SHITS ABOUT THIS TOWN WHILE IT'S DESTROYED AROUND US!
MY ACTIONS ARE THE RESULT OF YOUR NEGLIGENCE!
YOUR FAVOURITISM!
MY ARREST WILL BE THE RALLYING CRY!
UH... SAWYER.
AND, LIKE MY MESSAGE, MY STORE WILL STAND IN DEFIANCE OF ALL THAT WOULD RUIN IT! PROUD AND STRONG!
FOREVER!

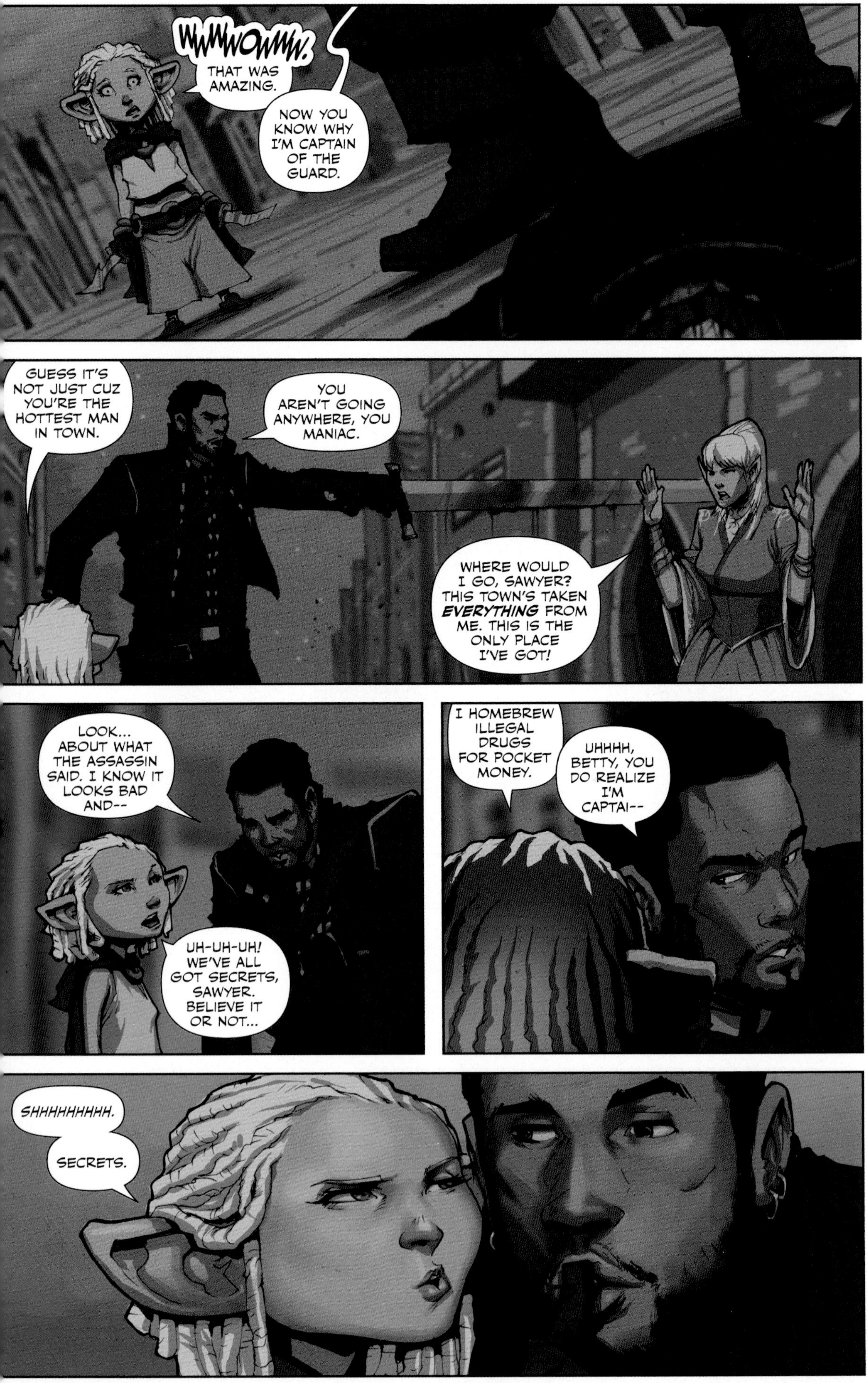
WWWOWWW.
THAT WAS AMAZING.
NOW YOU KNOW WHY I'M CAPTAIN OF THE GUARD.
GUESS IT'S NOT JUST CUZ YOU'RE THE HOTTEST MAN IN TOWN.
YOU AREN'T GOING ANYWHERE, YOU MANIAC.
WHERE WOULD I GO, SAWYER? THIS TOWN'S TAKEN EVERYTHING FROM ME. THIS IS THE ONLY PLACE I'VE GOT!
LOOK... ABOUT WHAT THE ASSASSIN SAID. I KNOW IT LOOKS BAD AND--
UH-UH-UH! WE'VE ALL GOT SECRETS, SAWYER. BELIEVE IT OR NOT...
I HOMEBREW ILLEGAL DRUGS FOR POCKET MONEY.
UHHHH, BETTY, YOU DO REALIZE I'M CAPTAI--
SHHHHHHHHH.
SECRETS.

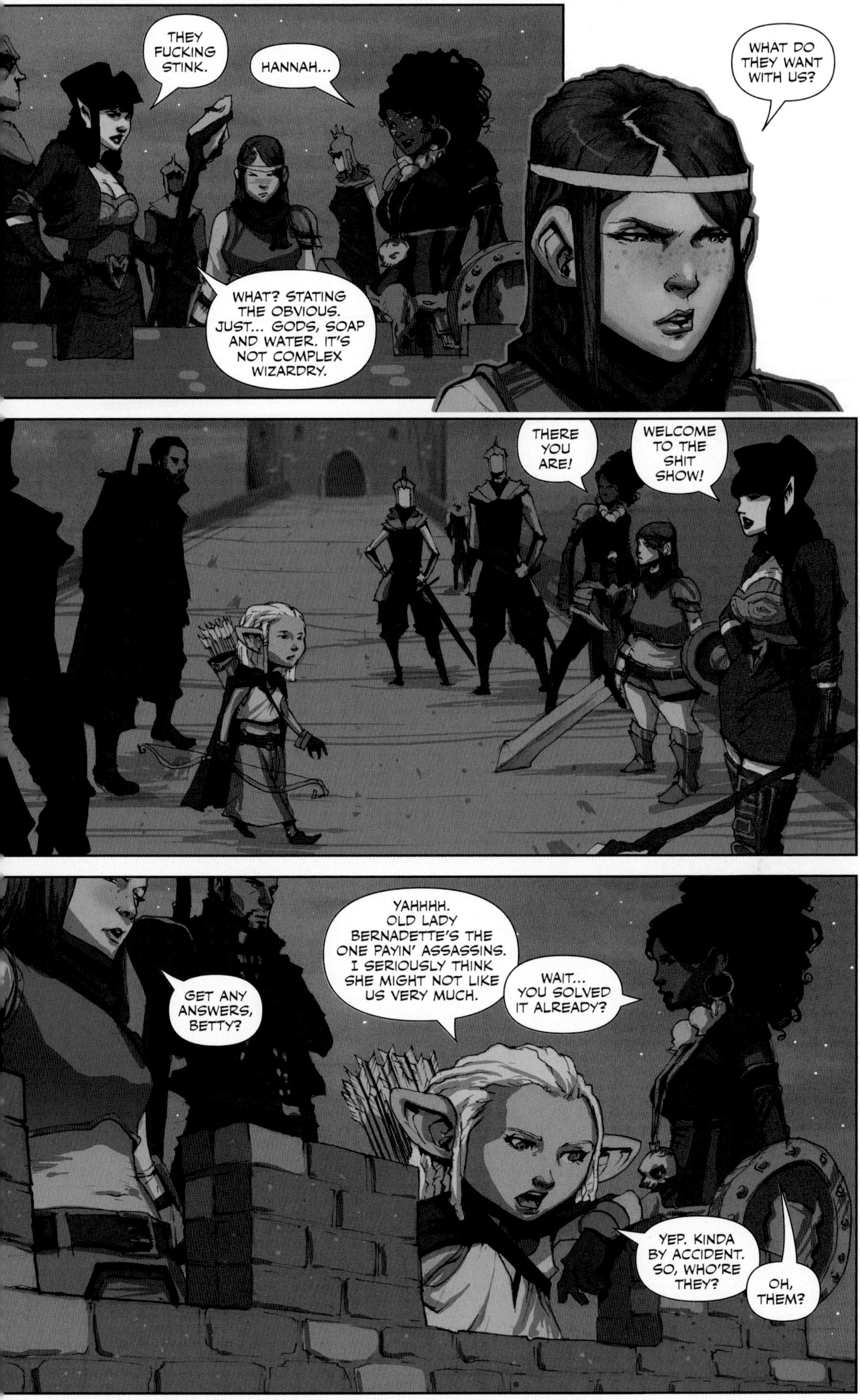
THEY FUCKING STINK.
HANNAH...
WHAT? STATING THE OBVIOUS. JUST... GODS, SOAP AND WATER. IT'S NOT COMPLEX WIZARDRY.
WHAT DO THEY WANT WITH US?
THERE YOU ARE!
WELCOME TO THE SHIT SHOW!
GET ANY ANSWERS, BETTY?
YAHHHH. OLD LADY BERNADETTE'S THE ONE PAYIN' ASSASSINS. I SERIOUSLY THINK SHE MIGHT NOT LIKE US VERY MUCH.
WAIT... YOU SOLVED IT ALREADY?
YEP. KINDA BY ACCIDENT. SO, WHO'RE THEY?
OH, THEM?

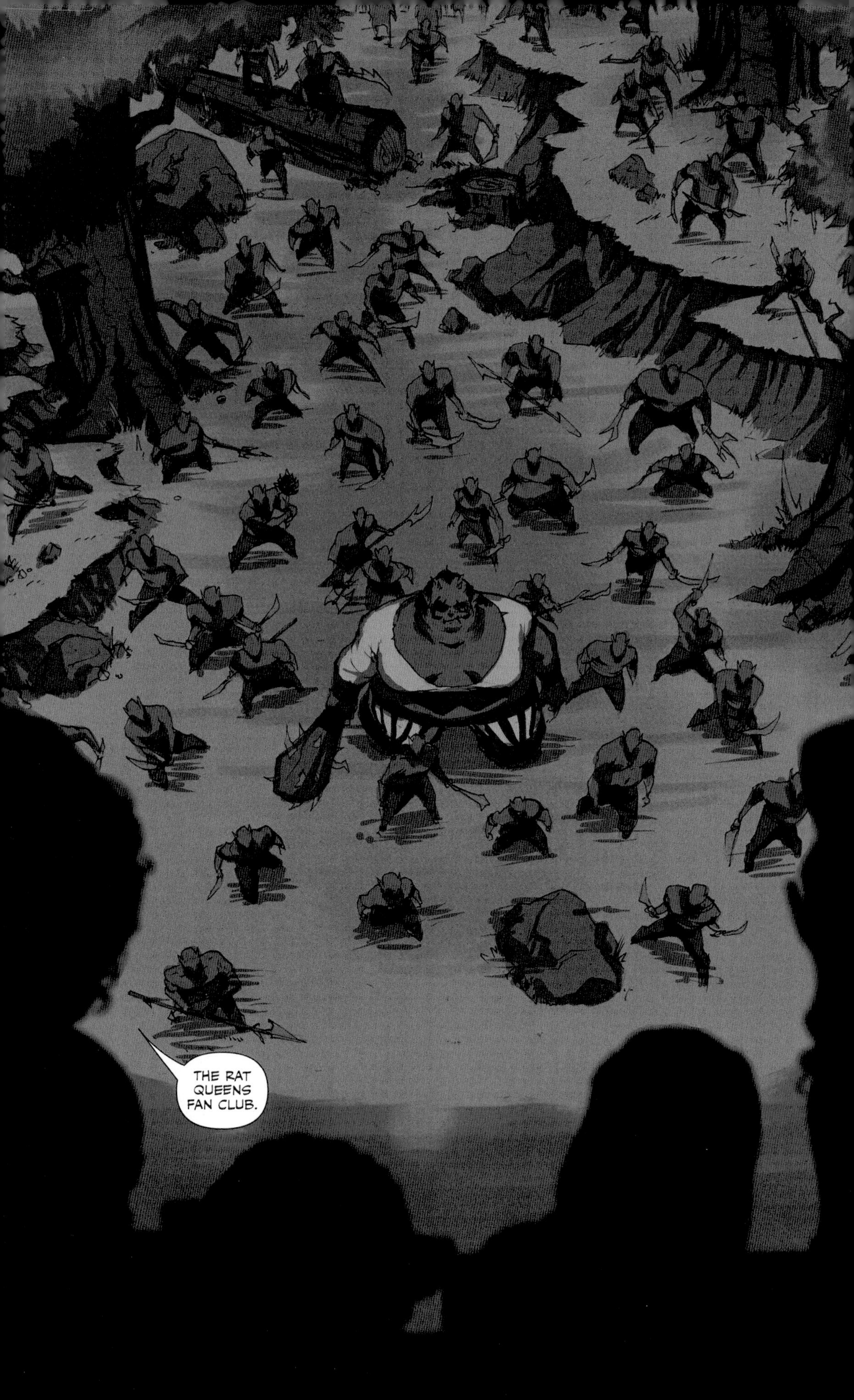
THE RAT QUEENS FAN CLUB.

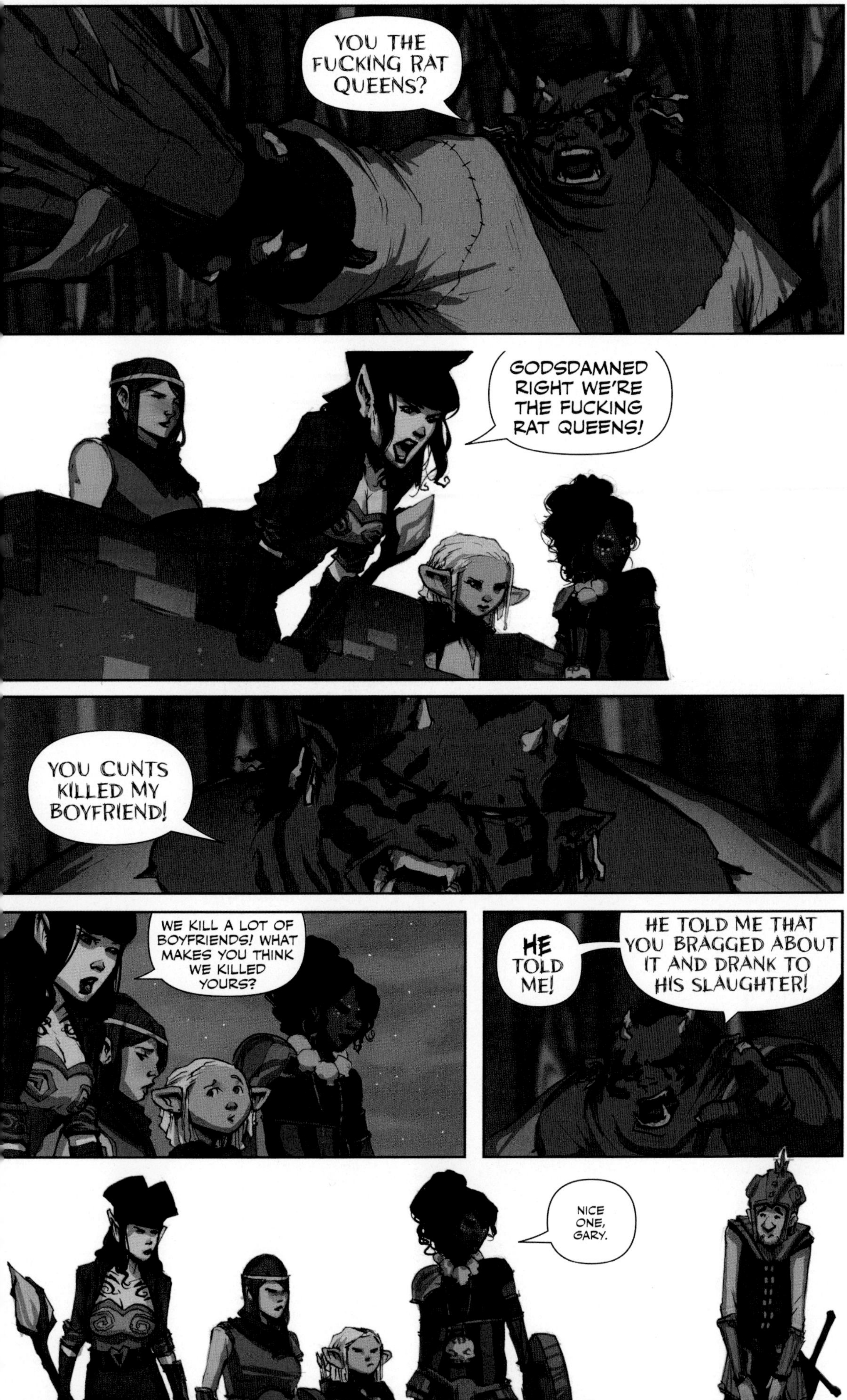
YOU THE FUCKING RAT QUEENS?
GODSDAMNED RIGHT WE'RE THE FUCKING RAT QUEENS!
YOU CUNTS KILLED MY BOYFRIEND!
WE KILL A LOT OF BOYFRIENDS! WHAT MAKES YOU THINK WE KILLED YOURS?
HE TOLD ME!
HE TOLD ME THAT YOU BRAGGED ABOUT IT AND DRANK TO HIS SLAUGHTER!
NICE ONE, GARY.

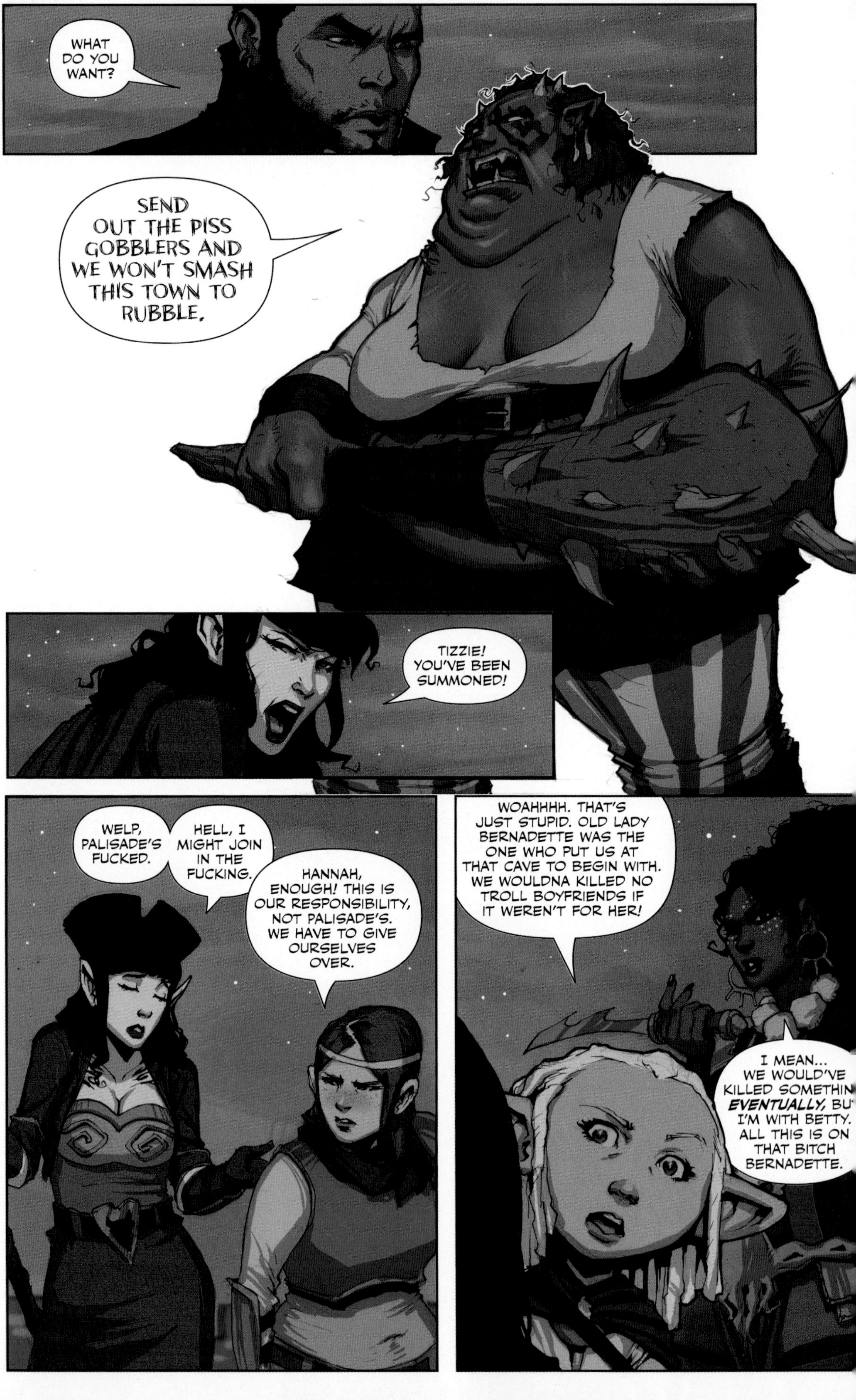
WHAT DO YOU WANT?
SEND OUT THE PISS GOBBLERS AND WE WON'T SMASH THIS TOWN TO RUBBLE.
TIZZIE! YOU'VE BEEN SUMMONED!
WELP, PALISADE'S FUCKED.
HELL, I MIGHT JOIN IN THE FUCKING.
HANNAH, ENOUGH! THIS IS OUR RESPONSIBILITY, NOT PALISADE'S. WE HAVE TO GIVE OURSELVES OVER.
WOAHHHH. THAT'S JUST STUPID. OLD LADY BERNADETTE WAS THE ONE WHO PUT US AT THAT CAVE TO BEGIN WITH. WE WOULDNA KILLED NO TROLL BOYFRIENDS IF IT WEREN'T FOR HER!
I MEAN... WE WOULD'VE KILLED SOMETHIN *EVENTUALLY,* BU I'M WITH BETTY. ALL THIS IS ON THAT BITCH BERNADETTE.

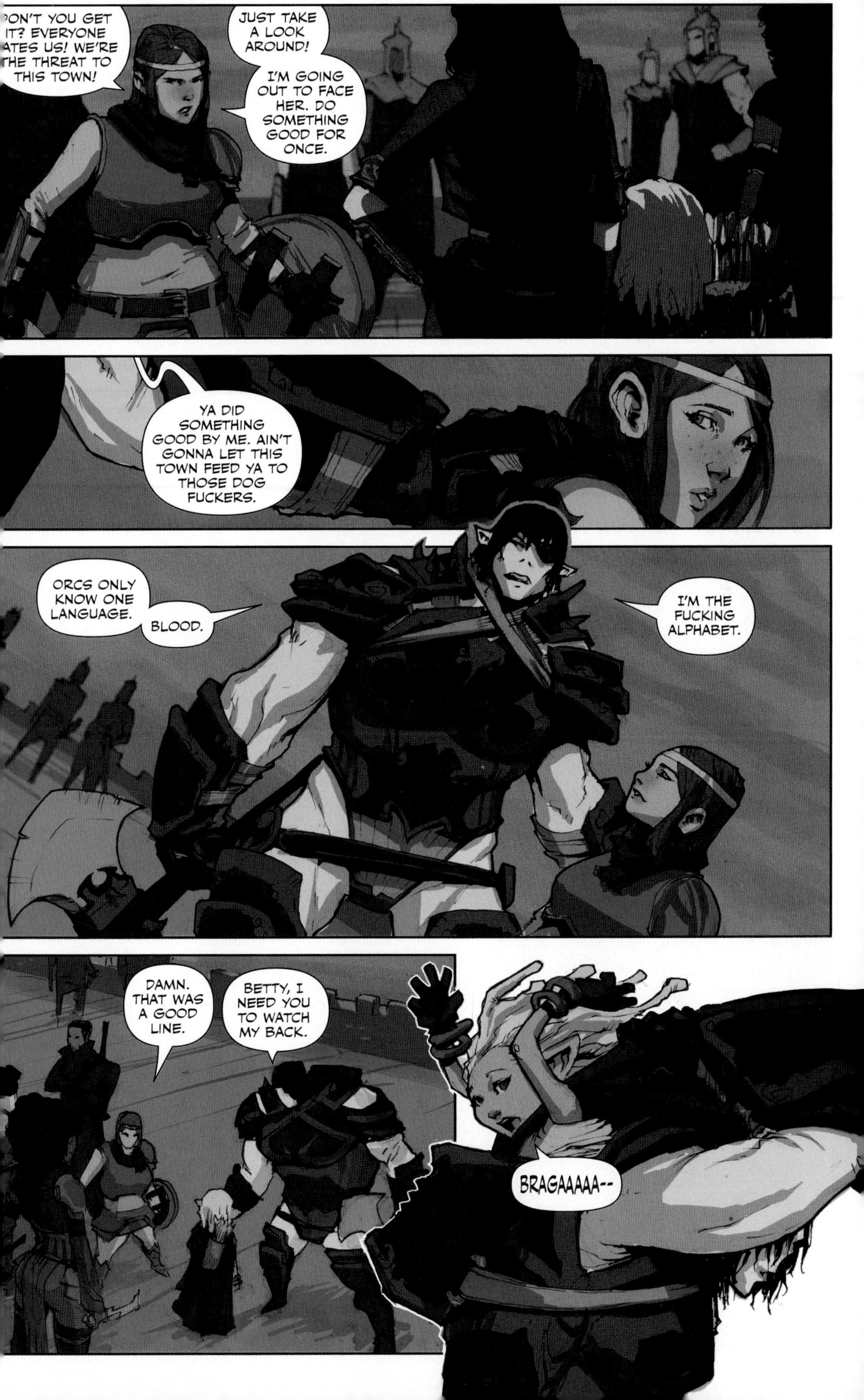
DON'T YOU GET IT? EVERYONE HATES US! WE'RE THE THREAT TO THIS TOWN!
JUST TAKE A LOOK AROUND!
I'M GOING OUT TO FACE HER. DO SOMETHING GOOD FOR ONCE.
YA DID SOMETHING GOOD BY ME. AIN'T GONNA LET THIS TOWN FEED YA TO THOSE DOG FUCKERS.
ORCS ONLY KNOW ONE LANGUAGE.
BLOOD.
I'M THE FUCKING ALPHABET.
DAMN. THAT WAS A GOOD LINE.
BETTY, I NEED YOU TO WATCH MY BACK.
BRAGAAAAA--

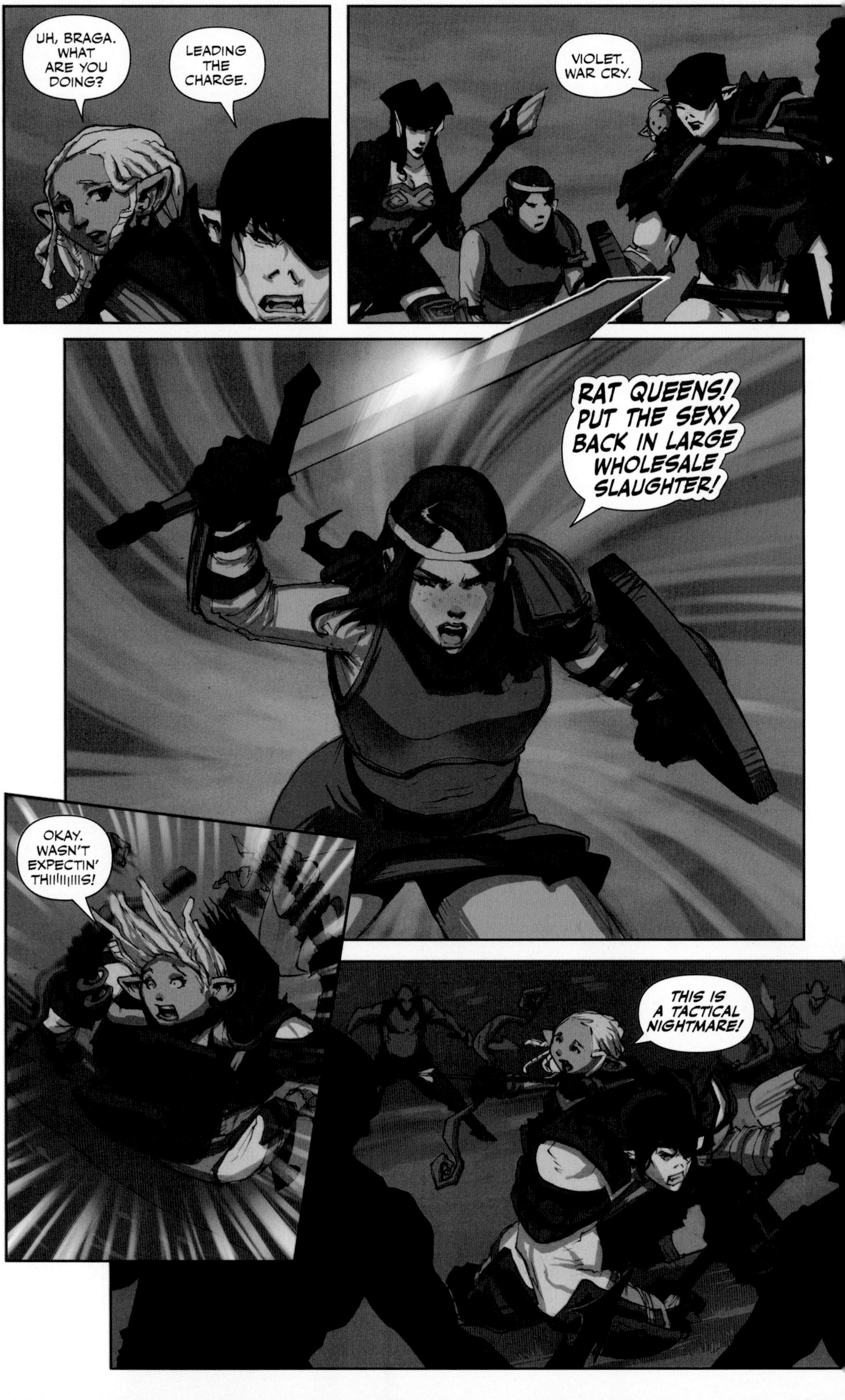
UH, BRAGA. WHAT ARE YOU DOING?
LEADING THE CHARGE.
VIOLET. WAR CRY.
RAT QUEENS! PUT THE SEXY BACK IN LARGE WHOLESALE SLAUGHTER!
OKAY. WASN'T EXPECTIN' THIIIIIIIS!
THIS IS A TACTICAL NIGHTMARE!

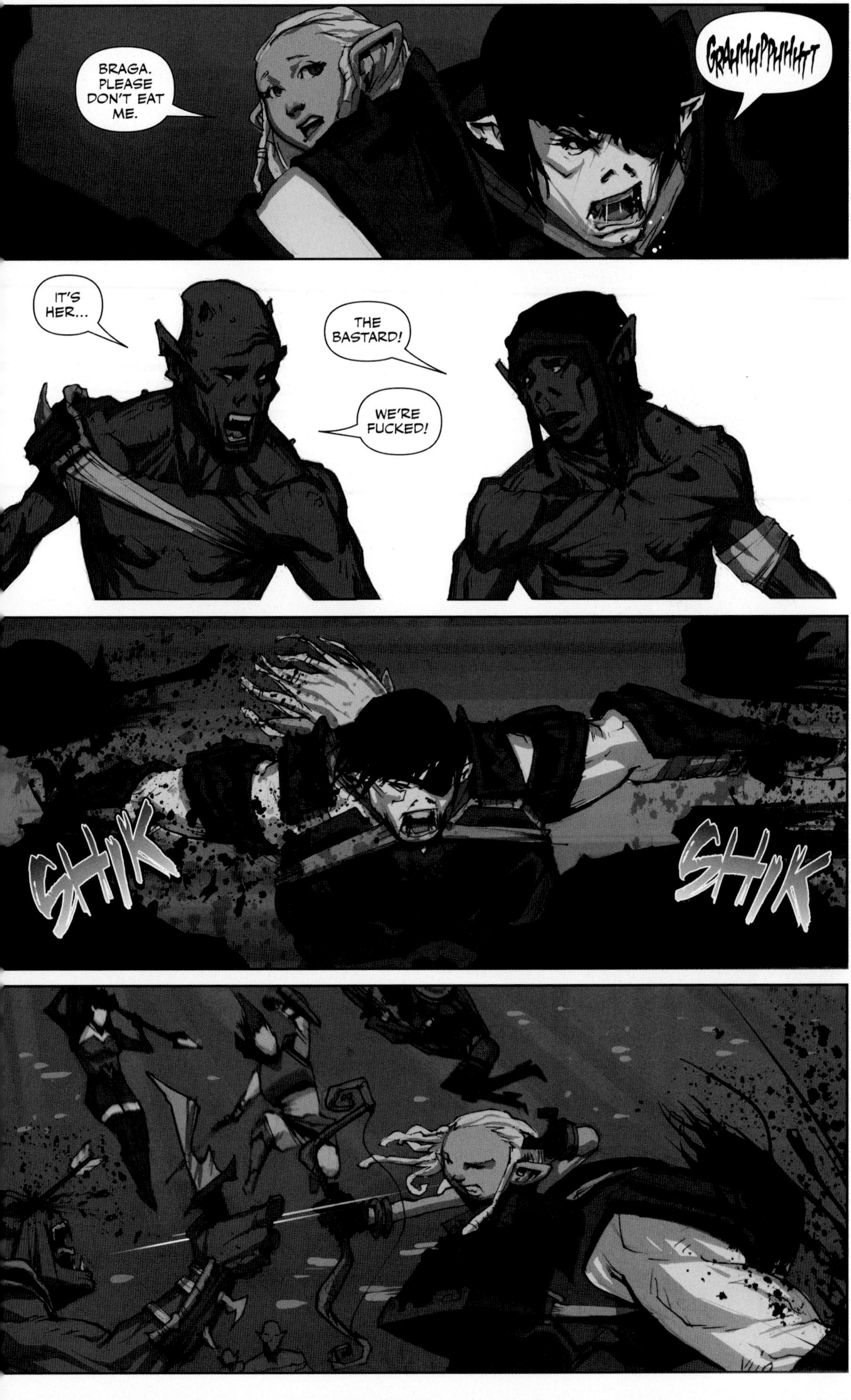
BRAGA. PLEASE DON'T EAT ME.
GRAHHHPPHHHTT
IT'S HER...
THE BASTARD!
WE'RE FUCKED!
SHIK
SHIK

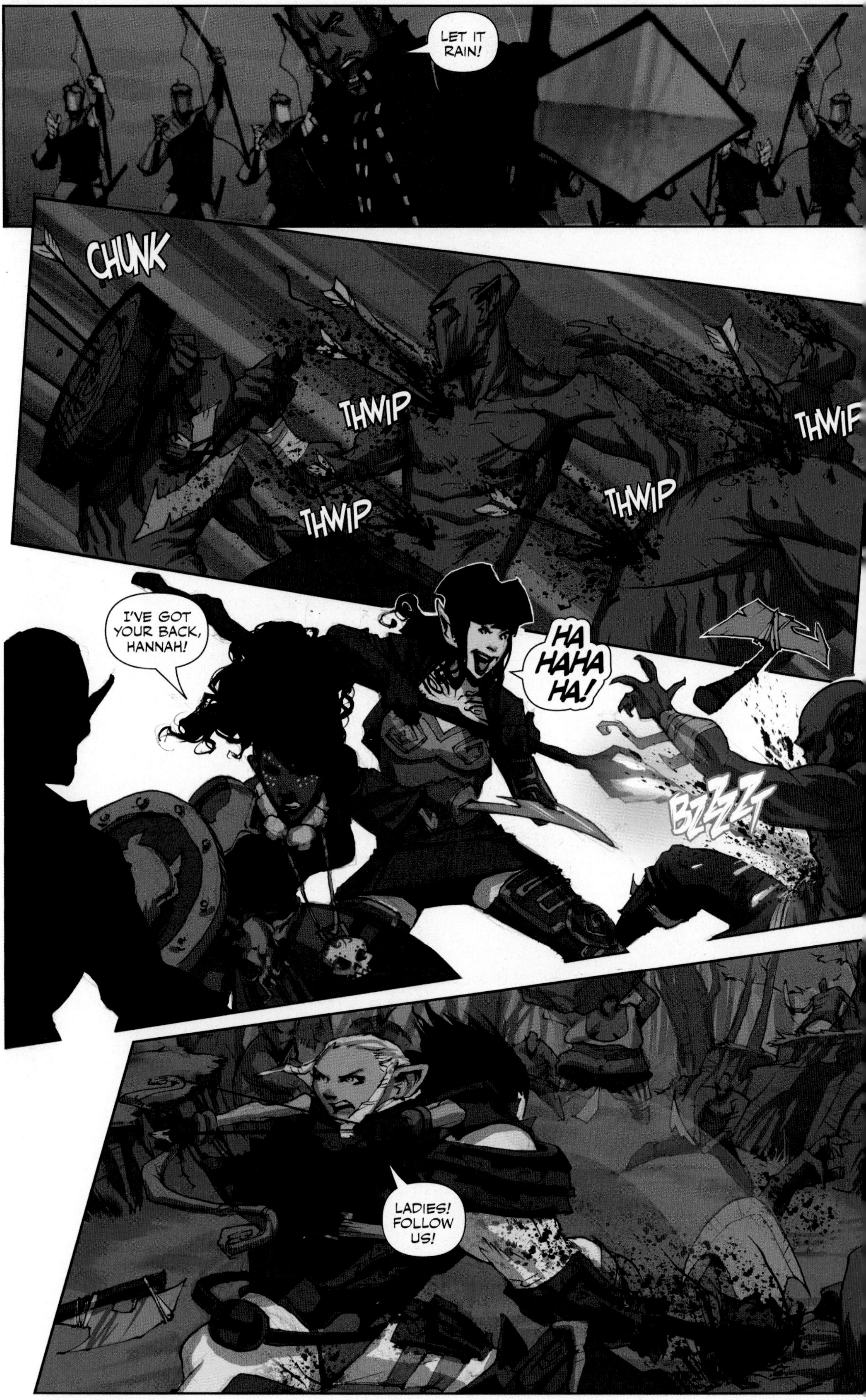
LET IT RAIN!
CHUNK
THWIP
THWIP
THWIP
THWIP
I'VE GOT YOUR BACK, HANNAH!
HA HAHAHA HA!
BZZZZT
LADIES! FOLLOW US!

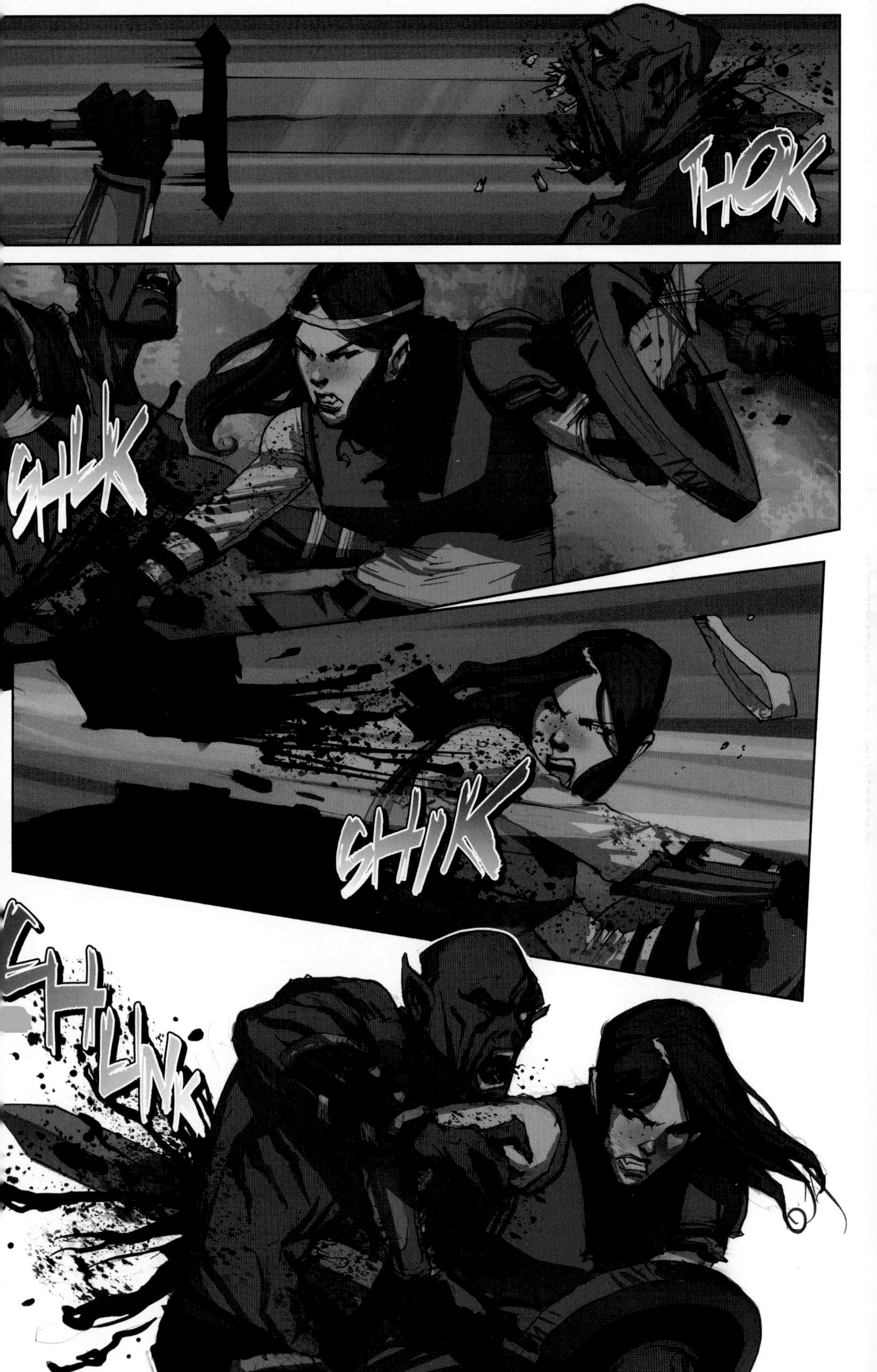
THOK
SHK
SHIK
SHLUNK

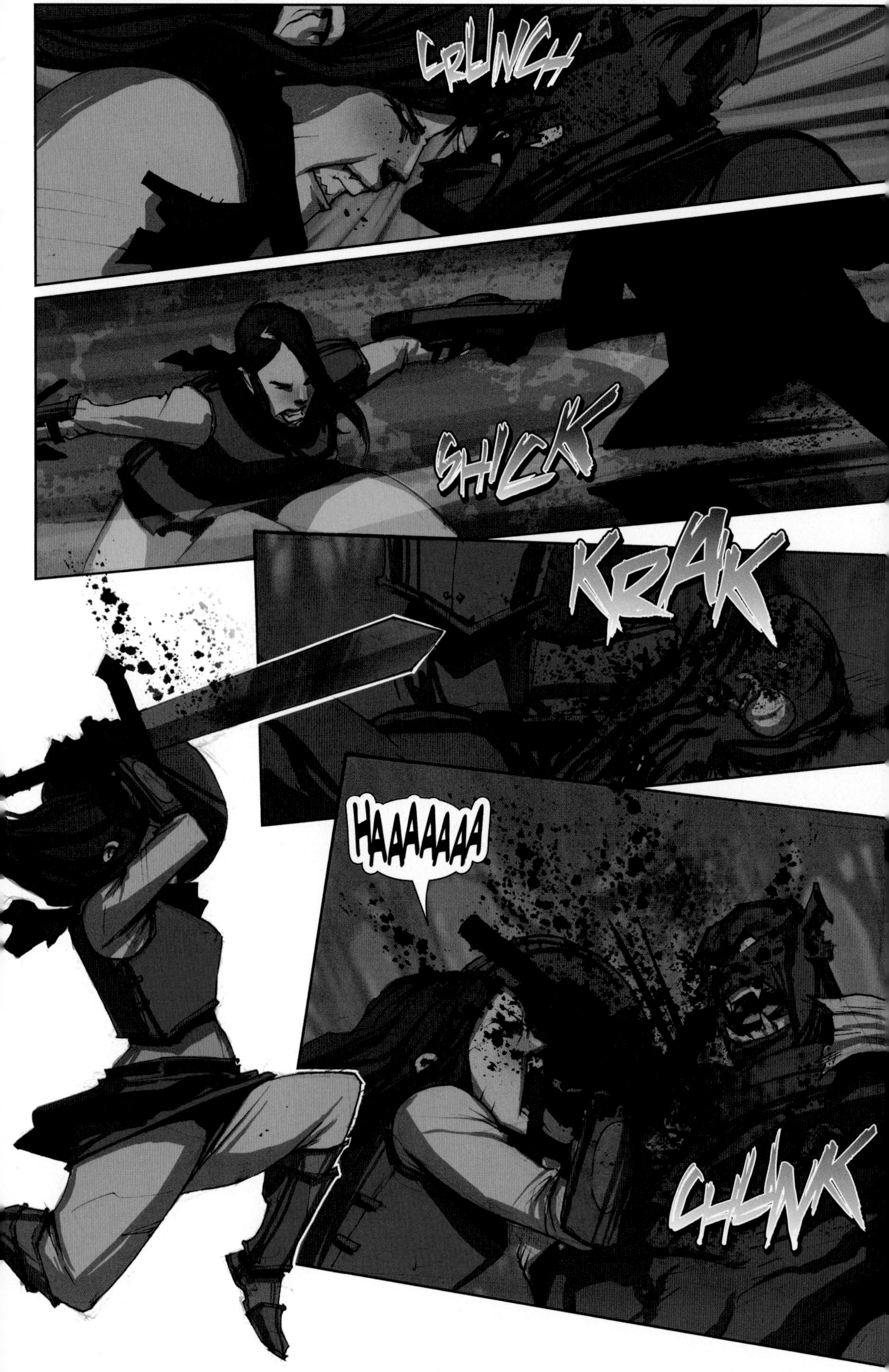
CRUNCH
SHICK
KRAK
HAAAAAAA
CHUNK

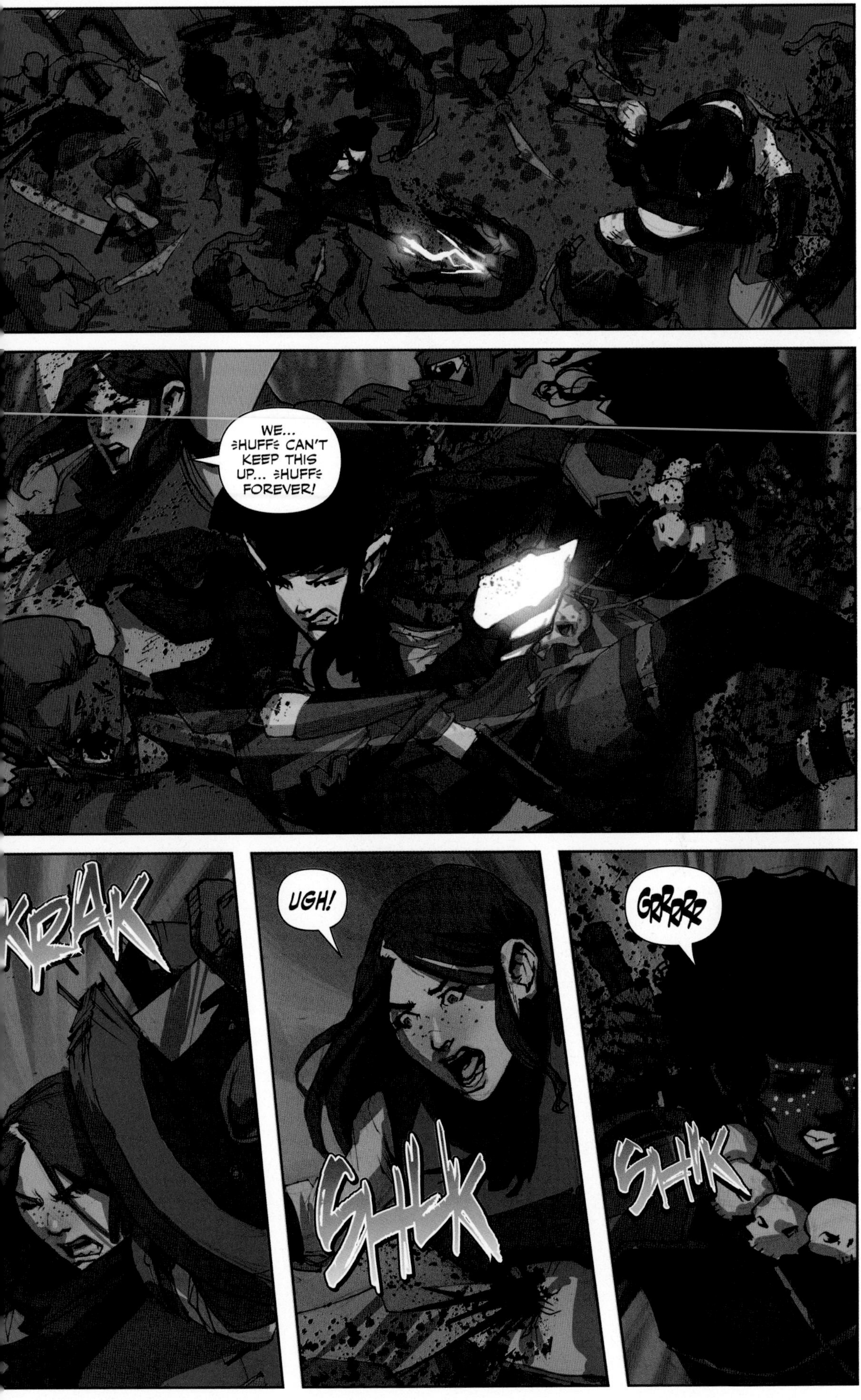
WE... ≶HUFF≶ CAN'T KEEP THIS UP... ≶HUFF≶ FOREVER!
KRAK
UGH!
SHLK
GRRRRR
SHIK

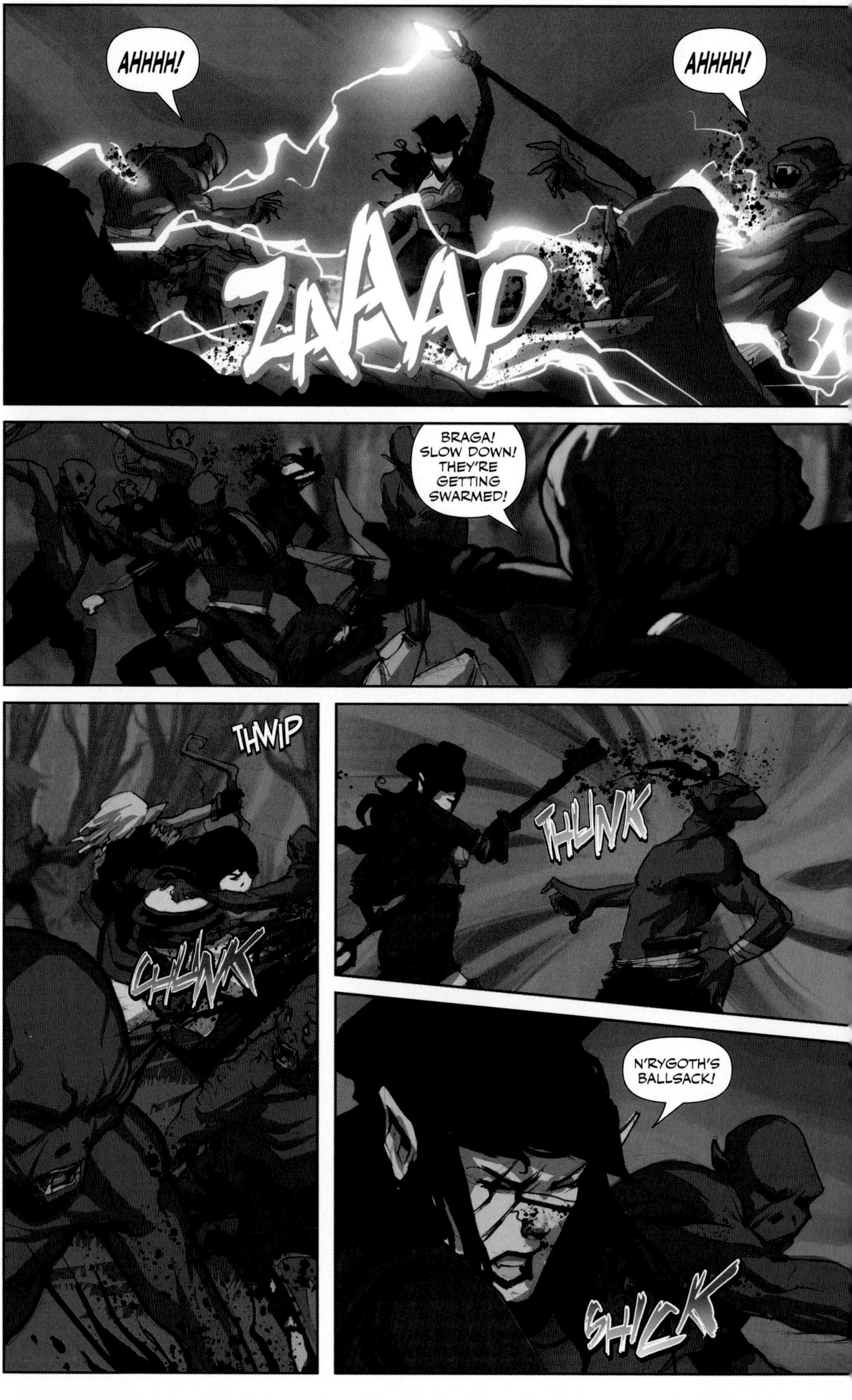
AHHHH!
AHHHH!
ZAAAAP
BRAGA! SLOW DOWN! THEY'RE GETTING SWARMED!
THWIP
CHUNK
THUNK
N'RYGOTH'S BALLSACK!
SHICK

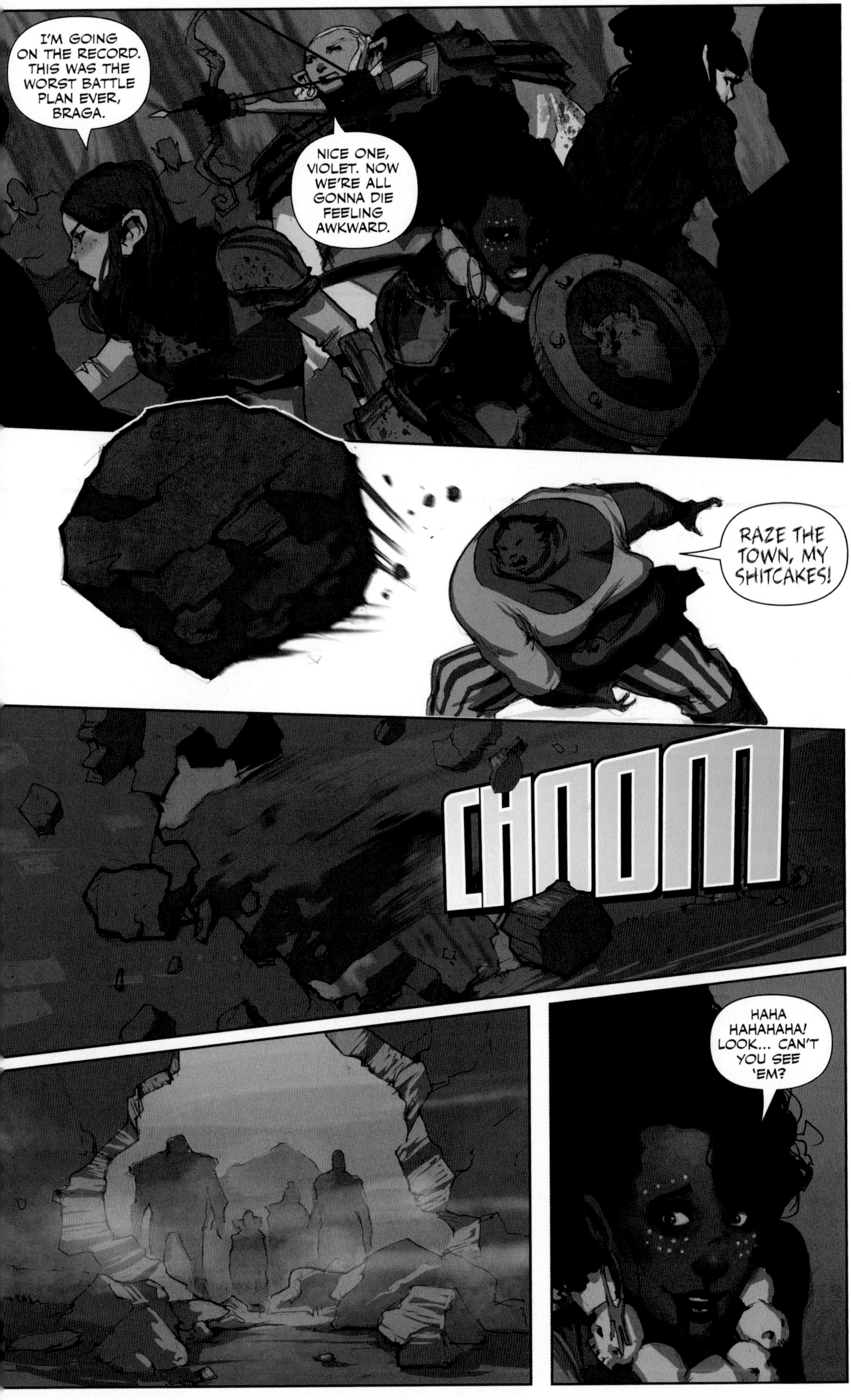
I'M GOING ON THE RECORD. THIS WAS THE WORST BATTLE PLAN EVER, BRAGA.
NICE ONE, VIOLET. NOW WE'RE ALL GONNA DIE FEELING AWKWARD.
RAZE THE TOWN, MY SHITCAKES!
CHOOM
HAHA HAHAHAHA! LOOK... CAN'T YOU SEE 'EM?

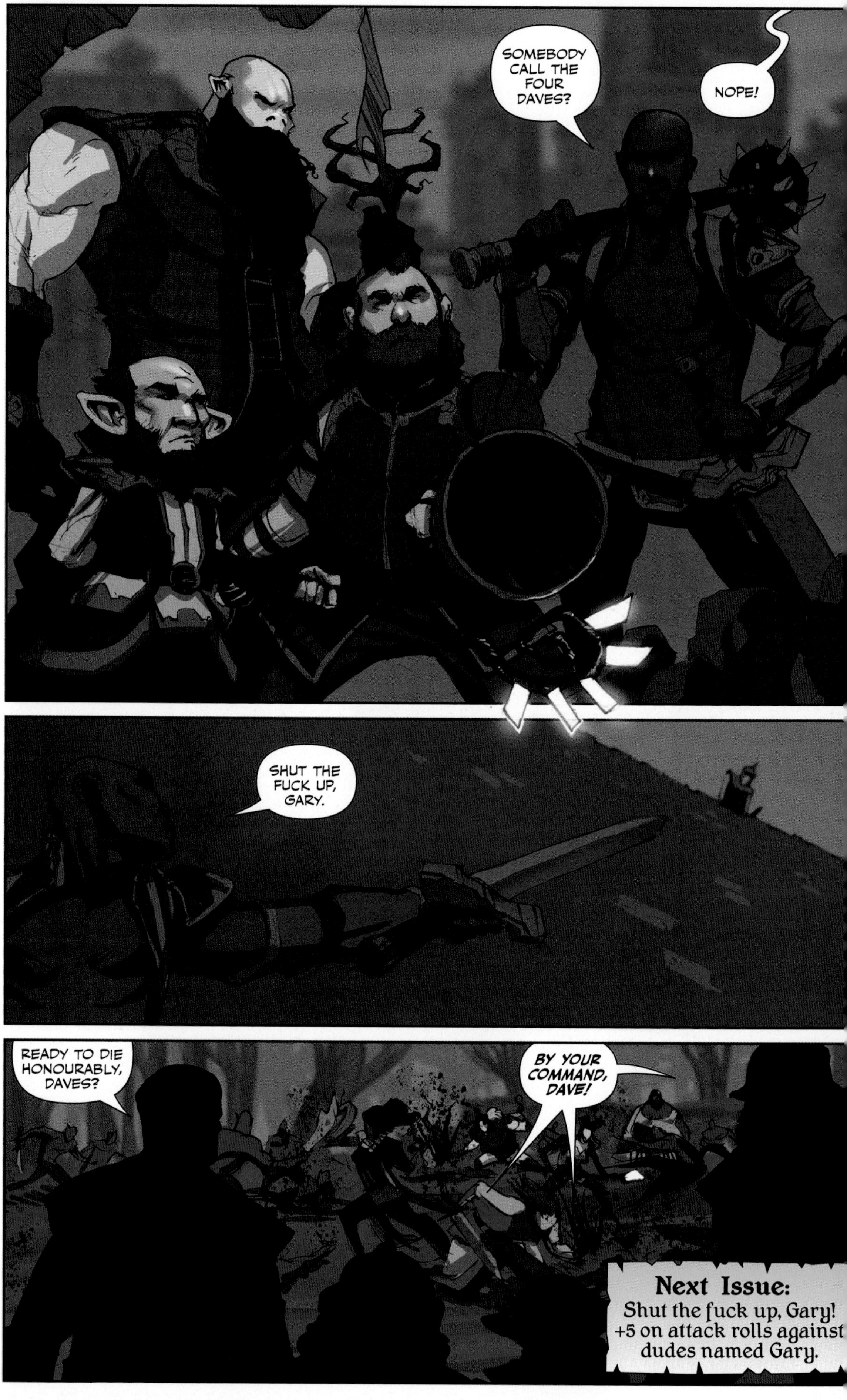
SOMEBODY CALL THE FOUR DAVES?
NOPE!
SHUT THE FUCK UP, GARY.
READY TO DIE HONOURABLY, DAVES?
BY YOUR COMMAND, DAVE!
Next Issue:
Shut the fuck up, Gary! +5 on attack rolls against dudes named Gary.

CHAPTER FIVE

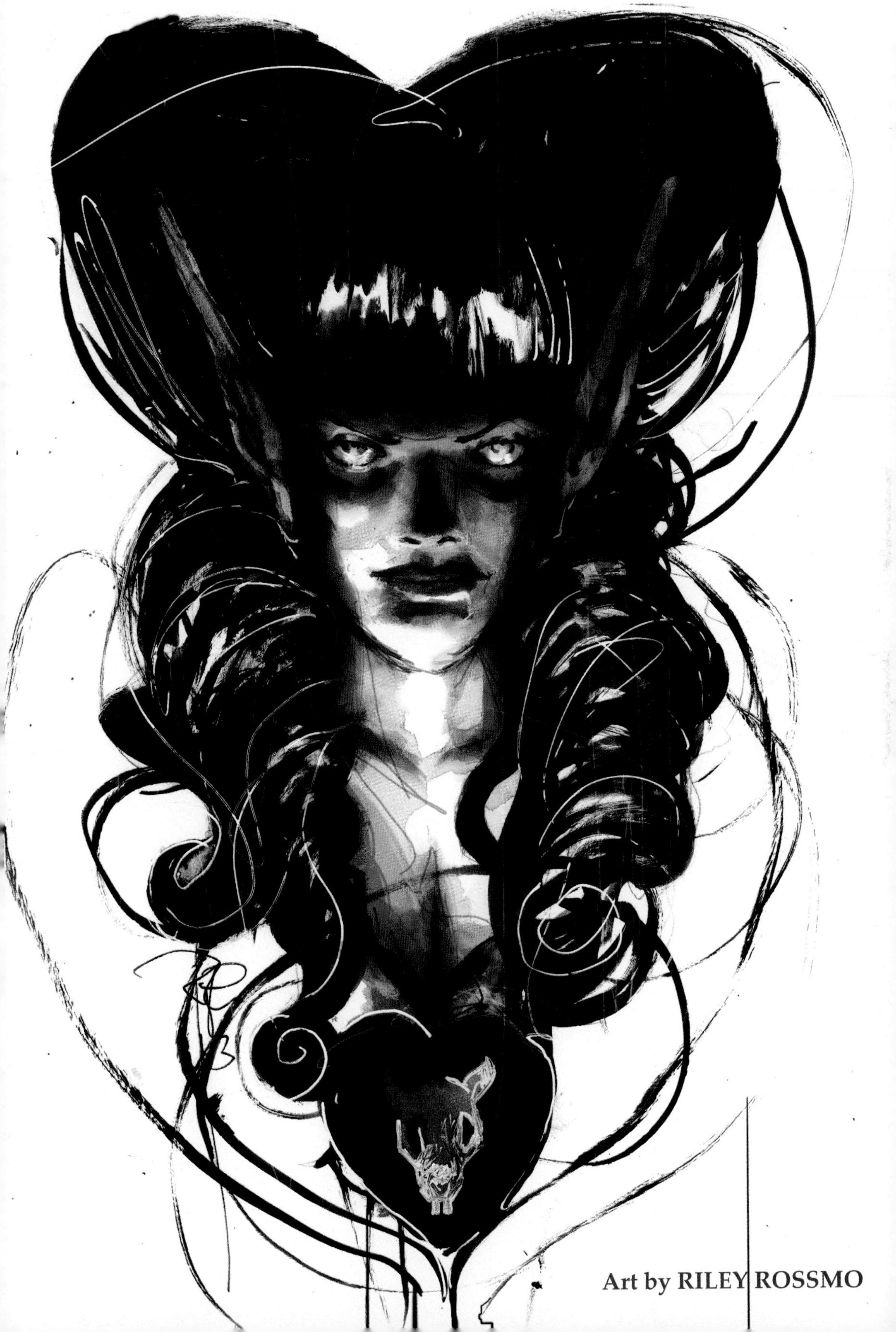

Art by RILEY ROSSMO

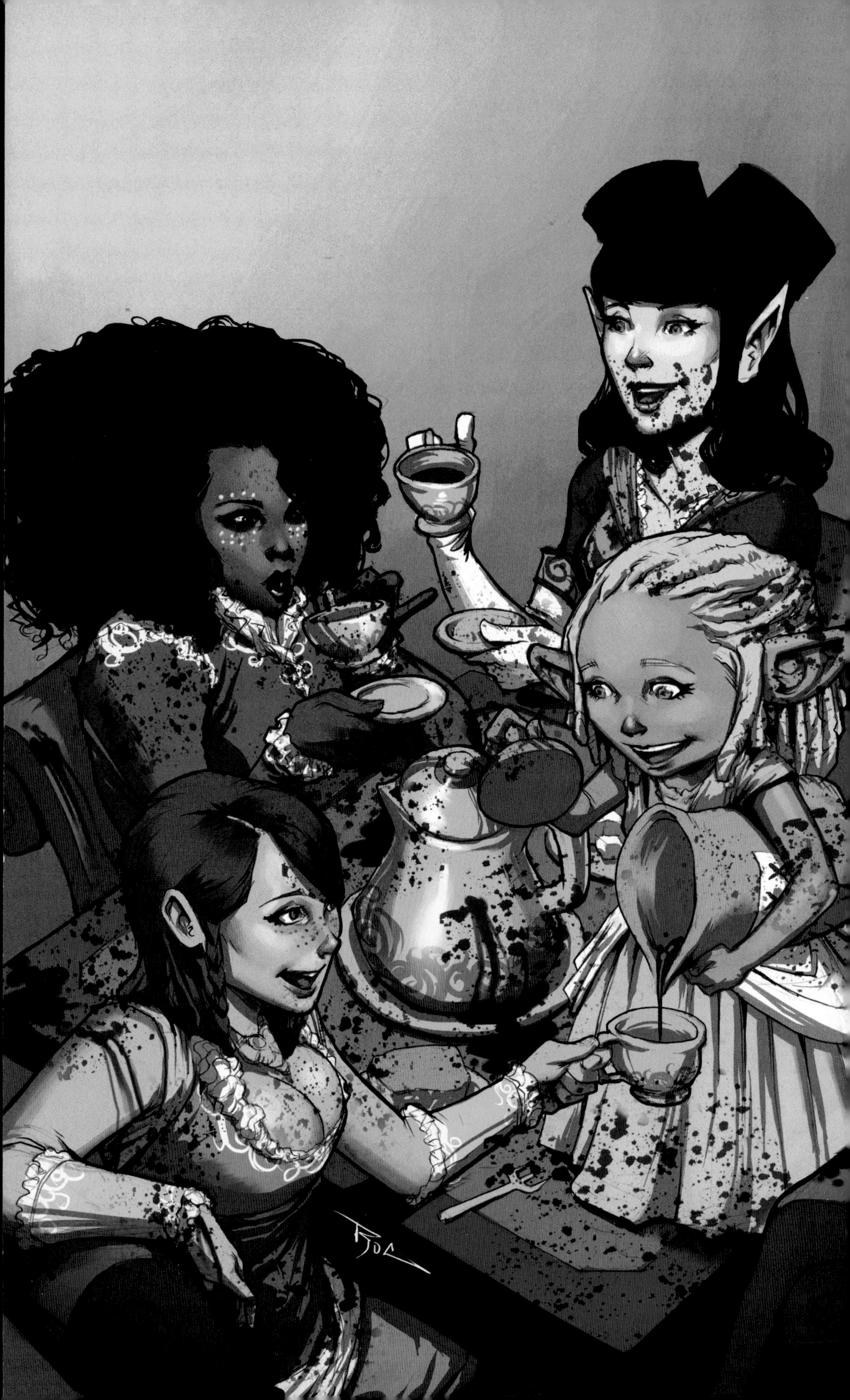

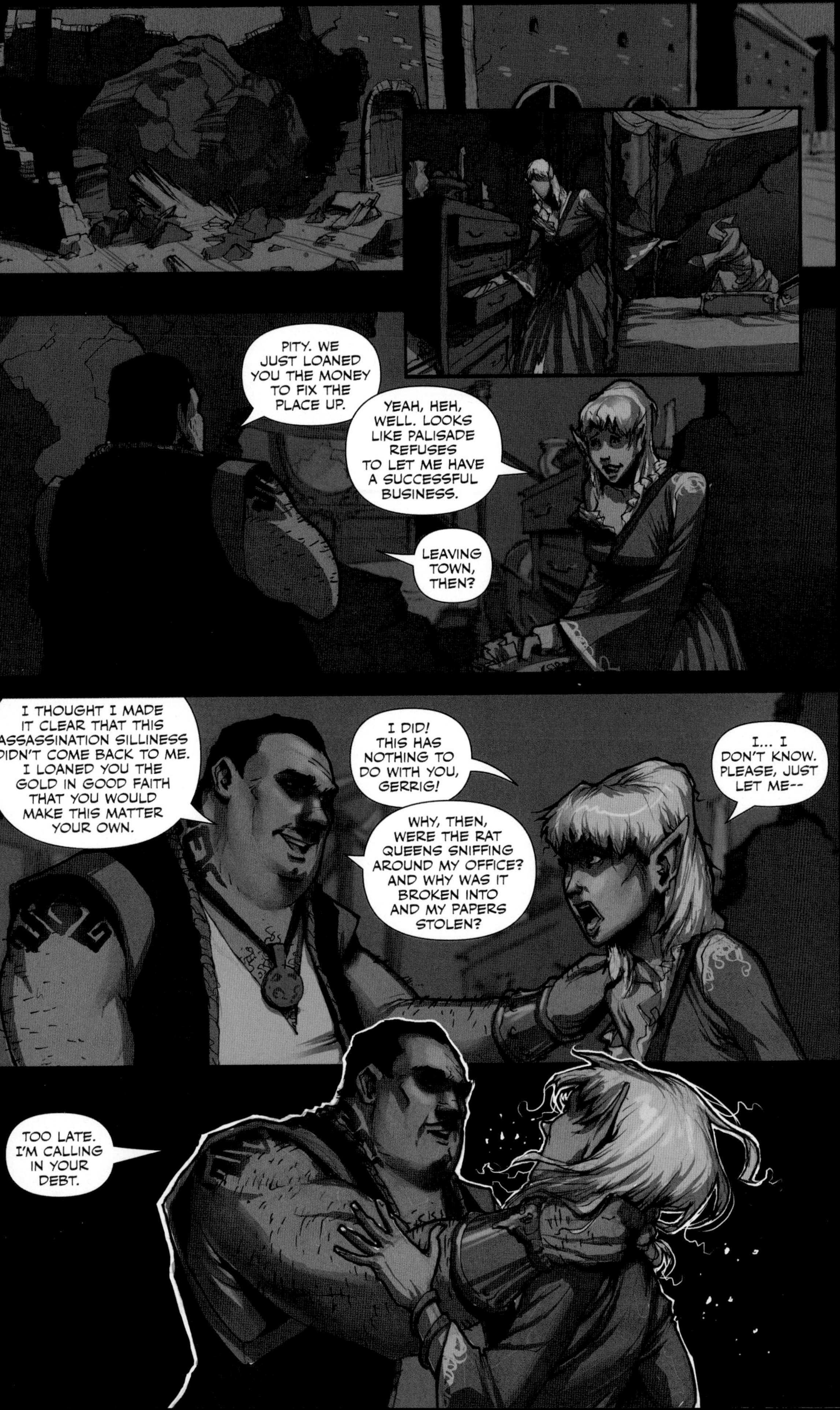
PITY. WE JUST LOANED YOU THE MONEY TO FIX THE PLACE UP.
YEAH, HEH, WELL. LOOKS LIKE PALISADE REFUSES TO LET ME HAVE A SUCCESSFUL BUSINESS.
LEAVING TOWN, THEN?
I THOUGHT I MADE IT CLEAR THAT THIS ASSASSINATION SILLINESS DIDN'T COME BACK TO ME. I LOANED YOU THE GOLD IN GOOD FAITH THAT YOU WOULD MAKE THIS MATTER YOUR OWN.
I DID! THIS HAS NOTHING TO DO WITH YOU, GERRIG!
WHY, THEN, WERE THE RAT QUEENS SNIFFING AROUND MY OFFICE? AND WHY WAS IT BROKEN INTO AND MY PAPERS STOLEN?
I... I DON'T KNOW. PLEASE, JUST LET ME--
TOO LATE. I'M CALLING IN YOUR DEBT.

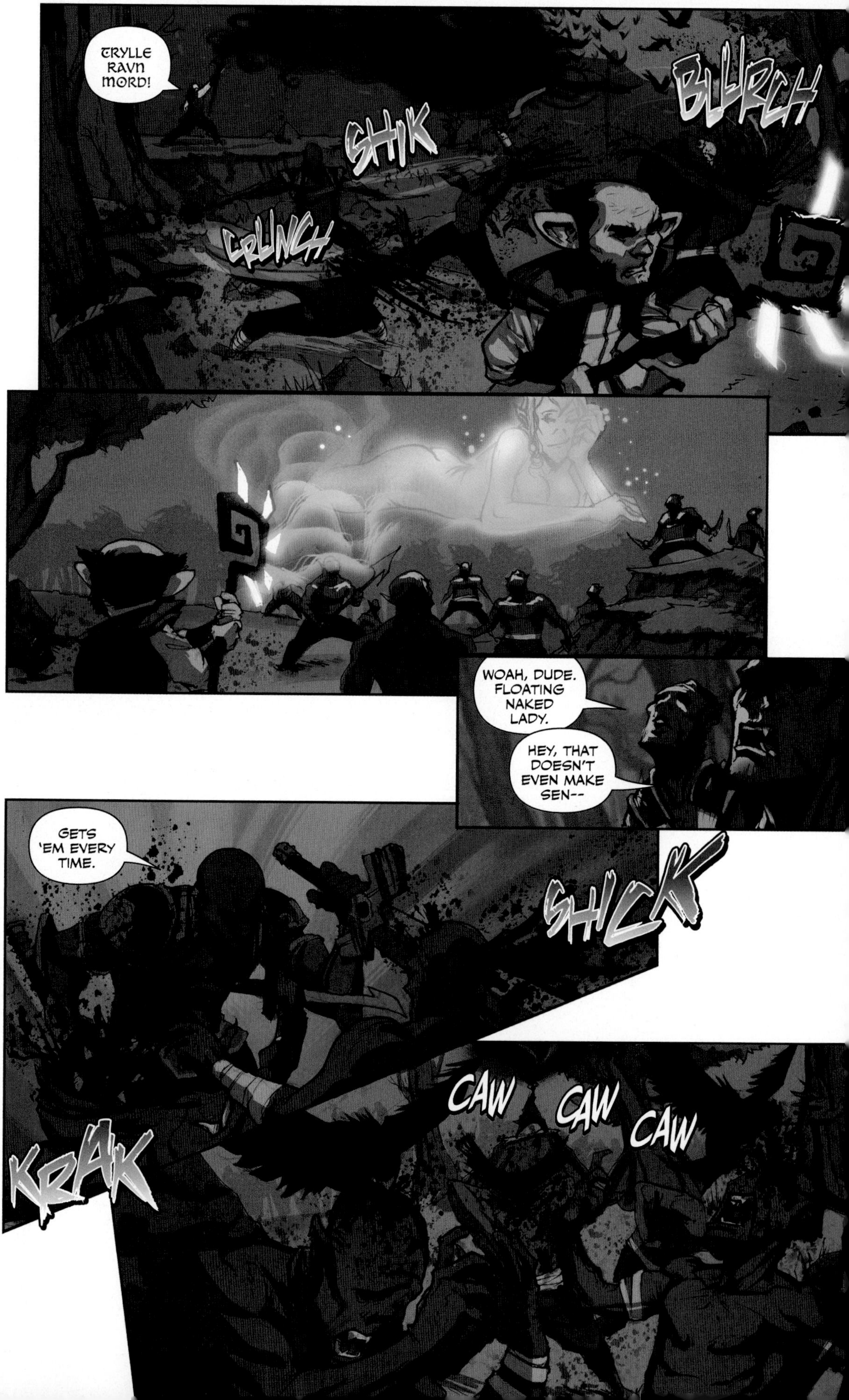
TRYLLE RAVN MORD!
SHIK
BLURCH
CRUNCH
WOAH, DUDE. FLOATING NAKED LADY.
HEY, THAT DOESN'T EVEN MAKE SEN--
GETS 'EM EVERY TIME.
SHICK
CAW
CAW
CAW
KRAK

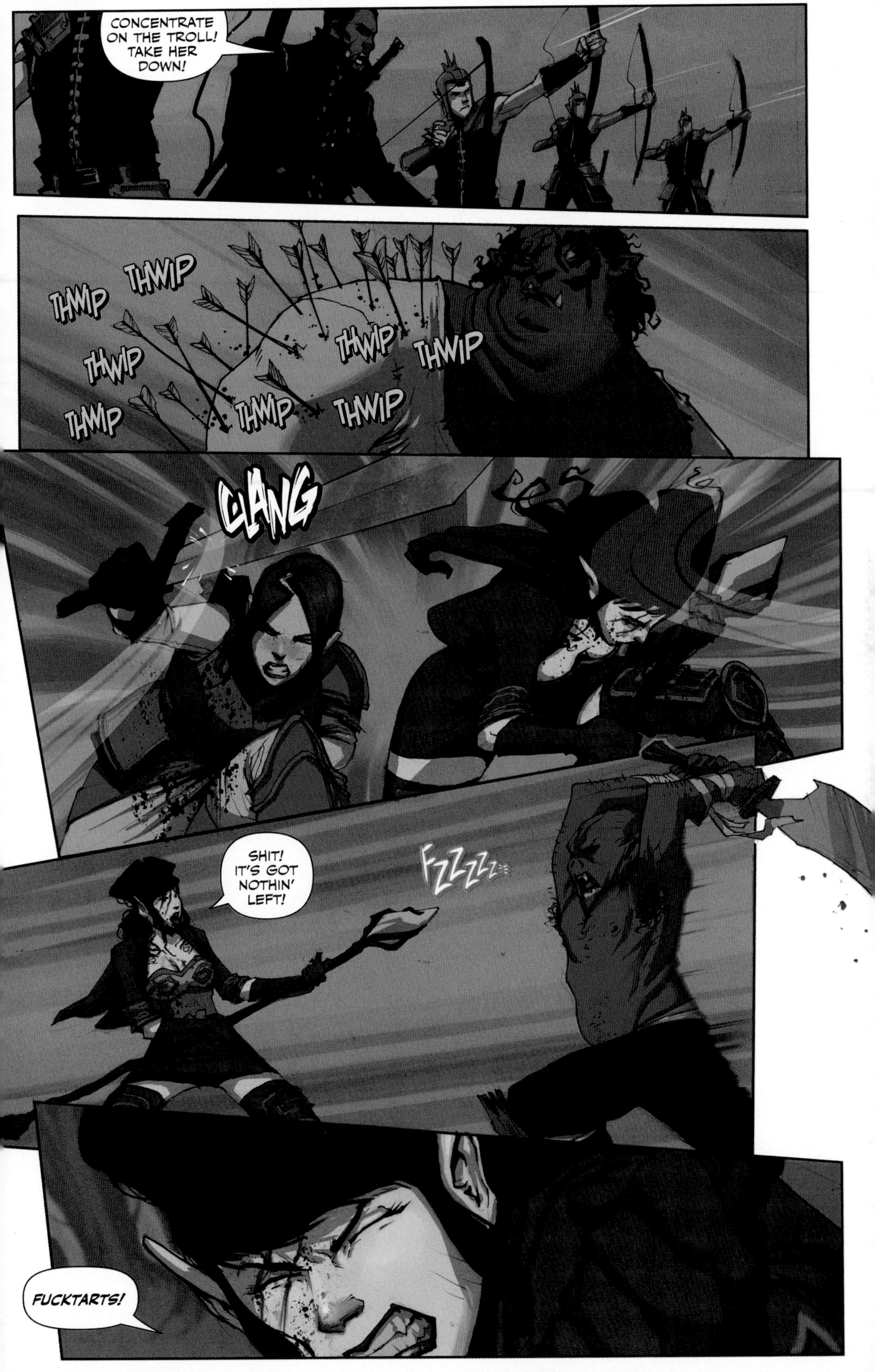
CONCENTRATE ON THE TROLL! TAKE HER DOWN!
THWIP
THWIP
THWIP
THWIP
THWIP
THWIP
THWIP
THWIP
CLANG
SHIT! IT'S GOT NOTHIN' LEFT!
FZZZZZ
FUCKTARTS!

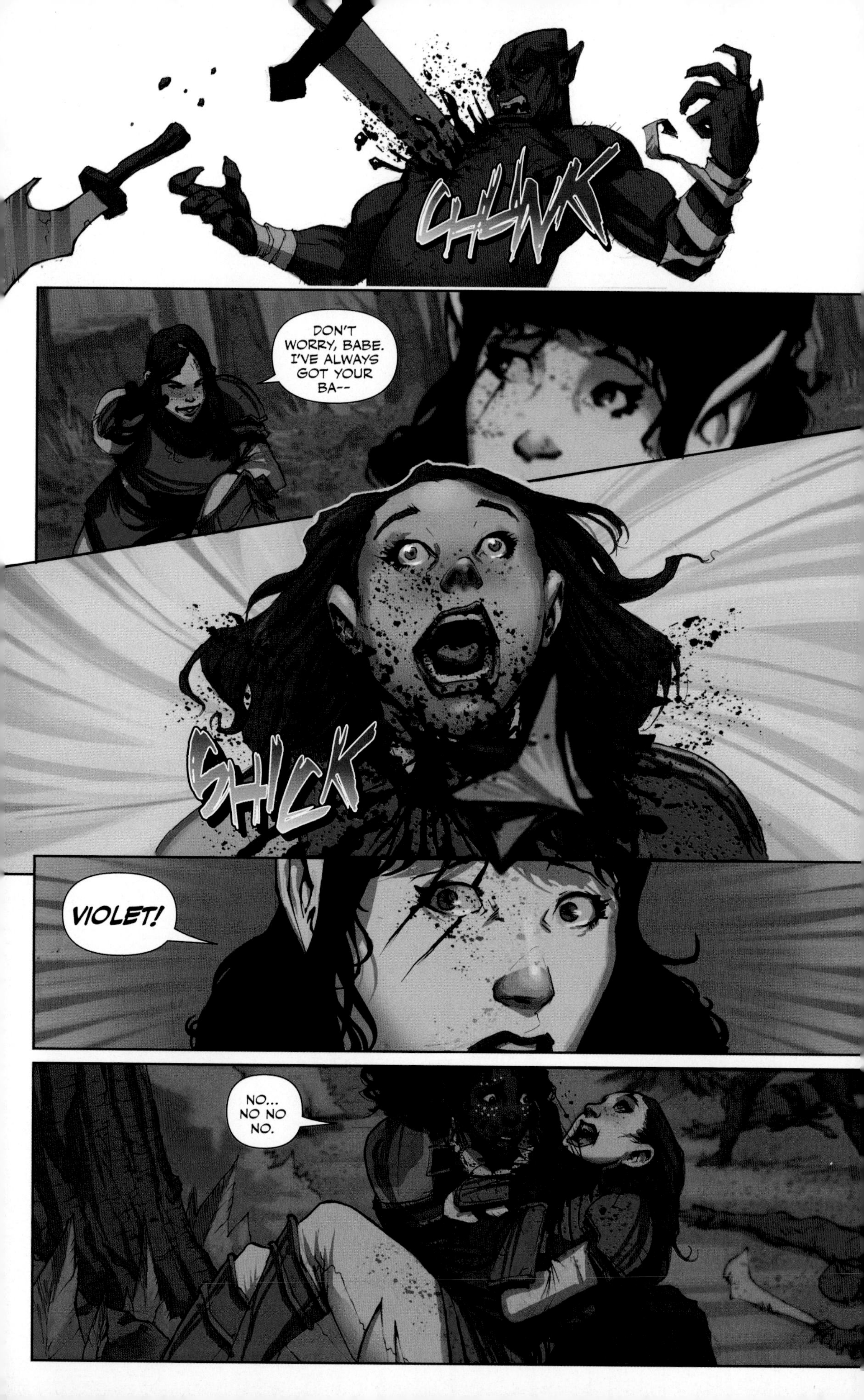
CHUNK
DON'T WORRY, BABE. I'VE ALWAYS GOT YOUR BA--
SHICK
VIOLET!
NO... NO NO NO.

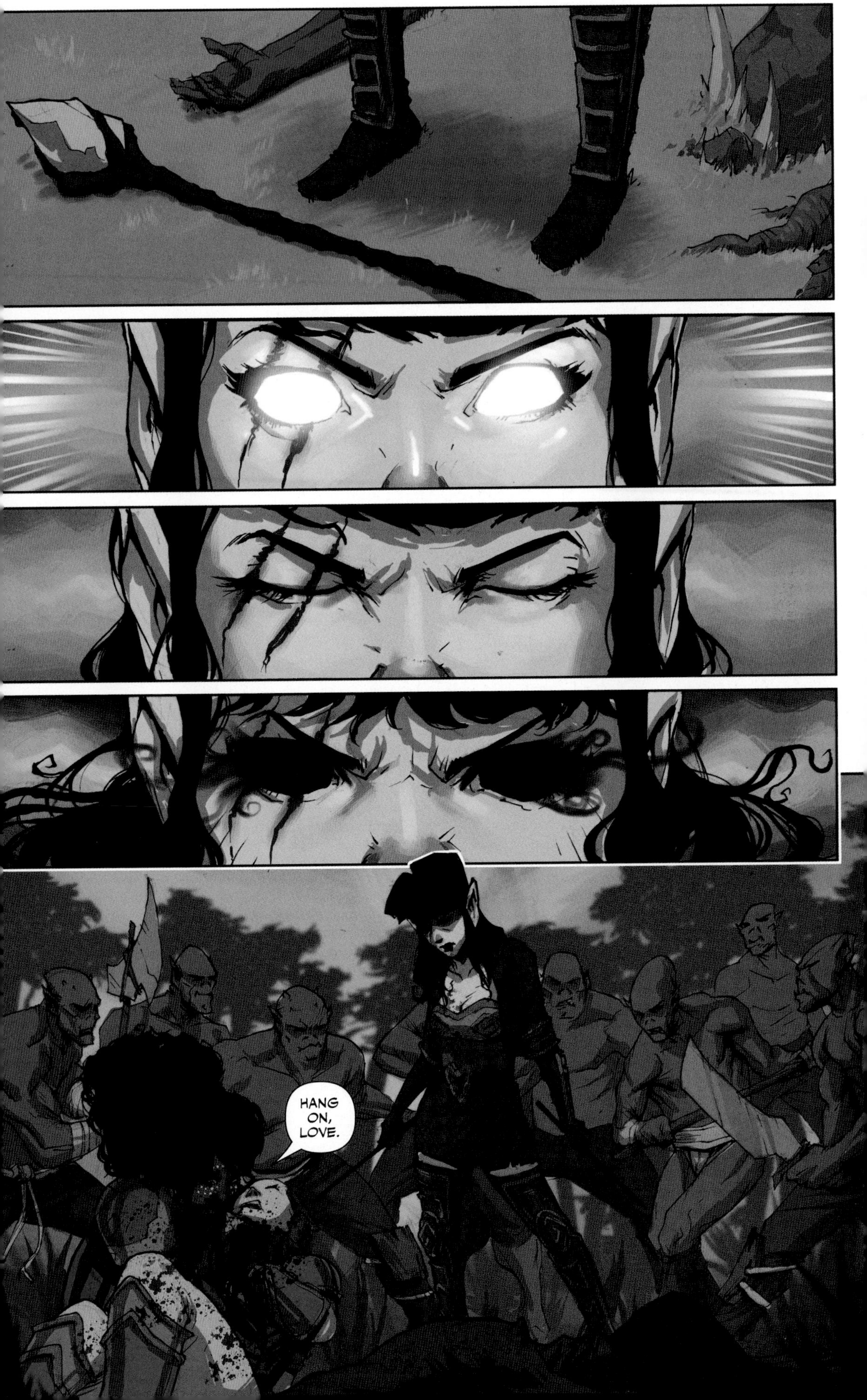
HANG ON, LOVE.

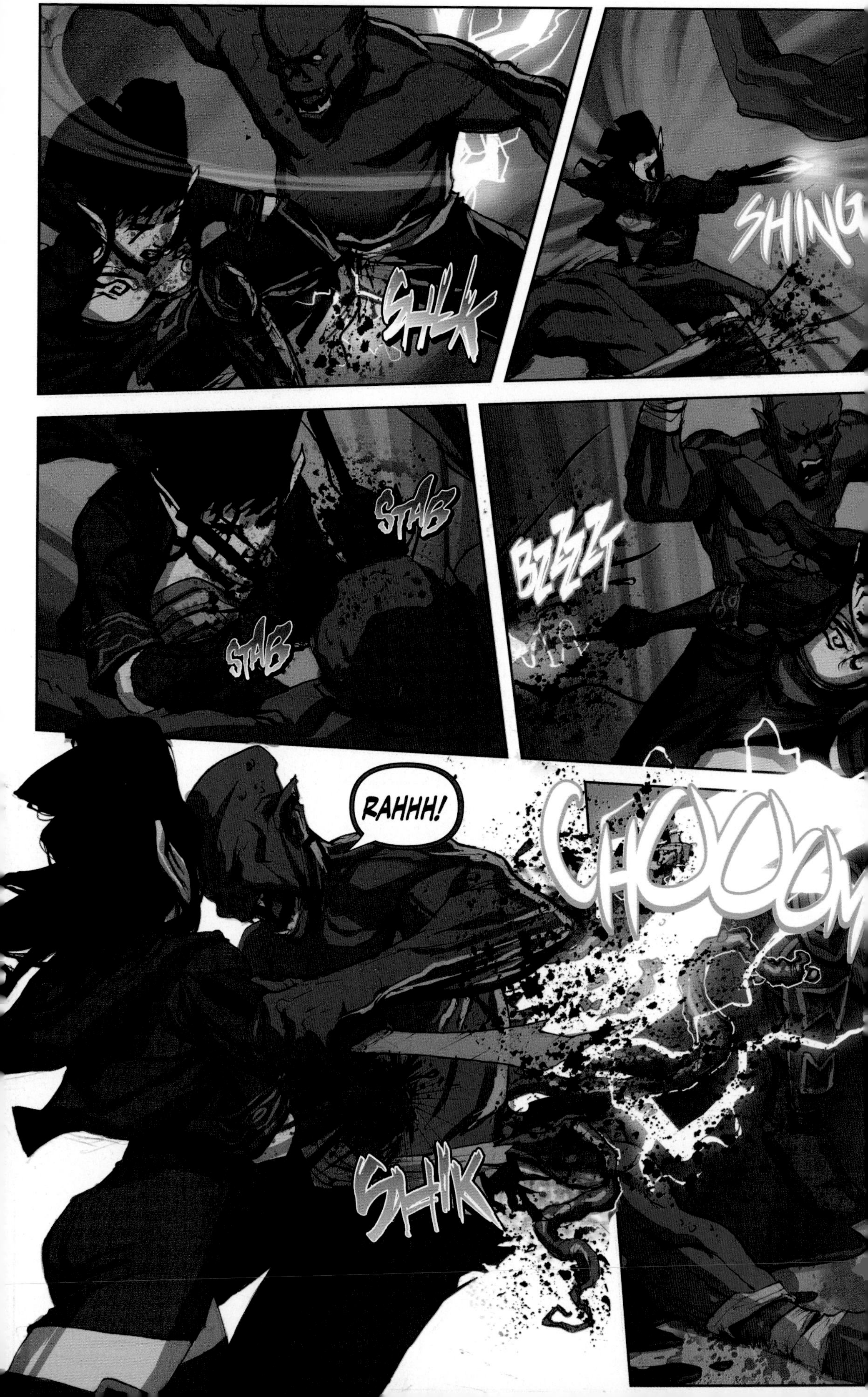
SHLK
SHING
STAB
STAB
BZZZZT
RAHHH!
CHOOOM
SHIK

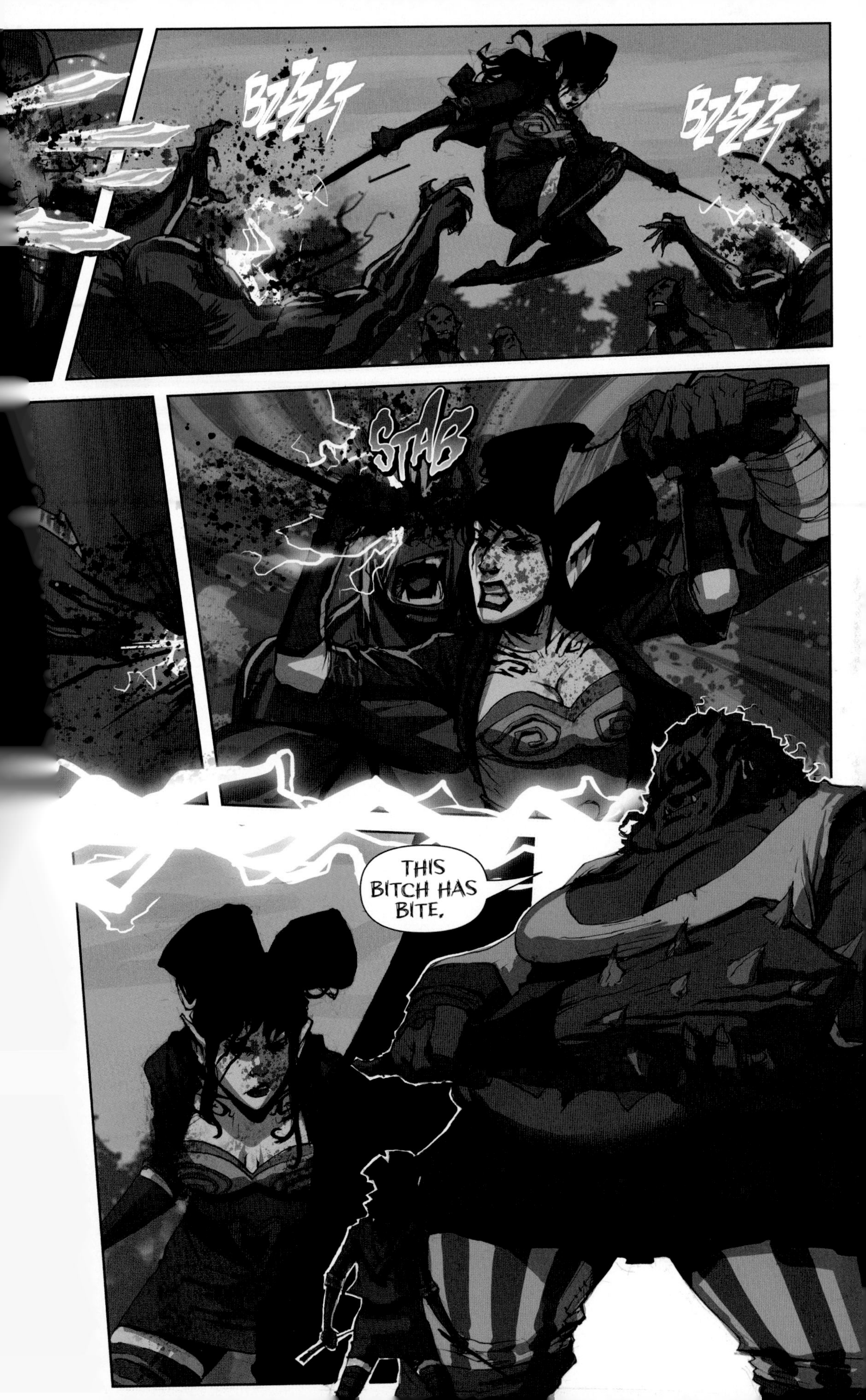
BZZZZT
BZZZZT
STAB
THIS BITCH HAS BITE.

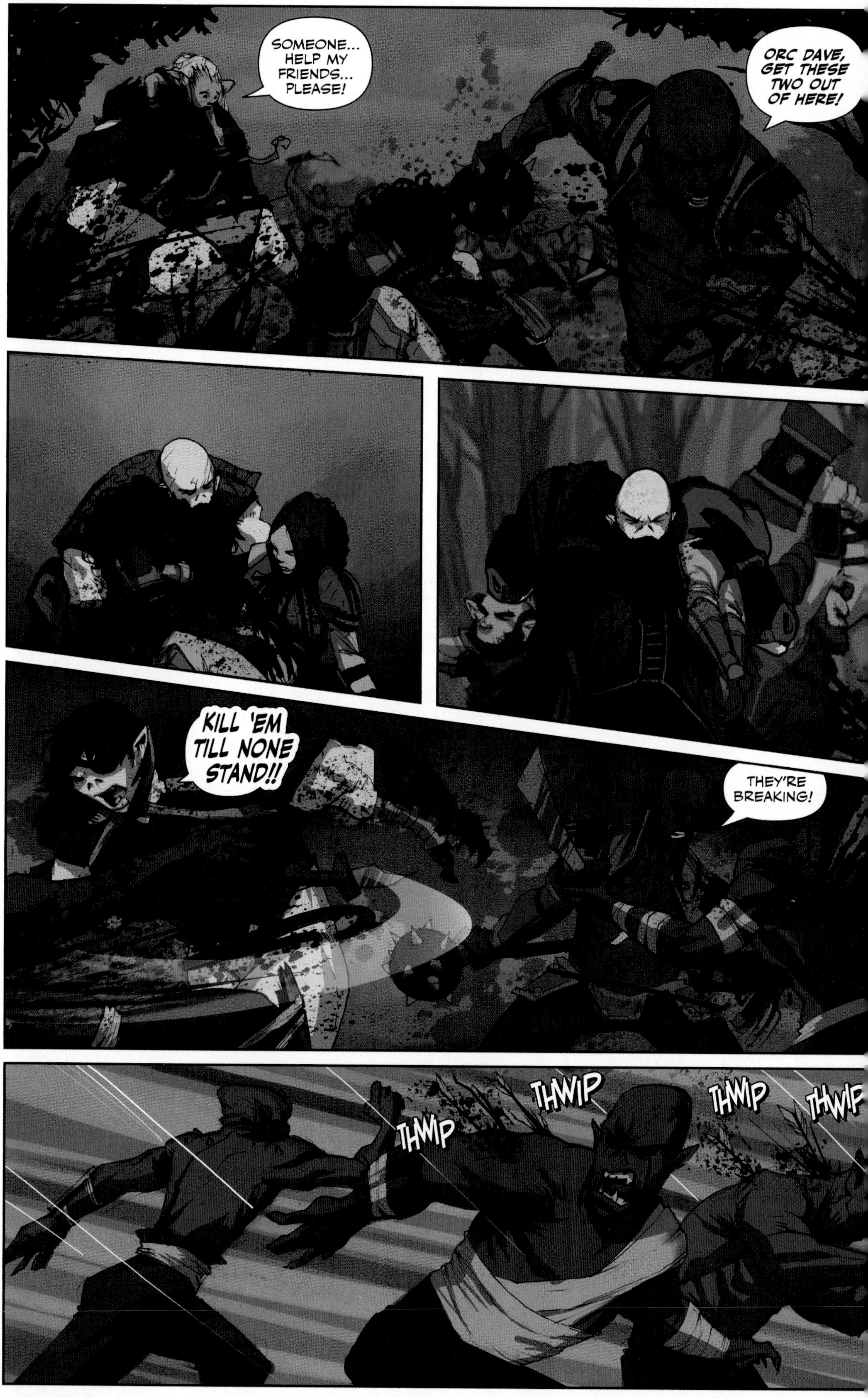
SOMEONE... HELP MY FRIENDS... PLEASE!
ORC DAVE, GET THESE TWO OUT OF HERE!
KILL 'EM TILL NONE STAND!!
THEY'RE BREAKING!
THWIP
THWIP
THWIP
THWIP

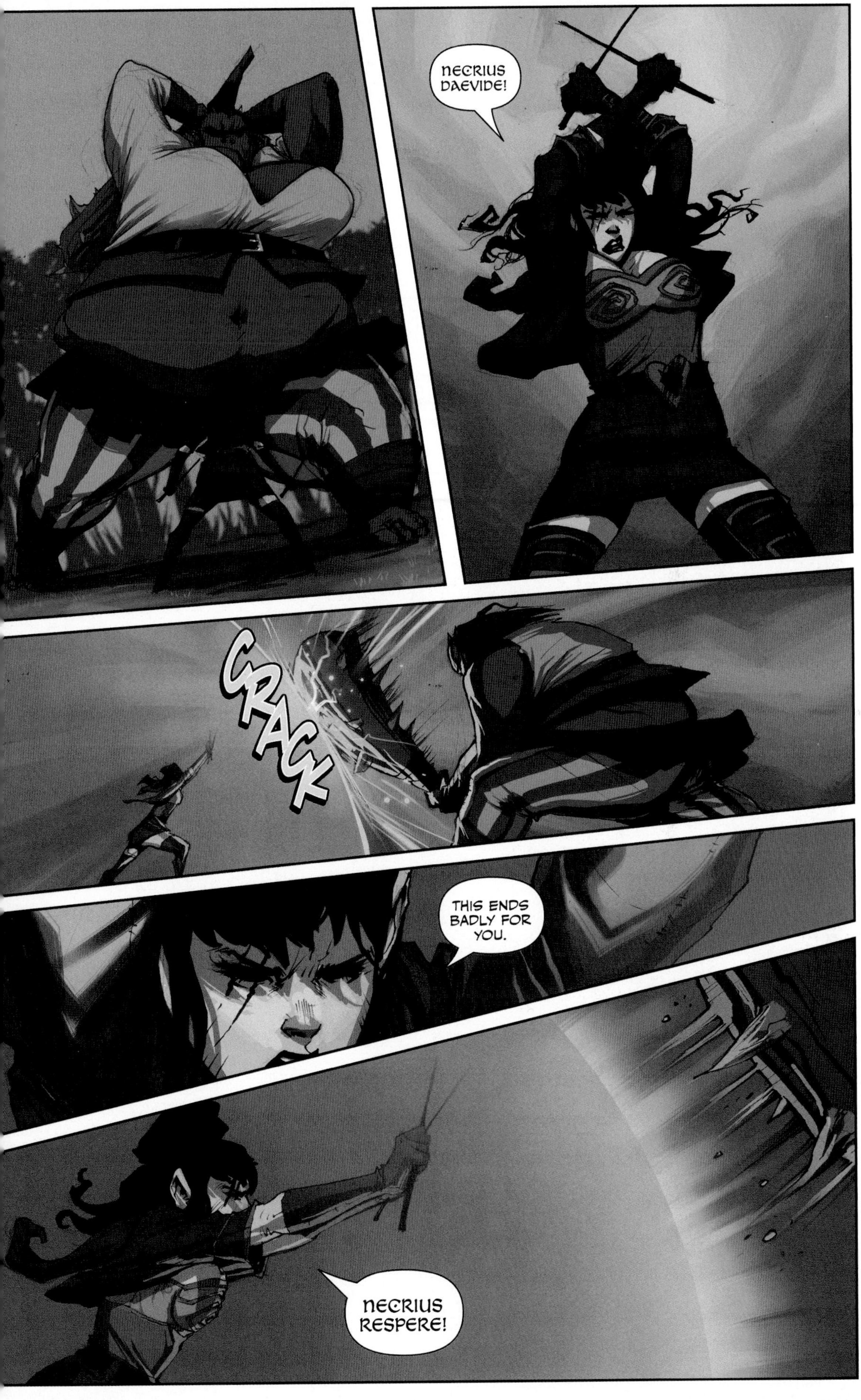
NECRIUS DAEVIDE!
CRACK
THIS ENDS BADLY FOR YOU.
NECRIUS RESPERE!

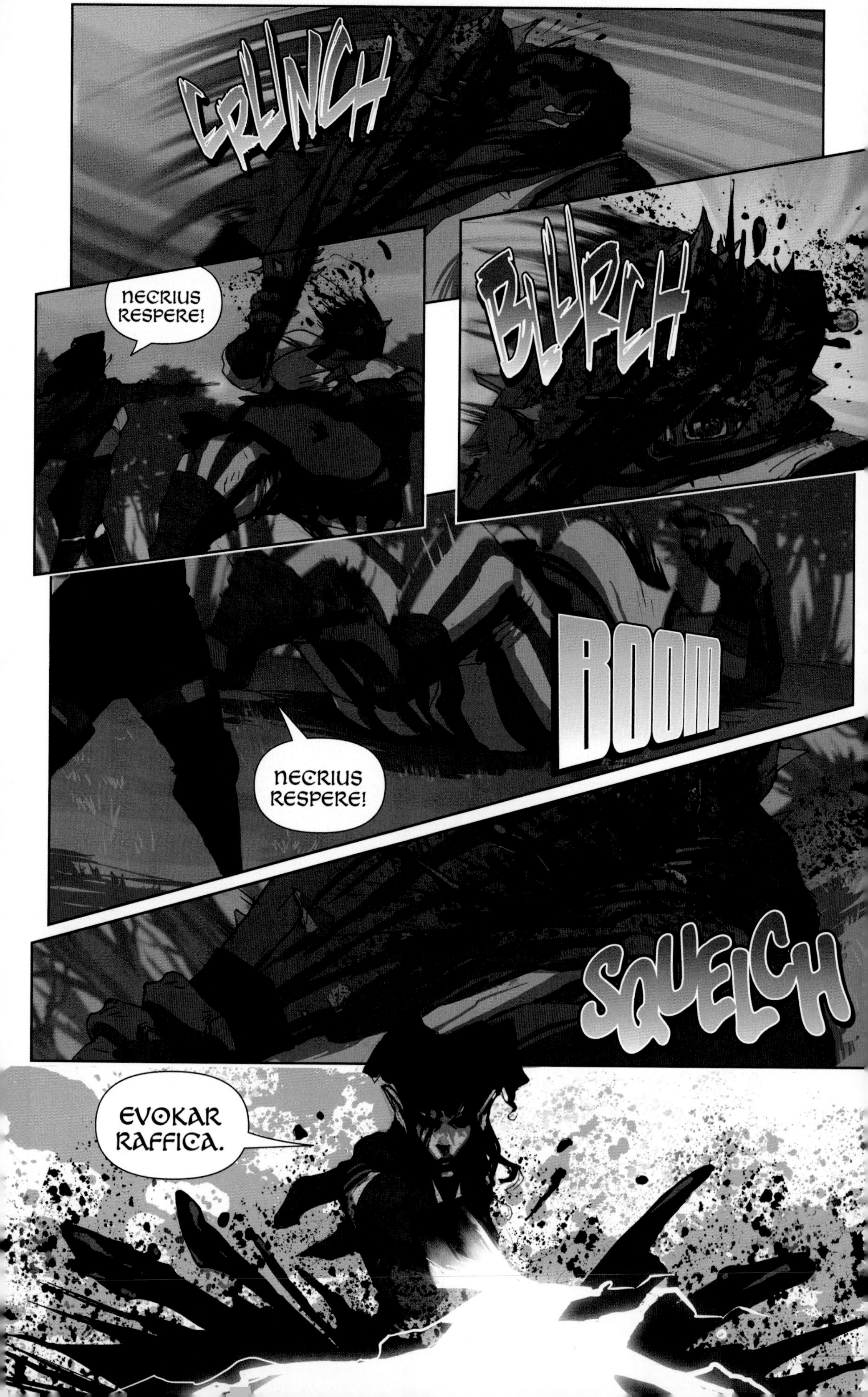
CRUNCH
NECRIUS RESPERE!
BLURCH
BOOM
NECRIUS RESPERE!
SQUELCH
EVOKAR RAFFICA.

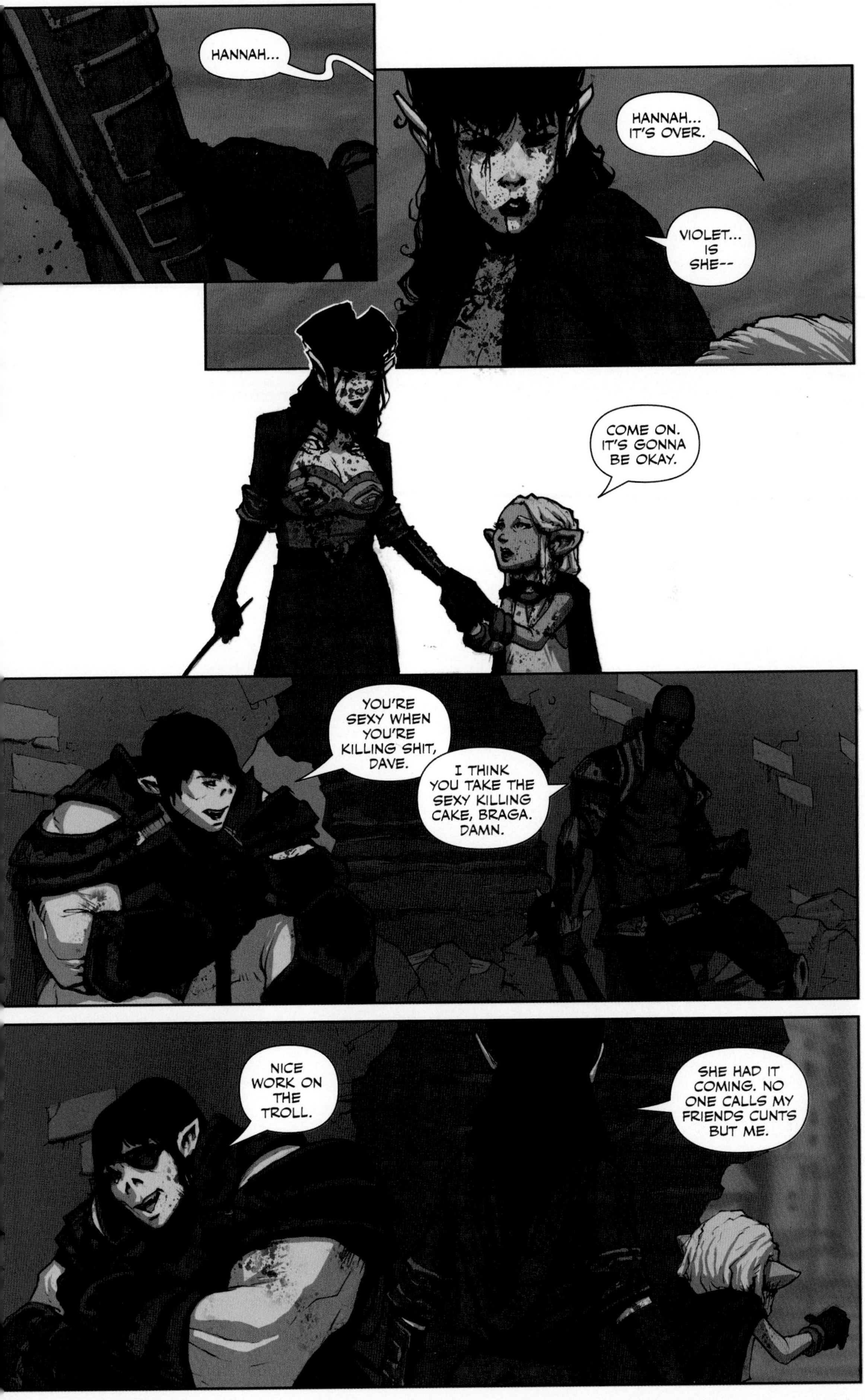
HANNAH...
HANNAH... IT'S OVER.
VIOLET... IS SHE--
COME ON. IT'S GONNA BE OKAY.
YOU'RE SEXY WHEN YOU'RE KILLING SHIT, DAVE.
I THINK YOU TAKE THE SEXY KILLING CAKE, BRAGA. DAMN.
NICE WORK ON THE TROLL.
SHE HAD IT COMING. NO ONE CALLS MY FRIENDS CUNTS BUT ME.

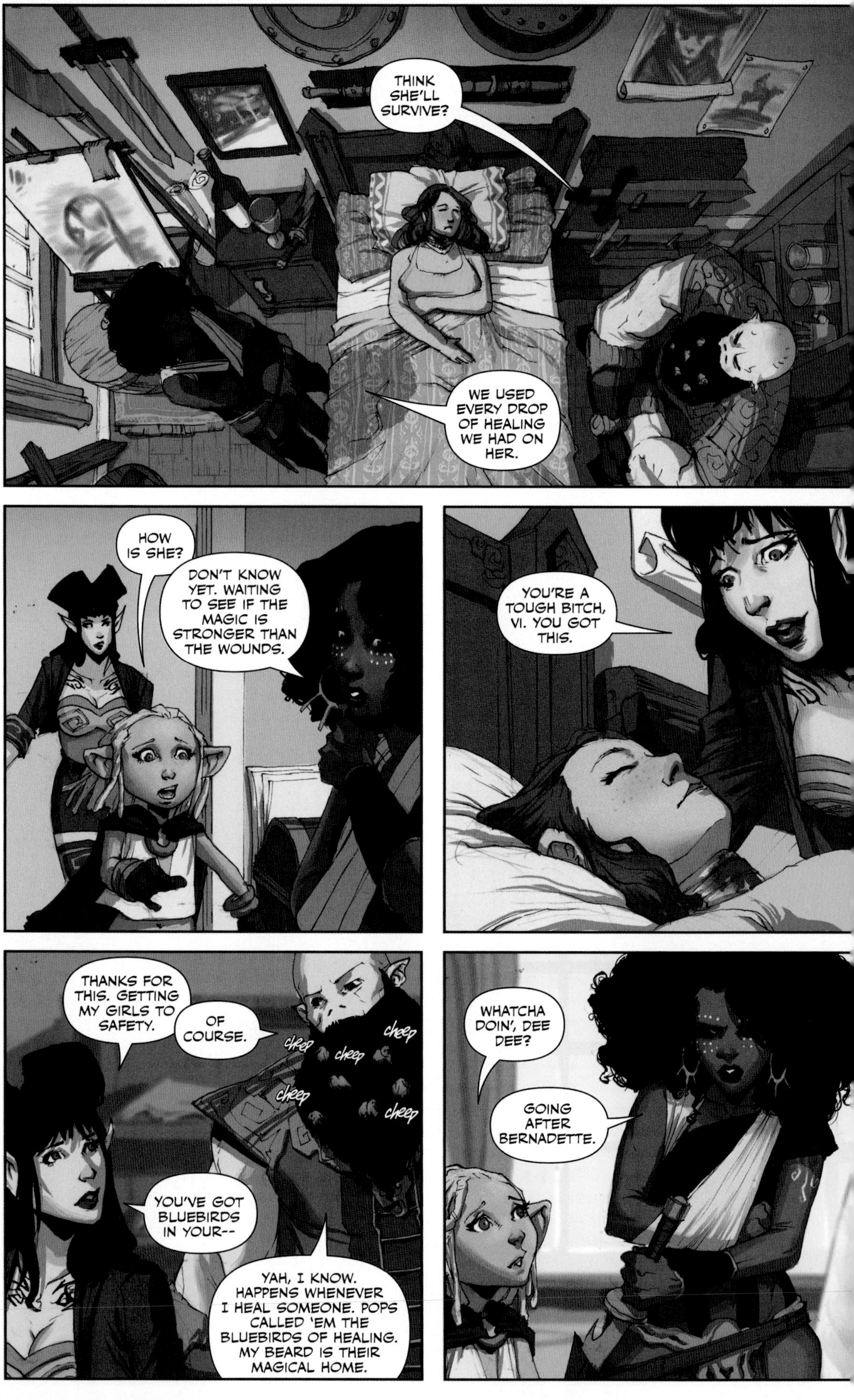
THINK SHE'LL SURVIVE?
WE USED EVERY DROP OF HEALING WE HAD ON HER.
HOW IS SHE?
DON'T KNOW YET. WAITING TO SEE IF THE MAGIC IS STRONGER THAN THE WOUNDS.
YOU'RE A TOUGH BITCH, VI. YOU GOT THIS.
THANKS FOR THIS. GETTING MY GIRLS TO SAFETY.
OF COURSE.
cheep
cheep
cheep
cheep
cheep
YOU'VE GOT BLUEBIRDS IN YOUR--
YAH, I KNOW. HAPPENS WHENEVER I HEAL SOMEONE. POPS CALLED 'EM THE BLUEBIRDS OF HEALING. MY BEARD IS THEIR MAGICAL HOME.
WHATCHA DOIN', DEE DEE?
GOING AFTER BERNADETTE.

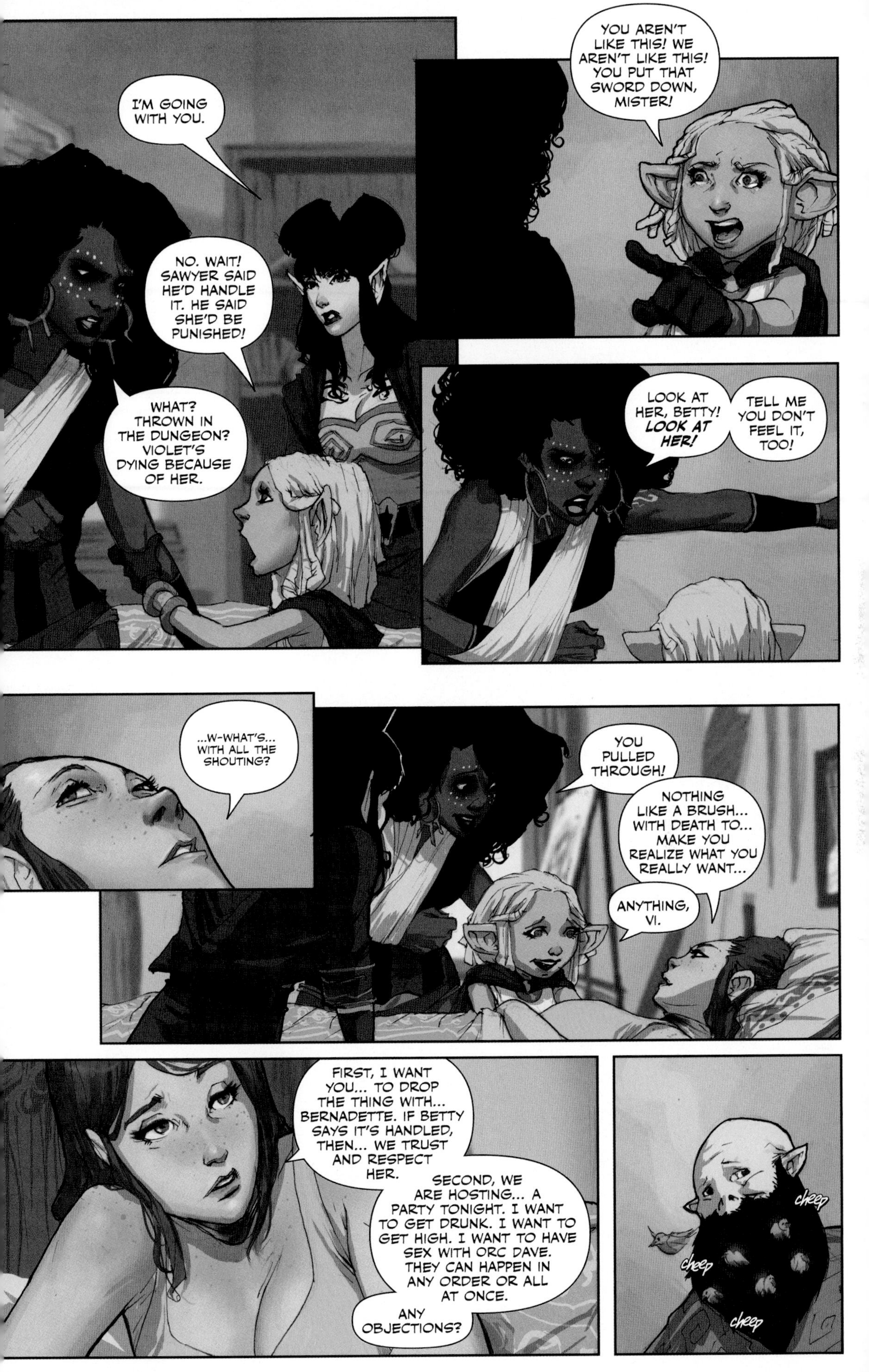
I'M GOING WITH YOU.
NO. WAIT! SAWYER SAID HE'D HANDLE IT. HE SAID SHE'D BE PUNISHED!
WHAT? THROWN IN THE DUNGEON? VIOLET'S DYING BECAUSE OF HER.
YOU AREN'T LIKE THIS! WE AREN'T LIKE THIS! YOU PUT THAT SWORD DOWN, MISTER!
LOOK AT HER, BETTY! LOOK AT HER!
TELL ME YOU DON'T FEEL IT, TOO!
...W-WHAT'S... WITH ALL THE SHOUTING?
YOU PULLED THROUGH!
NOTHING LIKE A BRUSH... WITH DEATH TO... MAKE YOU REALIZE WHAT YOU REALLY WANT...
ANYTHING, VI.
FIRST, I WANT YOU... TO DROP THE THING WITH... BERNADETTE. IF BETTY SAYS IT'S HANDLED, THEN... WE TRUST AND RESPECT HER.
SECOND, WE ARE HOSTING... A PARTY TONIGHT. I WANT TO GET DRUNK. I WANT TO GET HIGH. I WANT TO HAVE SEX WITH ORC DAVE. THEY CAN HAPPEN IN ANY ORDER OR ALL AT ONCE.
ANY OBJECTIONS?
cheep
cheep
cheep

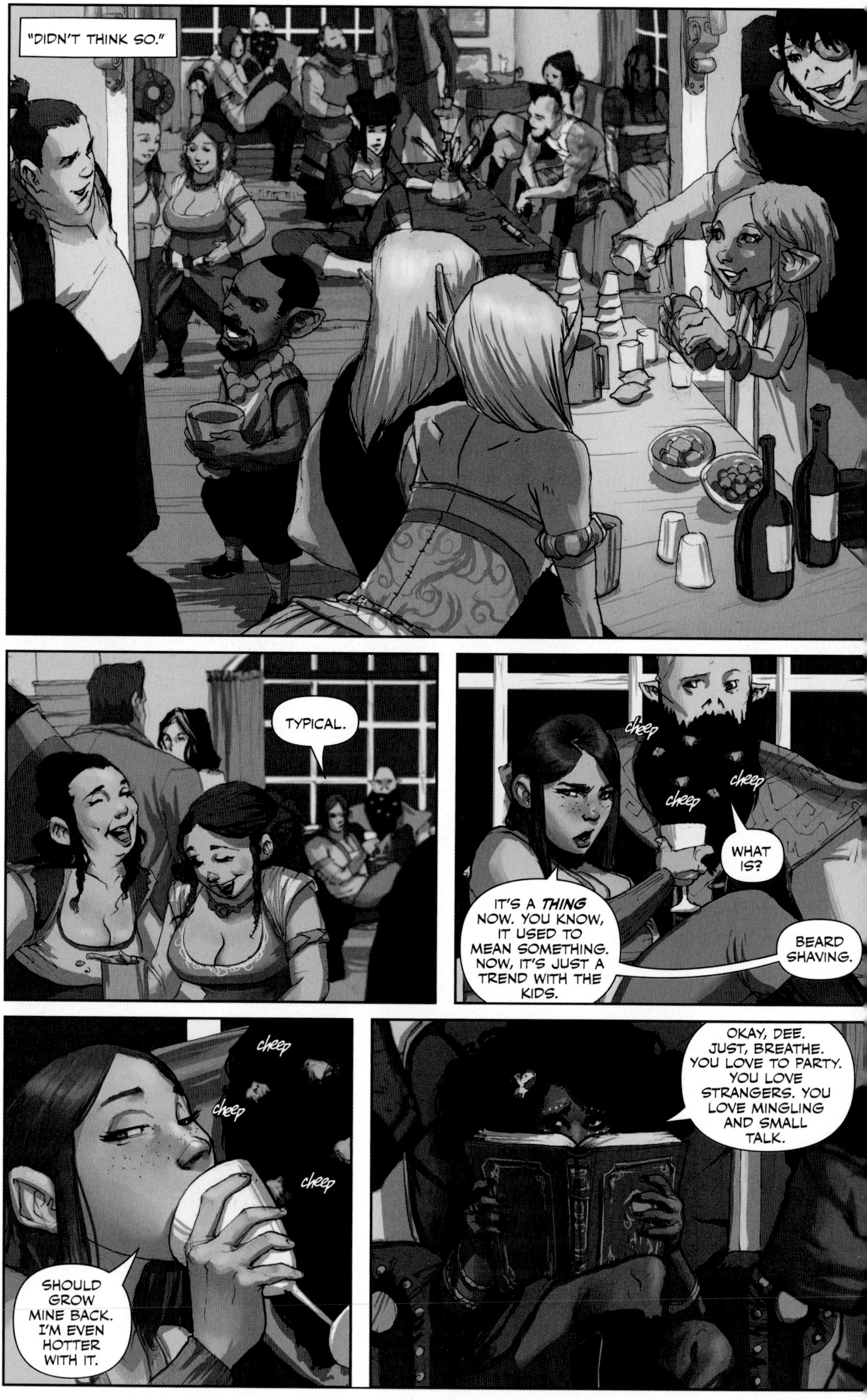
"DIDN'T THINK SO."
TYPICAL.
cheep
cheep
cheep
WHAT IS?
IT'S A *THING* NOW. YOU KNOW, IT USED TO MEAN SOMETHING. NOW, IT'S JUST A TREND WITH THE KIDS.
BEARD SHAVING.
cheep
cheep
cheep
SHOULD GROW MINE BACK. I'M EVEN HOTTER WITH IT.
OKAY, DEE. JUST, BREATHE. YOU LOVE TO PARTY. YOU LOVE STRANGERS. YOU LOVE MINGLING AND SMALL TALK.

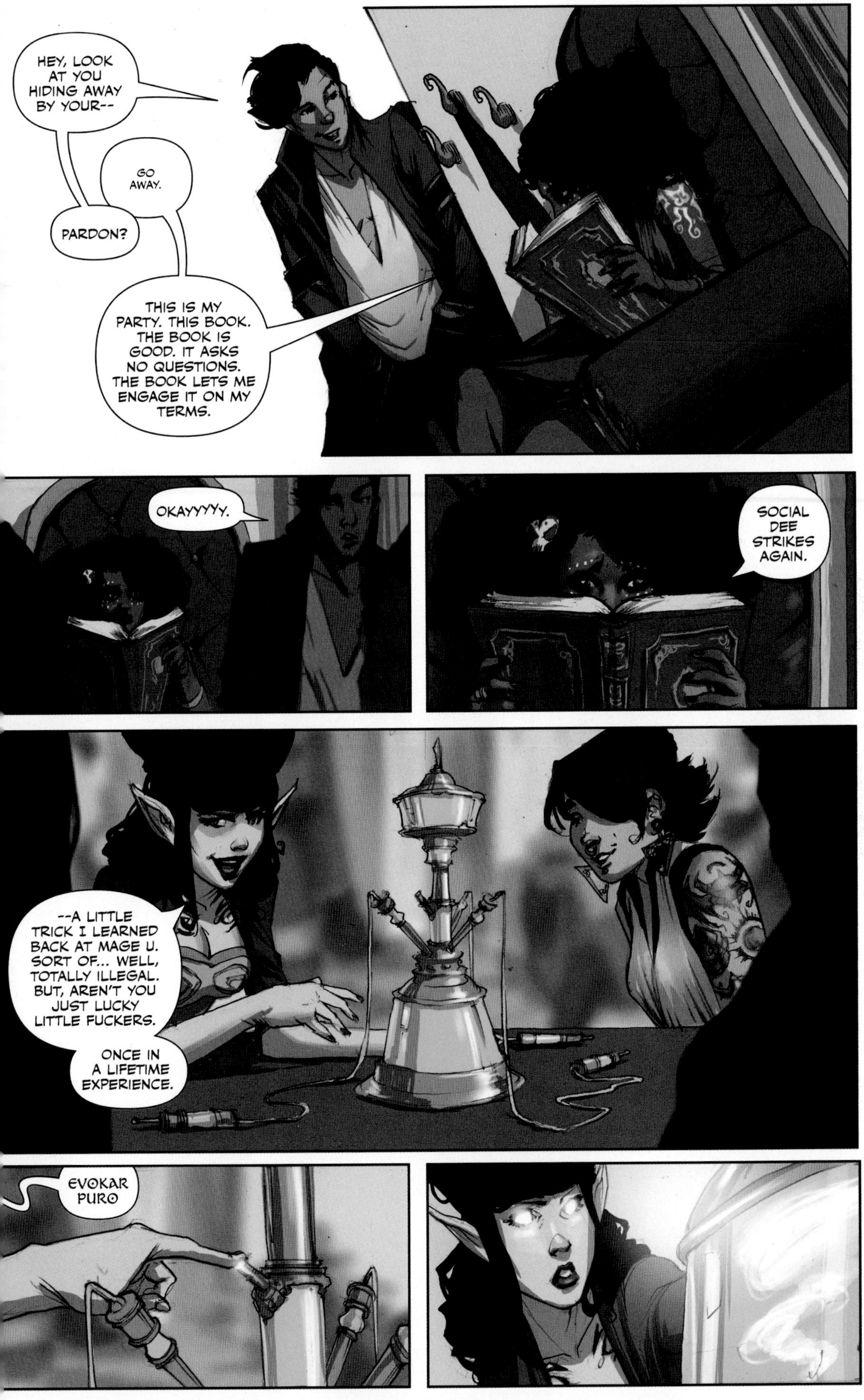
HEY, LOOK AT YOU HIDING AWAY BY YOUR--
GO AWAY.
PARDON?
THIS IS MY PARTY. THIS BOOK. THE BOOK IS GOOD. IT ASKS NO QUESTIONS. THE BOOK LETS ME ENGAGE IT ON MY TERMS.
OKAYYYYy.
SOCIAL DEE STRIKES AGAIN.
--A LITTLE TRICK I LEARNED BACK AT MAGE U. SORT OF... WELL, TOTALLY ILLEGAL. BUT, AREN'T YOU JUST LUCKY LITTLE FUCKERS.
ONCE IN A LIFETIME EXPERIENCE.
EVOKAR PURO

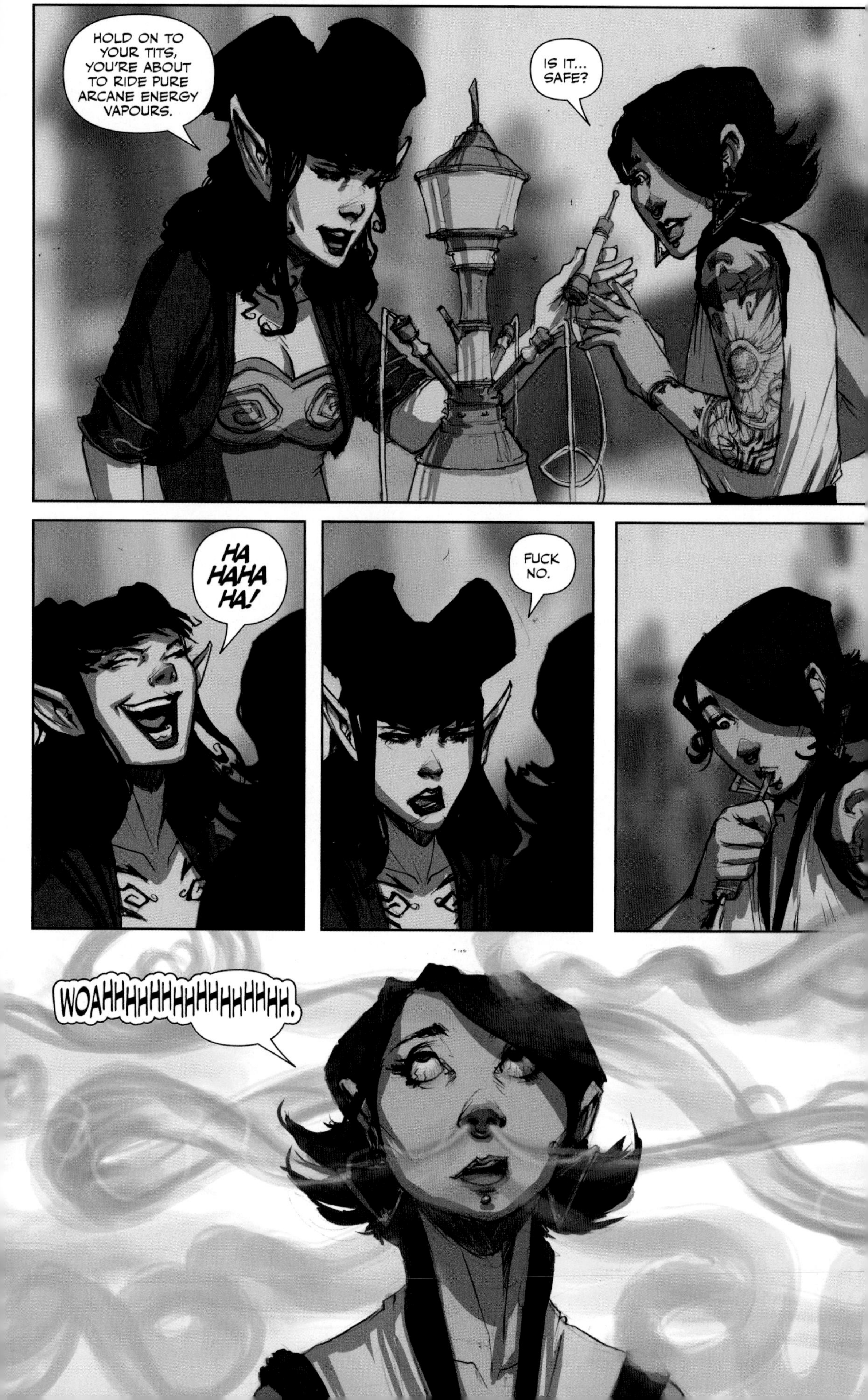
HOLD ON TO YOUR TITS, YOU'RE ABOUT TO RIDE PURE ARCANE ENERGY VAPOURS.
IS IT... SAFE?
HA HAHAHA HA!
FUCK NO.
WOAHHHHHHHHHHHHHHH.

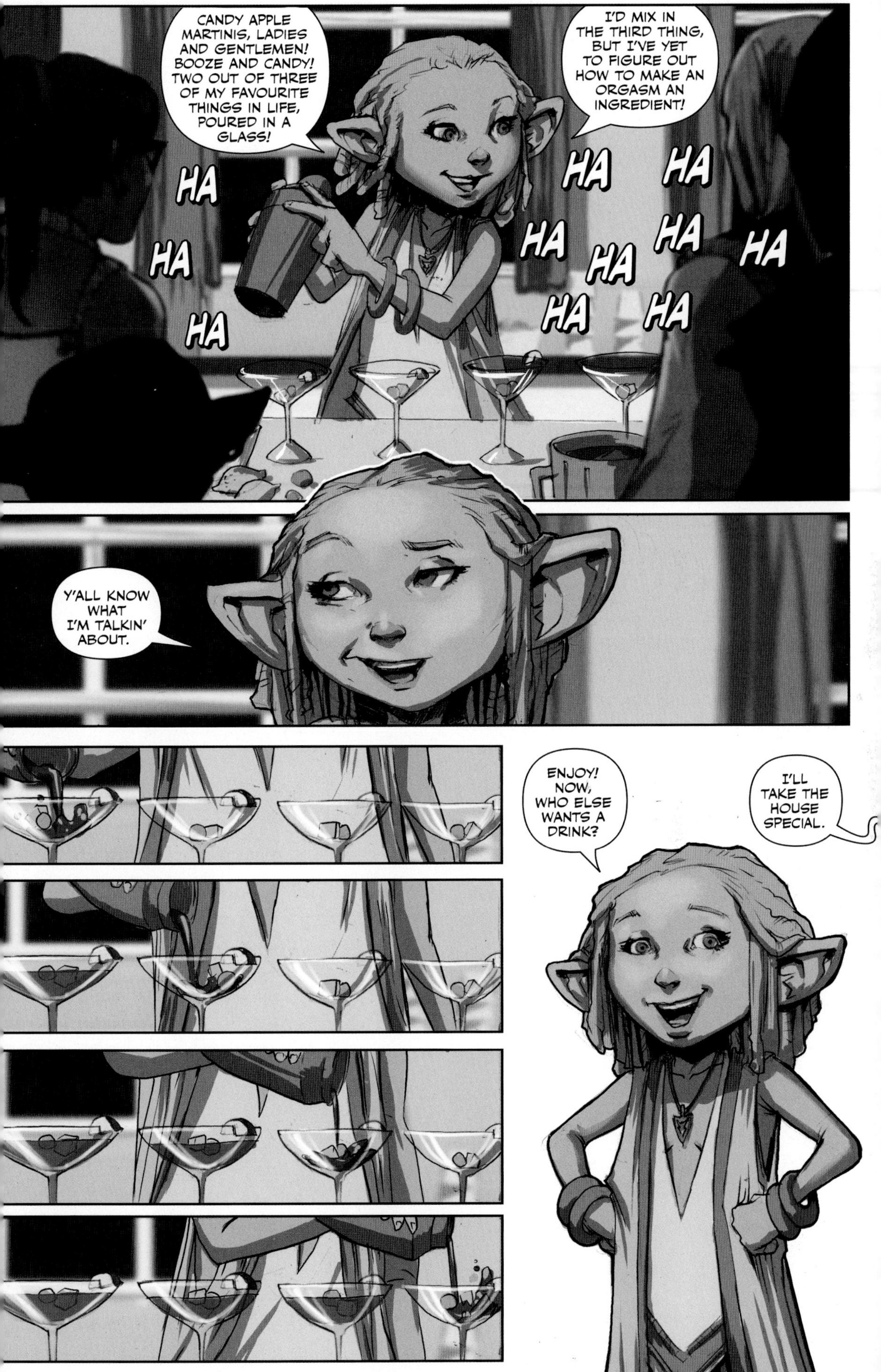
CANDY APPLE MARTINIS, LADIES AND GENTLEMEN! BOOZE AND CANDY! TWO OUT OF THREE OF MY FAVOURITE THINGS IN LIFE, POURED IN A GLASS!
I'D MIX IN THE THIRD THING, BUT I'VE YET TO FIGURE OUT HOW TO MAKE AN ORGASM AN INGREDIENT!
HA
HA
HA
HA HA
HA HA
HA
HA
HA HA
Y'ALL KNOW WHAT I'M TALKIN' ABOUT.
ENJOY! NOW, WHO ELSE WANTS A DRINK?
I'LL TAKE THE HOUSE SPECIAL.

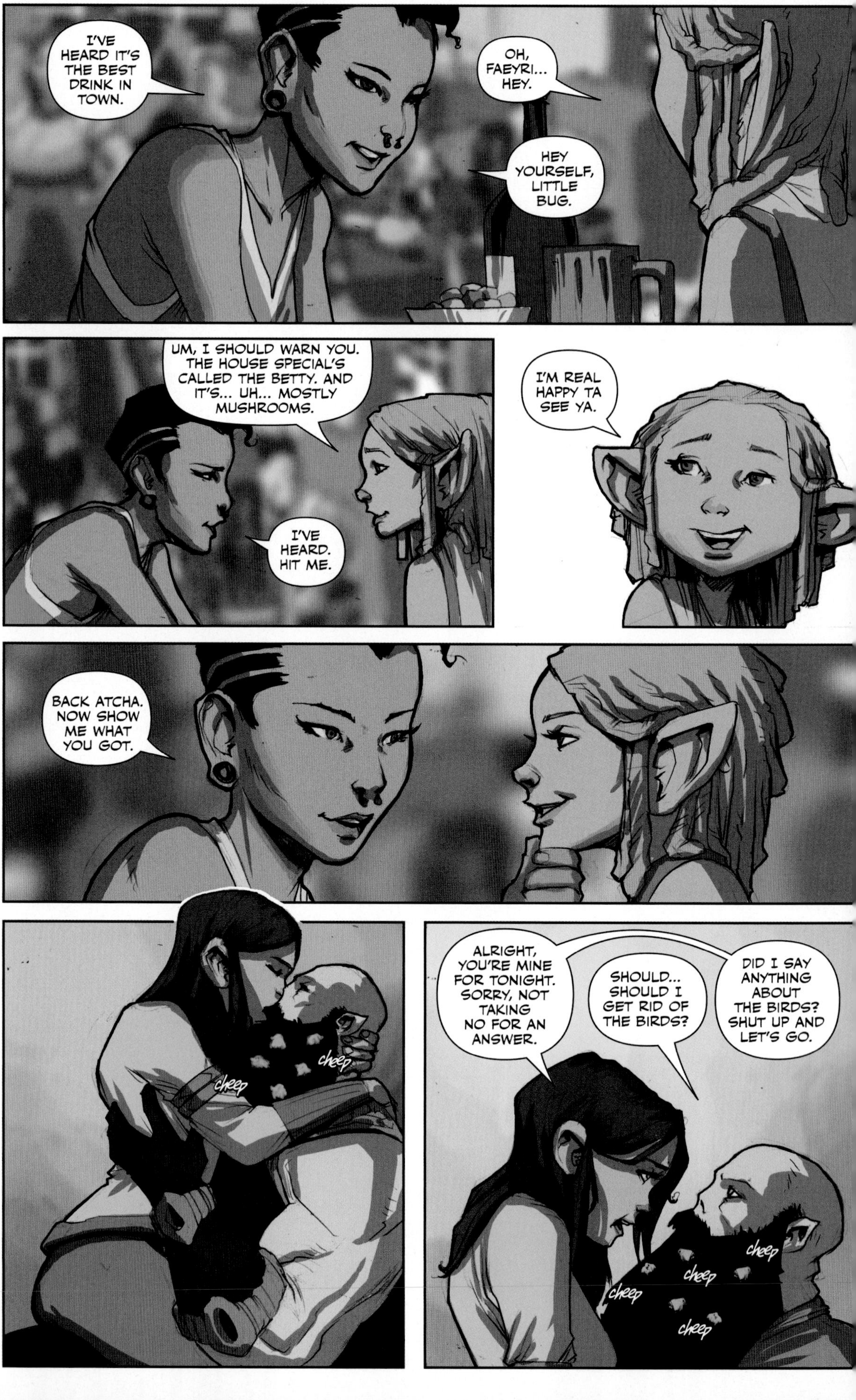
I'VE HEARD IT'S THE BEST DRINK IN TOWN.
OH, FAEYRI... HEY.
HEY YOURSELF, LITTLE BUG.
UM, I SHOULD WARN YOU. THE HOUSE SPECIAL'S CALLED THE BETTY. AND IT'S... UH... MOSTLY MUSHROOMS.
I'VE HEARD. HIT ME.
I'M REAL HAPPY TA SEE YA.
BACK ATCHA. NOW SHOW ME WHAT YOU GOT.
cheep
cheep
ALRIGHT, YOU'RE MINE FOR TONIGHT. SORRY, NOT TAKING NO FOR AN ANSWER.
SHOULD... SHOULD I GET RID OF THE BIRDS?
DID I SAY ANYTHING ABOUT THE BIRDS? SHUT UP AND LET'S GO.
cheep
cheep
cheep
cheep

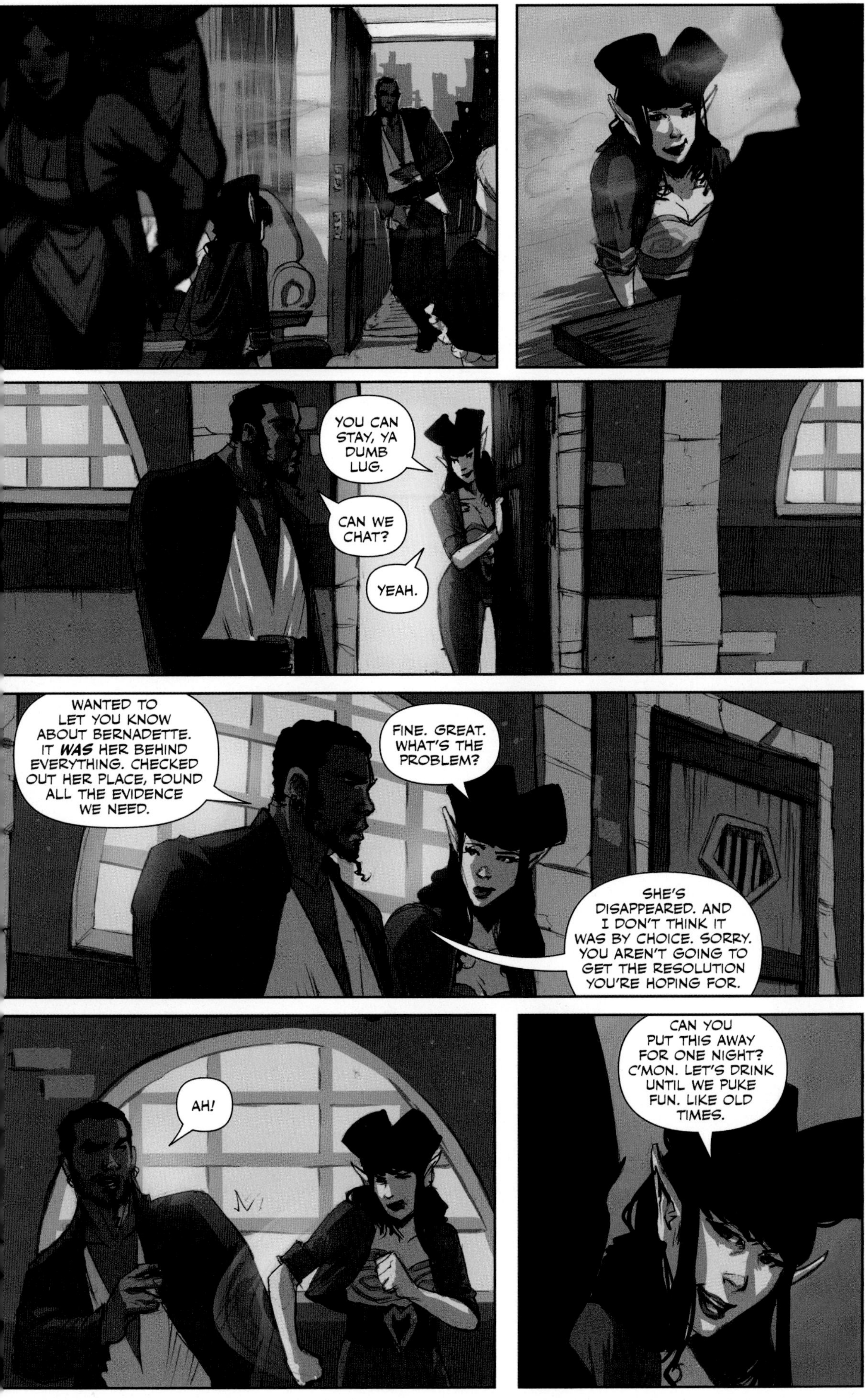
YOU CAN STAY, YA DUMB LUG.
CAN WE CHAT?
YEAH.
WANTED TO LET YOU KNOW ABOUT BERNADETTE. IT *WAS* HER BEHIND EVERYTHING. CHECKED OUT HER PLACE, FOUND ALL THE EVIDENCE WE NEED.
FINE. GREAT. WHAT'S THE PROBLEM?
SHE'S DISAPPEARED. AND I DON'T THINK IT WAS BY CHOICE. SORRY. YOU AREN'T GOING TO GET THE RESOLUTION YOU'RE HOPING FOR.
AH!
CAN YOU PUT THIS AWAY FOR ONE NIGHT? C'MON. LET'S DRINK UNTIL WE PUKE FUN. LIKE OLD TIMES.

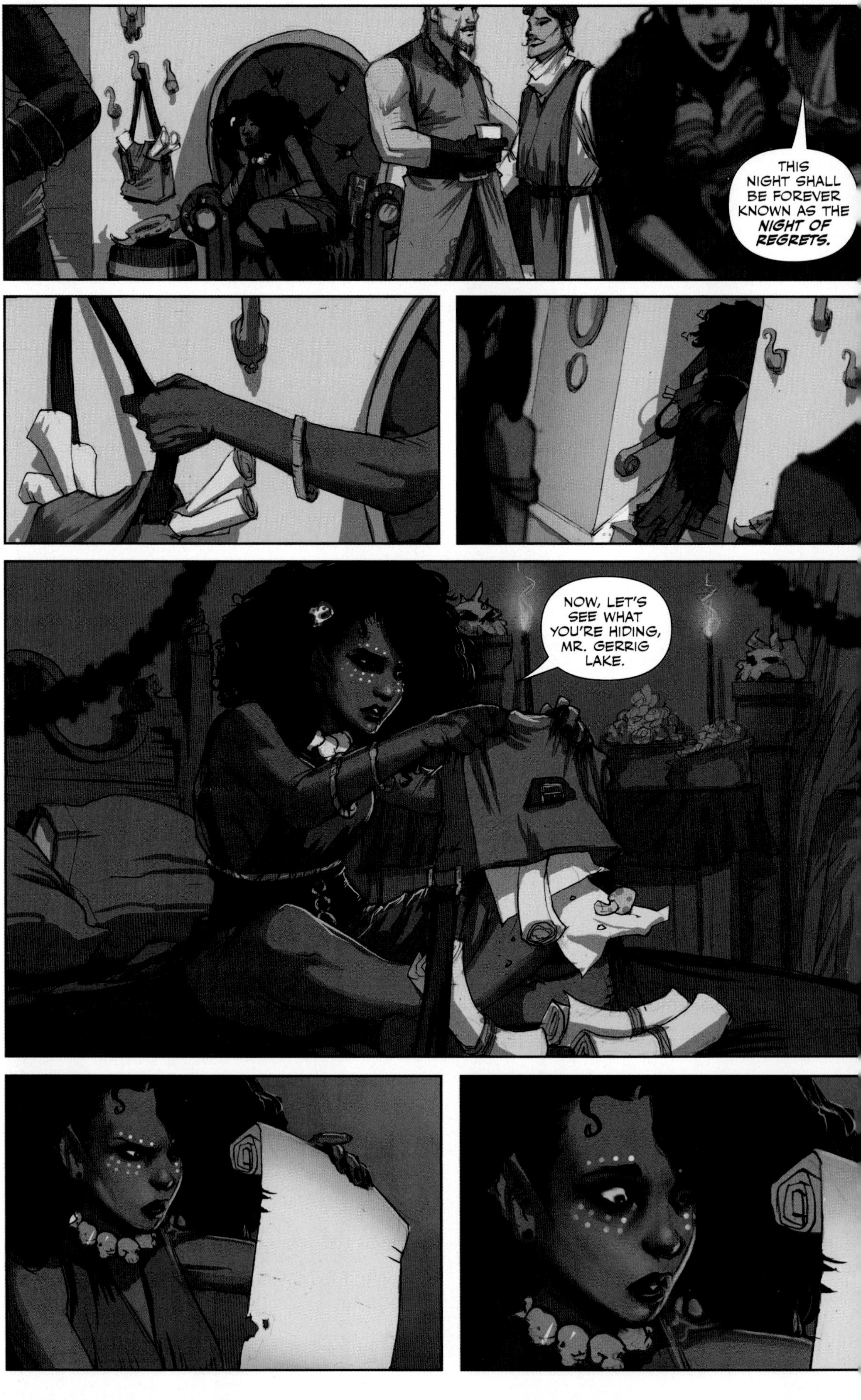
THIS NIGHT SHALL BE FOREVER KNOWN AS THE *NIGHT OF REGRETS.*
NOW, LET'S SEE WHAT YOU'RE HIDING, MR. GERRIG LAKE.

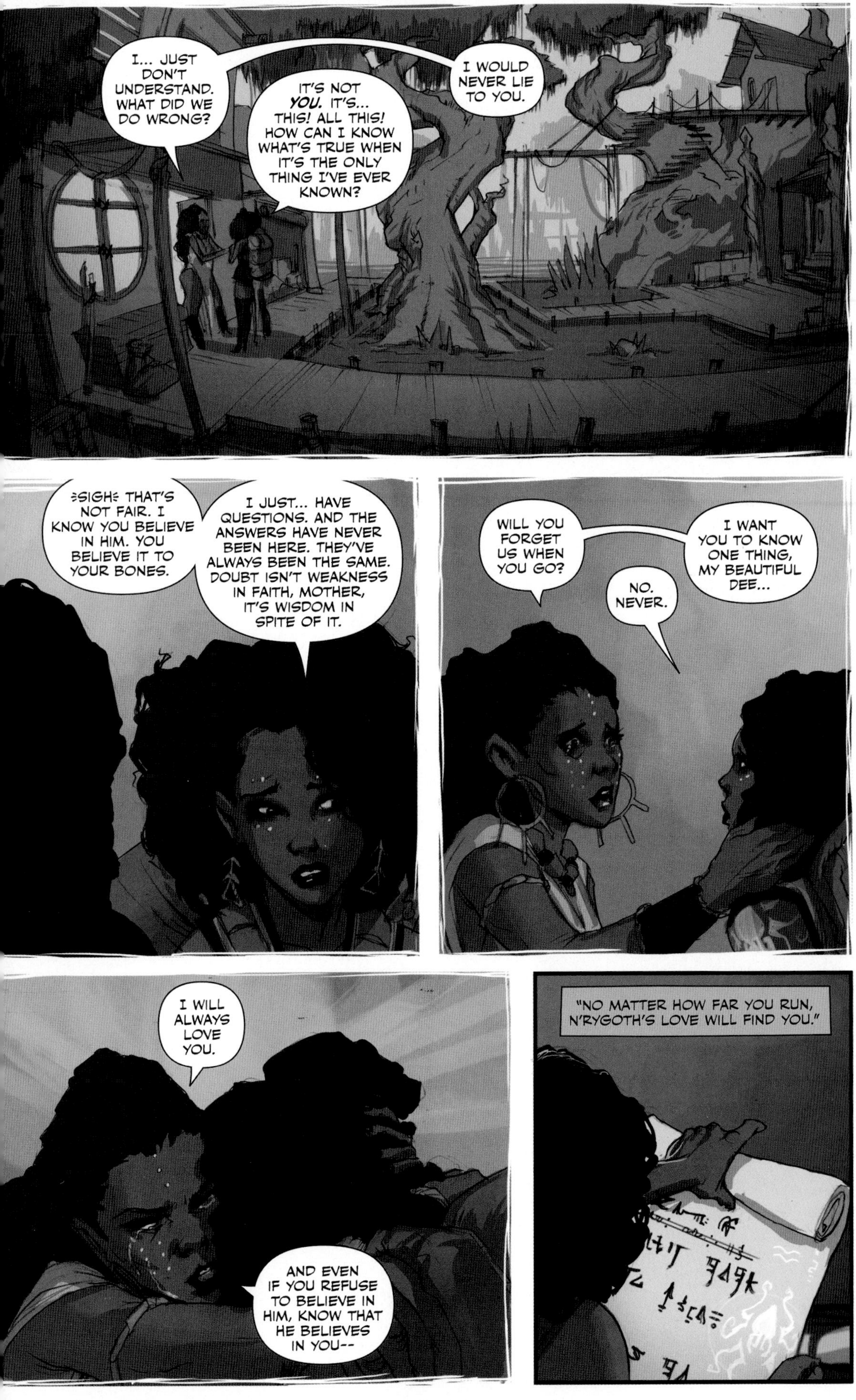
I... JUST DON'T UNDERSTAND. WHAT DID WE DO WRONG?
IT'S NOT YOU. IT'S... THIS! ALL THIS! HOW CAN I KNOW WHAT'S TRUE WHEN IT'S THE ONLY THING I'VE EVER KNOWN?
I WOULD NEVER LIE TO YOU.
=SIGH= THAT'S NOT FAIR. I KNOW YOU BELIEVE IN HIM. YOU BELIEVE IT TO YOUR BONES.
I JUST... HAVE QUESTIONS. AND THE ANSWERS HAVE NEVER BEEN HERE. THEY'VE ALWAYS BEEN THE SAME. DOUBT ISN'T WEAKNESS IN FAITH, MOTHER, IT'S WISDOM IN SPITE OF IT.
WILL YOU FORGET US WHEN YOU GO?
NO. NEVER.
I WANT YOU TO KNOW ONE THING, MY BEAUTIFUL DEE...
I WILL ALWAYS LOVE YOU.
AND EVEN IF YOU REFUSE TO BELIEVE IN HIM, KNOW THAT HE BELIEVES IN YOU--
"NO MATTER HOW FAR YOU RUN, N'RYGOTH'S LOVE WILL FIND YOU."

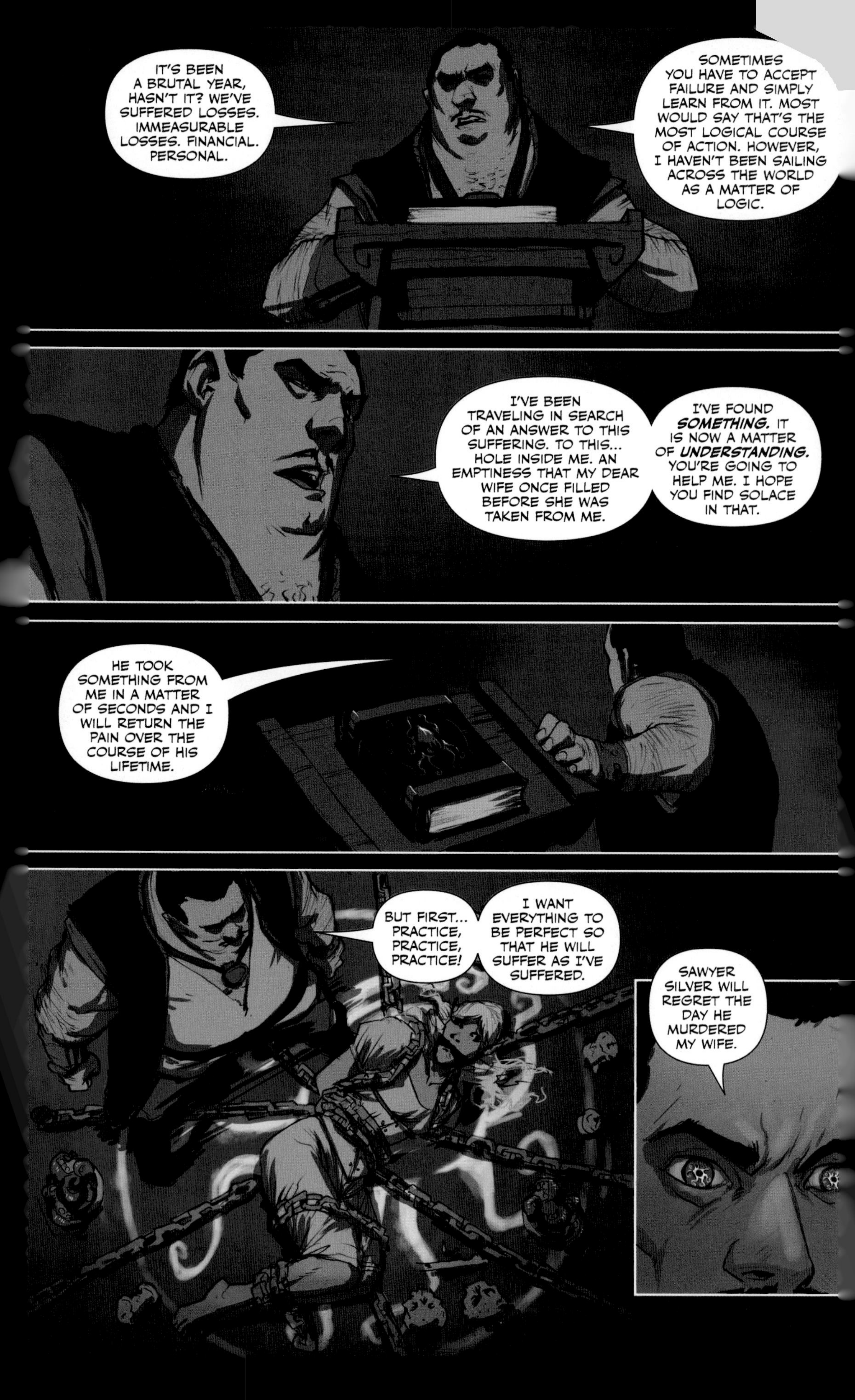
IT'S BEEN A BRUTAL YEAR, HASN'T IT? WE'VE SUFFERED LOSSES. IMMEASURABLE LOSSES. FINANCIAL. PERSONAL.
SOMETIMES YOU HAVE TO ACCEPT FAILURE AND SIMPLY LEARN FROM IT. MOST WOULD SAY THAT'S THE MOST LOGICAL COURSE OF ACTION. HOWEVER, I HAVEN'T BEEN SAILING ACROSS THE WORLD AS A MATTER OF LOGIC.
I'VE BEEN TRAVELING IN SEARCH OF AN ANSWER TO THIS SUFFERING. TO THIS... HOLE INSIDE ME. AN EMPTINESS THAT MY DEAR WIFE ONCE FILLED BEFORE SHE WAS TAKEN FROM ME.
I'VE FOUND ***SOMETHING.*** IT IS NOW A MATTER OF ***UNDERSTANDING.*** YOU'RE GOING TO HELP ME. I HOPE YOU FIND SOLACE IN THAT.
HE TOOK SOMETHING FROM ME IN A MATTER OF SECONDS AND I WILL RETURN THE PAIN OVER THE COURSE OF HIS LIFETIME.
BUT FIRST... PRACTICE, PRACTICE, PRACTICE!
I WANT EVERYTHING TO BE PERFECT SO THAT HE WILL SUFFER AS I'VE SUFFERED.
SAWYER SILVER WILL REGRET THE DAY HE MURDERED MY WIFE.

Books by Kurtis J. Wiebe you're bound to enjoy...

GREEN WAKE
VOLUME ONE
KURTIS WIEBE
RILEY ROSSMO

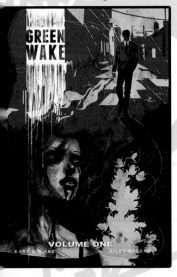

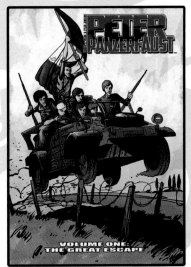

With Riley Rossmo

GREEN WAKE

VOLUME ONE

ISBN: 978-1-60706-432-9

VOLUME TWO:

LOST CHILDREN

ISBN: 978-1-60706-525-8

A riveting tale of loss and horror in the mysteriously forgotten town of Green Wake.

PETER PANZERFAUST
VOLUME ONE:
THE GREAT ESCAPE

DEBRIS

ISBN: 978-1-60706-720-7

After an attack leaves their people without water, Maya, the last Protector, sets out on a journey for pure water, to save the world before the monsters bring it all to an end.

GREEN WAKE
VOLUME TWO
LOST CHILDREN
KURTIS WIEBE
RILEY ROSSMO

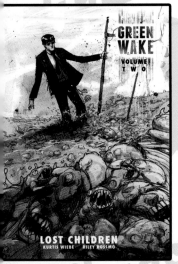

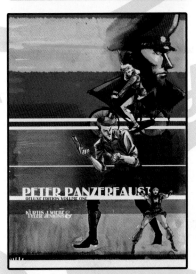

With Tyler Jenkins

PETER PANZERFAUST

VOLUME ONE:

THE GREAT ESCAPE

ISBN: 978-1-60706-582-1

VOLUME TWO:

HOOKED

ISBN: 978-1-60706-728-3

DELUXE EDITION

ISBN: 978-1-60706-968-3

The smash critically acclaimed sell-out series takes J.M. Barrie's familiar characters and places them in WWII!

"Might be the most interesting take on Peter Pan since the characters' creation."

BRIAN K. VAUGHN

PETER PANZERFAUST
DELUXE EDITION VOLUME ONE
KURTIS J. WIEBE &
TYLER JENKINS

debris
KURTIS J. WIEBE
RILEY ROSSMO

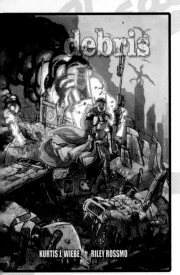

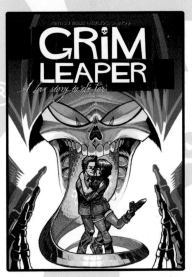

With Aluiso C. Santos

GRIM LEAPER:

A LOVE STORY TO DIE FOR

ISBN: 978-1-60706-629-3

Luo and Ella, two star crossed lovers...who can't stop dying!

GRIM
LEAPER
A love story to die for

OR MORE INFORMATION ABOUT ALL *Shadowline®* BOOKS AND WEB-COMICS, PLEASE VISIT US AT:

www.ShadowlineOnline.com

ollow SHADOWLINECOMICS on FACEBOOK and TWITTER

THIS is diversity! Graphic Novels For the Discriminating Reader

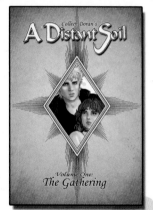

A DISTANT SOIL

Colleen Doran's legendary magnum opus completely remastered and re-edited with beautiful new die-cut covers. Five volumes.

BOMB QUEEN DELUXE

Jimmie Robinson's adults only satire of politics, sex and social morays. Not for the easily offended! Four Oversize hardcover volumes.

COMEBACK

Comeback is more than a company--we will bring your loved ones back moments before their untimely deaths...for a price.

COMPLETE normalman

The legendary classic paro series collected in o gigantic volume for the fi time!

COWBOY NINJA VIKING

Now in a Deluxe Oversize hardcover edition! Duncan has three distinct personalities...of course he's a government agent.

DEAR DRACULA

All Sam wants this Halloween is to become a real vampire! So he writes a letter to his hero, Count Dracula...who pays him a visit!

DEBRIS

Maya must find a source of pure water to save the world before the garbage monsters bring it all to an end.

DIA DE LOS MUERTOS

Nine acclaimed writers ar one amazing artist, Ril Rossmo, tell tales from t Mexican Day of the Dead.

FIVE WEAPONS

In a school for assassins, Tyler has the greatest of them all going for him...his mind! Jimmie Robinson's latest epic makes the grade.

FRACTURED FABLES

Award winning cartoonists put a wicked but hilarious spin on well worn Fairy tales in this not-to-be-missed anthology.

GREEN WAKE

A riveting tale of loss and horror that blends mystery and otherworldly eccentricity in two unforgettable, critically acclaimed volumes.

HARVEST

Welcome to Dr. Benjam Dane's nightmare. His or way out is to bring down t man who set him harvesting organs.